BLOOD BORNE

BLOOD BORNE (The Republic 3)
By Archer Kay Leah

Published by Ashborne Stardust Press

Copyright © 2019 by Archer Kay Leah

Second edition, August 2019
First published by Less Than Three Press, 2017

Cover designed by Natasha Snow Designs;
www.natashasnowdesigns.com

Map designed by Raelynn Marie

Print ISBN 978-0-9958275-4-7

CONTENT NOTES, WARNINGS, AND DISCLAIMERS

Blood Borne does not contain explicit content.

This story contains instances of transphobia and bigotry, including the deliberate and non-deliberate misgendering of a trans non-binary character and the use of that character's deadname. These instances are meant only to illustrate the harmful nature of the character's circumstances, directly related to the plot and character story arcs. The inclusion of such instances does not reflect the personal opinion of the author nor do they endorse discrimination or malicious treatment of trans and non-binary folk.

This story also contains violent situations, references to human trafficking and inferred violence against women and children, references to the kidnapping of a child, and mentions of a past suicide. There are also depictions of domestic violence and abuse (including psychological, emotional, and financial abuse) and exploitation, as well as an instance of nonconsensual touching and sexual harassment.

Please note the story does employ the use of gender-neutral pronouns *ce* and *cir*. These are not mistakes: they are the chosen pronouns of the character.

For everyone who wants the freedom to live who they are without fear and be appreciated for all that they are. Also for those who are still working it all out. Keep hanging on. You'll get there. <3

And for my Stitch, who inspires me even when I don't realize it's happening. You're in my heart for life. You're also on every single page. xoxoxo

Acknowledgements

With my deepest, humblest thanks to everyone whose experience and knowledge helped shape Adren and Ress. In particular, thank you to the folks on Tumblr: Anagnori for their invaluable insight, inner thoughts, and awesome glossaries; Ask a Non-binary and Chris (faerieli) for the list that opened up options for Adren; and Taz (jackalwedding) for the ce/cir pronouns that gave Adren belonging.

Additional thank yous to my partner, Megan Derr, Sam Derr, A.M. Valenza, and countless others for sharing what it's like being you, even when the path is difficult to tread. You are inspiration embodied. ~ AKL

BLOOD BORNE

THE REPUBLIC BOOK 3

ARCHER KAY LEAH

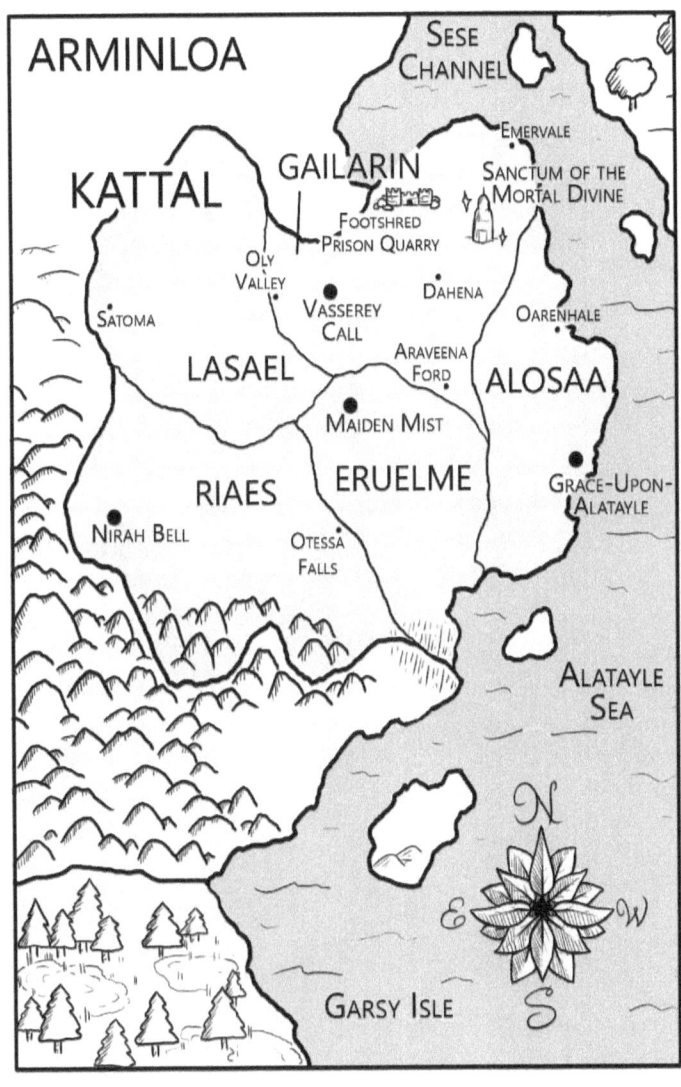

CHAPTER ONE

What a waste.

Shuffling down the dark corridor towards the bedrooms, Adren stared at cir grimy hands. Was the more tragic waste taking part in the job or the thief at the centre of the job itself? Dust caked cir skin, the stale scent lingering from the room where the thief had been restrained. His screams refused to stop assaulting Adren's mind. The piercing desperation of the man's terror echoed in cir memories, bouncing from one side of cir skull to the other, tearing holes through cir conscience. Every footstep resembled the sickening thump of the thief's body hitting the floor in his squeaky chair, his dismantled face three kicks away from being so broken no one could recognize him. His dried blood clung to the creases between cir fingers, as stubborn as the spatter on cir black leather long coat.

Serves me right for standing too close to Tethe—he's never liked a clean kill. Adren peered over cir shoulder to catch cir brother's dark glance. Tethe grinned and winked before blowing Adren a playful, exaggerated kiss, a habit since they were children. His affectionate gestures always increased whenever he owed Adren, but he saved the most emphasized for when he owed Adren for doing something ce hated. *Like making a dead body disappear and hiding the rest of the evidence. You're such a bastard, Tethe. Don't think I won't make you pay. You're buying me a new coat, especially if I can't get the smell of dead guy out of this one.*

"I don't think A's feeling too friendly right now," Mordane whispered from beside Tethe, lifting the metal lamp in his hand higher. In the candlelight, his dark, water-slicked hair gleamed, the ends curled around his ears to his jaw line. His brown eyes narrowed before he flashed a grin identical to Tethe's. Although short and not muscular like Tethe, their resemblance was undeniable. Like Adren, they wore all black, their shirts and pants covered by long coats that hung to their ankles in typical fashion. "If I were you, I'd sleep with both eyes open."

"If I were me, I'd not sleep at all." Tethe snorted, teasing his fingers through the tail of his shoulder-length hair. Similar to Mordane and their mother, his complexion and hair were dark, contrasts to Adren's light tan skin and long red hair in its tight, braided coil. "If little sis scared me, that is."

Adren stopped and turned, hissing and flicking cir fingers at Tethe. "Dare me, and I will.

14

You've taught me well. Maybe it's time I showed the master *exactly* how much I've learned."

Tethe beamed. Hand to his chest, he stumbled back a step and sniffled. "She called me Master."

"Ce," Adren muttered, wishing he could get it right after six years. *Especially when I'm too exhausted to keep correcting him.* "And let me clarify: you put the *ass* in '*mas*ter.'"

Mordane sucked in a breath before laughing quietly. "I'd hate to know where I stand in this."

"The 'Mord' in mortifying, perhaps?" Tethe arched one brow, his slender lips pursed. "The 'dane' in mundane?"

"A's right: you're an ass. And here's my room." Stopped outside of the closed door, dark red wood with an elaborate gold doorknob and knocker that resembled the head of a large cat, Mordane pointed down the hall. "Bedtime, both of you. We've got a meeting with the other faction bosses this afternoon."

"Which explains why it's almost dawn and we're *just* getting home." Snickering, Adren backed down the hall towards cir room. "How is it no one's managed to teach either of you timing?"

"Oh, ho! Look who's talking." Tethe crossed his arms and rocked on his boot heels. "Being the brat of a Boss swelling your head now?"

"No, just thinking that since you were alive a full seven years before me, you'd have figured it out by now." Adren shrugged. "It might kill you faster than I can."

"Or Mother will do the honours if the two of you don't shut up." Mordane pressed his fingers to his lips before flicking his wrist behind him, motioning to their parents' room. "She's asleep, and so is he. We don't need either of them asking questions."

"One, Father told us to shut this guy up, so his only question will be if the corpse is gone," Tethe drawled. "Two, I'll bet he's sleeping in his study, probably on his work." He squashed his cheek with one hand, contorting his lips. "Likely wearing it, too. Ink's such a pain." As his hand dropped, he rolled his eyes. "I'll go wake him up, tell him to go to bed."

Mordane sighed and craned his neck back. "I'll go with you. If he's too far gone, he'll be as bad as dragging a corpse." He glanced at Adren. "You good?"

Adren pointed to the door to cir left, a match to Mordane's door except for the knocker in the shape of a bird's head. "Fine. Goodnight, then?"

"Yeah, that." Tethe turned and followed Mordane back towards the staircase to the main floor below, waving his hand behind him. "Be at breakfast."

"Of course," Adren murmured, entering cir room. Breakfast was a daily, mandatory family meeting, divulging new information and pertinent warnings before any other meetings happened.

One of the secrets to success, cir father, Rivane, had insisted since Adren was a child. *"A unified family for a stronger family,"* was more than one of his beloved mottos; it was the solitary truth he had based his life upon. The one principle that drove his decisions for both their family and the Shar-denn gang faction he controlled. Given their family was still intact and cohesive like their faction, there was no point arguing with what he considered the most fundamental concept.

Now arguing my place within it... that's where it gets tough. Adren closed the door and crossed the grey room, passing through the spread of white moonlight on cir way to the windows. With the blue-silver curtains pushed to the opposite ends of the gold curtain rods, all four windowpanes were visible, taking up most of the exterior wall. The end of summer was coming, evidenced by the subtle colour change in tree leaves and the wilting flowers in the courtyard below. The cooler winds of autumn would begin in a matter of weeks, preceding the light dustings of snow that heralded winter, cir favourite season. Something about the crisp, cold air and brittle ice spoke more loudly than the other seasons, laughing at the secrets of the year to come.

A sigh slipped from Adren's lips, heavy and tired like the rest of cir. Still focused on the yard, ce watched crooked shadows play along the ground around the trees surrounding the gardens. Unfeeling shadows that danced and melded with the others without protest: always reliant on something else, unable to exist on their own. They were everything ce was expected to be.

Except I'm too stubborn to completely surrender, no matter who my father is, no matter what I do. On the way to the bed against the wall left of the windows, Adren unbuckled the silver buttons of cir coat and shrugged it off. Ce tossed the coat over the ornate wood footboard before sitting on the edge of the mattress. The room looked the same as ce had left it after dinner: dark, messy, and comfortable. None of the servants had bothered to clean it, abiding by cir request. *Mother's idea of tidy isn't worth the headache I get hunting for things or training people not to touch my stuff.* Everything had its place, often where no one else wanted them. The room was a hideaway, a place to keep secrets and be alone.

Adren drew cir hand over the red ribbon of the down-stuffed blanket beneath cir. Bright white, the blanket was a contrast to the dark grey stone walls and light grey wood panels of the floor, the same colours found throughout the house. The rest of the bed sheets were light blue with black accents like the rugs.

While the bed was close enough to the windows for Adren to see the tops of the trees, the remaining furniture was set back further. Two wide armoires, crafted from black wood like the bed, stood together near the door. Across the room was a long, black and red dresser split into three sections. The two sections on either side curved inwards, holding up metal boxes filled with Adren's jewels; the middle supported a large mirror and a washbowl. Large wood chests sat against the walls, overflowing with books, toys from a childhood long gone, maps, and the few weapons Adren considered useful. Clothes and books lay scattered around the room, their dispersal random only in appearance. Ce preferred to think of it as organized chaos.

Like the rest of my life. Then again, that's the Shar for you: they live to organize chaos. Hasn't done my family too bad, so why am I complaining?

Another sigh slipped out with the answer: *Because sometimes the chaos is too much.*

With another glance at cir hands, Adren rubbed cir fingertips together, cir stomach turning with the gritty texture. Tethe was right: their father had told them to make the man disappear permanently. Following dinner with their parents and several high-ranking faction members, they had gone to the dilapidated shack in the woods south of the family's elaborate house. Upon their arrival, the man they had been sent to terminate—a thief caught breaking into one of their cache houses—had been unconscious and tied to a chair in the dingy, candlelit sitting room. The men who had caught him had been gathered around a dust-covered table, playing coins and laughing loudly as they shoved each other.

The raucous demeanor had ended the moment they saw Tethe, who took control with few words and a dozen glances, each bearing a different meaning depending on who received them.

The thief had no chance of painless survival after that.

As was Rivane's way with those who preyed on the gang, Tethe's interrogation had been brutal, facilitated by angry force and relentless truth-seeking. No one committed crimes against the Shar-denn. No thief stole from them and lived, especially the sloppy ones like the man Tethe enjoyed torturing too much for Adren's liking.

Granted, Adren hated the idea of anyone stealing from them and hurting cir Shar-denn family, but ce never liked the pain forced on the offenders. Mordane had helped with the interrogation, asking questions with a calm, controlled tone while he circled the thief and Tethe. Adren had remained in the doorway. From what ce could tell, no one else there minded the piercing screams echoing through the empty shack or the blood seeping between the cracked floorboards. Although ce had wanted to command Tethe to stop, there had been no point. Ce had tried stopping him in the past, only to be pushed away and mocked. After what seemed like a thousand times, ce had stopped trying.

Instead, cir brothers handled the interrogations, coercions, and deals. Adren's role in their dirtiest affairs was simple: make the evidence go away. There could be no body, no documents, no blood—nothing to suggest they had done anything the High Council of Kattal considered illegal. Given Adren's unique magic that allowed cir to change the existence of people and things, ce was useful. If corpses were involved, ce dissolved the bodies and wove them into the dark fabric of their universe, dismantling their souls to give them peace in the void where no one could harm them again.

Not that it's merciful. Mercy would be doing it before *they ended up dead.* Adren lowered cir face into cir hands, scrunching cir nose at the stench. Mixed with the metallic scents of blood and knife handle was the musty scent of the shack. Ce yearned for the sweet scent of soap and its slick movement across cir skin. Anything to wash away the gloom and lies ce hated bearing.

"What I'd give to just say no to Father and rebel completely." *Maybe even leave Elsove Hillock, although that's a special form of torture in itself.*

How do you leave the only village you've ever known, especially when it isn't much of a village? Just our estate, a few houses, and enough gang members to pretend to be a legitimate settlement. Everything else comes to us. Adren forced cirself from the bed and dragged cir feet to the dresser. Ce debated whether or not ce had the energy to rip off cir shin-high boots and loose black pants.

The thought was dismissed as quickly as it appeared. Cir body was already threatening to topple over and hit the floor. *I'd probably smash my head open in the process, because that would be so very me.*

Lips in a tight scowl, Adren tugged the hidden stays in the high collar of cir black shirt and its cuffs, loosening the fabric before pulling the sleeves back. Tilting cir head from side to side until cir neck cracked, Adren adjusted cir leather belt, letting the belt sling loose across cir waist. As ce withdrew the pins and ties from cir hair, cir headache eased off, relief growing until cir braid hung free.

If only leaving the magic behind was as simple as undressing.

Or assuming a new place in the Shar's hierarchy. I wouldn't mind something that doesn't include people or crime. I could haul buckets and water the gardens or prune the trees and clean the floors. They'd be boring as anything, but blissfully so.

With a snort, Adren dipped cir hands into the washbowl, searching for the sliver of soap at the bottom. Never would cir parents agree to the alternatives. Rivane prided himself on their family and the involvement of his three children in the management of the faction. He was the first to boast about their achievements to the other faction bosses as though they were prizes to be coveted.

Their mother, Merasha, was no less enthusiastic and found a way to balance doting on them with pushing them to do better. Prim, skilled in strategy, and a quick-thinker in tough situations, Merasha was as desired by the other gang bosses as Adren's brothers were. Merasha's family had served Rivane's for generations, pairing their strategists and thieves with the enforcers and coordinators of Rivane's family. She was Rivane's second secret to success.

With all that good blood in the family, how could I ever—

Sharp sounds fractured the silence. Glass shattered, again and again, followed by shouts. Doors slammed on the level below. Voices raised battle against each other, deep, demanding, threatening. Men barked commands, short and repetitive.

Muffled cries of alarm.

Yanking cir hands out of the water and ramming cir knee into the dresser, Adren hissed as the washbowl tipped, splashing lukewarm water across cir waist. Ce dried cir hands on the towel beside the bowl and drew a knife from cir boot before charging towards the door. No one attacked their home and got away with it.

The door burst open, banging against the wall. Merasha ran into the room, barefoot and breathing heavy, her long, dark hair tangled and mussed. Dressed in a pale nightdress and dark lace dressing robe, she looked as disheveled as she was panicked.

"Eradrene!" Merasha whispered hoarsely, seizing Adren by the shoulders. Her shaking hands sent a shudder through Adren. "You need to leave. Hide. Now! Council can *never* get you, you hear? Don't let the soldiers catch you."

"But Mother—"

"Go!" Merasha looked to the hallway. "Hide!"

"I can't. I can't leave, not you. Not them. I'll go fight—" Adren pushed cir mother away.

Merasha clutched Adren's shirt in both fists and yanked cir close enough to touch noses. "You will go or I'll kill you myself! All our work can't go to waste," she snarled through clenched teeth, her menacing glare reminding Adren of how vicious she could be. "Hunters are raiding our home, arresting *everyone. I'm* telling you to get your ass out the door!" She shoved Adren and stumbled back. "Unless you want to be forced to suck the insides out of every councilman. They like 'em on their knees."

Adren sheathed cir knife and rushed to the armoires. There would be no winning against cir mother. Merasha never threatened to kill her children. Ever.

Given the look in her eyes, she meant it.

"How do you know it's them? We thought you were asleep." Adren grabbed a leather satchel from one armoire and hurried around the room, stuffing the bag. First with a lightweight dress then a handful of ribbons, followed by the gold and pearl bracelets from cir parents for cir sixteenth birthday, and the rings and chain ce usually wore. Finally, Adren threw in what little money ce was allowed to keep from the metal box hidden under one of the floorboards. There was no time to pack, but the items ce grabbed were vital. Without the dress and other things, ce would feel as though ce were in the wrong skin—tight, tense, and twisted up.

"I got up to see what you three were doing. I was on the stairs when the soldiers broke the windows." Head tilted, Merasha backed towards the door. "You're wasting time!"

"Come with me." Adren slipped on the satchel as ce headed for the door.

"I can't. I need to get the servants out. Veanne and her children deserve better than rotting in prison." Merasha pulled Adren into the corridor. The bellowing voices sounded close. Feet stomped the stairs. Beyond them, metal scraped and screeched. Men groaned and cursed. Objects banged the walls. More glass shattered. "Go!"

With a final shove, Merasha turned and raced up the hall, hoisting her nightdress up to her knees. She dodged the staircase, narrowly missing a man in dark clothes reaching for her. He roared for her to stop, stumbling up the rest of the steps before chasing her down the opposite hallway. Behind him, three other men made it to the top step, swords and knives drawn.

Adren dashed to the end of the hallway closest to cir room, focused on the second staircase spiraling up the back corner of the house. Screams cut through all other sounds in the house, high-pitched and desperate. As ce grabbed the wood banister, ce peered back.

Shadowy figures staggered at the other end of the corridor, hauling Merasha towards the main staircase. Kicking and hollering, Merasha struggled against the two men holding her. A third followed, prodding Merasha with his sword. They laughed as Merasha tumbled onto the stairs and to her knees.

When she refused to stand, they shoved her down the staircase.

Unable to breathe, Adren froze, tempted to go back and fling the men down the stairs until every bone in their bodies was broken, no matter what cir mother said. *Mother. Taken.*

Harmed. Because I didn't leave fast enough. Because of the housekeeper.

What a waste.

A waste Adren would make worse if Merasha caught cir disobeying her orders.

She really would kill me. If it meant keeping what I know from the Council, she'd kill us all. Then spend her life in silence and misery, damned for what I couldn't do.

The sacrifice would not be squandered. Adren fled down the stairs, praying cir knees did not buckle. At the end of the staircase, ce hopped over the last two steps and hit the floor of the main level hard, almost rolling on cir ankle. Ce skirted around the corner and ran down the second staircase towards the lower level. On the landing halfway down, Adren slammed cir shoulder against the wall, ramming open the narrow, stubborn hidden door enough to slip through. The moment ce was on the other side of the barely lit passageway, Adren leaned against the door until it shut, hoping the scraping sounds had not alerted the High Council's soldiers.

To the sound of cir heavy breaths, Adren descended the winding staircase, dragging cir fingertips along the jagged stone walls. Unpolished and filthy, the passageway was monitored by three guards every day and served only as a means of escape. Once at the bottom, ce turned sharply to the left and hurried through the long corridor towards the woods west of the house.

A bright yellow glow emanated from a torch at the end of the passageway, light flickering over a closed wooden door to another corridor. Beside the door, two men waited, their heads covered with the hoods of their dark long coats, their hands around the knives attached to their belts.

"You the only one?" one of them called gruffly. He drew back his hood to reveal disheveled, grey-brown hair to his shoulders and stern, sharp features. Darus, an enforcer hired by Rivane to lead missions and keep their faction members under control. Tall, broad, and strict in every facet of his life, he was difficult to ignore.

The second man nudged back his hood. "We were hoping there'd be more of you," Amelin said, raking a hand through his short, bright blond hair. The soft curves of his youthful face pinched. "Guess that answers that, then."

Growling, Darus thrust open the door and nodded at Adren. "Get in. We can't stand here all day. If you're it, you're it."

Adren obeyed, rushing through the door behind Amelin, careful not to touch him. A man who did what he did to women and children would never be someone ce wanted to be near. No matter how sweet his words, he was poison.

Darus joined them, slamming the door shut. After a touch to the small wood crate tucked into the corner, he ushered Adren down the hall, his rough hand on cir back. They broke into a run, following the long, meandering corridor to the next wood door. Amelin knocked twice, kicked once, and knocked once more.

"Enforcement D, Goods A, and little sister," Darus shouted.

The door opened. A short, bald man in dark clothes hovered in the entrance, snarling as he studied them and stepped back. "Get in here." One of Mordane's friends, Adren recalled, though ce struggled to remember his name. Jumbled thoughts blurred most of cir memories, feeding the panic underlying cir every breath.

With Darus's push, Adren stumbled into the hidey-hole. Ce hissed as Amelin caught cir.

Immediately Adren recoiled and backed against the cold stone wall, casting a glance over the murky cellar. Built underground in the woods, the cellar was one of four around the house, accessible by two points: the secret passageway and a door in the ground, hidden under leaves and secured by a guard. Each hideaway could support fifteen people, twenty at most. Stocked with barrels of water, metal crates of cured food, and metal chests with blankets and weapons, the hole offered enough protection for three days.

Adren breathed out, disappointment chilling cir blood. Other than cir, Darus, and Amelin, there were only three others in the cellar. None of them would have three days if the High Council's bounty hunters and soldiers were diligent. They would have to move soon.

Darus grunted and threw the four strong bolts on the door. He shifted his weight and leaned against the wood. "Best I can tell, they've got Rivane and the boys. Barely made it out myself. Took a couple guys down but not enough."

"They've got Mother, too," Adren added, cir gaze falling.

"Dammit!" Darus smacked the door with his palm. "Council's going to feel this if it's the last thing I do."

If we get that far. Adren stared at the square door in the middle of the ceiling. Maybe they would get lucky and no one would check the woods for stragglers until daylight. If they could use the last bit of darkness before dawn—

Boom!

The ground shook. Wood splintered. Stone cracked. Everyone inside the hidey-hole grasped the walls, steadying themselves until the trembling ended.

"What in the Four's name was that?" Adren peered at Darus.

"Escape plan," he muttered, pulling his knife and pressing his ear to the door. "Get ready to hoof it faster than you ever have. And shut it. I need to listen."

Adren held cir breath and crouched, fingers hovering over the hilt of cir knife as they waited in silence.

Ce jumped as the door rattled.

Two knocks. One kick. One knock. "Defence P," a man called from the other side.

Darus jerked back the bolts and yanked open the door. A man with dark hair sauntered in before Darus slammed the door closed and locked it.

"Pade?" Adren eyed his stocky form, obvious in his thick coat. His calm demeanor betrayed nothing of his keen ability to protect through any means possible.

"Like I'd ever let the bastards get me." Pade snorted and wiped his hands on Amelin's shirt. "Here. Blood, just in case you missed spilling some on your way out."

Amelin whined and pushed Pade away. "I hate your idea of gifts." He brushed at his shirt and coat.

"Sure you do." Pade's glance fell on Adren. "I have news."

"News?" Adren stepped forward, hoping his next words were about cir family escaping.

"Yeah, like why they're here caging us." Pade looked at Darus, growling. "Some ass from the Shar snitched us out."

"*What?*" every voice in the hidey-hole roared, the noise deafening.

"How?" Adren grit cir teeth. "How do you know?"

"I dragged one of the soldiers into the tunnel, got him to talk. I love the young ones—they're always so fragile." Pade laughed low and leaned against the wall. "I managed to get the name of their informant between the guy's screams." He drew a finger across his neck. "Now he's in bits with the rest of the tunnel down there. There's nothing a crate of explosive powder won't solve."

"You're seriously saying there's a traitor in the Shar-denn?" Arms crossed, Adren stomped towards Pade, cir fingertips digging into the crooks of cir arms. Whatever kindness had governed cir earlier was gone, silenced by the instinct to do exactly what cir brothers would. A familiar wave of heat poured through cir body, aching to act and send the traitor into death's darkest abyss with the snap of cir fingers. Cir guilt demanded to be appeased. "One of our own?"

"No, he's not even in our faction. Your father had him do work for us, though." Pade spat at the ground. "He's one mark the other factions hate to love—a difficult case."

Adren clenched cir jaws, enunciating each word carefully. "I don't care. He's going to die, *painfully*. I'll see to it myself." A flash of rage surged forth like the shock of lightning under cir skin, its burn barely disguising the fear that shook cir from shoulder to knee. The stern voices of cir father and mother collided inside cir memories, demanding ce act like their heir. Ce had to take charge, not surrender to panic. Words forced themselves out of cir mouth, foreign and sharp. "He took my family, so I'll take his life. I'll take his home. I'll take everything he loves and wrench out his heart so he can watch them die while he bleeds out. He's mine, and he's *dead*."

No one betrayed the Shar-denn and got away with it. No one.

They certainly don't get to hurt my family without paying for it. Revenge isn't sweet, it's necessary. I'm going to bring so much necessary upon this guy he'll feel it for all eternity.

Gripping Pade by the collar, Adren tugged him close. "Give me the name. Tell me whose blood I need to wear."

"Ress." Pade's lips curled into a smirk. "If you're going to do your daddy proud, *please* tell me I can come with."

Adren shoved him back. "Be my guest. There'll be enough guts to go around."

"There won't be anything if we don't shut up and get moving." Darus growled and snapped his fingers at the quiet, gangly man in the furthest corner. "You, Heweth, get that damn door open." He sheathed his knife as Heweth obeyed, dragging a short ladder with him from where it had leaned against the wall. "The rest of you *run*. Don't look back, don't give me sad eyes, don't give me lip. Head for cache houses in any direction that isn't where we're going or find one of the other hideaways. When you get there, spread the word that Rivane's gone down."

Heweth positioned the ladder beneath the ceiling door and climbed the steps. The door squeaked as Heweth opened it slowly, allowing dim light to creep into the hidey-hole. Adren bit back cir protest as Darus clapped a dirty hand over cir mouth, jerking cir against his chest.

"Shut it," Darus whispered, tilting his head and stepping against the wall, hiding in the safety of the shadows. No one breathed or moved, the perfect silence in the cellar disrupted by the soft sounds of leaves moving in the breeze. Heweth pushed the door open further and stuck his head out, glancing in every direction he could manage without falling.

"Clear," Heweth announced with a hoarse whisper, pushing the door open completely. "See you on the other side." He scrambled out of the hole and disappeared into the darkness, his footsteps heavy on fallen leaves, branches cracking in his wake.

Pade grabbed Adren's hand and yanked cir from Darus. "Your turn." He pulled cir towards the steps, gripping cir tight as he climbed the ladder and dragged cir with him.

From behind, Darus shoved Adren up the steps, jabbing cir in the back and pushing on cir legs.

Hands off, Adren almost yelled. If circumstances were different, ce would have turned around and punched him in the throat.

Things are already complicated enough. That bastard—that unbelievable, cock-twisting bastard of a little bitch—he snitched on us. Us!

Adren snarled at Pade as he hauled cir onto the grass, twigs snapping under their shifting weight. It should have been Mordane standing there with cir. It should have been Tethe pushing cir up the steps. Rivane should have been the first to run, not an overpaid lackey they would likely never see again. Not one of the men in the hole would ever measure up to the men that had raised cir. For all of Tethe's inner darkness and inconsiderate impositions, he was the staunch protector ce needed to feel safe in cir own home. When no one else could be trusted, Tethe was the one ce turned to, knowing his scathing hands would settle any danger ce could not ward off cirself.

And when no one else wants to be seen with me, there's Mordane, the only one who's ever cared enough to love me for me most of the time. He's the only one who bothers listening that little bit further.

Now they're both gone because someone couldn't keep their mouth shut.

As Darus pulled himself out of the hole, Adren flicked cir glance to the sky. Through the gaps in shaking branches and wilting leaves, ce glimpsed the stars and cursed. The last time ce had stared at the stars, ce had stood with Mordane and Tethe, laughing at the absurdity of wishing upon the night sky. It was so vast, so consuming, yet untouchable, unobtainable. A sea of cold emptiness waiting to crash down upon them and still people cast their hopes to the stars. Adren had agreed with cir brothers that would never be them, only one of the things they had in common. Stars would never dictate their future. Wishes would never fool them. They would make their own destinies, pulling each other along for the ride. None of them would be left behind.

Now that memory was tainted, muddied by a new memory of standing alone, wishing upon the stars for cir family to survive.

Darus snatched Adren's arm. "Let's go." He pulled cir to the north, charging between bushes without waiting for Amelin to catch up. Pade hurried past them, light on his feet, scanning every direction for danger. So far, the soldiers' focus seemed to have remained on the estate on the other side of the woods, though their luck could change at any moment.

"You expect us to go where?" Adren clutched cir satchel, picking up cir pace to match Darus's.

He sighed loudly, throwing an annoyed glance over his shoulder. "Cache house. We need information. Can't catch a snitch when you don't know where he is."

"We also need a plan," Amelin added, rushing up behind them, winded.

"That, too." Darus tugged Adren harder. "But we need to leave *now*, so keep up."

When he broke into a run, Adren followed, batting away leaves and tall grasses as they fled with Pade in the lead and Amelin behind. Each step that took cir away from home felt like a blunt saw shredding cir heart. The house ce had grown up in. The family ce loved. Both abandoned, both seized; both in the custody of cruel hands that would respect nothing about them.

Ress would die—a promise, not a hope. He would shed a drop of blood for every memory that haunted Adren.

For each comforting image of cir father playing a game with cir, teaching cir about rules and strategy, Ress would weep at cir feet.

For every time ce remembered cir mother's girlish laughter as they danced barefoot in the courtyard to the dulcet sounds of a string quartet, Ress would feel the lash of Adren's wrath.

For all the times ce relived the times Mordane and Tethe had embraced cir and wiped the fear from cir soul with the gentlest glance, Ress would scream for mercy.

Ce would teach him what loyalty meant.

I can just see him now: a sleazy, greasy, little man in expensive boots and cheap perfume. Not even worth the flimsy rag to wipe his guts from the wall. Or he's some lazy lowlife of a rodent, toothless and clawing at the scraps. No prospects except to run his mouth. I bet he's too foolish to hide.

Adren glanced at Darus, his long coat trailing behind him as he kept a steady pace, taking large strides with Pade through the harvested field before cir. They would find Ress and make certain he could never speak again. *Any plan, any strategy. I'll do whatever I have to do to shut him down, and these guys can take whatever shots they want. I'll make his soul writhe in agony forever, then I'll get my family back. If there's one life I'll end happily, one name I'll die saying without regret, it's Ress's.*

CHAPTER TWO

Another day, another set of tedious lies. Another reminder of what the Shar-denn had stolen from him. Another collision with the brutal truth that he would never truly love his wife in the way she needed, not like he wanted, despite how hard he tried. No matter how much she deserved it.

She would have been better off falling in love with a ghost.

Not whatever I am, stuck between here and there. Ress opened his dark eyes and faced the window to his left, hidden behind pale blue curtains barely moving in the cool air. The dim light of dawn chased darkness from the bedroom, the thin rays illuminating the walls and possessions Ress owned with Inesta. Nice, luxurious things with debatable value and no meaning, providing a life of comfort he never should have had.

A life paid for by others in ways that made currency seem like a child's game.

She doesn't even know the half of it. Controlling his deep sigh to keep from disturbing Inesta, Ress slid his glance towards her, his chin grazing the top of her head. At some point in the night, she had crept across the mattress to settle against his side. Her small body pressed against his lean form, her slender arm lying across his waist. They rarely slept so close. *Probably just needed the body heat*, he mused, pulling the blankets higher around Inesta's pale shoulders. The thin, pink nightdress she wore offered nothing in the way of warmth. *That's what I'm for, apparently. Huzzah. Found something I'm good at. Clap my hands and raise the bells, there's hope for our marriage yet.*

"I can hear you thinking," Inesta mumbled, her voice groggy. "It's too early for sarcasm." She huddled closer, rubbing her forehead along his cheek. Strands of her disheveled auburn hair tickled the end of his nose. "It's too early for everything." Her hand slipped along the waistband of his loose pants as she hummed. "Well, maybe except for this."

Fingers toyed with the ties of his pants before creeping down his groin, tracing the outline of his flaccid cock. The light touch turned playful, teasing him, commanding the tightening skin to do her bidding.

If only it were that easy. If only he could have felt something other than the excited skin that contradicted how he felt inside.

Even when her fingers snuck beneath the fabric to caress his half-hardened cock, he was divided. Try as she may, her efforts would go

40

unfounded. What she needed and what he could give would never be perfectly matched. Even if his traitor of a cock was in for the ride, the rest of him was not, and he had no intention of forcing himself that morning. Not like he had several nights ago during their monthly romp under the sheets. Or on the settee, as it had been, after she ambushed him in skimpy silver lingerie and practically begged him to make love to her. To see her smile, he had obliged. While he had felt nothing—no pleasure, no satisfaction—she had felt enough for the two of them.

Not now. The morning would remain his.

"You're trouble," Ress murmured, drawing her knuckles to his lips. "Start that and you won't want to go to work this morning."

Inesta pouted, her hazel eyes disappearing under lowered lashes. "You act like you actually want to go into the shop. I wish you'd stay and play a bit. For me?"

Had it been a matter of timing or responsibility, she would have won the argument. *There wouldn't be an argument to begin with. She'd be on me right now, riding her way into her next scream, hollering for more.*

He brushed back her hair, tangling his calloused fingers in its long length. "Wish I could, but it's not that kind of morning. It's not up for playtime," he said, leading her hand to his softening cock to prove his point.

"Oh." Inesta tucked her hand between her breasts, trapping it between her and him. "Sorry."

The dejection in her voice crippled him more than his bad knee did.

"Don't worry about it." Ress kissed her forehead, taking in the faint scent of spice from the soap she used. If he were different, able to feel arousal the way most men seemed to, he would have ravished her. Drunk in her essence and teased the spark of life burning inside her. Even if they never felt for each other what apparently a husband and wife were expected to, he should have given her that much. Like a real lover would. Like a sympathetic friend could.

The most he could manage was a sore attempt at being romantic, presenting her with unannounced gifts, showering her with endearments that felt rough as they left his lips, and killing himself to protect her. Everything else was foreign, strange. Unnecessary.

"We should get up, then." Inesta yawned and rolled away, stretching. "Bremary's opening the shop this morning, and you know she loathes doing it alone."

How could he forget? His cousin needed to be around people even more than she needed air. In most ways, she was the opposite to her older brother, Covran, who detested being in the presence of anyone except for family. Together, they achieved an almost perfect balance, a peculiar benefit shared with the metal wares shop they ran with Ress and Inesta. Covran was content to work with Ress in the forge and workroom while Bremary's friendliness blossomed in the front of the shop with Inesta and their customers.

In spite of everything wrong in their lives, the shop was their greatest blessing—and the most honest.

The last bit of honesty I've got, except for the fact I should be dead. No running from that nasty chunk of truth, no matter whose mercy I buy. One day, I won't have the right lie. One day, I won't need it because dead men don't need lies. The bastards just need to rot to fate's content.

Ress watched Inesta rise from the bed and tie her hair back with a bright green ribbon. Her wrinkled nightdress clung to her as she crossed the room to the round wood table in the furthest corner, situated under the last of the five windows spanning the wall to Ress's left. She swept a curtain back to let more golden light into the room before washing her face with water from the silver bowl on the table. A daily ritual, simple and mundane, but one Ress counted as blissfully normal and pure. An act of cleansing he witnessed every morning, aching to forget the filth soiling who he was.

A forgettable act so immersed in washing away the past, it screamed in the silence, beating him with the need to escape the blood dripping from his crooked, bruised spirit.

The only way out is dead, but not for you, Ines. Please, never for you. If I could have a single wish, it would be for you to have life. A blessed life that laughs in the face of the Shar's twisted notions. A life that makes them hurt for what they've done; for what I've done to you.

If only he could voice the words.

If only she would believe him.

Inesta flashed him a sad smile before picking up the white cloth beside the bowl and drying her face. There was a time when her smiles had been happier. The lies were easier to tell in those days, and they had purchased peace in their home.

That's all gone. Years and years tossed into the slop bucket. Swallowing another sigh, Ress drew his hands through his short, dark hair and locked his fingers behind his neck. Eyes closed, he listened to Inesta brush her hair, shed her nightdress, and browse the armoire across the room from him. In his mind, he could see her: naked and bountiful in proportion, enough to make mouths crave a taste of her pale skin. A tender package that gave her fiery spirit corporeal being, gracing their marriage with strength and determination he admired.

Except I don't love you like a lover does, not with all that romantic rubbish, never mind the sexual bollocks. I'm such a fool. Ress pressed the heels of his palms to his eyelids. *Taldris, that ass. I could kill him for leaving you. He loved you the way you want, the way you deserve, all heart and touch and pretty words. If he'd met you before the Shar-denn, he'd have never left and you'd have the life you've always wanted. One that doesn't include this pathetic sham we're treating like an actual conjugal relationship. Oh, wait, what's that? I think I hear the Goddesses laughing.*

"Hey, you, the deliciously edible man in my bed."

A tap on his foot forced Ress to jolt. Sharp pain shot up his left knee, clawing at his kneecap. Hissing, he sat up and massaged his knee until the seizing ache subsided. A befitting souvenir from the worst decision he had made as a youth, the wound refused to fully heal. To make matters even more frustrating, the injury hurt more with each passing year. He would be amazed if he could walk in his old age. Assuming he was lucky enough to *get* old.

"Oh, Ress. I'm sorry." Inesta jerked her arm back, grimacing. Her hair hung around her shoulders, smooth and straight except for the few locks with curls at the end. A handful of strands were twisted and tied back on either side, brightening her features. A green gown replaced her nightdress, the embroidered hems and pale green lace cuffs at her elbows echoing the fashions worn by the Grand Families and other aristocrats. "I'm sorry, dearest. That's not what I wanted." She stroked his right foot still hidden under the blankets. The ring on the middle finger of her left hand was a flash of pale red gold, a dainty marriage band with a row of alternating bright pink and white diamonds in the centre. "I just wanted to let you know I'm starting breakfast."

Ress nodded, grinding his teeth at the lingering threads of pain. This morning was not one of his better ones. All night, the dull pain had taunted him, waiting to be provoked. That, too, was worsening over time. A weekly occurrence, it seemed, instead of monthly.

Soon it'll be daily, and then what good will I be? Certainly won't be running from the Shar-denn in any measure of the word, and I won't even start on what High Council will do with me. I'm a thorn in the side of their national controls.

"It's fine." He pressed harder on the side of his knee. "I'll be there shortly. This old man's just going to roll his deliciously edible self out of bed and probably onto the floor."

Inesta laughed softly. "Did you want help?" She tilted her head, pursing her lips. "I could roll you into the kitchen if you want."

Ress waved her words away. "Let me keep *some* sort of dignity. I'm still self-rolling capable. Just ignore the really loud curses." He motioned to the closed bedroom door. "Go on. I'll be right behind."

"If you say so." Inesta patted his leg and moved to the door, her bare feet peeking out from beneath her gown. "Don't forget we've got that showing this afternoon," she said, grasping the gold doorknob. "That commission for Magistrate Galosa. Cove said he's nearly finished with the brooches. The collar's already complete, and so are the cuffs and bracelets."

"Yeah, because *I* completed them." Ress snorted. Covran excelled at planning projects, working the metal, and setting stones. His ability to complete the tasks well before they were due, however, remained suspect. "If he wasn't family—"

"You'd *still* have hired him. You don't trust anyone else."

She took the point in that match, Ress decided before she opened the door and slipped out. His knee reminded him how much trust could hurt, and how much he violated trust every day.

The fact Covran was family saved their shop, but it was Covran's love of smithing and attention to detail that helped them thrive. No matter his faults, Covran was one of the few people Ress trusted with anything, including the shop that bore more sentimental value than any object Ress owned. The business was a legacy from their great-grandparents, passed down to Ress's mother, Sebina. After she had fled Kattal with Ress's father and sisters, taking Ress's advice to get as far from the Shar-denn's hunting ground as possible, the shop's fate had been placed in Ress's care. Regardless of his gibes and annoyances with Covran, he was grateful his cousins cared about the business, running it whenever he disappeared on business for the Shar-denn or High Council.

Then there's the matter of Cove knowing about the Shar at all. With slow movements, Ress slid his left leg over the edge of the mattress, followed by the right. *Not that* everyone *doesn't know of my involvement with them. Thanks, Taldris. Remind me to kick your ass for that. Oh, wait, sorry. You're calling yourself Tash now, aren't you? Bastard. New name, new boyfriend, new life.* He gripped the sheets, flattening his feet on the floor and flexing his muscles before they followed through on their threats to cramp. *Meanwhile, I get stuck with the same old pains, and the lies, and the enemies. Ever since you sold my name to Council, I've got even more enemies. Nothing like having bounty hunters breathe down my neck while a dangerous gang stokes the oven for my roasting. Some best friend you are. When you destroy lives, you really go for it.*

But that was only part of the truth. For all the anger he harboured towards the man he once knew as Taldris, Ress carried triple the blame towards himself. They had agreed to join the gang as individuals, each responsible for their own choices, no different than their other two best friends, Varen and Nimae. Even if the only other option was death, there had still been a choice. At fourteen years old, Ress had made the best choice he could to survive.

Twenty-two years later, he was still surviving. To say he lived was a joke.

Maybe anger was not what he felt towards Tash, the man who had emerged from the ashes of Ress's childhood friend—a friend who had run from the Shar-denn and abandoned Ress, Varen, and Nimae. A friend who was branded a traitor, forcing the vengeful appetites of not only their faction's boss and members, but the members and bosses of other factions, putting Ress, Varen, and Nimae on a list of suspected future defectors. No, anger was inaccurate.

Sanity-devouring jealousy, that's what this is. Ress stood and padded across the wood floor to the table in the corner. Washing his face with the lukewarm water, he stared at his fragmented reflection, ignoring the droplets traveling down his neck. After Ress's attempts to work against the Shar-denn and stop them from hurting innocent people, how was *Tash* the one with a new life safe from the gang's retribution? Tash, who used to defend faction leaders as a guard, willingly violent and selfish in his pursuit of working up the ranks? While Ress had grappled to sabotage the gang without being caught, Tash had unleashed his anger at their circumstances onto the Shar-denn and was rewarded for participating in their crimes.

Yet it was Tash who was granted a reprieve by whichever goddess loved him best.

Not only had he left the Shar-denn and hidden well enough to become a priest, Tash had found redemption through the High Council, the republic's governing body and supreme authority. With a list of names, Tash had purchased forgiveness from the twelve councilmen, skirting around the same laws that would see Ress executed. Tash walked free, at the cost of turning in Ress, Varen, Nimae, and dozens of others. Some of whom no longer lived, having taken their own lives rather than confess their crimes.

Varen was among the dead, released from the chains of the gang that owned them. A freedom Ress wished he could have, so much he could taste the need bleeding from his soul.

Disgusted, Ress sneered at his reflection and slicked his hair back. Silently cursing the puckered scar marring his right jaw, he dried his face and neck then tossed down the towel. One day, he would get out from under everyone's commands, both the Shar-denn's and the High Council's. Until then, he had to play their games. The Shar-denn commanded he work for them, coordinating the transportation of goods and producing counterfeit currency, among other things. The High Council forced him to stay to commit crimes and report back on his accomplices.

The gang wanted ultimate power over the republic, stealing control from a council of bureaucrats they blamed for everything wrong with Kattal. The High Council saw a nation plagued by a social disease they had to contain and cure, pointing fingers at the Shar-denn for terrorizing Kattal's citizens with delusions of anarchy. It was a game both would inevitably lose.

In the grand scheme of it all, neither master cared where Ress ended up.

Caught between the two, he aimed to reclaim his life. Although the councilmen disapproved of his vigilante behaviour, he would continue to sabotage the Shar-denn and leave the High Council to deal with the consequences of their plans.

And though the Shar-denn frightened everyone, including him, he would drive the knife of betrayal into the back of the gang over and over until they bled submission.

Then maybe, one day, he would take Tash to task over leaving Inesta to fend for herself.

One fight at a time. Limping through the room to the sounds of Inesta moving clay plates in the kitchen, Ress approached the armoire. Wide and constructed from dark brown wood, the vine-engraved armoire was one of the only things he'd kept from his parents' old home. Carved by his father, Telumic, he had argued with his parents over taking the armoire before they left for Arminloa, the neighbouring country. They had insisted he keep it, wanting a piece of them to remain in Kattal, home to their family for generations. More than that, they had wanted Ress to remember them and their family's happy past. Before he had brought fear into their home.

He drew a hand over the leaves on the left door. Sunlight illuminated the scrapes left by his younger sister, Trenna, after she had stumbled into the armoire as a child. At the time, she had been almost as tall as him, her head reaching halfway up the door. Several hand lengths above the scraped patch was the end of the vine, embellished with five open flowers. The flower at the top was his favourite, having been at eye level with both his mother and older sister, Lalaern. The curved petals warmed him with memories of both women standing beside the armoire in his parents' room. That had been when things were simpler, wholesome. When he had been a boy excited with the prospect of being a man.

Ress opened both doors, returning the memories to their safe place. Without glancing at the dark tattoo on his left forearm, he chose an embroidered black tunic from the pile of folded shirts on the top left shelf. From the shelf below, he grabbed the first pair of pants he saw, the dark brown leather soft to the touch, loose and barely worn. Both the shirt and pants were Inesta's doing, her preferences tidier and more fashionable than his. He was happy in dingy, dark clothes, especially since they got dirtier in the forge, doused in sweat and smoke. If not for their visit to Araveena Ford's magistrate that afternoon, he would have dressed in his shirt from the previous day. To keep his wife happy and avoid sullying their shop's reputation more than he already had, he would present himself as a gentleman.

Settled on the edge of the bed, Ress yanked off the pants he had slept in and tossed them over the footboard. As he pulled on the fresh pair of pants and tunic, he stared at the light and shadows playing through the room. Above him, the black wood beams appeared new, hiding the fact they were dusty and creaked under heavy rain. The walls were just as dark except for the red sheen revealed by sunlight. On either side of the bed, against the wall, were two small tables with candles. A standing wooden case for jewelry sat next to the table on Inesta's side of the bed, a mate to the armoire against the wall beside the door, encasing the two fine gowns and other expensive possessions Inesta rarely wore.

My fault, Ress admitted, tugging on his boots without dislodging the red and gold knife in the sheath sewn into his right boot. He gave Inesta nice things only to deprive her of occasions to wear them. Had the Shar-denn not claimed him, he would have escorted her to the balls, dinners, and holy observances for which they received invitations. Although he had little interest in the events, he would have loved to see Inesta dressed lavishly like the women from the high-born Grand Families.

Instead, he was the anchor keeping her from a life she deserved to enjoy. Rules kept him in Araveena Ford. Demands shackled him to his home. Inesta was a prisoner by proxy.

"I do this to keep you safe," he muttered, peering out the open doorway. Inesta bustled around the table in the middle of the kitchen area, humming as she stepped and spun, light and quiet on her uncovered feet. The skirt of her gown danced with her movements, the loose, pleated fabric barely settling before she moved again. When they married, he had never expected to take comfort in watching her do something as routine as set the table. Twenty-four years old and scared, his intentions had been to keep the Shar-denn's hands off her.

Twelve years later, seeing her still in their home astounded him. Although their marriage was a failure beneath the forced smiles and fatigued efforts, she made their house a home more than the wood and stone it was built from. His ruse had succeeded this far, justifying why he would continue to play the role of husband, holding on to a relationship that had been strained nearly to the end of its very existence, pushed and pulled in too many directions, none of them kind or even vaguely sympathetic. Sometimes he wondered if they had simply perfected being falsely cordial with each other, enough to deceive even themselves in order to keep going. At best, they were friends who slept together. At worst, he was her jailer, compassionate and gentle but still no better than the gang members in the Shar-denn's trafficking ring.

Goddesses, forgive me.

With a deep breath, Ress retrieved his marriage ring from his bedside table and pushed up from the bed, slipping on the understated gold band as he strode from the room. The rest of the single-level house filled his sight, spacious without walls separating every room. To his left was the small storage room where they kept linens, adjoined to the main bedroom. Beside the storage room, the side door that opened onto the yard and a stone pathway towards the back of the house, occupied by a small forge and work area. To his right was the smaller bedroom with a larger storage room next to it, built back further than the other rooms. The kitchen and sitting room waited before him, separated by a patch of black wood floorboards, lacking the elegantly woven blue rugs that sat beneath the dining table, chairs, and settees. Only the kitchen hearth was lit, leaving the sitting area cool. Beyond the sitting area was the double-door entryway, leading to the front yard, garden, and the red dirt road that ran towards the village square.

Inesta looked up from the washbasin, her hands growing still around a partially peeled pink fruit. "Almost ready." She brushed the back of her wrist across her forehead before nodding at the hearth to her left. "Just warming the last of the meat. I'll send Bremary to the butcher later, get her to fetch a few things for both our households. It's her turn, anyway."

"Sure. I'm all for getting her away from Cove for a bit. She's been hounding him about the girl that keeps making eyes at him. I told him he needs to move out of that house. Bremary will kill him before he ever lays a girl flat." Ress leaned against the table, eyeing the wooden bowl filled with orange, savoury fruit and the wooden board with half a loaf of bread, already sliced. Empty, brown clay plates and metal settings waited on the table next to metal goblets filled with water. In the centre of the table sat the glass vase he had given Inesta for the first anniversary of their wedding day. Large, white coronni flowers with vibrant golden centres stood in the vase, their thick green leaves spilling over the edge. Enveloping the fragrant white petals were tiny leaves of dark orange ferns, reminding him it was autumn once more.

A quiet autumn, he hoped, unlike the autumn before.

"Ha! As if that's his greatest worry." Inesta arched a brow, breaking apart the fruit in her hand and placing one half on each of their plates. "She's been making eyes, herself. If he's not paying attention, he'll wake up one morning and find out he's suddenly the brother-in-law to the daughter of a certain twice-decorated soldier. The same girl Cove eyed for months last year and didn't have the gall to court."

"No."

"Yes."

"He doesn't know, does he?"

"Not a wit or so Bremary says. So she's taking full advantage and getting that girl's attention better than Cove did." Snorting, Inesta dipped her hands into the water in the washbasin. "Then again, you can't trust either of them to know what's going on with each other even under their own roof. They're wearing blinders, both of them. They're brother and sister, for the love of the Four. You'd think they'd have stopped with the games a while back and talk it out." She gestured at the table as she dried her hands.

Ress obeyed her silent command and moved towards his seat at the furthest end of the table. On passing, he curled his arm around her waist. "Nah, they live for it. Out of the four children in that family, those two always ran my aunt straight into raging frustration." He kissed Inesta's cheek, his lips lingering near hers. "Still, it's entertaining, so I'll take it. Never a dull moment with them." His next kiss was chaste on her lips. "Thanks for breakfast."

"Have to eat," she answered, shrugging out of his embrace. "Now go on, sit."

Not to be told again, Ress sat down and waited. After retrieving the roasted meat from the hearth and placing it on the table, Inesta joined him, sitting adjacent to him in the chair to his right. They were silent as they filled their plates and began to eat. If not for Inesta's unusual fidgeting and the drumming of her fingers on her chair, he would have considered the morning the same as any other.

"What's got you?" Ress cast a questioning glance at her shaking leg.

Inesta stilled, rigid and awkward. "Nothing." She breathed out. "Much."

Ress reached for her, his palm up. "Go on, tell me." When she slipped her hand in his, he squeezed her fingers, hoping it was enough reassurance.

No answer came. Instead, Inesta stared at her plate and toyed with a piece of bread.

What did I do now? Ress held back a sigh. He was accustomed to silence at meals, while other meals were so loud he wished he had never heard a word. The tenseness in between the two extremes worried him more. "Ines, what is it?"

The reply was a frustrated breath. "I received a letter yesterday from Eloras, one of my friends growing up. You remember her, don't you? She married and moved out to the Alosaa tract."

"The blonde one, tall and skinny and shal—" Ress caught himself before finishing the insult. Inesta was nervous enough without him calling one of her closest friends shallow and pretentious. He cleared his throat. "Living in one of the big cities now, you said. Her husband works for the Commerce Assembly or something."

"Assistant to one of the Chief Assemblymen, yes. They're in Grace-upon-Alatayle, close to the port."

Grace, the largest city in Alosaa, the regional tract of Kattal attached to Gailarin, the region in which Ress had lived his entire life. From what he knew, Grace-upon-Alatayle and the surrounding towns were posh and refined, supported by half a dozen Grand Families and a dozen more aristocrats, most of them members of the Commerce Assembly and frequent users of the seaside port. The Shar-denn equated the value of Grace and its neighbouring districts to that of Alosaa as a whole. Should the factions completely infiltrate Grace, they would control one of the primary waterways into Kattal and could scare the rest of the Alosaa tract into compliance.

But first, they would have to bring down Alosaa's Tract Steward, Kayte Oaren, a man as formidable as his family's history of success in battle. The politician in Kayte safeguarded Alosaa with strong words and well-trained guards, commanding the region with dedicated task forces and skilled committees no one dared cross. If that was not deterrent enough, the soldier in Kayte was ready to pierce the heart of the Shar-denn despite his diplomacy. He only needed to be set in the right direction.

Temptation to give him that direction plagued Ress. One message, four names—that was all it would take.

Had Ress wanted to start a war, he would have sent Kayte on the chase. If a civil bloodbath was what Kattal needed, Ress would have sent an identical message to Aeley Dahe, Tract Steward of Gailarin. Aeley would battle and bleed for the tract she controlled, no less than Kayte would his. Her soldiers could give Kayte's a fair fight, herself included. Together, Kayte and Aeley would do more damage to the Shar-denn than the discreet, cleanly executed methods of the High Council.

Unfortunately for Kattal, Ress was not that foolish.

While the Shar-denn harmed or sold their share of citizens, the consequences of a full outing would be disastrous for the republic. Retribution from the Shar-denn would be messy. He knew what would happen if the deepest fears of the Shar-denn factions blazed and their inhibited rage went on a rampage. It was destruction he would not be responsible for. The safer choice was a slow boil over the controlled fire set by the High Council.

Blinking back everything he could not tell Inesta, Ress forced a smile. "What about Eloras?"

Inesta dug her spoon into a piece of fruit but did not eat it. "She's invited us to Grace."

"So she wants to show you around."

"No, not to visit." Inesta laid down her spoon. "To live."

"Oh." Ress withdrew his hand from hers.

She pinned his wrist to the table. "Wait, dearest, please. Eloras says it's beautiful there, so peaceful. She's never been happier. It's better than living here in Araveena, she said. There's more of everything, and it could do us just as good." Inesta's voice softened, twisting Ress's heart tighter than the sickening effect it had on his gut. "She says she's found the perfect place for us to live, you and me, and there's a small building around the corner that's good for a shop like ours. It's fate, she said, and it's all *hers*. Eloras can do whatever she wants with these places, and she's offering them to *us*. Just us."

"Ines—"

"Ress, *please*." Her fingers gripped his. "We could go. Leave this shop to Cove and Bremary and cause a stir in the city. We're good enough.

You're good enough. Your work is so flawless, so perfect. Eloras has been flaunting our pieces at showings and events and everyone loves them. *Everyone.* They want those pieces, dearest, all those wonderful things you make. They're willing to pay, too. There's talk of people wanting to commission even larger pieces." Inesta's clasp tightened. "It's Grace, a big, big city. There'd be more sales, more recognition, and more customers, especially the wealthy kind. Do you know how many benefactors you could get?"

He could guess, but there was more to his decision than money.

As if reading his thoughts, Inesta clamped both hands on his arm, her fingertips caressing him. "It would be good for us, too. We could start fresh," she said, tears wetting her eyes. "We could leave everything behind—the pain, the long nights of waiting, the constant looking over our shoulders. Grace could change everything, and we could use a little grace in our relationship. Something that isn't *this*." With one hand, she motioned to the house. "We could go away. For years. For decades. There'd be so much to see, to do. We could make all new friends. Wipe it all clean and build again."

One tear slipped down her cheek, followed by a second. Inesta all but fell off the edge of her chair. "Please, Ress. Do this for us. I promise I won't ask you for something like this again. I need this, and I think you need it, too. Please. Just this."

Closing his eyes, Ress wished they could restart the morning and avoid the entire discussion. If time worked backwards, he would have crawled into a hole and died the night before. "No."

He pulled his arm from Inesta's hold, nauseous from her slackened grasp. His eyes did not have to be open for him to see the disappointment on her face. The hitch of her breath and strangled sob etched a clear enough picture on the darkness in his mind.

"I can't leave, Ines." When he opened his eyes, he focused on the table. "I understand why you want to leave—I do—and I wish I could, but I can't. There's people here I can't leave. Bremary, Cove, other people in this village—I can't leave them to fend on their own. They don't have anyone else standing between them and the Shar. I can't just run away. I'm not Taldris."

Inesta's fingers curled into fists. She promptly drew them into her lap.

"I'm sorry," Ress apologized quietly. "Really, truly sorry. Maybe one day, just not now. Not…"

Ever. Not ever, that's what I should be saying. He dropped his gaze to the food on his plate. *You want to know the real reason why I can't leave Araveena? The real reason you're crying? I can't go anywhere without Council's permission, and certainly not permanently. I go where they want me to go, on Shar business only. I'm their toy, their ugly little errand boy, and I'm not allowed to go play with anyone else. Not until they get everything they want. By then, I'll be dead.*

He stole a glance at Inesta's bowed head. *But I can't tell you any of this, my shame runs so deep. I can't tell you the truth about my release from Council's custody and their rules. I can't tell you about being an informant or that I'm trying to make amends. All you see is the lowlife bastard you married because of some other, even lower lowlife bastard. I feel so guilty, so bad. I wish I could cry every one of your tears for you, but I can't.*

"There's a reason why my work is flawless." Ress braced himself for the partial truth. "It's because I'm protecting people I care for, including you. That's never changed, and it won't. I can't pack up our life and leave."

"I get it." Inesta raised her hands. "You can stop explaining. I'm not a child. I don't need to have it spelled out for me." She faced him, her eyes red and puffy. "The saddest part is that's *exactly* what I expected you to say. Thanks for not disappointing my disappointment."

Before he could apologize again, Inesta pushed back her chair, collected her dishes, and took them to the washbasin. The plate and utensils clattered in the metal tub. Without another word, she hurried towards the bedroom. The door slammed shut, as hard and loud as he expected she screamed inside.

"Welcome to just another day," he mumbled, standing to clean the dishes. They were lucky he worked in the back of the shop while she worked in the front—he could avoid her for most of the day. Otherwise, she would be tempted to kill him where he stood.

He would be the first to let her.

If there was one thing Ress appreciated most about his cousins, it was their ability to sense when things were bad enough that silence was the only way they could help.

Bremary and Covran noticed the frigid responses and space between him and Inesta, but neither addressed the matter. Instead, their gazes bounced between Ress and Inesta before flicking towards a distraction. Their curiosity was not subtle, apparent from the scowls and quizzical expressions, but it was sympathetic.

Just as well, Ress mused, standing in the doorway of the workroom as he surveyed the rest of the shop. Even if one of his cousins *had* bothered to ask him what was wrong *this* time, the conversation still would have ended the same: "I messed up."

Words that should've been in my marriage vows, followed with a string of apologies to buy me some leniency. Arms crossed, Ress leaned against the doorframe, watching the patrons in the shop. Two men in faded shirts and loose work pants browsed the daggers and swords hanging on the walls, occasionally turning around to the middle portion of the shop that boasted boxes and displays of goblets, candle holders, statues, and other assorted wares. At the front of the shop, to the right of the front entrance, two young women in brightly coloured tunics and skirts chatted with Bremary and Inesta over the jewels kept in glass cases.

From Inesta's friendly manner, it was not easy to tell she was still upset with Ress. She was talented at hiding her true feelings. Only when she met Ress's glance was her anger noticeable. The truth scorched him every time.

"So wait, you're meeting Galosa *when*?"

Ress rolled his eyes. "Midday," he repeated for the third time that morning. To relieve pressure on his good leg, he shifted his weight before peering over his shoulder. "Get the brooch done or I'm disowning you."

Covran laughed and fidgeted on his stool, his brown eyes gleaming. The bright blue diamonds of the white metal brooch in his hand glinted in the sunlight from the windows in the wall behind him and the ceiling. "You've been saying that for twenty years. Time to get a new threat. You could at least find one that works. Something frightening would be refreshing."

Moving closer to the workbench against the right wall, Covran resumed working on the brooch, his head bowed over the standing frame of a jeweler's lens to ensure the smallest details of the piece met Ress's standards. Steady and careful, he set the last diamond in the pattern: a flower in full bloom, with a ribbon around a stem crafted from silver pearls. "Scare me, why don't you, just once. Make me believe," he added, sliding off his stool, the brooch sitting in his palm. His boot heels clicked across the wood floorboards as he disappeared through the back door into the forge, his black leather apron scraping the doorframe.

Several retorts came to Ress's mind, none of them appropriate. He turned back into the workroom, waiting for Covran to finish in the forge. Had the meeting with Galosa not been important, he would have accompanied Covran and helped him add the final touches to the brooch, melting the metal to ensure the stones remained in place.

Instead, Ress abided by Inesta's request to avoid the flames and heat. The least he could do was appear as polished and presentable as she wanted him to be. Professional presentation was even more important given Galosa's knowledge of Ress's involvement in the Shar-denn. As village magistrate and liaison with the High Council, Galosa was invested in the safety and survival of citizens, governing Araveena Ford with strict ordinances and sharp logic. He could easily make Ress and Inesta's lives more difficult, including shutting down their shop and exiling them from Araveena Ford altogether.

To Ress's relief, Galosa had not gone that far, not yet. The only thing saving them was Covran and Bremary's shared ownership. They were perfect, law-abiding citizens. Worse, their mother was Ress's aunt, Herias, a notorious barrister known for her ability to make criminals weep at their trials.

Of his family, his aunt scared him the most. She could barely look at him, let alone say his name. Her disgust over his choices ran deep, her sympathy unsalvageable. Their relationship had shattered when he turned twenty—the same day he admitted to his parents he was in the Shar-denn. To his surprise, Herias had not turned him into the authorities herself, but only because she wanted to protect her reputation and their family. What loyalty she had was to everyone else, not to him. He had tarnished that gift.

To add to the strained family matters, Covran and Bremary took after Herias in appearance. Unlike their other brother and sister, Arnanthe and Raeda, they were not fair and round-faced. Instead, they were like Ress, with the tan skin and brown eyes prevalent in their maternal bloodline. Bremary wore her straight, dark hair long to the middle of her back, often sweeping it up into a tail and embellishing it with small pins, combs, and the occasional flower. Almost as tall as Ress, she favoured the height of the men in their family rather than the women.

Covran resembled Ress even more, his face just as slender and sharp, his body lean and arms muscular from constant use. His dark hair was short with small curls around his nape. All their lives, strangers had mistaken Covran and Bremary as Ress's siblings. In many ways they were, having spent as much time with his family as they did their own.

While the biggest difference between Ress and Bremary was in personality, the most notable differences between him and Covran were professional. Covran paid little attention to time, preferring to get lost in the skill of smithing. Most of his interests centred on weapons and larger pieces that required less attention to tiny details and more emphasis on hard use. The sweat-inducing heat of the forge never bothered him.

Ress, however, found peace in working with precious metals and stones, preferring to work in cool, crisp air. As a child, his attention had constantly wandered to the particular shine of the jewelry created by his parents, leading him to believe that was where his crafting hand needed to be. In truth, he could work with anything, a skill he had honed as an apprentice to his parents. Finely engraved pieces for display, serving ware, and statues. Locks and keys. Arrowheads, knives, and other weapons. Currency. The ability to craft them all was why the Shar-denn kept him, even after his arrest two and a half years ago. Even though the gang suspected he was an informant.

Once more, he cursed his abilities.

"It's done now," Covran announced, entering the workroom. He drew his arm across his forehead, wiping away sweat and ash with his black tunic. "All of them. The whole set."

Stopped at the workbench along the wall to Ress's left, Covran opened a wide, black wood box with gold latches. Inside, tucked snugly in grooves lined with soft, red fabric, lay the other pieces commissioned by Galosa. A thick, jewel-studded gold collar with white crystals lay beside a pair of matching cuffs. Narrow, silver bracelets with blue jewels lay surrounded by half a dozen brooches of various hues, all set in white metal.

"Thank you."

"Yeah, sure. You know me, always making someone else happy." Covran laid the last brooch in its place. "Some gift, though, right? *So* not even a matter of business." He peered over his shoulder. "Galosa courting someone? Is there going to be a Mistress Magistrate? Maybe a Master Magistrate, for all we know?"

"I don't know, and I don't care." Ress raised his hands, easing back onto one foot. "Ines and Bremary take the orders; I ensure we make them. I don't care who he's giving it to or who he's playing tongues with. It's better if we don't know these things."

Covran's lips twisted. "You're no fun." He closed the box and latched it shut. "Still, just to make things interesting: when you deliver these to him this afternoon, think of him naked and on his knees, tonguing the body parts for which we make *no* jewelry." A wicked grin spread across his lips. "I can think of somewhere else we could put jewels. Rings, too, depending on who he's licking—I mean, *entertaining*."

Ress slapped his forehead and squeezed his eyes shut. "Cove! Don't do that damned sex stuff to me. I don't need to know. For the last time: we're not going there. If you want to decorate what's in your pants, be my guest. You don't have anyone to suck your cock, anyway, so I don't see the point." Before his cousin could argue, he forced his eyes open and pointed at Covran. "This isn't a bawdy house of intimate goods. Get yourself together or I'll send you to your mother."

Laughter filled the workroom. "*That's* an even worse threat than disowning me." Covran snorted. "Face it, Ress. The only scary thing you've got going for you is the Shar. Well, that and your face."

As Covran returned to the forge, Ress covered his right cheek with his palm. They had hurled the insult at each other since childhood, but it struck him harder now. His scarred jaw reminded him to choose his friends more wisely and turn them in at the first sign of betrayal.

He sighed, pawing the puckered skin.

"Cove's a fool. Don't listen to him," Bremary's soft voice advised from the doorway. "You're still a looker."

Dropping his hand, Ress turned to Bremary. He hated being caught in vulnerable moments. "Not what I was thinking, but thanks."

Bremary stepped into the room, a gentle smile on her painted lips. "Sure. I'll believe that if you want." Hands clasped, she leaned against the workbench. Dressed in a pale mauve tunic with a dark purple skirt, she reminded him of summer, as though she wanted to ward off the colder season with fabric alone. "But here—" She removed a bronze pin from the twisted plaits in her hair and held it out. "Take this in case you eventually want to pop that lie and start being honest. You can be human. Go on, I won't tell."

Ress shook his head. The offer was appreciated, but he was not ready to surrender to candid honesty. Not with her, not with Covran, not with Inesta. Maybe he never would be ready. Maybe there was no one he could be that honest with.

Smirking, Bremary worked the hairpin back into place. "Well, if you ever do, you know where to find me. In the meantime, someone's asking for you." She motioned behind her with her thumb. A woman in a voluminous black cloak stood in the middle of the shop, her head covered with a grey shawl. "That woman's back. Our merry mistress Ines is about to put both feet up her backside. She's already on her last nerve."

"Fine, I'll deal with it." Ress sighed and followed Bremary out of the workroom. The day was on a downward spiral into misery.

His sanity spiraled straight into agony the moment the woman turned around.

Kirra. Oh, come on, fate. You couldn't have found someone else to destroy today? Seriously?

"Ress, honey! It's so lovely to see you!" Kirra greeted, her nasally, pitchy tone dripping with insincerity. Arms waving erratically, she walked towards him. "Oh, we simply *must* talk and catch up on all those terribly adorable things you do here. And my boyfriend—well, he'll just *have* to visit with me *one* of these days. Goddesses know he keeps breaking *every* piece of metal we own, including the teeth lodged in his teensy, tiny head."

Bremary stepped aside and kept stepping, staying close to the wall as she moved towards the glass cases. The two women standing with Inesta at the desk in the front of the shop glanced at Kirra then quickly looked away.

Inesta glowered at Kirra, one hand fisted.

Kirra fluffed the lightweight shawl covering her honey-coloured hair and pouted. "So, darling, let me see them. Let me see all the pretties. Show me your shiny toys, honey love, and I'll show you what a girl can do with them. While you're it, I need you to fix something."

Fury flared in Inesta's eyes. She pointed at Ress then sliced through the air with her finger, hard and fast, motioning to the workroom—her silent way of commanding him to kick Kirra out.

Without a doubt, he would hear about Kirra's display later. If Kirra continued with the charade, he would not be sleeping in the second bedroom or on the settee in the sitting room. He would be sleeping outside on the road, buried underneath half of his favourite things.

Inesta might not love him, but her jealousy did.

"Get in here," Ress muttered, yanking Kirra into the empty workroom by her elbow. Her cloak parted beneath its wooden toggle clasps, revealing thin metal chains sewn to her black leather bodice. From the angle, he recognized the glint of a small knife tucked between her breasts.

When Covran entered the room from the forge, Ress released Kirra.

Covran flushed, hesitating, caught between going forward and pivoting back. "Sorry. I'll just—" He whirled around and walked away. A moment later, the high pitch of a hammer pounding metal filled the air, quick and hard. The ground beneath Ress and Kirra vibrated with each strike.

"One of these days, you're going to get one of us bludgeoned into the afterlife, you infuriating trollop." Ress crossed his arms. "Get my meaning?"

"Oh, *honey*." Kirra's golden eyes narrowed, her voice sliding into her natural tone, low and smooth. "You know I'm not as easy as your wife thinks I should be. I love hiding in plain sight and being someone I'm not." She stepped closer, pressing against him. The knives at her hips dug into his waist. "I don't believe for one moment that little girl of yours can do damage. A nasty glare and the threat of her gorgeous little fist aren't anything to fear. You're far likelier to be gutted by a wildemouse."

"Then say your piece and run along." Ress nudged her back. "I'm sure your *boyfriend's* just waiting to yank your chain."

Kirra smirked. "He always is. You should hear him scream my name. He's the bestest best friend a girl could have." She rose onto her tiptoes, her mouth finding his ear. "He wants to see you tonight. Here. Midnight," she whispered.

Ress let out a frustrated breath. He hated bounty hunters. Even more, he hated whenever they called him to heel.

"Got it?" Kirra stepped back.

"Got it."

Appearing satisfied with his answer, she primped her hair and shawl. As she slipped into the doorway, Kirra erupted into a fit of giggles. "You're such a darling! Thanks for fixing that for me." The insipid tone was back, as was the deliberate way she moved through the shop, acting clumsy in her footing. If she were not one of the two hunters who had arrested him and hauled him to the High Council, he would have wondered how she could catch anyone.

Bremary, Inesta, and the two women pulled back as Kirra passed. Behind Kirra's back, Inesta made a clawing motion, careful to hide the gesture from their patrons.

The shop filled with the feeling of collective relief as Kirra left, stumbling through the door and knocking elbows with the person on their way in.

Good, I can finally get back to work. Ress headed for his office, a small, windowless room inside the workroom, separated from the front of the shop. With Galosa's commission finished, he had other things to worry about, especially since he needed to give a report that night about his gang activities. Three jobs were difficult enough to balance without adding the threats of arrest and punishment should he turn up nothing.

Paused in the office doorway, he snapped his fingers. Before he hid, he should instruct Covran to leave him alone and fend off anyone wanting to interrupt. What Covran knew about Ress's criminal activities was too much for an outsider, even if Covran wanted to help bring the Shardenn down. The fewer things he saw in Ress's hands, the better for them both. Bremary and Inesta needed to know even less.

Spinning back towards the forge, Ress took a step.

One look into the shop stopped him cold.

Red. All he saw was red.

The woman moved slowly, browsing the knives on the wall across from him. Long red hair trailed down her back in gentle waves, its hue lush and intense. When she turned to pick up a small statue, he noticed the light tan skin of her unsteady, unpolished fingers. Red dirt clung to the ragged hem of her loose, white dress. Specks of what resembled leaves stuck to the tiny, pale pink pearls dotting the discoloured embroidery. A dark red shawl with frayed ends draped around her haphazardly, the thick, tightly knit fabric bunched around her neck. Bracelets clinked faintly as she drew a light finger over the metal wares, seeming to be lost in thought.

Unable to stop watching her and the particular sway in her steps, Ress struggled to think of her name. He wanted to know her. Not to feed his pride, not for a measure of safety, not to satisfy a hungry desire that eluded him. Because he simply wanted to.

If his natural inquisitiveness was not to blame, it was whatever she had brought into the shop. The longer she lingered, a subtle change in the air grew from a whisper to a shout, an invisible shift in the atmosphere, so uncomfortable and wrong it was liberating and right, slicing through the foul tethers between him and Inesta.

Every attempt he made to look away failed. He moved quietly into the doorway, his arms shifting from crossed to uncrossed, unable to find ease. His mind fought to reconcile what he saw with what he felt. She was flesh and blood, hiding a curious story with her simple dress and hint of wealth in the details. They were a distraction in comparison to what life exuded from her, a presence extending beyond her body as if her spirit could engulf the shop and everyone inside.

She turned towards him, her head lowered while she inspected a silver goblet. The moment she returned the goblet to its display crate, she stiffened. Slow and controlled, she raised her glance to his.

Young with too-old eyes, she filled him with fear and awe, stunning him into perfect stillness.

Coolness swept through him, dancing under his skin, leaving bumps in its wake along his arms and neck. The distance between them seemed smaller than it was. The unseen connection pulled taut, twisting an alarming darkness around the lightness that lured him in.

A flicker of rage sullied her gaze before she smiled, banishing the tension and yanking back the darkness, leaving only her strange presence and the chance to say hello.

He was too confused to do anything but gawk.

"Can I help you?" Bremary's voice jolted Ress back into rational thought. She approached the woman with an outstretched hand. "If you're looking for something specific, I'd be happy to point you towards whatever we have."

The woman started to shake her head but stopped. "Nothing in particular today," she said, the lyrical tone of her voice carrying across the shop. "I'm considering something for the near future, though. It'll be my birthday soon. I'd like something to make me smile." The words were quiet, almost a murmur.

For all the joy they should have carried, all Ress heard was sadness.

His heart ached for her, even without a reason.

Bremary's eyes widened as she nodded and led the woman towards the glass cases at the front. "In that case, birthday girl, we have the *perfect* things. I see you're wearing a couple of gorgeous bracelets. We have rings and necklaces that might match. Or we can craft some that do..."

The woman followed without protest, eerily quiet and precise as she stepped around the displays and stopped beside Bremary. In her strides, there was neither a feminine daintiness and lightness nor a masculine stomping and heaviness. Her movements were something in between: a fluid grace disrupted by a swagger Ress usually associated with the Shar-denn, alternating between the two.

There were too many details that set her apart from the people he knew. Too many irrational emotions that drilled into his thoughts, demanding he speak to her.

And if he opened his mouth, he would sound like a fool.

There was no reason, no sensible explanation, only the truth: if he tried to speak to the woman, he would scare her off and fall prey to Covran and Bremary's mocking for the rest of the day. His did not need to make a fool of himself over someone he found interesting. *Another point for the most disappointing husband in the world.*

With a sigh, Ress returned to his office. The woman was nothing but a customer, a distraction, a stranger who would leave. He needed to focus on working for the people who held his life in their hands until he placed a weapon in their grasps.

The door clicked closed before he threw the bolt, locking out the rest of the world. The small, lamp-lit room was little more than a cage; the locks on the door and his desk drawers a means to keep the secrets of his immorality from tainting the innocence of Inesta, Covran, and Bremary.

He crossed the unadorned room to his desk and fell into the wooden chair, jerking his injured knee in the process. Sucking in a sharp breath, Ress drew his fingers along the underside of the bottom drawer to his right, the lowest and largest of the three drawers on that side. When his fingertips dipped into the crevice containing the drawer key, he pulled the key free and unlocked the bottom drawer. A stack of papers greeted him as he opened the drawer.

Out of habit, he glanced at the door before withdrawing the stack and separating the papers into small piles on his desk. No one needed to see the schedules for the few goods he was still allowed to transport or the maps and drop locations, even if the maps were nonsensical to anyone outside the Shar-denn. Certainly no one could see the designs for the weapons he crafted, dangerous items no one should have.

Ress eyed the knife lying in the drawer, unsheathed and unpolished. The knife resembled the one he carried in his boot. Gold bands circled the bright red hilt, and specks of crushed jewels caused the red metal to glimmer in the light. Engraved in the dull, grey blade, a closed-mouthed skull rested on a fist—the emblem of the Shar-denn. The same symbol he bore on his left forearm, tattooed in black ink.

He rubbed the tattoo, not bothering to roll back his sleeve. To everyone else, the mark condemned him as a member of the gang. To him, it was a memory of better days, frightening as they were. Every time he saw the tattoo, he recalled the days he had agonized over his choice to get it. While not the fondest memories of his late adolescence, remembering still brought warmth to his heart. In those days, he found security in friendship, fighting to hold onto sanity with the boys he loved like brothers.

Varen and Nimae had been the first to get tattoos, proudly displaying the skulls and twisted branches with thorns on their upper arms. The marks had appeared identical except for the script along one thorn-less branch, paired with a single flower small enough to overlook: each other's names, betraying their hearts and confirming what Ress, Taldris, and their families had already known. The truth of what others in the gang had suspected about their close relationship.

A relationship that had ended when Varen killed himself—the same night Nimae disappeared, fleeing the Shar-denn to hide from the authorities.

The life they had together had been torn apart like everything else. What hope love gave them had been smashed and burned, leaving Nimae on his own to fend for himself.

They had never been alone.

Varen and Nimae had always been in Ress's life. They had grown up together, bonding like brothers. Considering the only siblings they had by birth were sisters, they had treasured their connection. Together with Taldris, they had formed a family of their own, protecting each other and offering strength.

Until Taldris ran away, then became Tash and broke their family.

Tash, whose tattoo had gained him respect and admiration from other members of the Shardenn because of its size and complexity: a bird that spanned his entire back, requiring more than one day to complete and left him in pain for several days afterwards, though he had not complained.

In the wake of the attention paid to Tash, Varen, and Nimae, Ress had been at a loss. Gang custom dictated that its members be tattooed in its honour. Had he refused to follow tradition, they would have questioned his loyalty.

To prove his commitment, he chose the Shardenn emblem with the hope it convinced others he was worthy, especially after being stabbed by a faction boss. The last thing he had wanted was to be considered whiny and submissive. To show he had guts, he got the tattoo where it could be hidden or revealed easily, even by the authorities.

The gang members had laughed, clapped him on the back, and welcomed his audacity. They considered it a mark to taunt the republic and dare the authorities to take him down.

He returned his gaze to the knife in the drawer. Dried blood clung to the crevices where blade met hilt. It was all Ress had of Colare, the man who had made the Shar-denn's trust necessary, stealing Ress's life and those of Varen, Nimae, and Tash. The knife took him back to the day it had been jammed into his leg, a warning to never question a faction boss again. At fourteen, he had been too young to understand what the Shar-denn truly was.

Once that blade tore into him, it changed everything.

Colare would never know that after he was killed in his sleep by his brother, Traise, that brother had given Ress the very knife used to cripple him. A payment for Ress's worthy service and loyalty to the faction's real leader, they had agreed.

Now the knife was a reminder of his mortality. A guide, a talisman, a punch in the head from the Realm of the Dead, forcing him to work for the people he despised. A taste of what would befall his loved ones should he forget what was at stake.

Failure would never be worth the price.

CHAPTER THREE

"I'll be home soon. Just need to check on something in the shop before I forget again," Ress told Inesta, his hand on the handle of the front door.

Inesta sank further into the grey settee and huddled under a blue blanket, her back to him. She had yet to speak to him, her anger from the discussion at breakfast unresolved. Even during the appointment with Galosa, she had skillfully avoided addressing Ress directly. Once they had closed the shop for the day and returned home, the silence had been heavy with dread.

I know where I'll be sleeping, and it won't be anywhere near her. Ress closed the door and crossed the creaking porch to the skip down the steps. Hands jammed into the pockets of his pants, he followed the pathway of grey stones to the red dirt street, walking between the gardens of golden flowers and green ferns. At the end of the pathway, he passed through the engraved silver archway he had built, leaves brushing his skin from the dark green vines wrapped around the latticework. On either side, the archway was held up by a stone wall that ran around the house, waist-high and red as the earth.

He turned towards the village square and continued along the straight road. While not yet midnight, his timing was close, enough to reach the shop before Rathen snuck in through the back door of the forge. The meeting was something between an annoyance and a blessing. Inesta's silence was nothing new, but he needed more than being ignored.

Not that fighting's any better. Ress regarded the houses, wondering if the lives of the inhabitants were complicated like his and not the friendly, open pictures they portrayed in public. The elegant homes on both sides of the road were built more than two dozen paces apart. As part of the wealthier districts of Araveena Ford, the expensive stone and polished wood houses were a visible source of pride to their owners. Well-kept and pristine on the outside, adorned with immaculate gardens and shiny frippery, they hid any physical or emotional disarray on the inside. They were not like the rundown dwellings in the poorest districts on the outer edges of the village. Nor were they like the worn but comfortable buildings around the village square. The houses here were meant to put the others in their place, to remind people of their caste. To confine what dared not be shown.

To be a cage.

Would the girl he had seen in the shop earlier agree? Or was her cage the one they all struggled with, a matter of flesh and thought chaining them in feelings too complex to fully unravel?

Ress shivered, drawing close to the sinister black metal gates and railings of the house to his right. Why was he thinking about the girl *now*?

Not that you haven't been thinking about her all day, he chastised himself. Since the strange woman had snatched his attention, his thoughts kept drifting to her state and his apathetic response. From her slow movements and despondent tone, she could have used more than his silence and worry. He had known it, recognizing the same unhappy things in her that haunted him.

Still, he had done nothing.

He could have asked if she was all right. Or saved her from Bremary's bombardment of overwhelming friendliness and restrained excitement. Instead, he had been a coward, paying the price with unasked questions and foolish wonderment. At the very least, he would have settled for knowing her name, but he wanted to understand who she was. The strong presence reeled him in; the flicker of inexplicable anger in her gaze pushed him away. His curiosity piqued and famished for answers, he wished he could have redone the moment she had smiled at him.

But I can't. Time doesn't work that way. Ress pulled into himself against the cool air, pushing his hands further into his pockets. He turned into the alley between the last two houses on the road. *I'm lucky I didn't speak to her—Ines would've seen and this night would've been that much better.*

If Inesta knew the truth of what was on his mind—that her anger had not been at the forefront of his concern all day—she would have shouted her jealousy without listening to his defence. After Kirra's ostentatious display, he would not have convinced Inesta that his constant thoughts about another woman were nothing to worry about. Inesta already doubted his disinterest in carnal activity.

Teeth grinding at his incessant need to rationalize, Ress exited the dark alley, coming out between the butcher's shop and the stone mason's building. He wove around the closed merchant carts marking the edge of the village square and entered the open space. The square was empty save for the dais and flagpole in the middle, the green and gold flag of Kattal hanging limp. Moonlight illuminated everything except where yellow light spilled out from the doorways of two taverns.

Ress continued to the opposite side of the village square, ignoring the hollers and laughter pouring from the taverns. Never had he frequented the establishments or drunk to excess. There had never been a safe time to do so. From the day Colare stabbed him, he had sworn to never let his guard down or compromise his judgment.

Stopping at the doors of his shop, he pressed his palm to the cold metal gate over the wood and metal doors. If he turned around, he could skip the meeting and visit one of those taverns. Just once, he could get lost in the raucous noise and forget everything else.

Yeah, do that and Rathen will have my head in a bag so fast, I'll spend my afterlife dizzy. Ress removed the loop of keys from the twine cord around his neck and unlocked the gate. After pushing it open, he unlocked one of the doors and slipped into the shop, closing the door and locking it behind him. Paused on the spot, he listened for footfalls and breaths.

When he heard nothing, he continued through the dark shop, sidestepping displays and cases on his way to the moonlit workroom. On the other side of the doorway, he glanced at the closed door to the forge. The door was still locked. Perhaps he had beat Rathen to the meeting after all.

Determined to make the meeting quick and efficient, Ress unlocked the office door and entered the pitch-black room.

"Took you long enough."

Ress jumped at the gruff voice. He squeezed the keys tightly, the sharp ends protruding from between his middle fingers, ready to jab the intruder.

"Relax, it's me. No one poaches my marks." Rathen stepped out from behind the door but remained in the shadows. A dark cloak covered his tall, broad body, hiding everything from his face to his toes. With the flash of a ring as it caught a sliver of light, Rathen drew back his hood slightly, revealing his hard gaze.

"Bastard," Ress muttered, closing the door and surrounding them with darkness. "I hate when you do that."

"As if I *love* playing messenger for your sorry ass." Rathen paused long enough Ress could imagine his sarcastic expression. "No, wait, how'd you put it to K? Yanking your chain? Yeah, I *love* yanking chains, you snarky little dung mutt." The air moved with Rathen as he stepped away, followed by a knock on the desk. "Come here, dungy dog. Come here. Be a good boy and I'll give you a treat."

Jaws clenched, Ress toyed with his keys. "What? Want me to roll over and lick your boots? How about I piss all over them and we'll call it even?"

The answer was a snort followed by the scratch of a matchstick on the box on Ress's desk. Flame caught as Rathen lit a small white candle on the edge of the desk. "Mutt's got fight, I'll give you that." Rathen pushed back his hood, uncovering his short, unkempt blond hair and strong features of his face. His cloak fell aside to show his black leather long coat and the knives strapped to his thigh. "Next time, don't disrespect K. You may have fight, but my bite'll kill you, especially where she's concerned."

"Then muzzle her next time. Don't send her barking into my hole." Ress threw his arm out, gesturing to the front of the shop. "I'm *not* the only one here. One of these days, she'll blow the operation wide open. Get her a new cover. At least teach her some new tricks."

Rathen let out an annoyed breath. "Fine, I'll mention it." His glare raked over Ress. "But not for you. I care about her safety and our contract with the Council. Everything else is a bunch of whining I'm not hearing." He motioned to the desk. "Now get to it. I'm not staying here all night."

"Thank the Four for that," Ress mumbled, reattaching the keys to the cord around his neck before crossing the room. He retrieved the desk key from its crevice and unlocked the bottom drawer. Without hesitation, he pulled out the papers for the High Council and smacked them down onto the desk. "The few drop schedules I have and a map. Mostly just designs. Shar's getting impatient. They want the new weapons realized in the next three years."

Rathen thumbed the papers, tilting his head to read them. "What are we talking? More explosives? Redesigned blades?"

"Partially, but worse." Ress crossed his arms and stepped back. "They have new explosives. The stuff blows up and sends metal bits in every direction, embedding in anything soft, then all *those* bits blow up simultaneously. Nasty little things."

"How'd they manage that?"

"No one's talking about it. One secret they're keeping close." Ress tapped the papers. "Now the worse I mentioned is in this. Other weapons they can use without being anywhere *near* the victim. Or not so close, anyway. Projectiles that can be launched from a small, concealed weapon—no blades involved, unless they're part of the projectiles. They want to trade them with other nations, in addition to showing up Council soldiers who don't have the same toys."

Ress pulled a cylindrical piece of charcoal-coloured metal from the open drawer. "This is part of it." He peered at Rathen through the empty centre running the length of the tube. As long as his forearm, the cylinder was lukewarm and heavy. The thick edges were smooth, having taken him more than two nights alone in the smoky forge to perfect. Crafted from a design he had settled on after four months of modifications to suit the sketches he had been given, he was certain it would work with the other components he was expected to create. "The projectile passes through this. At this end, there's supposed to be a bit you hold and click back. It triggers a mechanism and shunts the metal bits through the other end. It'll put a hole in whatever it's aimed at. It'll pierce flesh like it was butter."

"And you're *giving them* these? Are you *that much* of a fool?" Rathen held up his hand. "Wait. Criminal. Why am I asking?"

"Yeah, because that's your answer for everything, isn't it?" Ress grunted, laying down the tube. "I'm not exactly alone in this. There's a group of us working on them. *They* worry about making them actually work and how the pieces fit together and what material does what. *I* just contribute ideas, materials, and labour. They're secret projects—few people know *anything* about what's going on." He motioned at the papers. "It's the whole reason I'm still alive. They know I know things. They know I can *do* things. Really painful things, and with the same weapons they have me make. I could be sitting on explosives a hundred times worse than what they have now and bring down every faction boss's estate without any help. They don't know what I can and can't do. Considering I'm kind of used to breathing, don't be all over me for wanting to keep that going."

"Nice. The survival excuse. Couldn't think of anything better?"

"Kiss mine." Ress straightened, jutting his chin out. "If you want the information, you need me alive. So yeah, I'm going with survival. Take the papers to the Council and tell them what I said. Also tell them we have a small problem."

"Oh, great, bad news for Severn. My favourite."

"Shut up, errand boy, because she'll want to hear this." Ress rocked on his heels, pain flaring up his knee. "I'm being weaned off. Shar's not telling me things like they used to. It's *exactly* what I expected. They don't trust me now. After you arrested me, that was it; they'll never take me into their confidence in the same way. Not the bosses, not the other members. Even the lackeys are careful around me."

Rathen collected the papers and rolled them around the metal cylinder. "Yet you managed to get this." He tucked the papers and cylinder into a pocket inside his coat.

"Because they're limited in who can do what. Metalsmiths aren't jumping at the opportunity to work for them, especially those who can design weapons and smuggle illegal goods better than most. That doesn't mean they can't hold back."

"So you're going to be a piss-poor informant in the future."

"Especially if they turn around and kill me."

Silence fell between them. Rathen's eyes narrowed, his lips twisting as though he was giving Ress's words honest consideration.

"What happens when I'm no longer useful as an informant?" Ress asked.

"I don't know," Rathen answered quietly. "It's not up to me. That's all Severn and Cota. Since they're councilmen, I can't even begin to guess." He flipped up his hood and pulled it forward until it covered most of his face. "They're not your friends, though, so find yourself a priestess and start praying."

A nicer answer than I expected. Ress closed and locked the drawer, returned the key to its hiding place, and snuffed the candle. Light and quiet, Rathen hurried across the room. Pressed against the wall, he waited for Ress to exit first.

Without anything more to say, Ress left the room and closed the door. True to their routine, he unlocked the door to the forge before leaving the workroom and going to the front of the shop. Rathen would let himself out through the back and lock the doors behind him. *At least I got one of the smart bounty hunters who can pick locks, not that it's any consolation. I'd give anything for useless most days.*

Once the front door and gate were locked, Ress turned towards home, slipping the cord with the keys under his shirt. He crossed through the empty square, ignoring a small group of men and women as they stumbled out of the tavern, singing and cheering. As he stepped around the merchant carts, someone yelled, the high-pitch, mangled words followed by deeper, demanding voices shouting back.

Behind him, the sound of the singing group faded into the distance.

When he neared the alley between the butcher's and the stone mason's buildings, the yell sounded again, calling for help. Grunts and insults answered back, mingled with the sounds of a struggle. Someone begged to be released—the voice of a woman or child.

I don't care who you are. You're not pulling that in this village. Ress drew his knife from his boot and snuck into the alley, holding the blade downwards, pointing it behind him. Three figures scuffled in the dark alley. Two men dressed in dark clothes and hoods tugged on the distraught woman between them, faces covered except around their eyes. A bag lay on the ground, neglected as the woman pummeled her fists against the men, striking their chests and legs.

The woman. Ress squinted to better see her in the faint moonlight between the buildings. He recognized her body, the shawl hanging over one shoulder and dragging across the ground, the red hair…

The girl from the shop—the one he was connected to, even if only through an unspoken misery. He felt her now, the presence reaching out, daring him to do something. Anything.

"Hey!" he yelled, charging ahead with long strides.

The assailants stopped, their heads jerking up. "What's it to you?" the taller man answered, snatching the girl back.

At the same moment, the girl surged forward. The taller man fumbled and cursed, fighting to hold on. The moment she was out of his grasp, the shorter man caught her arm and jerked her back into him.

"Let her go and find out." Ress stopped three paces away. When the panicked girl met his gaze, he tilted his head and slid his glance towards the wall to his left, hoping she understood what he was trying to tell her.

Her eyes widened. She nodded once before tilting her head towards the same wall, suggesting she understood what he wanted her to do.

"We're two, you're one," the shorter man snarled. "A lame one, at that. What are you going to do? Stomp on us?"

Ress smirked, fingers flexing around his knife. "You'd be surprised."

He jerked his gaze to the left. The girl yanked hard on her attacker. Turning mid-pull, she slammed them both into the wall.

In the distraction, Ress lunged for the taller assailant. He dodged the punch to his throat and swiped his arm between them, dragging the knife blade across the man's face.

The man cursed and slapped his hand to his cheek, covering the torn fabric. Not waiting for him to recover, Ress kicked the side of the assailant's knee hard enough to send him to the ground. Writhing and groaning, the man struggled between soothing his knee and his face.

Before the second attacker could react, Ress wrapped his arm around the shorter man's neck and pulled him close, ripping him away from the girl. "Let's talk surrender. I let you run, and if I see you again, I'll make your faces match." He flipped his knife and tapped the blade against the assailant's knee. "How much do you value this?" His chokehold tightened as he pressed the blade down, breaking skin around the kneecap and drawing blood. The man gagged and spat, fighting the hold, digging his fingertips into Ress's forearm. "Have I made myself clear?"

"Yes," the man hissed.

Ress shoved him aside, satisfied as the assailant staggered and tumbled onto his partner. *That's what you get when my best friend was a guard. He taught our little family well.* He stepped closer to the girl and sheathed his knife, not looking forward to cleaning the blade. Taldris, Nimae, and Varen had never minded using force. They had accepted it as part of their roles: Taldris as a guard, and Nimae and Varen as fighters in raids whenever they were not protecting thieves and other gang members on missions. Unlike them, Ress never liked using weapons.

I'm never going to get used to being alone, either, not like this. I'd give every moment of being the odd one just to have them back.

Disgusted by the poor timing of his nostalgia, Ress sneered at the wounded assailants. Both men stood and hobbled past him towards the village square. As they disappeared around the end of the alley, he turned to the girl and offered a weak smile. "Are you all right?"

She hesitated, responding with an uncertain, pained glance. Her long hair was disheveled. Her white dress was askew, the neckline digging into her neck on one side, the rest hanging off her shoulder. The red shawl was torn and soiled with dirt. Several rings hung on a gold chain around her neck, gleaming where light touched them. Even after being attacked, she carried a faint, sweet scent. Like a stubborn flower that had survived a rainstorm with fist-sized hailstones.

No doubt she's going to have bruises the size of fists tomorrow morning. They needed to get out of the alley. She needed to sit down and warm up.

"I'm better," she answered, her voice quiet and hoarse. "Thank you." Her eyes narrowed. "I saw you earlier, in the shop of beautiful jewelry and metal things."

"Yes, you did." He offered his open hand. "I'm Ress. I own the shop, actually."

She stared at his hand as though the customary greeting were foreign.

"Call me Adren," she answered, gripping his wrist.

Just as quickly, Adren recoiled and fussed with her dress and shawl until she resembled the way she had in the shop. Without hesitation, she picked up her discarded satchel and dusted it off before slipping it over one shoulder. The fabric stretched tight from how much was in the bag. Shuddering, she glanced up and down the alley, her fists tight around the satchel's strap.

Ress could guess at her concern. "Let me take you someplace safe. My home isn't far from here. We have an extra bed, warm blankets, and a place to wash. Food, too, and drink."

Adren's odd expression threw him. She looked confused. Cynical. Disgusted.

Have you never had anyone help you before? Or is this shock?

"Sorry. Did you want me to walk you home?" He frowned, at a loss for what he should say. "Or are you staying in one of the taverns? Maybe the inn?"

When she shook her head, Ress held back a sigh. At least it was an answer.

"No, I'm just—it's just me and I'm—I can't—" Adren stared at the ground.

"Maybe we'll start small. I'll take you to my house and you can sit for a while." With Adren's nod, Ress motioned to the alley. "This way, then."

They walked side by side with slow steps, quiet except for the sound of their boot soles on the road. Ress stole glances at her, noticing how she focused on the road ahead. Something was wrong, beyond the assault. Yet for all of the clues her reactions gave him, he had no guesses.

Once they reached the archway in front of his house, he stopped, focusing on the two blue doors forming the front entrance. *And I'm a fool. Such a big, had-it-coming fool. This is where I need to forewarn you about Ines. She's going to rip me a new hole over this.*

"Here's the thing," he started, grimacing. "I'm married. But that's not the thing. Well, it is, sort of. Just my wife, she's—we're—a bit... off today. So if things seem tense, it's not you."

Expecting Adren to respond with silence, he eyed the window shutters. Blue like the doors, the shutters were vivid with silver flecks. In the moonlight, the flecks glittered, giving the shutters a jeweled appearance. *My pretty little prison.*

"It's all right. I can deal with an angry wife." Adren shuffled her satchel from one shoulder to the other. "If she doesn't put a fist in my face, I'll be good."

Ress bit back his surprise at her answer. Perhaps she had more fight in her than he anticipated.

Hopeful that Inesta might be sympathetic to the circumstances, Ress urged Adren ahead. When they stepped inside, Inesta peered over the settee. Her eyes were red and swollen as though from crying, the blue blanket wrapped around her shoulders.

She jumped up, the blanket falling to the floor. "What are you doing?" Inesta demanded, grasping her hips and glowering at Ress.

"This is Adren." Ress closed the door. "Two men attacked her in an alley and beat on her. She needs a place to rest and something warm to drink."

"Ce," Adren said.

Both Ress and Inesta stared at her. "Sorry. What?" Inesta asked before Ress could.

"If we're going to be accurate, I'd rather you refer to me as ce, not 'she,'" Adren replied wearily. "I'd rather not explain, not right now. Not while I feel like someone's beaten songs on my ribs and I'm about to fall over."

Ress blinked, trying to comprehend Adren's words. The first part he would ask about later. The falling over concerned him more.

"Here, sit." He guided Adren to the second grey settee. Although Inesta's gaze followed them, Ress ignored it. As long as she treated

Adren with a measure of respect, she could yell at him later all she wanted.

To his relief, Inesta retrieved the blanket from the floor as Adren sat on the settee then tucked it around Adren's legs. "Here. I'll get another couple blankets," Inesta said softly. "Then we'll see about all the other little things. Do you need a place to stay tonight?"

Adren nodded, still clutching the satchel.

"Then you'll stay here. We'll figure it out." Inesta patted Adren's shoulder. "Everything will be better in the morning." She gestured to Ress then the storage room with linens inside. "We'll be right back."

They crossed through the sitting room and kitchen together. Inesta entered the storage room, pulling Ress in with her before closing the door.

"I don't like this," she whispered in the dark. "Something's off with her."

"Are you sure you aren't just—"

She slapped his arm. "I'm not 'just' anything. I tell you: something's not right with her."

"She's had it rough." Ress shook his head. "I mean, *ce's* had it rough tonight. They weren't asking for directions to the tavern, Ines. They were all hands and intent." He rubbed her shoulders. "Give it tonight. Let Adren rest and move on in the morning, all right?"

Inesta was silent. Braced for an argument, Ress held his breath.

"Fine, but if she touches anything that's mine, she'll answer to me. I'm *more* than hands and intent." Inesta opened the door, took a pile of blankets from the shelves, and walked away.

Please tell me this was the right decision. Ress flicked his glance to the ceiling. *Call it charity. Call it being gallant. Call it pity. Whatever it is, I know I have to do this. It's a necessity. I don't know why. Just don't let this blow up in my face.*

Then it was dawn. Do I place bets on who's up first, or is that too much?

Ress turned onto his side on the settee and studied the closed doors of the bedrooms. Curling one arm under his pillow and drawing the blue blanket up to his chest, he slowed his breaths, listening for movement in either room. Adren had slept in the guest room beside the main bedroom, where Inesta had slept with the door locked. Despite her misgivings, Inesta had taken care of Adren until neither of them could stay awake. Then they had left him to the comforts of the sitting room.

At least I got to sleep inside. He peered over the end of the settee to the kitchen. *Plus I have the food.* His gaze swept over the cloth-covered bread loaf on the table, fresh from the night before. *I should probably do something about that before Ines gets up. It's the least I can do after yesterday's disaster.*

Stifling a groan, he forced himself up and tossed the blanket over the back of the settee. His knee was in no better shape than the day before. *No more playing hero, not today. Everybody can save themselves. I'll just sit on my backside and get Cove to do everything. Make him earn his owner's title.* Ress hissed and hobbled to the kitchen, thankful he had fetched clean water from the well the night before. He needed a day where things went right, not started wrong and spiraled into ridiculous.

Here's to hoping today's all sunshine and pretty flowers. At least Ines finally spoke to me. He lit a fire in the kitchen hearth, waiting for the flames to catch before sliding a small pot of water onto the rack inside the hearth. As the water warmed, he cut half of the bread Inesta had made and arranged it on a clay plate on the table.

The door to the guest room opened.

Ress paused, his hands hovering above the plate, the knife in his right hand steady. Adren padded out of the room, fully dressed and blinking as though fighting to stay awake.

"Morning," Ress said, tossing the bread knife into the washbasin behind him. "Go ahead and sit. I promise I don't bite." Once Adren sat in the chair furthest from him, he withdrew a bottle of bittersweet cider from the cupboard to his right. After pouring half of the cider into a small metal pitcher, he placed the pitcher on the heating rack beside the pot and plugged the bottle with its stopper. He turned and leaned against the counter. "Sleep well?"

"I guess. I don't remember much between hitting the pillow and waking up to the light."

"How about the pain?"

"That I could do without," Adren muttered. "I can't even begin to count the bruises." Ce gave him a crooked smile. "I'm pretty colourful now. Guess I will be for a few days. When I get tired of the blue it'll be green before I know it. Though the yellow—I wouldn't mind passing over that."

Good to know you have a sense of humour. Ress took the pitcher from the rack and poured two cups of cider. "I understand. I've been known to get a bit colourful myself." He gave Adren one cup and kept the other, sinking into his chair carefully. "Do you need anything wrapped?"

Adren appeared surprised. Before he could ask why, ce waved his question away. "I'm fine. Just need to go where I'm supposed to be today. Easier than last night's awful shortcut."

"Shortcut to where?"

"Exploring." Ce took a breath and gripped cir cup. "I was curious about the village. I wanted to see what it was like when it was all quiet. Everything's so different during the day. All I wanted was a walk. Then those guys came out of nowhere, dragged me into the alley, and, well, you know the rest."

"Yeah, I do." Ress sipped his cider as Adren stared at the table. An uncomfortable silence snuck between them. For all the words they had exchanged, he still knew little about Adren. "You're not from here, are you?" he asked, unable to sit still.

"No."

When Adren did not elaborate, Ress cleared his throat. "Visiting?"

Ce drank slowly before continuing. "I was looking into job prospects."

"Who with?"

"That's a secret, and you ask a lot of questions."

Ress held up his hands. "All right, fine, I'm too curious for my own good. Call it a nasty habit. Some people think it's endearing. Sort of." He laughed, recalling the way his sisters used to tease him, often answering his incessant questions with their own until their mother demanded they stop. "Though I have one more, if it doesn't bother you: the thing about being called—"

"Ce? Yeah, I know. I was waiting for you to ask. I did throw it at you at the strangest time." Adren scowled and flicked the table. "Usually I say it better. I guess I was more affected by what happened than I thought."

"No, it's fine. Then again, the when doesn't really matter, does it? Just that it's said at all."

A smile brightened Adren's face. "Something like that, yes." Ce sighed. "Honestly, though? I'm used to the question, and I used to think it needed a long, convoluted reply—until I realized it didn't, and I could just embrace it without always justifying the details. So here's the simple answer I give everyone: imagine you're living your life, being you, but then every time someone says a certain word, it feels like they're cutting you in two and only looking at the one half. They see the other half—and the whole—but it doesn't make sense, and they don't have any explanations or a word to call it, so they push it away." Adren smirked, more with annoyance than amusement. "You'd get pretty frustrated, enough to want to set it right. So that's what I did; I came up with a word. It's comfortable, it's mine, and it stops me from feeling like I'm being divided into pieces."

"I can also imagine it's not been easy getting to this point," Ress said gently.

"No, but nothing comes easy. That's life." Adren shrugged. "Most people have a difficult time with it. I still can't get most of my family to refer to me as 'ce' or 'cir,' especially my brothers." The last two words were barely a murmur before Adren's voice cracked. Adren's glance flickered downwards, cir shoulders sagging as a flush spread across cir cheeks. A crestfallen expression accompanied Adren's strained tone, cir words a peculiar contrast of easy and forced, as though ce wanted to avoid saying them but was determined to make them heard. "They've always had a hard time adjusting and don't deal well with change. They don't like being ripped out of what they know. They kind of flounder and stumble through until someone sets them right. I was always the one who picked them up and set them straight. I'd still be if someone hadn't taken it away."

Small bumps rose along Ress's neck as he shivered. In a matter of moments, Adren had gone from confident to forlorn, a sharp, dark tone underlying the words. They were a lament more than recollection.

As much as he wanted to know more, his instincts told him to leave the issue alone.

"So you'd rather use a word that means all of the parts of you. You want to truly be you, without having to hide. That's not so hard to understand," he said softly, shifting in his chair. "It's not easy being different when everyone wants you to be the same. I understand that, too. Doesn't matter how hard you try, you can't really be what you aren't. Either you make everyone else happy and live in misery, or you completely confuse them and be happy with who you are." Ress flashed Adren a weak smile. "I have to admit, I like the confusion part more. Makes them think. Makes them actually see you because they're too caught up in trying to figure you out."

Once more, Adren's face brightened, eyes glistening with what Ress prayed were not tears. He could not deal with crying, not for a second morning in a row. "Yeah."

"So then I'll call you whatever you wish. Is there anything else you want me to know?"

Adren eyed the bread. "Um, I'm hungry?"

Ress laughed. "I think we can do something about that." The door to the main bedroom opened as he stood, drawing his attention to Inesta in her purple gown, her auburn hair pulled back in a loose tail. "Since we're all up, I should get breakfast finished."

Inesta approached the table, frowning while she looked from Ress to Adren and back to Ress. "Am I missing something?"

"No, dearest." Ress untied the burlap bag of crushed baked oats mixed with soft grains, savoury herbs, and sweet spices sitting on the counter. "We're just talking." He scooped a red clay bowl through the oat mixture, filling it more than halfway. "Did you sleep?" he asked Inesta, setting the bowl down in front of Adren.

"A little." Inesta took her seat. "How about the two of you?" She folded her hands in her lap as Ress filled her bowl and set it down.

"Quite a bit, thanks," Adren said.

Ress remained silent as he filled his bowl. In truth, he had barely slept. Grateful when Inesta seemed to ignore his lacking reply, he wrapped a thick cloth around his hand, removed the pot from the fire, and poured water into each bowl. After giving Inesta and Adren their spoons, he sat down and mixed the water into his grain meal.

They ate quietly, the loudest noise being their spoons scraping the bowls. Inesta's subtle glances at Adren did not escape Ress's attention. Why she chose silence over simple talk was beyond him. She had nothing to lose, nothing to worry about. *Then again, Adren's not talking, either, and ce's certainly not looking at anyone.*

Breakfast ended almost as fast as they had started. Inesta collected the bowls and dropped them into the washbasin. Adren said a hasty thank you and disappeared into cir room. When ce reappeared, ce wore cir shawl and satchel.

"Wait." Ress jumped up from the table. "You're going already?"

"I need to get on. Thanks for the breakfast, though, and the place to sleep." Adren glanced at Inesta, who said nothing as she washed the dishes. "I appreciate your concern."

"Where are you going? I can take you, if you—"

"No, that's not necessary." Adren held up cir hand. "Thank you for helping me, but I need to get going. I have things to do. Home won't wait." Ce stepped towards Ress, hand extended. "Thanks, though. I can't say how much it meant to meet you."

Ress stared at the calloused skin of Adren's outstretched palm. Where was ce going? Where did ce live? What had happened with cir brothers to cast a spiteful shadow across cir emotions? What Adren had let slip was a precious piece of who ce was, a small portion of what he expected to be a painfully complicated life with dozens of stories worth telling, but that was all. Whether by coincidence or Adren's intention, he knew almost nothing.

What he did know was he doubted Adren's excuse for leaving. The message between the words was more significant than Adren made it sound. Even cir presence was off—small, confused, and shy rather than the strong, room-engulfing entity he remembered.

He clapped his hand around cir wrist. "I'd feel better if I could take you where you need to go. After last night…" Ress squeezed Adren's arm. "Please?"

Adren stiffened. Ce shifted cir feet, clutching the satchel strap tight. "You're nice, but I don't need a guard. It's daylight. I'll be fine."

Ress said nothing to Adren's curt tone. He released cir wrist. "All right, I'll drop it. If you need something else, anything, tell me. You know where to find me."

His last word sparked a glimmer of interest in cir eyes. "I'll remember that." Adren waved at Inesta and headed for the front doors, walking with the peculiar grace-and-swagger movement Ress attributed only to cir.

As Adren slipped out the door, the image of cir walking away burned into Ress's mind.

"Finally," Inesta muttered, drying the bowls. "At least she didn't steal anything."

"Ce..." Ress corrected, stopping himself before Inesta pinned him with a deeper glare. "It's fine. No harm came to anyone. We're out a bit of food, but that's it."

"I still don't think it's safe." Inesta wrung out the thin towel. "No matter what you say, we still need to leave Araveena. Just like I think something's wrong with our *guest*, I swear it's not safe here. Really, *really* not safe."

Great, we're back to this again. Ress sighed. "I told you—"

"And *I'm* telling *you* we need to take the offer from Eloras." She pointed at the front doors. "How many Adrens will there be? How many more attacks? If it's not safe for young women to be out at night, how safe do you think it is for me? Or for you, since you've already been arrested once?" Inesta threw the towel onto the counter. "Things are *not* going to get better. Let's go somewhere safer."

Except it isn't safer; it's much more dangerous. "I'm not changing my mind," Ress said. "We've had this conversation. Let's leave it there."

To avoid Inesta's angry mumbling, Ress strode into the bedroom and closed the door. No amount of arguing would bring them onto the same side.

He stripped off his tunic and leather pants, replacing them with a loose brown shirt and pants. With a quick shave and the slicking back of his hair, he finished grooming and rejoined Inesta in the kitchen. The fire was out and all evidence of breakfast cleaned away. Silent but patient, Inesta waited as he pulled on his boots and motioned for them to leave. Their walk to the shop was no less taciturn than the morning before.

Inside, Covran and Bremary bustled around the workroom and shop, bantering while they rotated objects in the displays and prepared for the day. Inesta joined in, teasing Covran and cackling with Bremary.

Ress barely heard what they said, his restless thoughts jumping between Inesta and Adren. He had caught Bremary's cheerful greeting but nothing more. Even as he sat in the workroom, tinkering with fine chains for necklaces, he listened to little of what Covran said to him. Most of it was a joke, followed by Covran's laugh. When the comments related to their work, Ress brushed aside Covran's words with a nod. In the back of his mind, his answers were appropriate, but if anyone were to ask him to repeat anything anyone said, he would have been speechless.

If anyone were to ask about Adren, however, he could have told them plenty. How ce had the will to fight and a tough edge softened by a pretty appearance and smooth tone. How ce could talk at length about who ce was inside where no one could see the truth, but retreated into silence around Inesta.

How Adren's eyes did not match the rest of cir.

While ce appeared to be in cir early twenties, Adren's eyes were all wrong. Green with a gold ring around the outer edge, they were normal except for their age. At his best guess, they were twenty years off. Older, weighted with burden. Sparks of emotion had played through them, always fleeting, always hiding before he could understand why. There was a story to Adren. Agony and misery haunted cir gaze with the bitter remnants of trauma, and not only from the assault. During their talk, ce had hinted at loss.

Still, he had let cir walk away without knowing more.

Not completely your fault, he reminded himself, squinting as he fought to focus on the gold links in his hand. *Adren basically told me to back off without actually saying it. Ce didn't want me to follow. That's up to cir, not me. I asked too many questions as it was.*

Questions were all he had. For each one he wanted to ask, another two dug their way into his thoughts. At the top of his list was why Adren affected him at all.

By the time noon arrived, he had as many frustrating thoughts as he did links in the three chains he had crafted, each a foot's length. In the same time it had taken him to finish the chains, Covran had paraded around with a newly finished set of three small daggers, each engraved with a name, polished, and safe in a fresh leather case tied with gold cord. Daggers Covran had started the day before at the same time Ress had begun the first chain.

It's going to be a long day. Ress laid the last chain on the workbench and wiped his face with his hands.

"Looks like you're having fun," Bremary said from the doorway, smoothing her grey dress and kinked hair. "I'm headed to the baker's. I'll bring you back something special. It might just perk up your mood." She pointed to the front of the store. "We have a visitor, by the way. Our favourite flouncing seamstress has dropped in to say hello. So stop being all people-stay-away and come be friendly."

Ress could only stare at Bremary. *Sure, because the past two days haven't hurt enough.*

"Right behind you." Ress sighed and slid off his stool. Following Bremary into the shop, he forced a smile as Allaysia came into view.

"Ress!" Allaysia greeted, stepping back from the clear glass cases near the front window. Her blue eyes bright, she strode towards him, arms outstretched beneath her green knit shawl. The skirt of her dark brown dress swished across the floor, elegant and lavishly embroidered with glimmering green beads. Bright green ribbons were woven through her wavy brown hair. From appearance alone, it was difficult to tell she was in her early forties and not her late adolescence. "It's been days and days and days." She drew him into a tight embrace, twisting back and forth slightly. "I've missed you."

"Hey, Ally." Ress buried his face into her neck, squeezing his eyes against the memories pummeling him. It was not her fault she was the older sister of his former best friend. Allaysia always treated him like a little brother, using the six years between them as an excuse to coddle him when she was not teasing. Her parents were no less kind, having been in his life since he was born. As much as he wished he could stay away from them to avoid remembering the past, they were family, tacked onto his own.

"Hey, Little Pup, what's wrong?" Allaysia pushed him back, frowning. "Having a bad day?"

"How would you know the difference?" Bremary slipped behind the front desk to stand beside Inesta. Leaning forward on her elbows, she rested her chin on her raised palms. "You're talking to a master of silence if ever I've known one." She looked at Inesta, who continued reading and writing receipts as though Allaysia were not present. "All right, make that two, and they're in competition."

Ress and Inesta grunted.

Bremary held up her hands. "Pardon me for making observations. I'll go get the food, then, since that's all I'm good for." She blew a kiss to Allaysia then skipped towards the front doors. "Until next time, assuming I don't catch you before you leave. Give your parents a big hug from me."

"I will." Once Bremary left the shop, Allaysia turned back to Ress. "Don't think that distracted me. What's wrong? You're a bit... eh, more than usual."

No answer was the right answer. To avoid digging himself further into the marital hole, he tilted his head towards Inesta and slid his glance in the same direction.

Allaysia pursed her lips, a gleam of understanding in her eyes. "Fine, don't tell me," she said loudly. "Just thought I'd ask."

Grateful for her discretion, Ress dipped his head.

Inesta ignored them, her customary response whenever Allaysia visited.

"I know what'll lift your spirits." Allaysia tapped Ress's chest, a playful smirk turning the corners of her pink lips. "Dinner with us."

"Ally, I don't—"

Allaysia thumped his chest with a light fist. "Don't go reasoning yourself out of it this time, you little pain in my thumb. We haven't seen you in a while. I miss you, and so do Mother and Father. Mother's been harassing me to ask you over for weeks. If you don't come, *she'll* start doing the asking, and I'm pretty sure you don't want that."

The threat of her mother visiting the shop to give him an earful was not a bad thing, Ress wanted to argue. With the rest of his family in Arminloa, Parase was the closest thing to a mother he had. Some days, he wished he could be mothered, even for a moment. He had made a mess of his adulthood.

Except being in their house reminded him too much of how it used to be when Tash was still Taldris. *Back when things were good. I haven't been able to see them without thinking of him, and I haven't seen him in a year, not to mention the eleven damn years before that. I don't know what I'd do if I saw him now. Not that I would. He's too busy to bother with the likes of us. Still, it'd be good to talk with Parase and Kilienn. I could use advice in dealing with Ines, even if there's not much left I haven't tried. At least maybe it'll distract me from thinking about Adren. I can't solve one problem while obsessing over the other.*

"I don't know." Ress glimpsed Inesta. "I've got a lot of work to do, and Ines and I…"

"It's fine," Inesta said without lifting her head. "I won't be home anyway. Me and Bremary are heading to Gretty's for a party. It's supposed to be just us girls." From behind the tangles of her hair, she peered at Ress. "It's just as well. We could use some time, couldn't we?" She motioned to Allaysia with a weak hand. "Being in their house makes my skin crawl, but they're family to you. You definitely should go."

Ress needed no other words to catch her meaning. A reprieve from each other could help.

Allaysia's lips contorted with visible annoyance. "Yes, you definitely should," she echoed, not saying what he suspected she wanted to. Her tightened fist on his sleeve said enough.

"Guess I'm coming to dinner." Ress breathed out. "Better go tell your mother. She's probably going to stuff me until I can't move."

"That's the plan." Allaysia grinned, mischief in her eyes. "And what we plan, we always make happen. This'll be the best dinner yet."

CHAPTER FOUR

Any further and he would be on the small lot owned by Parase and Kilienn, one step closer to fulfilling his commitment to dinner.

Standing in the dark, on the side of the red dirt road, Ress stared at the house, one of many in a row of houses. Although not one of the wealthiest districts in Araveena Ford, the houses were well-constructed and kept, built close together to allow for more families. Each lot offered a house large enough to support a family of six, many with a small building in the back of the lot for horses or work areas like his forge.

The house before him was elegant, even if the black wood walls were worn, needing to be replaced or stained, and the white stone chipped. The window shutters were bright yellow like the frames around the black doors. Yellow flower boxes hung from the windowsills, filled with wilted orange flowers of various hues, their petals clinging to the stems despite the cold autumn gusts. The flowers in the garden on the front lawn fared worse, many of their torn, dull petals ripped away and scattered across the ground. Only the glossy green ferns and golden bushes stood strong.

Ress took a breath and walked the path of flat grey stones leading to the front door. He could get through dinner. Of all the things in his life to fear, a meal with his second family was not one. How many times had he stood before a faction boss or taken a beating? Being ambushed by bounty hunters and interrogated by Councilman Severn was more terrifying.

Still, he feared the present. Even as he stepped onto the stoop and reached for the door, he wanted to leave. His hand stuck to the silver door handle, fingers frozen in an awkward, curled position. One day, he would come to the house and no longer be welcome. One day, he would have done something too foolish to be considered family any longer. For all of their support despite his bad decisions, his second family would leave like his blood family or push him out. There was a limit to kindness and sympathy, particularly when his actions could endanger them.

He jerked his hand from the door. Perhaps it was best not to drag his troubles into their safe space. They wanted a pleasant family dinner, not another round of what he had done to tear another hole in his marriage.

Except Ally will probably march through the streets and bang on my door if I don't show. She knows things aren't good. There's no stopping her from trying again, not with Ines away. I still can't tell who's more stubborn, though Ally scares me more. She always has.

With a sigh, Ress pushed open the door. Voluntary attendance at dinner was better than a blustering Allaysia in the middle of the night, especially if Inesta returned home. That was a fight best delayed.

"Ally?" He entered the foyer and closed the door. The foyer was painted white like most of the walls in the house, prim and bright in the light from the gold lantern on the ledge to his left. Above the lantern hung a polished mirror in a bronze frame, its corners gilded in yellow gold. The mirror was similar to the larger mirror on the wall to his right, beside the standing rack of shawls, long coats, and short jackets. On the other side of the large mirror stood a tall, rectangular vase with stalks of summer wheat and slender boughs of golden tree fronds. Beyond the vase was the open door to the sitting room.

Voices floated through the air, followed by Allaysia's giggles.

"Al-ly." Ress peered through the doorway ahead of him into the brightly lit dining room. The black table was set with pristine white linens, white clay plates with clear, smooth glaze, and gleaming glass goblets. The white candles in the glass candleholders were not yet lit, but the scent of spices, melted butter, and roasted meat suggested dinner would be served soon.

More laughter sounded, then the voices of men.

Two too many men, neither of which were Kilienn.

The short hairs along Ress's neck bristled. *She wouldn't...* He charged into the sitting room. White walls with dark red wood panels greeted him, the large room warm from the fire in the hearth. The vibrant red window curtains and gold adornments did nothing to distract him from his suspicions. *Please tell me you didn't.*

"Ally!" Stopping in the centre of the room, the thought of going further turned his stomach.

The laughter and chatter stopped, cut off by harsh shushes. Feet shuffled. Allaysia burst into the sitting room from the doorway across the room, her cheeks red and eyes beaming. Over her brown dress, she wore a black leather bodice, laced at both sides with black ribbon. Strands of black beads and green jewels had replaced her green hair ribbons.

"You made it!" Allaysia hugged him tight around his neck. "I'm glad you got away from the perilous beast of Araveena. I'm surprised she hasn't swallowed you whole." She pushed him back, scowling. "Though I'm pretty sure she's sunk her teeth into you enough. You look like you've gone ten rounds with her claws on the inside. You poor baby pup," she said, kissing his cheek and embracing him again.

A figure stepped into the doorway. "Ally, who did you—"

Ress snapped his head up, finding the person he had feared it would be: Tash, dressed in the fine red veil and vestments of a priest, staring wide-eyed as though he had the right to be surprised.

Jaws clenched, Ress gently pushed Allaysia away, barely stopping himself from shoving her. He should have seen the betrayal coming. He never should have entered the house.

"Forget this," Ress spat out, spinning away.

"No, wait—" Allaysia clutched his arm. "Please." She gave him a gentle tug. "I know this isn't what you want, but I think it's what you need. Both of you," she added, glancing at her brother. "I wasn't lying when I said I missed you, Ress, but it's not just you. I miss *both* of you. I miss how it was. It's not easy being in the middle, not when I wish you'd put aside your differences and make up. You've both done terrible things, but ignoring each other forever isn't doing anyone any good."

As Ress glowered at her and stepped back, Allaysia jerked him closer, throwing him off balance. She held her other hand out to her brother. "I can make your life a living nightmare if you two keep making me pull out my hair over this." She thrust her hand further. "Do *not* make me play the old maid card, Little Bird, because I will, just as I'll play the wounded sister hand for Little Pup. I know what twists your guts better than your lovers do. I'll stand here and cry until you decide you're worth forgiving enough to *at least* stand in the same room."

"She will, too," a man added from behind Tash. He slipped into the doorway, his long, black hair tied back in a loose tail. Dressed in an unembellished black shirt laced at the collar, tight black pants, black bracers, and black boots with one knife in each, Mayr appeared the same as the first time Ress had met him. Brawny and quick to bite with words, he fulfilled Ress's expectations of a Head Guard for a high-ranking politician. The black tattoos around Mayr's neck presented a silent demand for him to be taken seriously. "For the love of all that's sacred, *do not* make her go full-on moat building. We don't have enough buckets."

Mayr's grey gaze turned onto Ress, hardening as he spoke. "Make your decision a good one. I'm not cleaning up the mess." His features softened as he looked at Tash. "The same goes for you. You can't keep coming here and creeping in the corners to avoid him."

"I know," Tash muttered.

After another glance at Ress, Mayr leaned into Tash and whispered in his ear, their hands entwining between them. Tash nodded, his bright blue eyes lowered.

When Mayr stepped away, Tash took a shaky breath. "I was the one who did him wrong," he said, moving to stand by Allaysia's side and take her hand. "I'm with you. I'm just hoping you are, too, Ress."

His name was spoken so softly, Ress wondered if he had imagined it. Unable to speak, he studied Tash, reminded of Tash's shared resemblance with Allaysia and their father, Kilienn. Not only did they have the same brown, wavy hair with blond streaks, but their skin was the same light tan tone. Tash was not clean-shaven like his father but kept a close-cropped beard. In his shimmering red robes with gold embroidery and long, trailing veil draped over his head, he appeared smaller than when he had served the Shar-denn, his broad build lacking the extra muscle he had boasted as a guard.

Yet for all the changes, Tash still wore dark leather bracers, shielding his forearms like he had in the Shar-denn. He also wore a ring shaped like a talon, the metal curved over the middle finger on his right hand from knuckle to fingertip. A chain of silver links connected the base of the talon to a small metal ring on his bracer, pulling tight whenever Tash made a fist.

A ring and chain Ress had forged for him, five years before Tash had fled the Shar-denn. They had been a gift for Tash's eighteenth birthday, honouring the bird that was his namesake.

You actually kept them. I can't believe you're still wearing them, you bastard.

Allaysia, Mayr, and Tash watched him in the silence. Ress ground his teeth, trapped in a debate over his options. *One: run and never face Ally or her family again. Two: stay and yell at Taldris. Three: stay and try not to rip out body parts he might need and have his boyfriend kill me in the process. Four: continue standing here like a fool and have Ally fall apart and goad me into giving in. Then have the boyfriend lecture me about how messed up it is to make women cry. Really don't need that one, especially since I'm so good at it.*

Ress glimpsed Allaysia's hopeful expression, his stomach sinking at the fear in her eyes. She was trying to do a good thing, and while he could accuse her of being malicious, he knew better: she was trying to do what Ress could not do on his own. Forgiveness was difficult. He needed to be led to the cliff of opportunity and pushed over the edge.

Luckily for her, he would fall.

"For you," Ress murmured, easing Allaysia's grip from his arm. He kissed the back of her hand and held it to his chest. "Because neither of us could stand you crying—or the idea of you suffocating us in our sleep."

"Don't think I still won't." Allaysia drew them close, wrapping her arms around their backs. "I'm just trying to channel my powers for the greater good."

Tash kissed her cheek. "May the Goddesses lend you aid when you make the rest of us lapse into ruin, and may They run fast and far when you finally haunt the Realm of the Dead."

Allaysia laughed and nudged Tash with her elbow. "Next prayer, you should put in a kind word on my behalf. Maybe They'll let me live forever."

Mayr whimpered in protest. "Oh, please, *no*. Kill me if that happens." Arms crossed, he leaned against the doorframe. "I can put up with anything but that. Or my sister living forever. Or my sister-in-law. Or even Ae, because some days I wonder why I didn't run when I had the chance."

"Is the poor baby having sister problems?" Allaysia pouted. "Would you like to talk about it, Little One-I-have-no-name-for-yet?"

"And I'm done." Mayr held up his hands in surrender and turned into the corridor. "I'm going to talk to the grown-ups," he called over his shoulder before walking towards the kitchen.

Tash laughed quietly. "Don't mind him. His family's been giving him a rough time. A little too much advice he never asked for."

"Oh." Allaysia's lips twisted. "Should I apologize? I'd hate to make your visit terrible. He's been fitting into our family so well."

"Just be yourself. He'll sleep it off." Tash brushed her hair back. "Besides, you've got me, and it's my fault he's in this mood to begin with. Don't worry."

Ress caught his breath, unable to recall the last time he had seen the tender relationship between Allaysia and Tash. In that moment, it was as if time moved backwards, skipping over the painful parts and faltering on the joyful memories. No matter Tash's crimes, he had never been unkind to his family.

In part, that was what hurt the most after Tash left the Shar-denn. Not only had Tash hurt his blood family, he had given Ress, Varen, and Nimae up with them. That pain was not easy to forget. Or forgive. Not even if Allaysia cried a sea's worth of tears.

"Is this a good time to tell you dinner's ready?" a quiet voice asked from behind them.

Startled, Ress spun around. Parase stood in the doorway to the foyer, wearing a white apron over a light blue dress with cuffs of dark blue lace around her elbows. Her dark hair was gathered in a long braid, and her blue eyes shone like her daughter's, the resemblance to her son obvious in her face.

"My favourite seamstress," Ress said, moving towards her for a hug.

"Your first seamstress, more like." Parase laughed into his shoulder and held him tight. "Thank you for entertaining an old woman's wish and coming tonight." She pulled back and eyed her daughter with a scowl. "Even if it was under false pretense."

Allaysia raised her hands. "You said invite him for dinner. You *never* specified under which policies that dinner was required to happen."

Parase snorted. "You're sounding more and more like your brother."

"That's what I've been saying," Mayr shouted from the dining room. "Living with one is fun enough. Getting them both together is inviting disaster *right* in."

"Excuse me. I need to go sort this." Allaysia picked up her skirt and hurried out of the room, brushing past Parase. "Get over here, you darkly beast," she called loudly. "You might be cute, but I'll still bury you."

Chairs scraped the dining room floor. Feet scuffled. Allaysia cried out, followed by laughter and snorts.

Ress smiled at Parase's smirk. She looked happier than she had in twelve years—maybe even longer. Neither he nor Tash had made life easier for her. *Not like we should have.*

"How about I take you to dinner?" Ress held up his arm.

Parase curled her arm around his. "I wouldn't mind it in the least." She followed his lead through the foyer and into the dining room with Tash behind them.

The dining room was spacious, the white walls broken up by alternating red panels in bright and dark red. Gold lanterns hung on the walls, each housing a thick white candle. The table in the centre of the room was set for six, with newly lit candles positioned between the platters of food. Golden liquid filled the glass goblets—mead, he suspected, one of Kilienn's homemade libations. Allaysia and Mayr stood in the open doorway to the kitchen.

Kilienn bustled around the table, filling a glass plate rimmed in gold with food from each platter and serving bowl. White cord held back strands of his shoulder-length brown hair from his face. Prim like the house, he wore his dark green tunic belted at the waist beneath a black vest that hung to his knees, the hem falling just above his brown boots with red soles.

"Go on, pick your seats," Kilienn said, licking his thumb before gesturing to the table. "I'll take this to the altar." With the plate and a goblet in hand, he left the room through the door to the kitchen. From there, he turned into the corridor leading to the bedrooms and the altar at the end of the hall.

Parase stood at the head of the table. "Ally, love, you're here with me, and Little Bird, you sit here," she instructed, pointing at the seats adjacent to either side of her.

No one argued. Allaysia stood to Parase's left as Tash claimed the seat to her right. Mayr stood next to Tash, leaving Ress to stand at the chair between Allaysia and Kilienn's place at the end of the table.

In the silence, Ress glared at Allaysia. How many painless ways could he exact revenge for setting him up? From the expression on Tash's face, he had known nothing of her plan, either. They had the right to be angry with her and get payback for her deviousness.

Assuming I survive through dinner. Mayr's suspicious glances were obvious: he expected Ress to cause an outburst and give him reason to react.

Ress could not fault his expectations. They had met only once, when Tash visited Araveena Ford to publicly confess his actions in the Shardenn. After Tash had served punishment for his crimes, being tied to the flagpole in the village square for three days, Ress had found a spark of will to help Tash return home. A year had lapsed since, along with his compassion.

His jealousy, however, raged like destructive flames from the divine.

Ally, Ally, Ally. If this goes badly, I'm taking you down with me.

Kilienn entered the room from the kitchen. "Now that we're all here—" He stopped at his seat and lifted his goblet towards Tash. "Son, you have the honours."

Tash raised his goblet towards the candle closest to him. When the others did the same,

Ress relented and lifted his goblet, not feeling the reverence he suspected they did.

"To the Four, goddesses of life, being, and divine understanding," Tash began, his voice clear and steady, "I ask blessing upon the meal before us and all those here, in physical form and spirit. As your humble servant, Emeraliss, I seek favour upon this family and the kindness of Our Most Beloved Navara, Hastal, and Laytia. May Your gentle grace be upon us, Your unconditional love uplift us, and Your bountiful gifts be cherished with a full heart. Blessed be the Four."

"Blessed be the Four," Allaysia, Parase, and Kilienn echoed before drinking. Mayr's response was quieter, though his expression was pensive as he grasped Tash's hand.

"Blessed be," Ress muttered against the rim of his goblet, tempted not to drink. Who would notice? Who would care?

Not to insult Kilienn or his mead, Ress took a quick sip and sat down with the others. They passed platters and bowls around the table, filling plates to the sound of praise for Parase's cooking.

That's the easy part. Wait until we get to the actual dinner. I wonder if Ally has any suggestions for topics. Ress eyed Tash. *I don't know what to say to him. What* can *I say? 'Thanks for wedging an axe in my back. How about taking my head next?' How did she expect this to go? We're not five. He didn't break my toy. He didn't steal my sweets. He didn't call me nasty names. He ran away then shot his mouth off and got me arrested. What else is there to say other than 'I hope you die really painfully, you selfish ass'?*

As Mayr leaned into Tash to whisper in his ear, Ress was curious. He knew little about Mayr other than his position with Tract Steward Dahe. Too hurt and angry to care, he had never asked Allaysia to elaborate on the relationship between Tash and Mayr. From what he could tell, Mayr was considered family, no different than Ress. Despite their differences and positions on opposite sides of the law, they would have to keep the peace for Parase and Allaysia's sakes.

Tash laughed as he eased Mayr back, his low tone stopping the chatter between Parase and Allaysia.

"Hey, not fair!" Allaysia scooped mashed purple vegetables onto her spoon and tilted the spoon upwards, keeping the food in place. "No secrets at the table or you're getting pelted. I've improved my aim."

Mayr grinned. "Careful. I've been well-trained in everything from sister sabotage to filling heads with all sorts of things you'll never be able to forget. I'm incredibly adept at taking orders, especially with the right master." He glanced at Tash, his grin sliding into a smirk.

"Hey, now." Parase tapped the table. "None of that talk during dinner. Save it for after. We old folks need to be entertained." Her eyes gleamed as she winked and sipped her drink.

"Yes, because that's the whole reason we have children to begin with," Kilienn added, chewing behind his smile.

True to Ress's predictions, an awkward silence filled the room, complemented by hesitant glances in his direction and the occasional cough. If they wanted him to converse, they expected too much. While he would not yell his frustrations and ruin their dinner, the ability to put words together in a casual, coherent sentence passed him by. From the way Allaysia's leg bounced under the table, a habit whenever she was nervous or bored, he suspected she was also at a loss of what to say. The last time he had been in the house with the entire family, Tash had been close to death.

"So," Parase said, clearing her throat. "Mayr, when we saw you two months ago, you'd made plans to visit your daughter. How did that go? I know you were looking forward to it."

Surprise flitted across Mayr's features. "Good, I think." Swallowing hard, his stunned expression melted away. "We got along just the way I'd hoped. Better, actually. She made our visit everything I'd never dreamed of." He flashed a proud grin. "She's perfect, too, smarter than I ever was. And friendly. I swear she'd make friends with anybody and anything. Throw one of those vicious, snarly beasts from the old stories at her and she'd charm them into being cuddly and cute."

"Don't forget the locket Betta gave you," Tash murmured.

"Oh, yeah, right." Mayr tugged a chain out from under his shirt and slipped it over his head. An oval locket dangled from the chain along with a small, colourful ring. "This is her. This is Iliane," he said, opening the locket before passing it to Parase.

Parase leaned towards Allaysia and held the locket between them. "She's absolutely lovely! Already a real beauty." She passed the locket to Allaysia. "Sorry, I forgot: how old is she?"

"Twelve," Tash answered.

Mayr pursed his lips, giving Tash an annoyed glance. "I swear you do this to test me." He returned his attention to Parase. "Eleven. Twelve in three months."

Allaysia giggled into her goblet, the locket in her free hand. "Give it a few years and she'll be breaking hearts *everywhere*. There's going to be so many crying boys left in her wake, no one will know what to do. It'll be a mess of depressing proportion. Someone get the buckets."

Instead of laughing with Allaysia and Parase, Mayr stiffened. Eyes lowered, he reached for his goblet, staring at the liquid but not bringing it to his lips. The apologetic gaze Tash swept over Mayr was not lost on Ress, nor was the way Tash held Mayr's hand on the table.

Mayr recovered quickly and smiled. His lips twitched, suggesting he forced the expression, though Ress could not understand why. When Allaysia handed the necklace to Ress, Mayr's attention followed the locket.

A priceless item in questionable hands. The modest weight of the locket sat comfortably in Ress's palm. Both the locket and the chain were of yellow gold. Out of habit, he inspected both, searching for imperfections in the craftsmanship and weak links. The clasp was sturdy, the links of chain tight and thick, able to withstand the stress of a soldier's life. They were more than enough to support the vine-engraved locket, the artistry pleasing on the eye with smooth, connected lines.

The ring with it weighed little, woven from purple, red, and gold threads knotted into bands. While the locket was crafted with an experienced hand, the ring boasted imperfections. The knots were neither perfectly aligned nor tightened enough, and the banded pattern was slanted in places. He could see where the ring began and ended, with the final knots larger than the others and out of place, their ends frayed as though created by a child.

For all I know, maybe his daughter did. It's small enough to fit a child's finger. Ress considered the painting inside the locket. The girl's dark hair hung in thick curls around her round face and spilled over the shoulders of her blue dress. She looked youthful and happy with an infectious grin. If the artwork was an accurate representation, he could imagine her effect on others.

"So you have children. How many?" Ress passed the locket to Kilienn.

"Only the one." Mayr shifted in his seat, fingers tightening around his spoon. "And sort of." He cleared his throat. "I was with her mother when she was born. I took care of her for a while. Mostly just watched over her, walked around with her to get her to sleep, and changed nappies. I figure it counts. If it acts like a father and talks like a father, maybe there's a chance they can be one, right?"

I wouldn't know, Ress wanted to say but stayed silent. There was no reason to spoil dinner with stories of him and Inesta.

"Are you planning on raising any more children?" Parase's eyes brightened with her hopeful smile.

"Not yet, no," Mayr answered.

"The possibility isn't completely ruled out," Tash added softly.

Mayr scowled at Tash before facing Parase. "We're waiting to get some things sorted first. He hasn't been an Uldana priest for a full year yet. We're still adjusting. The *two* of us."

"As I said," Tash interrupted, "the possibility still exists. Then we'll find a way to adjust all over again. For the rest of our lives, I imagine."

The glare Mayr pinned on Tash reminded Ress of Inesta's expression whenever he trampled on a sensitive topic and would not keep his mouth shut.

"Are you married, the two of you?" Ress asked. *You certainly act like it.*

"No. We're close enough without making it official." Mayr shrugged, pushing food around his plate. "It doesn't change much for either of us."

"But we would make it official if there were children involved," Tash clarified.

"Really?" Mayr dropped his spoon, the metal clattering on his plate as he turned to Tash. "You want to have that conversation again, right *here*? *Now?* In front of *everyone*, before we even get to the desserts?" He snorted. "I can guess why. No doubt your mother and sister will be completely on your side, just like my mother, Tara, and Orlee. Then I won't get any sweets because we'll get stuck talking babies. You promised me, you pretentious,   holier-than-your-boots troublemaker."

Tash shook his head. "I'm just making the answers as accurate as possible—maybe even reminding you of *your* promise."

Mayr let out a loud, frustrated sigh. "And they call *me* impatient," he mumbled. He picked up his spoon and tapped Tash's wrist with the handle as he spoke, accentuating his words. "Meanwhile it's. All. You. *All* you. But *I'm* getting all the attention. Stop it. I like it when they ignore me."

Parase covered her mouth, muffling her chuckles. Allaysia sputtered and giggled against the back of her hand. Kilienn said nothing, the laughter visible in his eyes.

Yet despite the domestic banter, Ress caught Tash's smirk before he shrugged and winked at his mother. Even more subtle was Mayr's smile as he looked away, his head lowered. There was another story, a truth with a light heart and gentle honesty.

We used to have that, me and Ines, sort of. Ress stared at the patch of tablecloth in the centre of the table, his eyes unfocused. During their third and fourth years of marriage, Inesta and he had enjoyed happy, optimistic perspectives of their future. Their conversations had been sweet, their hopes high, as close to a deep, romantic love as he could offer.

None of the goodness had lasted. The light, joyful aspects of their relationship plummeted into the greedy, insatiable pit of pessimism and the realization they could never have what either of them needed. They had never been entirely together, never truly in harmony. What constituted playful spats between lovers had evolved into fights, followed by years of silence and indifference, sharing a life without sharing themselves. They rarely spoke of their emotions or fears, even though he suspected they shared the same feelings. Equally trapped, equally unsatisfied. Equally alone.

After his arrest, what little they'd had twisted into something ugly. Their relationship became an apathetic, unfeeling picture of him throwing himself at Inesta's mercy while she froze him out and berated him with paranoia.

I don't even know what it is now, or how much more either of us can take. What I do know is we never felt strongly about having children. I've never wanted to be bothered with them. Ines... she's never been certain. Maybe she'd want them with the right man, but she can't meet him when she's stuck with me.

Ress's gaze caught Tash's over the dancing flames of the candles. *If only you'd chosen her and run away together. She could've had a family. She begged you to choose her, to love her. I never wanted her. I never wanted the life that should've been yours. I just wish you could take it all back. Make this better. Fix what you broke. Make me believe in you again.*

As if he heard Ress's thoughts, Tash hung his head. An instant later, he raised his glance to Ress's and nodded, his features strained with apology.

"I'm sorry," Tash mouthed, the corners of his eyes softening with sadness.

For one wistful moment that could forgive lost time and shred undying memory, Ress almost believed him.

Dinner had crawled by at a miserable pace, but the clean-up was agony embodied.

Left alone at the table with Mayr and Tash as Parase, Allaysia, and Kilienn cleared the table, Ress tried to avoid looking at them. His offers to help had been refused. He was certain Parase was taking advantage of Allaysia's sly trick to force Ress to speak to Tash. They had not exchanged words since Tash's silent apology, only glances.

Every one of those glances stabbed him deeper, digging into another part of him. His sadness, his anger, his hate. Anything that could be agitated was poked and prodded. The silence choked on unspoken words, suffocating with the strain of remorse and spite.

For every word he wanted to yell at Tash, he wished for better. If only they could return to being children, reviving the promise to be friends for the whole of their lives. They had made the oath as innocents, four years old and excited about their futures. That vow had bound them as brothers, giving them someone to turn to whenever life was cruel.

Do you even remember any of it? Does it even matter anymore? Ress dared to glimpse Tash's face as Tash spoke quietly to Mayr. *How much do you really care?*

"Well, that's the end of that," Parase said, gliding into the dining room from the kitchen with Allaysia and Kilienn behind her. No longer wearing her apron, she smoothed her dress. "Let's go sit in the other room, shall we?"

Mayr stood and offered his arm to her. "Let me escort you. Being a gentleman's the least I can do." He raised his other hand to Allaysia. "How about you and me call a truce for the night? You can think of all the ways to sister me later."

Allaysia made a face as she accepted his hand. "I *suppose* we could. Might be boring, I'm just warning you now."

"Trust me, after spending days in the Temple, I think I can handle boring." Mayr threw Tash a pointed glance and led the women from the dining room. Kilienn followed, chuckling under his breath.

The door closed behind them.

Well, that's not deliberate. They couldn't have made it any more obvious if they'd barricaded the doorways. Ress scowled at Tash, not sure what to expect.

Tash cleared his throat. "I know what I owe you." He stood and pointed at the kitchen. "If you're willing, we could try talking. I know I don't deserve any of your time, but you deserve the chance to say whatever you need to."

Like I hate you and miss you all at the same time, and it absolutely disgusts me?

Ress swallowed back the rest of his snide comments. The last time he had seen Tash, he had let his anger speak. Perhaps it was time to unleash what he wanted Tash to hear: the painful consequences of Tash's thoughtless actions, destructive and vicious in their affects on their loved ones. He wanted Tash to feel the crushing weight of grief.

He wanted to stop feeling alone.

"Fine. After you." Ress followed Tash into the kitchen and shut both entrances, careful not to push on the clear windowpanes in the top half of the doors. When he turned, Tash stood at the table in the middle of the room, staring at the chair next to him. Light from the hearth along the wall beside Ress filled the room. "Do you even know what to say?"

Tash smiled sadly. "Only a thousand variations of 'I'm sorry.' I don't know what to apologize for first." With slow hands, he removed his veil and draped it over the back of the chair. He raked his fingers through his hair, pulling the wavy strands over his shoulders. "There's nothing I can say that will change what matters. I cannot pray your rage into nothingness. I cannot restore what has been taken. Still, apologies and explanations are what you are owed. They are the only thing I can give." He held both hands out to Ress, his palms up. "I have nothing, but offer everything."

"How about an answer?"

"To what?"

Of all the questions Ress wanted to ask, only one found its way to his lips. "You're still wearing the ring I made you?"

Surprise flitted across Tash's face as he rubbed the talon ring. "It's not something I wish to sacrifice," he said softly. "I've made a lot of bad choices, but your friendship was never one of them. I wear it in remembrance."

"Of better times."

"No. Of guilt."

The sincerity in the correction made Ress pause, offering him comfort and saddened satisfaction. "You used to wear it on your left hand."

"I know." Tash held up his right hand. "Keeping it on this one reminds me not to punch anyone lest I break the ring. Though it's more likely I'd break my finger. I'm not fond of either option."

Ress snorted and crossed his arms. "I'll give you that." Against his skeptical doubts, he stepped towards Tash. "You're a no-good rank bastard. A complete and utter ass who's thought only of himself and damned everyone you supposedly loved. I'm *barely* keeping it together for the people you're supposed to protect." He thrust his hand towards the sitting room. "And that damned foolish confession of yours last year? Guess how fun *that* was for me to fix. If there's *anything* you owe me, it's your gods-awful face on fire and rotting."

"I know."

"No, you don't," Ress spat out. "You had the Shar crawling up my backside and itching to kill someone. If not for *me*, you wouldn't have a family to visit. They'd be dead. It's about as foolish as leaving the Shar to begin with!" Pointing a trembling finger at Tash, his face warmed as his voice grew louder. "You damned egotistical, selfish bastard! Stop getting the people who love you nearly killed. We're *not* paying your debts."

"I never asked you to." Tash clasped his hands before him. "I'm well aware of the Shar-denn's interest in me. I went into the confession knowing they could be part of the consequence. Mayr cautioned the same. They could have taken me, but they didn't have the gall." His gaze lowered. "I know you've tended to my family, and I can't tell you how grateful I am. One of those debts you mentioned, one I can never repay."

"Ha! You're telling me. You have *no idea* what I've had to do for everyone here and the whole damn village." Ress ground the toe of his boot against the floor.

"So tell me. Make me understand the depth of your anger."

"Now you're being pretentious. Someone should gut you."

Tash shook his head. "You want to tell me how badly I hurt people, so do it. Tell me how it really is."

"I've given *everything* I have, is *that* good enough for you?" Ress yelled. "I keep losing sleep over how I can save your family and the village, but your family matters most because they're my family, too." He swallowed hard, choking back the sickness roiling in his stomach. "I had to *beg* the rest of my family to leave Araveena so they'd have a better chance. Now I can *never* see them because I'll be followed. *Your* family didn't want to leave. They've stood by me, even after I got arrested. The same with Cove and Bremary. Most days I don't understand how they could or why they'd bother," he murmured. "I'm just going to end up dead. I'll probably take them with me."

"I know the feeling," Tash said quietly. "I'm surprised I'm allowed to enter this house."

"Then get on your knees and kiss my boots because it hasn't been easy saving them." Dry-mouthed and caught on the verge of confessing truths he never shared, Ress crossed the kitchen to the counter with the washbasin. Difficult as it was, he needed to say something to someone.

He was tired of keeping secrets. Tired of being the only one who knew what he did.

Ress snatched a clean wooden cup from the cupboard to his left and filled it with water from the pitcher on the counter. After drinking half of the water in the cup, his thirst barely satisfied, he stared out the window above the washbasin. In the dark, only the outline of the garden and stable in the back of the lot were visible.

"I've been buying their protection," Ress admitted. "You know what I do for the Shar—melting stolen goods, turning them into sellable pieces and counterfeit coins and weapons. Since I was already doing it, I did more, but I stole things on my own. Some of it I took from the Shar, which was risky, but doable. I've taken on extra jobs to buy out the guards and bosses. And favours—I've done several to strike the deal that no one would touch Ally or your mother," he muttered against the rim of the cup before taking a sip. The thought of either of them being taken by the Shar-denn made him sick.

"I've done everything I could to help people without getting killed in the process," Ress continued, placing the cup on the counter. "But you know what *really* kills me?" He spun around to face Tash. "That you turned me in to the High Council and *really*, truly, *so completely* messed *everything* up. I'm not talking family. I'm talking *much* bigger." Leaning against the counter, he crossed his arms tight. "I'm talking sabotage, which you've ruined. All because you couldn't keep your damn mouth shut."

Tash stepped back, his brow furrowed. "What sabotage? What are you talking about?"

Ress sighed. "The sabotage I've pulled most of my time in the Shar." He slid down the red cupboards beneath the counter and sat on the floor, his knees raised. "Ever since they moved me up to coordinating the transport of goods, I've... made adjustments. Sometimes crates don't arrive. Items get mixed up. Girls haven't made it to the Breakers in the cache houses. They've been re-routed." Head resting against the cupboards, he focused on the ceiling beams. The truth dredged up sick memories that made his darkest nightmares seem kind, almost generous. How many times could he open a crate or carriage of trafficked victims and *not* be horrified to find them terrified, beaten, and malnourished? He heard their desperate cries even after they were long gone, embedded in his mind like the tears of the survivors who had been freed. The worst of it was the knowledge that no matter how many he saved, there were always more he could do nothing for. "I haven't been able to do any of it as frequently as I've wanted, though. It's difficult finding reasons to blame others and not get caught. Or set up instances where the lackeys have no way out except to surrender. That's too damn expensive.

So is buying kidnapped victims a way home without being caught again."

He pointed at Tash, his forearm resting on his good knee. "*You* went and made it *that* much harder. Got me arrested and *now* the Shar won't trust me. I can't intervene like I used to, and hunters are pissing circles around me."

"I didn't know." Tash let out a long breath and sat on the nearest chair. "I'm so sorry. I didn't realize..." His eyes narrowed. "If you'd started before I left, why didn't you tell me?"

"I couldn't trust any of you—you, Varen, Nimae. I figured you were all too far gone on Shar-denn lies, I'd be dead if I said anything. Goddesses know I could've used your help, but for all I knew, you'd have turned me in or at least stopped me."

"That's not true."

"Please. The three of you were so deep in doing the bidding of the faction leaders, you could've made a permanent home up their ass. One word from you and I'd have been gone."

Tash left his chair and crossed the room to where Ress sat. With his layered robes gathered in his fist, he sank to the floor beside Ress and clasped his raised knees. "That's a lie. I wouldn't have said a word."

"What? Like you didn't say anything to Council?"

"Ress—"

"No, don't you go telling me I overreacted. You turned out to be a liar and a double-crossing snitch. Then you ruined my work, just like I figured you would. Different time, different means, but still ruined it. You became *exactly* what I feared you were." Ress rubbed his injured knee, soothing the ache that had returned. "And you know what else? I hate you. You don't even know what you did. Not the extent of it. So go on, ask me what you did."

"I don't—"

"Ask me!"

Tash jerked away, raising his hands. "All right. What did I do?"

"You killed Varen and Nimae," Ress whispered.

Even in the dimming firelight, Ress could see Tash pale.

Tash shuddered, drawing his hands into his lap. "That can't be right. I didn't—that wasn't—"

"Varen's dead. *Dead.* And Nimae ran off before the hunters could get him. Wherever he is, he's not coming back. They're gone forever. All of that's on you." Ress hoped Tash felt sicker than he ever had, vomiting guilt and shame and everything in his treacherous stomach. Was it difficult for Tash to breathe? Did Tash's lungs feel as though they were being shredded and crushed? Did it feel as though someone reached into his chest with barbed gloves and squeezed his heart until it stopped beating?

Everything I felt when I found out.

"You know, it's funny," Ress continued, his voice hard with spite. "Even with everything you did to *me*, I can't tell you how much I hate you over *that*. You *knew* how in love they were. Dammit! We were the first ones they told; the only ones they could trust to see them kiss or hug or do anything vaguely romantic for those first few years." He glowered at Tash. "What did you think would happen? Didn't you care what it'd do to *them*?"

Tash's lips moved without sound as he folded his arms over his legs. Blinking back tears, he lowered his head onto his arms.

"Everyone says Varen killed himself to keep from betraying the Shar, but I'm pretty sure he did it to protect Nimae." Ress cleared his throat, fighting the grief clawing at his emotions. "Just like I'm sure they were connected right up to Varen's last breath. There weren't many reasons why he'd kill himself, especially with a knife to his throat. It definitely *wasn't* out of loyalty to the Shar—he hated those bastards. But he would've killed and died a thousand times for Nimae."

"I'm sorry," Tash whispered, facing Ress, his head still down. "That's not what I wanted."

"That's what we got. If Nimae's not dead-dead, he's dead on the inside. It's *all your fault*." Ress scratched the floor with his nails. "Their house is abandoned with all of their things. It's covered in cobwebs and dust and dirty animals that piss everywhere and leave smelly, rotting corpses. It's a tomb, not a home. Varen's family should've buried him there and burned the whole thing down. I can't even step foot it in anymore," he admitted, no less disgusted with himself than the state of the house. "Too many ghosts, none of them satisfied."

Tash buried his face in his sleeves, wiping his eyes. "I didn't know. No one told me what happened. Council's document said Varen was dead, but not how. They didn't even tell me they had him."

Ress snorted. "Yeah, well, that's how much you loved us, isn't it? Council probably didn't want to admit they messed up." He pointed at the scar on his jaw. "And since you so kindly *haven't* asked: I got this lovely gift after you ran from the Shar. Some of our more caring gang brothers thought I knew where you'd gone. When I told them I didn't, they tried to beat it out of me. Thankfully, they finally believed me and stopped, but the scars stuck.

"On that note," Ress continued, "you've got *no right* to chastise me for not telling you about what *I* was doing. *You* left without a word to anyone. Don't *ever* tell me I should've trusted you when you didn't bother trusting me."

"I'm sorry, I'm sorry, I'm sorry." Tash held his head in his hands, his elbows trembling on his knees. "I couldn't take it anymore, but I couldn't tell you—I just had to leave. I was too scared to tell anyone. Then when I gave the Council your names... It wasn't supposed to be like this." He looked at Ress, his gaze clouded with tears. The moment the tears trickled down his cheeks, he wiped them away. "You might think it was easy, that I was happy to do it. You think I was being malicious and spiteful, but it wasn't like that."

"Right, I've heard that before."

"It *wasn't*," Tash argued angrily. "I didn't want to turn you in. I debated it for years. Yes, it was easy to turn in the names of the other Shar members, but you three... I didn't wake up one day and decide you should be arrested. I kept moving your names on and off the list. I agonized to the point where I couldn't eat or sleep. After I finally gave the list to the Council, I didn't leave my room for days. I kept praying for your forgiveness, and I still do, every day."

"Oh, *come on*. What good is prayer and forgiveness when your friends are *dead*!" Ress thrust both of his hands into the air. "I can't believe after *all* these years, *that's* your excuse. If you're going to insult me, at least come up with something good."

"You want me to lie? How is that any better?"

"Because then I'd know you really care!" Ress yelled.

"*That's* the reason I turned you in to begin with!" Tash shouted back. "I will take your abuse and anger and punishment, but I will *not* lie to you. I'm not going to make up stories just to appease whatever you feel for me. If you don't want to hear it, there's the door. I'm *not* the one who asked you here, but I *am* willing to lay out the truths, no matter how much they hurt or how much you don't believe them."

Tash slammed back against the cupboard and crossed his arms. "I turned you in because I wanted you out of the Shar. *That's* the reason I don't have a good excuse. You want to hear I didn't care about you, that I wanted you punished. You want me to say I'm the Council's puppet. You want me to say I never thought of you, but I can't give it to you. It's not real."

"Don't make this my fault."

"I'm not," Tash argued. "I was trying to make it better. It just went wrong."

"'Make it better'? How did you *ever* figure that?"

"I knew how miserable the four of us were. After I left, I found a second chance at life. It wasn't much, but it was better than living with a dying soul. I wanted the same for you."

"So, what, you wanted us to be priests like you? Groveling and praying and making up pretty little dreams?"

"No, that's not—" Tash sighed. "I've never stopped caring. In fact, it only got worse because I wasn't with you. I didn't have your help. I felt alone, even when I was surrounded by priests. I wished you could've run with me and found safety. I knew I ruined your chances to get out alone, so I found another way. I wanted to make it up to you."

"You turned us in to get us out?"

"Yes."

"Have you lost it?" Ress sputtered. "That's one of the most ridiculous things you've *ever* done, and I've seen you do *a lot* of ridiculous things. I had to get you out of half of them."

"I know that *now*, but I wasn't thinking clearly *then*. You were always the rational one. Varen was the spirited, optimistic one, and Nimae always put everyone else's needs first. I was the one who acted without thinking and did whatever the three of you told me to do." Tash hugged his legs and rested his cheek on his knee. "I was on my own, making decisions without talking to people who knew me. I wanted to see you without getting skinned for trying. I wanted to save you. I wanted to be the hero, the brother who put everyone back together."

"In the end—"

"I broke us up even more." Tilting his head back against the cupboard, Tash closed his eyes. "I figured the crimes you'd committed weren't as bad as mine. Even Varen and Nimae didn't hurt people the way I did. I thought Council would give you a lighter sentence or you'd negotiate a deal. You three were always good talkers—I assumed you'd talk yourselves into something better than prison. Still, I begged Council for leniency for you. I gave them detailed explanations of the Shar's inner functions in return for that leniency. They said they'd take care of it."

"Oh, they did." Ress grunted and picked at the threads of the worn sole on his boot. "They leniencied Varen into suicide and me into being an informant. Then they lenienced Nimae right out of sanity. They took real good care of us."

"I promise that wasn't what I wanted. I wanted to rescue you," Tash said softly. "I thought they'd honour their deal with me. I thought being a priest meant something. I wanted to help."

"Thanks," Ress muttered, "but you can stop helping now. You've got your temple, your priests, and your sheltered second life. Don't waste your time on a lost cause like me." He wiped his face with both hands. "I won't have long left, anyway. The mess I'm in isn't entirely your fault—I've done substantial damage on my own."

Except I have no idea how I'm getting out of any of it. I don't even know what to do with what you've told me. Sighing, Ress stretched out his legs and flexed his aching knee. Did he believe Tash? Had Tash turned them in because of loyalty and poor strategy? Could he have been foolish enough to believe the High Council would offer them escape? Tash's apology appeared sincere, the hurt in his voice genuine. What would Tash gain from lying? The damage was already done. There was nothing to be had, save resolution and forgiveness. In all possibility, Tash's flimsy, pathetic excuses were the truth. In a twisted way, they *had* to be true. Lies would have been more fanciful and easier to accept. Lies would have fueled Ress's bitterness, ensuring he never spared another moment on Tash.

The truth left him more conflicted than he already had been.

If anyone was responsible for their mess, it was Ress, Varen, and Nimae. Without them, Tash never would have joined the Shar-denn. The three of them had worked for the gang before discovering what it truly was, doing small jobs that made them feel grown up, happy to join another friend of theirs, Lyfar, and his older brothers. Tash had followed them into it, wanting to be like them and prove himself to his family. By the time they realized they were employed by a gang, the game was set and the four of them were game pieces, directed by threats of a faction boss with no qualms over stabbing boys for their insolence.

Was it any wonder Tash wanted to be the one that saved them all?

He was the last to join and the first to go. Ress glimpsed the sadness in Tash's face as he stared at the floor. *He was always the one needing acceptance and wanting to prove he was worth something. But he never had to, not to us. Then we got him involved in something that demanded he keep proving himself in order to survive and he couldn't take it anymore. How is it any different than me rationalizing myself into staying when it's more logical to run?*

A blur of movement stole Ress's attention. Looking up, he found Mayr standing on the other side of the door to the dining room. Contrary to his friendliness at dinner, Mayr watched Ress and Tash with a tightened expression.

"You have a shadow." Ress elbowed Tash in the ribs.

Tash glanced at Mayr. "A warm shadow."

As Tash raised his hand, Mayr dipped his head. In an instant, the offensive glare of warning melted into a languid gaze of adoration. A moment later, he turned and walked away.

"He's really in love with you," Ress said.

The response was silence. Tash smiled and lowered his chin.

"And you're in love with him."

Tash's smile deepened. He lowered his head further, closing his eyes.

"And if anyone hurts him or tries to force you two apart, you'll tear into them."

An ugly darkness warped Tash's expression as his eyes opened. "I might be a priest, but I didn't forget how to protect." He raised his chin.

"If there's anything people can't keep me from, it's my devotion to the Four and to him. They're all I need, and I'll die for both. Honestly, though, I'd sooner break bones before that happens, with or without the priesthood's belief in peace. Hastal understands. She's a remarkably understanding goddess that way."

Ress drew his fingertips along the floor, tracing lines and swirls without creating a pattern, imitating his chaotic thoughts. "It must be nice, finding a love like that. You're one of the lucky ones."

"I know, and I thank the Four every day for him." Tash laced his fingers together in his lap and bowed his head. "He's helped restore me to who I ought to be. Where I used to hope I'd merely survive each day, I'm hoping for more—a family, because I can do that now. I can be that man. I have everything I need, everything I've wanted, and now I want that little bit more to complete our lives. I want to make it *our* life."

"That's what his issue was during dinner, I take it?"

Tash laughed. "His family is so excited with the prospect they're smothering him into making a decision. Still, he wants us to take our time. He wants everything to be perfect before we disrupt it again. Before him, I wanted nothing more than to be a priest, groveling and dreaming, as you'd say. Now, I want more of the life I have with him. After seeing him with

Iliane, I know what I want for us. I want to see Mayr as happy as he is with Iliane every day, and with a child we can raise together. A child he doesn't have to lose."

Shifting, Tash stretched his legs out. "But you have love," he continued, his tone laced with sadness. "You have Inesta. She wouldn't stay with you if she didn't love you. She certainly wouldn't have married you."

Bless your ignorance, you love-spoiled fool.

"You'd like that, wouldn't you? You'd like to know she moved on after you. Found someone better." Ress laughed derisively at Tash's assumptions. "We aren't married because we're in love, and we certainly don't have the kind of relationship you do. Ines and I are friends only, even it doesn't always feel like it. We're not romantically tied. We share the same bed, nothing else."

"I don't understand. That's not like her."

"No, it isn't, but she changed when you left." Ress glared at Tash. "I married her *because* you left. I didn't want to see her hurt, so I told the Shar she was mine to begin with. I told them she'd been using you and they couldn't touch her without answering for it. Then I paid them to make sure it stayed that way."

Tash lowered his crestfallen gaze. "So then you… and her…"

"It's a marriage of concern, intimate but missing all those things we wish it had. I love her in my own way, and I'll always do everything I can to keep her safe, but safe isn't enough. *Concerned* isn't enough. She can't even get everything she wants from me. She has needs I can't meet." Ress sighed and craned his head back. "Sometimes I can give her the pleasure she's after, but I'd be happier if we were completely celibate. I've never wanted anyone like she wants to be wanted. She's as frustrated with me as I am."

Hit with the familiar sensation of feeling too old, Ress drew his hands down his face. "It's a mess. I want her to be happy, so I do what I can, going through the motions. It's not that I don't *want* to love her that way, it's just never fallen into place. And as much as I want to *be* in love—the deep, disgusting kind of romantic bollocks that makes us complete fools, so far gone we'd die for a taste—I haven't found it. Not the real thing, only a mockery. And I wish I didn't want it, I really do, because it isn't fair, and it'll never be fair to her."

"I'm sorry for that, too," Tash murmured.

"Yeah, I figured. Ines and I need to stop pretending, but I don't trust what'll happen if I do. Some days, though... some days it's difficult to pretend."

Difficult enough I'm tempted to give the house to her and live with Cove and Bremary.

"Perhaps there's purpose," Tash said. "Perhaps the Goddesses have a—"

Shouts rent the air, muffled and familiar. Bangs followed. The angry voice continued, moving closer.

The kitchen door to the dining room swung open and slammed against the wall. Sharp snaps sounded from the windowpane, cracks bursting from the centre.

"And there you are!" Inesta yelled, storming into the room. Her hair tangled around her shoulders, framing her reddened face. Her black shawl slid down her shoulder, exposing her disheveled dress.

She stopped short, gaping as Ress and Tash scrambled to stand. "You're with *him*?" she roared, her green eyes widening. Stepping back, she almost bumped into Mayr in the doorway behind her. With a loud growl, she lowered her chin and sneered at Tash. "You despicable, lying bastard! How *dare* you stand there with him, in this house, like you belong, you disgusting, filthy, lying coward. You should be dead for what you've done!" Both hands out, she lunged at Tash.

Mayr yanked her back by the arm.

Inesta whirled around, poised to slap him. "Don't touch me!"

"Then keep your hands to yourself," Mayr responded coolly, seizing her wrist. As she struggled to get free, he held her in place. "Hit him and you're mine. Just you, me, and the law."

"Mayr." Tash stepped forward, one hand raised. "It's all right. Release her."

Mayr exchanged glances with Tash, his fists still clamped around Inesta's arms. A moment later, he released her with a gentle shove towards the wall to Ress's right. "Fine, but I'm not leaving." Arms crossed, he stood in the doorway, taking up as much space as he could. He lowered his chin and glowered at Inesta. "If you so much as lay a *finger* on him, I don't have *any* problems arresting you. Assault charges are a real bitch, but not half as much as I can be."

"Good for you." Inesta hissed at Mayr and rubbed where he had gripped her. She turned to Tash. "So you found yourself some top ass to hide behind. Congratulations. You can keep ruining lives."

Tash moved closer to her, holding both hands up. "Inesta, I know you're angry, and I know why. I won't take that from you, but we can all remain calm and talk—"

"*Talk?*" Inesta thrust her arm out towards Ress. "That's how we're here in the first place! Nobody talks to me until the damage is done. Then all they do is lie!" Reaching into the dipped neckline of her dark dress, she pulled out a crumpled piece of parchment. "Like what they're doing and who they're doing it with!" She stomped past Tash on her way to Ress. "Like this—nothing but a dirty lie." The bundle crunched in her fist before she threw it at Ress.

The paper bounced off his chest and fell to the floor.

Ress bent down to retrieve the parchment. He froze, recognizing the schedule of drop-offs for the Shar-denn—a list that had been locked in his desk in the shop.

"Yes, I found it. *All* of it." Inesta stood rigid, her rage making her seem larger than she really was. "I left the party early because Bremary got talking, saying you were keeping secrets. Saying you've been working on some dangerous things and getting Cove to help you. So I went to the shop. I found the key—what a damn awful hiding place *that* was. Then I found this. I'm not a fool. I can guess at what it is. I came to take you home and confront you."

Face flushed as her voice grew louder, she gestured to Tash. "*Then* the ass he has sucking his cock answered the damn door and I find out *you're* here with *him*! Not only have you been lying about what you *haven't* been doing with the Shar-denn, you're consorting with the man I hate most! You're sitting around, licking wounds after telling me you weren't talking to him!"

Ress reached for her. "Ines, it's not like that."

"Slap me silent it isn't." Inesta wrapped her arms around herself. Tears slid down her cheeks, glistening in the firelight. "No more. I'm done. I can't put up with your lies. I can't stand who you are."

She spun and strode towards the door, the heels of her shoes clicking across the floor. Approaching Mayr, she stomped to a stop, waiting for him to move. He stepped aside, his dark gaze following her across the threshold as she hurried into the dining room.

"Ines, wait!" Ress charged past Tash and Mayr, limping through the rooms after Inesta. Sharp pains stabbed his knee as he stumbled into the foyer and clutched the doorframe to keep from falling. "Wait."

Inesta stopped in the open doorway of the front entrance and turned, her pained expression stealing Ress's breath. *"Don't* come home tonight."

Without another word, she fled from the house.

Ress stared after her, dumfounded. He was going to kill Bremary.

A gasp sliced through the tense silence. When he peered into the sitting room, Parase, Allaysia, and Kilienn gaped, dazed with pale faces. Allaysia covered her mouth with both hands, her wide, misting eyes filled with horror.

"Ress, I'm sorry," she apologized, fumbling over the words as her voice wavered. "I've never respected anything she's done, but I didn't mean to make things worse. I—I—" Allaysia burst into tears, hiding her face. Kilienn drew her into his arms, swaying gently. "I just wanted you to make up with Little Bird," she managed between sobs, the stammered words muffled. "You've both been hurting and I—I wanted to help. I'm so sorry. So, so sorry."

"You couldn't have known, Ally." Tash slipped around Ress to stand in the foyer. "If anyone's responsible, it's me. I'm the one who started it." He clasped Ress's shoulder. "You've paid the price for far too long. Now you're being punished. I'm sorry."

Ress stared into the darkness of the outside world, the road and houses blended together in his blurred vision. *Not as sorry as I think I'm going to be. I might as well burn alive straight until morning and wake up in the Realm of the Dead. Welcome to the tragic beginning of the inevitable end.*

CHAPTER FIVE

In the middle of the night, Ress wandered the streets, tempted to close his eyes and test his ability to reach his shop without sight. After all the nights spent walking off fights with Inesta, he knew the paths and alleyways intimately.

Except this was no ordinary fight. It was Inesta taking the final word. Unlike her relationship with Tash, she was not offering Ress an ultimatum. She was making the choice and ensuring he knew his place.

The worst part was he knew she was right. Even worse still, he had little fight left in him.

As much as he wanted to charge into their home and demand they talk, the hard tone in her warning suggested she meant every word. Too tired of fighting and apologizing, he could not bring himself to find out what would happen if he violated her wishes.

Ress shoved his hands further into his pockets and pulled his sagging shoulders forward, drawing into himself against the biting chill in the air. He should have borrowed a coat from Kilienn or taken one of Allaysia's shawls. Had he not been desperate to get out their house, he would have considered what he needed. Time was the first luxury to be sacrificed when he was running from unending apologies, suffocating humility, and unwanted pity. While he appreciated the sympathy, he wanted to be left alone. Whether or not Allaysia, Bremary, or Tash were responsible for Inesta's fit was irrelevant. In the end, only Ress was to blame. No amount of comforting gestures changed the truth, nor did they make him feel better.

If anything, they made him feel worse.

He did not deserve the kindness, especially when there was no one to comfort Inesta. Although Tash's family treated him like a victim in his marriage, disregarding Inesta with disgust, they were wrong. He had never been the one who needed the most care or someone to take hits—the burdens were always hardest on Inesta. Dragged into a world she never should have been part of, she was the one who needed the most support. She was the only one worthy of it.

That's why I'm not sleeping in a warm bed tonight. I don't deserve it, either. Just me in a chair with blanket in the shop. Or maybe I'll sleep on the floor since that's where I belong. All the comforts of prison wrapped up in a shiny box of jewels.

Ress sighed and turned down an alley to the village square. Head lowered, he walked the narrow, moonlit path. Both Parase and Kilienn had argued with him after he refused their offer to stay the night, threatening to tie him to a bed to make him stay. They surrendered only after Tash had argued on Ress's behalf, but not without scowls and grumbling their disapproval.

Disappointment he could handle. Allaysia's teary requests for forgiveness were a different story.

All the more reason to get out of there. He kicked a stone and watched it tumble up the middle of the alley. The stone stopped several paces away, but his gaze continued, catching on the dark mound near the other end of the alleyway. In the dim white light, the motionless pile resembled a heap of black cloth, patches of dull leather jutting out from beneath a tattered black blanket with snarled fringe. If not for the sudden slight movement between fabrics, the mass could have been mistaken for misplaced laundry.

Instead, it was a misplaced person, huddled against the wall. They had drawn up their legs, scrunched into a ball as best as their upright position would allow. Their arms were curled around their knees, allowing the blanket to cover more of their body. Wrapped around them from the front, the edges of the blanket spilled across the red dirt, its top corners pinned to the wall by shoulders. No feet poked out from beneath. No colour showed, not even skin. A hood drawn all the way forward stole the possibility of seeing the face buried in the blanket over the person's knees.

Ress frowned and stopped. No one slept in the alleys. Araveena Ford had always succeeded at ensuring no one needed to, especially with Magistrate Galosa in charge of their village. It was one of the magistrate's ongoing campaigns, a promise from when Galosa had taken office during Ress's childhood: everyone would have a home. Everyone would have a warm place to lay their head at night. Even while the Shar-denn stole from people and left them homeless, Galosa had not balked from his promise. Although Ress and Galosa had an uneasy relationship, Ress respected Galosa for the efforts. The more the Shar-denn took from citizens, the more strain they put on Galosa.

Has to be some drunk who couldn't make it home. Everyone else knows to bang on Galosa's door and beg for a bed, even in the middle of the night. He breathes to be needed by someone.

He stepped closer, struggling to pick out details. A man, judging by what he could see of the clothes, but that was all. No names came to mind, just the nagging suspicion that he should recognize them.

And a familiar, numbing tug on his subconscious that beckoned him closer.

A foggy whisper of doubt leapt into his thoughts. There was little to see but too much to feel. Each step took him further into an invisible mist, guided by the light of a spirit determined to shine away the shadows of secrecy. *It can't be...*

"Adren?" he whispered, reaching out.

The mass startled. Limbs moved quickly. A knife swiped out from under the blanket, driving Ress back. "Back it up," the deep voice commanded, followed by a growl. "Enough watching. Run or lose parts."

When the figure lifted their head, Ress's breath hitched. Adren peered up, cir green eyes widening.

"Ress." Adren's grasp on the knife loosened, cir hand lowering slightly before tightening again. "What are you doing here?"

Ress arched one brow. "You're one to be asking." His gaze swept over Adren, taking in the scuffed leather of cir dark long coat, now uncovered by the fallen blanket. He paused on the metal rings ce wore, one on each finger, all of them different. "You said you were going home."

"I am home." Adren slipped the knife into the sheath strapped to cir thigh, further disturbing the blanket. "Any street—any alley—can be home when there's nowhere else to go."

"You said none of this earlier *why*?"

"You couldn't fix it so what was the point?"

Ress craned his neck back, growling in annoyance. While he would never declare himself a staunch practitioner of philanthropy, his generosity could be tapped more easily than people gave him credit for. "You should've said something."

"Not how I do things."

"And sleeping on the street is?"

"Safer than busting into a shop or being caught in a barn." Adren shrugged. "It's dark, secluded, away from people. A good place to think."

"Because an inn won't work."

"Not when they're full-up and I have no money."

"You're telling me you'd rather be cold, alone, and broke than actually ask for help."

"Yeah, because help isn't free." Ce snorted and crossed cir arms. "I've seen what 'help' looks like. Not pretty."

Kind of like this lovely attitude? Memories from breakfast skipped through Ress's mind. Appearance was not the only change in Adren. A chilling sensation crept over his skin, demanding he stay his ground and challenge Adren's stubbornness with his. For all the roughness, something deeper festered in cir tone, and desperation clung to every word like an echo. The same confused darkness strained the air. Adren's essence danced around him, entreating him to stay while the rest of cir pushed him away.

Both he and Adren seemed equally haunted by conflict, unable to discuss the why and how of their circumstances, hiding behind silence. Perhaps that was why he wanted to get to know Adren, Ress decided. Though he still lacked an explanation for how he had found cir in questionable situations twice. Or why he was attracted to cir, wanting to tease out what it was he found so pleasing.

"This can't happen," he muttered. "*You* might not care that you're wasting away in a dingy alley, but I do, especially since I rescued you from one last night." Ress scowled. "I imagine you're still feeling the bruises—or do you like gambling your safety away?"

"Not much of a gamble when I'm dressed like this. People avoid the scary ones." A dark expression passed over Adren's face. "Today is not yesterday. Yesterday was a matter of surprise. Tonight is a matter of survival. Bruises heal, but I'm more interested in breathing. Homeless doesn't mean dead."

"It also doesn't mean throwing yourself into harm's way. It's not a life sentence." Ress held out his hand. "Come on."

"I don't need saving."

"You weren't too proud to accept my help last night."

"I know, and I'm thankful for it, but this isn't that."

"No, this is you being so full of yourself you can't be kind to someone who might have something to offer. With talk like this, someone might think you're fishing for pity and stomping all over the person who gives it to fool yourself into feeling better." Ress thrust his hand further. "Can't play the misery game with me, not when I'm so deep in the rules I could've invented the concept. So come on. If you want sleep, I've got a space with walls and roof and no people. Might even be willing to share some of the food I have stashed away, unless you've given up on eating because it's completely beneath you?"

"However could you guess?" Adren smirked, hesitant as ce grasped his fingers and tugged him forward. "There are two problems in your logic. One: this smacks of charity. Two: I have no desire to spend time with your wife. It's clear she didn't want me in your home."

"Suits me fine," Ress mumbled. "We're not going to the house." He straightened and stepped back, gently pulling Adren's hand. "Though who said this was charity? I was proposing a deal."

"Deal?"

"Yeah, like I give something, you give something, and we meet in the middle?" When Adren started to draw away, Ress clutched cir cold fingers tighter. "Place to stay plus food and necessities in return for simple jobs around the shop. Helping Cove and me, mostly. Keeping the fires stocked, cleaning the floors, other small things. All legal, all hands-to-ourselves. Maybe even a bit of money for your purse so you don't have to make it an extended stay."

Adren was silent, staring at Ress from beneath cir dark hood. The instant he saw rage in Adren's eyes, he loosened his grip. Why was every quiet moment between them spoiled by a flash of anger, rage, or another inexplicable emotion? They were as frustrating as the rest of the feelings he sensed from Adren, none of which he could separate from the others. Everything was tangled in a perplexing mess, no different than his thoughts and emotions whenever ce was around.

"Consider the deal struck," Adren murmured, yanking on Ress until ce stood. Ce caught the blanket before it pooled on the ground and shook the dirt loose. Against the wall by cir feet was cir satchel, not stuffed as full as Ress recalled. "Lead on."

Ress turned towards the village square, waiting for Adren to pick up cir pack while he contemplated Adren's appearance. Gone were the pretty dressings and feminine air, replaced by a bulky long coat with broad shoulders and dull silver buttons. Under the coat, ce wore loose, dark pants and a shirt with a high collar, both belted with a strap of woven leather. The legs of cir pants were tucked into dark boots.

Had he not seen Adren before, he could have taken cir for a young man.

One of the Shar-denn boys, at that. His glance fell to the knife strapped to Adren's thigh. The knife was a lacklustre piece with a black hilt and no visible embellishment, an inexpensive weapon that could have been purchased from any market. *Hardly Shar-denn fare.* Not that the common knife alone could preclude Adren's possible involvement with the gang.

By the grace of the ever-loving Four, I really hope ce isn't part of the Shar. Give me this one thing, you beloved, most cherished goddesses. Something the Shar hasn't touched. Something I haven't broken. Please, please, *put me on par with Taldris, just this once.* Ress peered at Adren beside him as he led cir to the metalsmith shop. *I'm not asking for much, just someone who doesn't hate me or want to use me. I wouldn't mind someone who needs me as much as I need them. Really wouldn't mind someone I could confess to on a daily basis without them wanting to run away, but who am I joking?*

They were silent as they reached the darkened shop and Ress let them in through the front doors. Once they entered, he closed the gate and doors behind them, locking everything before palming the keys.

"It's not pretty, but it's warm," he told Adren, guiding cir to the back rooms. "We can set you up with a simple pallet tonight, but tomorrow

I'll come up with something more comfortable."

They entered the moonlit workroom.

The door to his office was open.

Cursing silently, Ress hurried inside, scanning the room for evidence of Inesta's visit. To his relief, no papers were strewn across his desk or piled on the floor. When he tugged on the bottom drawer of his desk, the drawer remained closed. The drawers above were also locked.

Surprised more than relieved, he slid his hand along the bottom of the lowest drawer. Inesta had returned the key to its hiding spot.

Bless you for being discreet even when you want to rip my guts out. Quick to hide the key in his pants pocket before Adren could see, Ress opened the metal box of matches on his desk. One of the few expensive luxuries he allowed himself, he struck one matchstick along the grated lid until a spark caught.

"I can set you up in here," Ress said, lighting the candle placed in the centre of his desk. He gestured to the floor between his desk and the wall to his right. "It's a big enough space to sleep. I can vouch for its potential."

"Slept here a few times, have you?" One of Adren's brows arched.

"Give or take a lifetime." Not interested in speaking about his problems with Inesta, Ress crossed the room to the tall, wooden armoire along the left side of the room. He took out all four blankets and a scrunched pillow then moved back to where Adren stood. The heaviest blanket was the first to be tossed down, a grey mass of thick fabric that provided satisfactory cushioning. Next were two blue patchwork quilts, followed by a blanket knitted from bright purple yarn, each lighter than the last. He dropped the pillow at one end of the makeshift bed. "That should do. It's not as uncomfortable as it might look."

"It's better than numbing my backside in the dirt." Adren placed cir satchel at the end of the blankets opposite the pillow. Ce drew back cir hood, revealing a tight, braided bun sitting low on cir neck. "Thanks… for this," ce said quietly, breathing out as though in defeat. "I'm not used to people like you being so… giving."

"If you ever want to talk about it—"

Adren pressed one palm to cir forehead. "Not really. I just… I can't… honestly, I just want to sleep. It's been a long day. An even longer night. Headache's grinding my skull."

Ress resisted frowning, unable to ignore his disappointment. They had talked freely at breakfast, almost like kindred spirits. Now, Adren skirted issues when not being abrasive. "If you want." He pointed to the workroom. "I'll be out there. I'll keep it quiet. Let me know if you need anything. Latrine's out behind the forge. Water's in the workroom. Food's available if you're hungry."

"Thanks. Just need sleep for now."

"Sure." Ress picked up the candle and moved towards the door. "And it really is a deal," he said, standing in the doorway. "I want to help, no lie. We can work out the particulars tomorrow with Cove. I'm sure he wouldn't mind someone to talk to other than me."

Adren sat on the blankets, watching Ress with a blank expression.

"Night." Ress stepped into the workroom. Behind him, the quiet sounds of buckles being undone broke the silence. He placed the candle on the tidied workbench and sat on a stool. As he stared into the flame, he reached for the silver flask tucked between two small, headless bronze statues on the back of the workbench. Quick to uncap the flask, he sipped the biting alcohol, wincing at the searing burn as he swallowed. Fulore was Covran's drink, not his, but anything was better than a perpetual dry mouth.

Adren. Inesta. Tash. Inesta. Adren. Adren…

It was too much to think about, even in small doses. How was he going to deal with any of it?

He sipped the fulore again. While his issues with Tash could never be fully resolved, they could be helped. Their talk had given him a sliver of peace. Despite Tash's ridiculous reasons for his actions, at least he *had* reasons—ones that suggested his heart was not as far gone as Ress had feared. Although Tash had made poor choices, their intent was valid. His grief over

Varen and Nimae appeared real. In those long moments, Ress could have sworn he had his old friend back.

Inesta was a different problem. Her feelings were clear, but not her intentions. When he finally returned home, what would he find?

Home... Ress glanced at the office door. Adren was a riddle he wanted to solve, but he grappled with the questions. No home, apparent problems with family, deep-rooted misery not spoken of, and a spark of life existing outside of cir body despite cir problems. *I can't let you live on the streets. Ines is right: Araveena's dangerous. It's been dangerous ever since the Shar took an interest in it, long before I was born. They'll never let Araveena out of their clutches, and there isn't a damn thing I can do about it. The only thing I really have control over is whether I choose to care about people or not.*

He sneered at the flask, his distorted reflection casting an uglier look back at him. Caring—he did too much of that. *That's how I got here in the first place. It's an addiction, maybe the only one worth dying over.*

Ress raised the flask to the headless statues, no longer remembering why he had forged them. *Here's to caring too much. Maybe it'll actually help someone. Maybe we'll end up happy in the end. Maybe there's a better life ahead.*

Two days later, he started to believe his exile was permanent.

Ress sighed and regarded the sunlit workroom, absentminded as he polished silver goblets. Inesta had not entered the shop since she last saw him, and she had refused Bremary's visit the day before, a painful first that brought Bremary to the verge of tears. No one knew what Inesta was feeling or what she was doing. How long would she avoid them?

At least Adren's talking to me. Ress's gaze stopped on Covran and Adren standing in the doorway to the forge, his skin tingling with the sound of Adren's laughter. Once again, ce wore the white dress with its pearled and embroidered hem, cir dark red shawl wrapped around cir waist and hanging to cir knees. Cir hair cascaded in tight waves around cir shoulders. Gone were the black clothes, contained in the satchel tucked in a cluttered corner in his office. Even the defensive and skeptical attitude was gone, replaced with the friendlier, chattier Adren he recalled.

Ce's acting like ce's been here all along. Contrary to his concerns and the awkward first day, Adren had charmed his cousin. The day before, he had worried Covran would disapprove of Ress's decision to let cir stay and Adren would run away. Adren had spent the day in the shop, quiet, cautious, and dressed in cir dark clothes, keeping cir head down. Covran had cast more than one intrigued, doubtful glance at Ress.

Now, everything was different. Adren had come out of the office with new clothes, a bright smile, and a singsong greeting for both of them. Ce wore cir rings on the gold chain around cir neck. Cir boots had been turned down at the shin and again at the ankle. From what Ress could tell, ce did not carry cir knife.

Each detail only reminded Ress of what he wished he knew about Adren. Where had ce come from, and what could have happened to drive cir to Araveena Ford instead of one of the cities, where job opportunities were more plentiful? Or had Adren fled from a city, running from whatever bothered cir deep enough to hide so carefully?

Ress focused on the goblet in his hand, carefully laying it in the cloth-lined wood case with its mates. Maybe he would ask Adren to tell him more about cir after their dinner with Covran and Bremary. Perhaps he could even entice Adren to speak as candidly as ce had before, when ce had sounded pleased to let him into a part of cir life. The discussion would give him something to think about other than Inesta. He needed the distraction, the same reason he was considering taking Bremary up on her offer for him and Adren to stay with her and Covran. *Besides, Adren could use a nicer place to stay, and*

Bremary... I know she'd feel better if I stayed with them, especially with Ines ignoring her. Oh, Bremary, sweet Bremary. You're not a kid, but you still want everyone to be your friend. Your heart's so big and soft, it's easily broken. After all these years, you really know how to make it difficult for me to say no.

"Well there's a serious I-need-to-vent face if ever I saw."

Startled by Adren's voice, Ress blinked. When had ce moved to his side? "What?"

Adren clutched the handle of the broom and leaned against it. "Looks like you could use a barrel of something strong and a night of ranting. If you wanted to start now, no one would blame you. Getting drunk at noon *sounds* like a social scandal, but it happens more than anyone admits." Ce tilted cir head, hair falling forward. "Or if you want to talk, I'm sure Cove wouldn't mind me not sweeping the floors for a bit. He's dragging his dirty boots like he's dragging his ass. What dirt I sweep out he brings right back in."

"I heard that!" Covran shouted from the forge between hammer strikes. He peered around the doorframe and flicked his fingers at Adren. "Mouthy excuse for help. I'm going to make the slop buckets your next priority."

"Good luck with that," Adren called back, not parting glances with Ress. "I'll take slop over staring at your face all day."

Covran's nose scrunched. "No wonder Ress is keeping you. You're as bad as Bremary. Get new friends," he said, pointing at Ress before disappearing into the forge.

Or new family, Ress almost said, the silent insult hitting him hard.

"So?" Adren smiled weakly, the expression strained as though forced. "Tell me more about this fight you and the wife are having. I've already heard the gist of it. You might as well give me details."

"Not much to say." Ress closed the box of goblets. *Not about that, anyway, and not to you. Why should you care? It's a series of bad decisions I can't tell you about without putting you in danger.* "I've made mistakes, and she's had enough. Nothing more to it." Standing, he carried the box to the workbench across the room, placing it with other items to be sold.

"You're one of *those*," Adren muttered.

"One of what?"

"Nothing. Didn't say a thing."

Before Ress could argue, Adren swept a path through the workroom and continued into the shop. Cir offer was kind but posed more problems than he could handle. Part of him wanted to unload the bitterness and disappointment onto a friendly shoulder, particularly cirs. He could see himself telling Adren everything, though he had no idea why. Nor could he understand why he imagined himself seeking comfort from Adren. Covran and Bremary were family, and talking to them was normal, but Adren was nothing to him. Merely someone he helped.

Except for the flicker of a light deep within that shone brighter whenever ce was near. Or the noticeable tug on his emotions, forcing him to watch Adren, sensing cir even when they were in separate rooms.

Nothing about it made sense. The more he tried to rationalize it, the further he found himself falling into a chasm, knowing nothing.

And yet he wanted to say everything, for no reason at all other than it was what he should do.

I'm officially a mess. Maybe I should go and—

"Ress!" Bremary yelled. "Get out here."

"What now?" he mumbled, dragging his feet on his way to the front desk where Bremary stood with Adren.

"This just came." Bremary held out a folded piece of beige parchment. "It's in Ines's hand."

Ress opened the parchment quickly and breathed out. "Ines wants me to come to the house. She also wants me to bring Tash."

"Umm, why?" Bremary stepped back. "Doesn't sound like a good idea, not after what you've told me."

"How would I know? I'm not the one who kicked me out." Ress folded the paper and tucked it into the back pocket of his pants.

Dread twisted in his gut, pleading him not to go. "I'm going to do what I'm told, though."

He glanced at Adren and Bremary. Would leaving Adren with his cousins result in disaster? Although Adren got along with both, they knew little about Adren. The possibility of cir being a thief or worse crept into his mind more than he wanted, enough that he had removed all traces of the Shar-denn from his office and burned the documents in the forge. Still, every time he thought Adren might be something more than what ce portrayed, he forced himself to believe in more than conspiracies and paranoia. Life was too precious to waste it on seeing potential enemies in everyone. "Keep busy without me, yeah? I'll be back soon as I can."

"Sure, shouldn't be a problem." Bremary grinned. "We've got plenty to do, mostly herding Cove into his box and driving him into the ground."

"Whatever you say." Ress looked at Adren. "I'll be back soon, honest."

"Go!" Bremary shooed him out of the shop, waving both hands.

Unwilling to stall further, Ress obeyed, his steps hurried as he journeyed through the village. When he stopped on the stoop outside Tash's family's house, he knocked and waited, his hands buried deep in his pockets. He felt like a child again, calling on his friend and waiting to feel welcome.

The red curtains in the front windows swayed and parted slightly. A moment later, the front door opened.

"Ress," Allaysia greeted, eyes widening. She stepped aside and held the door further, drawing back the trailing skirt of her light green dress. "Come on, get in! Don't know why you didn't just walk in anyway."

"I didn't know, with how things went, if I'd..." Entering into the foyer, Ress cleared his throat. "Is your brother still here?"

"Tash? Him and Mayr aren't leaving for a couple more days." Allaysia pushed the door closed and turned towards the back of the house. "Little Bird! Stop preening your boy and get over here."

"Apparently we need to discuss the differences between your eyesight and what's actually going on," Mayr said, walking through the sitting room with Tash behind him, his dark clothes overshadowed by Tash's red robes. "Because I swear, Ally, you're looking for—" He stopped in the doorway, raking a hard glance over Ress. "You're back."

"Mayr," Tash scolded, slipping into the doorway beside him and placing a hand on Mayr's back.

"Hey, merely making an observation." Mayr leaned against the doorframe, eyeing Ress. "Settled the wife down yet?"

"That's why I'm here." Ress flicked his attention to Tash. "We've been summoned."

"Both of us?" Regret crept into Tash's gaze as he nodded. "It's just as well. It's past due time."

Mayr straightened, his palm grazing the hilt of the knife on his belt. "I'm coming along."

"No, you're not." Tash kissed Mayr's cheek, his lips lingering. "I have to settle this on my own. You'll only upset her more. So before you argue: I'll be fine. She can't do anything to me she hasn't already done."

Mayr turned his head, catching Tash's lips in a quick kiss. "Yeah, *that's* a short list. And you wonder why I worry." The pointed stare he gave Ress was as firm as his voice. "Take care of him."

Or you'll take it out on me, Ress finished, nodding his understanding. Beneath the sarcastic response he wanted to give, he admired Mayr's protectiveness of Tash. As he followed Tash out of the house and down the road, Ress's mind wandered. Would he ever find someone willing to stand by him, no matter his faults and criminal life, or was the chance long gone?

"How is she?" Tash asked quietly.

"Don't know. Haven't seen her." Ress shrugged. "She sent me a note and said we needed to meet her."

"Oh." Tash's steps matched Ress's hurried pace. A long silence followed, their boots scuffing the dirt the loudest sound. "How are *you* doing?" Tash asked as they turned down a road.

"I don't know. A little terrified?"

"Understandable."

"Like the rest of my marriage—built on a whole lot of understandables."

"At least you cared enough to try. No one else would have." Tash peered around the edge of his veil. "Goddesses know I was selfish enough to leave her alone. You're better for her than I ever was."

Ress snorted. "There you go, daydreaming again. Do you even believe half the things that come out of your mouth?"

"More than half. I'd go so far as saying I believe all of it."

"Stop it. You're annoying." Fighting a smirk, Ress shoved Tash gently. "Stop talking like you're suddenly an optimist. You'll turn me into one."

Tash laughed. "Maybe that's the plan."

"It's a terrible plan. Change it back."

"Where would be the fun in that?"

Ress turned down another road and slowed his steps. When he finally stopped, he looked at the house to their right. Only partially relieved to see his own home, he wondered what they would find on the other side of the front door. "About as fun as this is going to be."

"One word at a time," Tash advised, clasping Ress's shoulder and guiding him forward. They climbed the porch steps with heavy footfalls as though attending their own execution.

Inside, the house was silent and cold. The bedroom doors were open, allowing sunlight to spill into the rest of the house. In the centre of the sitting room sat six closed wood trunks of various hues and four large, burlap sacks, the fabric strained from how much they held.

"Ines?" Ress ventured towards the trunks. Behind him, Tash closed the door almost silently.

The moment he turned his head, he stopped. Inesta stood at the kitchen table, disheveled and statuesque, dark circles under her eyes. A priestess in voluminous red robes and veil stood beside her, her long blonde hair falling to her waist in loose curls.

"Good, you're both here." Inesta gestured to the priestess. "This is Lorea."

Ress dipped his head. "Priestess." He glanced at Tash, hoping Tash knew her.

The confusion on Tash's face did nothing to soothe Ress's nerves. "Sister Lorea." Tash's voice lowered to a near whisper. "Inesta."

"Brother Halataldris, Ress, come." Lorea motioned to the table. "Please, join us." Her voice was smooth with a pleasing high pitch, but she did not smile.

This is bad, very bad. Ress moved cautiously, waiting for something to attack him. The only comfort was Tash at his side, braced for whatever was coming.

They stopped at the table. Ress stood across from Inesta while Tash claimed the place across from Lorea.

"I don't want to drag this on," Inesta started, her hazel gaze flicking to Ress's face. "I want a divorce."

Ress's stomach felt as if it had dropped out of his body, dragging down everything else struggling to stay inside. "Ines, please—"

Inesta shook her head and held up her left hand. Her marriage ring was missing, its lack hitting Ress as fiercely as her words. "I'm leaving. I can't do this anymore. I have to find my own life, and I have to do it *now*. If I don't, I'll talk myself into staying. Again." When her hand started to tremble, she lowered it. "I've got to do it while I have the courage."

He choked on a ragged breath. How long had he expected her to say she was finished with him? How long had he expected her to withstand their life? If anything, it was a miracle she had stayed at all.

Despite everything he wanted to say, no words formed. No sound, no excuse, no apology. Helpless, he wished someone would say something instead of watching him.

The corners of Inesta's eyes softened, tears slipping down her cheeks. "Can you understand why?" Her gaze hardened, sliding towards Tash. "I'm angry *all* of the time, at everything. I hate the Shar-denn—what they are, what they represent. They ruin *everything* they get their grubby, greedy hands on." She brushed tears away, her voice cracking between words. "They ruin the people I care about."

As Tash hung his head, she turned back to Ress. "I've tried to fix things and straighten you out. Now I just feel let down. Lied to. Disrespected. All because you can't trust me, because of what you're involved in. It makes me feel small, worthless."

"You're not worthless," Ress whispered. "You never have been."

"I am when it comes to most of your life." Inesta gestured towards the village. "I'm good when I'm playing shopkeep. I'm good when you want someone to talk to. I'm just no good for anything else." Wrapping her arms tight around herself, she stepped back from the table. "Honestly, I get it: in comparison to the Shar-denn, I'm nothing. I'm your poor, useless wife. I have to be, which is really damned hilarious since I am what they've made me," she murmured. "I wake up at night scared and angry and scarred. I'm full of rage. It never used to be in me, not until Taldris. Then *you* kept it burning."

Ress's shoulders sagged. "I didn't mean to hurt you. I wanted to try and make you happy."

"It's been a nightmare." Inesta gripped the back of the chair in front of her, her knuckles whitening. "I can't trust *any* of you, ever. I have to find out for myself if there's any way to get anything good back once it's been stolen and smashed apart."

"I'm sorry, Inesta." Tash moved closer to Ress and reached out to Inesta. He drew back almost as quickly. "I accept everything you say about me. I accept the blame. I've made mistakes, and I take responsibility for them. But please, don't be rash in this decision. What he's done, he's done to protect you. It's not safe for you to be on your own."

"Safe? I'm not safer with any of you!" Inesta stepped away from the chair, her lips twisted in disgust. "'Rash decision' this: you ruined my life *three* times. *First*, you chose the Shar-denn over me. *Then*, you ran from them *anyway*, after saying you were staying for *me*! Funny enough, the Shar-denn wanted me more than you *ever* did. They wanted to hurt me as much as they did you. It's the reason why Ress married me, destroying my life all over again. Not to mention how horrible I felt because of it. All I took from it was that you never loved me, *not ever*.

"Then, *oh and then*," she continued, yelling and flinging her arms, "you got Ress arrested, shoving our marriage and reputations further down the hole. Actually, wait—" Inesta laughed, craning her head back. "Now that I think about it, you've ruined me four times, starting with the day you met me." She lowered her chin. "This is where we're ending it."

When Tash opened his mouth to speak again, Inesta held up her hands and backed away. Lorea reached across the table to tap Tash's arm, shaking her head until he closed his mouth and backed away from Ress, putting more distance between him and Inesta.

"Stop trying to talk me out of this," Inesta snarled. "If I'd never met you, I'd never have needed Ress to take care of me or feel like he had to." Her gaze softened as she looked at Ress. "I *know* you do everything you can to protect me. Except protecting me means you *have* to lie—and it's those lies I can't stand anymore. Most days, my whole life feels like a series of lies and half-truths. I need to go where people remind me of what truth looks like. What actually *living* feels like, because I don't remember. There's always going to be distance between me and you. You'll never be truly mine. My *life* will never truly be mine... unless I leave."

"So this is how it ends." Ress clutched the chair before him. "This is everything you've never been able to say to me. All those fights, all that silence... You're going, even if it means leaving yourself open for the Shar to..." He could not bring himself to say the words, let alone think of all the things they could do to her.

"I have to," Inesta argued. "I always feel like I'm being punished. All I did was fall in love. I gave my heart to someone who threw it back in my face and broke me. The worst thing, though?" She stared at the vase in the centre of the table. "Some sick part of me still loves Taldris, at least who he was."

With a sniffle, Inesta wiped the drying tears from her face and rubbed her eyes. "I'm more than what you've made me. This divorce is my last shred of dignity, the tiny bit I've kept safe. Let me keep it. Don't make me beg," she whispered. "Don't make me like one of those girls the Shar-denn captures and sends to Goddess-knows-where. I'm *not* going to plead for mercy. I'm not going to do a damn thing more for them. Eloras has offered me a home in Grace, a life, and I need to have my freedom to have that. This is me taking it back."

"And I'm here to help her get it." Lorea hugged Inesta around the shoulders. "I have both the document and the tools for the Severing Ceremony. We can do it right here. There's no need to visit a temple or involve anyone else. I will act as officiant and signer as a beholder of the Goddesses' most sacred trust."

Her sad, golden gaze turned onto Tash. "Brother Halataldris, you are requested to be the witness and second signer."

Inesta reached for Ress. "If you really do care for me, grant me this." She glanced at Tash. "And if you really have changed, if you truly want to help me, you'll sign off on it."

"What choice do I have?" Ress drew away from Inesta's reach. "You've made it clear you won't stay. You've also made it clear you hate me, even without saying it. There's not much else to be said, is there? Really no point in me agreeing or disagreeing. It's done, either way."

"I don't hate you. I just can't stay with you. There's a difference."

A difference that felt like no difference at all.

He could live with her not loving him, but to have only her contempt and fury, to know nothing he had done was good enough—how could he accept any of it with peace or apathy? Not that he doubted her misery. That was easy to understand, and he would never blame her for it. Yet understanding did not stop the pain of rejection and being stabbed by truth.

After all the years of fighting, he was finished. The raging fire that fueled his need to protect her was dying, vanishing in a cloud of smoke.

The worst part was how relieved he was.

"I can't make you stay against your will. You know where I stand, why I married you. If that doesn't matter to you, nothing I say matters anymore." Unable to meet Inesta's gaze, Ress looked at Lorea. "What do we have to do?"

"Stay where you are while I prepare things," Lorea answered, lifting a brown wicker basket from the floor. "It'll be a short ceremony, nothing tedious." She faced Tash. "Help me?"

With a hesitant glance at Ress, Tash assisted Lorea in placing objects onto the table. They arranged four white candles and five glass goblets around the vase. As Lorea lit the candles, Tash filled the goblets with mauve-coloured wine, both muttering the names of the Goddesses as they moved. On the table between Ress and Inesta, Lorea laid a rolled parchment, ink well, quill, and a serrated knife with a white hilt adorned with red jewels. Next to the knife sat a white metal keepsake box with flowers engraved in it. Inside were two coiled strands of braided white and silver ribbons.

The same ribbons from the day Ress had married Inesta, kept in the box he had made for her.

"Come, stand before me," Lorea instructed, beckoning Inesta and Ress to join her at the end of the table with the parchment and ribbons. Once they stood side by side, Ress on Inesta's left as he had been at their marriage ceremony, Lorea gathered the ribbons. Around Ress's right elbow, she tied the end of one strand, knotting it before repeating the same actions with the second strand around Inesta's left elbow. Slow and precise, Lorea looped the strands together and wove the strands around Ress and Inesta's arms, binding them in a pattern of crisscrossed ribbons, creating an intricate web. When the pattern of ribbons reached their wrists, Lorea tied the loose ends together.

Ress stared at the ribbons. It was as if Lorea knotted his heart. The bindings stole his breath, forcing him to remember the day he had married Inesta. How tight the ribbons had felt then; how weighted by promises he wanted to keep. They felt no different while waiting to hear the words that would separate him from her. The promises were broken. The bindings would become only ribbons.

He would be alone.

Lorea stepped back, facing them and Tash, who hovered behind Ress at the table. "We have gathered today with a shared solemn heart," she started, clasping her hands. "Love is a sacred blessing, a gesture of soul from the most reverent, most radiant Goddess, Emeraliss. Love, the most worthy of gifts we can bestow onto others: a precious, fragile part of us that is to be cherished and guarded above all others. It is uplifting, it is forgiving, it is honest. It gives our spirit breath, binding us one to another.

"Still, like all delicate things, the bindings of love may be broken, for one reason or another. It may not be that we chose poorly, but that we were not ready for it, or that we must pull away to be one with ourselves in self-love. So it is for you, Inesta and Ress, two hearts that have chosen to untangle to become one with the self. Before these bindings are unwound, I offer you a chance to say words of parting." Lorea motioned to Inesta and bowed her head.

Inesta took a deep breath and let it out slowly. "I'm sorry, Ress. When I married you, this wasn't how I expected it to be. I married you out of good faith, but I can't... This is for the best, for both of us. I won't be stuck here, and you won't be stuck with me. So find someone. If there's anything I wish for you, it's that. Find someone who will love you the way I can't, someone who you can let in completely." She planted a gentle kiss on his cheek. "You have wonderful things to give, but someone else deserves those wonderful things, not me." With a sad smile, she nodded at Lorea.

"Ress?" Lorea turned to him.

What could he say? What did he *want* to say? He was still wrapping his thoughts around what was happening. *You really know how to spring it on someone, don't you?*

"I'm sorry I couldn't give you what you wanted," he said, glancing at Tash before returning his attention to Inesta. "I'm sorry I couldn't be *who* you wanted. Everything I did, I did because I thought you deserved it. I'm sorry it all went wrong. May you find everything you're hoping for."

There, that's it. I can't think of anything even vaguely kissy-kissy, not when I feel like slamming a few doors. If it sounds bitter, then fine, I'm bitter.

From the sadness in Inesta's falling gaze, he supposed he sounded as curt as he thought he did.

Lorea indicated nothing of what she thought of the exchange. "With the words between you forging a new path, I shall sever the ties joining you as one." Silent, Lorea picked up the knife and cut the ribbons up the middle. Scraps dropped to the floor, leaving separate strands hanging from Ress and Inesta's arms.

Untying the remainder of the strands, Lorea withdrew the ribbons and stepped back. "With my brother priest as witness, so are you unbound, as seen and lamented by our most radiant Goddess, Emeraliss." She slipped between Ress and Inesta to lift up the goblet closest to them. "To bind you to your new paths, drink of the sweetness of life. Remember, today you have chosen to walk with your heart alone, but it is not the end. Doors do not remain closed, no matter how stubborn or locked they may be. Every door is meant to be opened as every breath is a new chance at life. So shall it be."

"So shall it be," Inesta murmured, taking the goblet from Lorea and sipping the wine before returning it.

Ress accepted the goblet. "So shall it be." He drank a mouthful and handed the goblet to Lorea, refusing to look at Inesta.

"Now we'll sign the document and be finished." Lorea placed the goblet on the table and unrolled the parchment. She signed her name at the bottom in black ink and offered the quill to Inesta, who signed as quickly as she jumped back.

Lorea held the quill towards Ress. "Your turn."

Taking the quill, Ress stared at the parchment, picking out their names, the date of their marriage, and the current date from the rest of the document. The words 'divorce proceeding' and 'Severing Ceremony' almost jumped out at him, demanding to be seen. This was his last official act as a husband.

But she doesn't want me. She wants me to find someone else. Haven't I wanted that for all these years? Rather than treating this like I'm losing something, shouldn't I be thanking her for giving me the chance to find something new? Someone I can talk to. Someone like…

Unable to finish the thought, Ress signed the parchment. He handed the quill to Tash.

Tash looked at Ress then Inesta, followed by another glance at Ress. "I'm sorry." His shoulders sagged as he peered once more at Inesta. "For everything." He signed the parchment and slid it towards Lorea.

"Thank you, all of you." Lorea rolled the parchment and slipped it into a leather case. "I'll take it to the High Council's Records Hall and ensure they note the changes." Immediately she blew out the candles and emptied the goblets.

As Lorea began to pack, Tash moved around Ress to stand close to Inesta. "It's not safe for you to travel alone," he told her, cupping her elbow with one hand. "If you're wiling to wait a little longer, I'll ask Mayr to escort you. He's made his life protecting members of a Grand Family. He'll make sure you're safe and cared for, and that you get there in one piece."

Inesta snorted. "Thanks." When Tash drew back, looking wounded, Inesta's tone softened. "It's a kind offer, but I've already arranged for someone to take me to Grace—friends, a couple houses down. They're waiting to pick me up, and we'll be on our way."

"I'll let them know you're ready," Lorea said from the other end of the table, putting the last of her things away. She closed the basket and lowered her head, pressing her hand to her chest. "Brother Halataldris, Inesta, Ress. I wish you health and better days. Brother, I will see you again in Sacred Assembly. Peace be upon you and yours."

With little noise, Lorea hurried to the front doors and let herself out.

Ress stood in the awkward silence, staring at the floor. His marriage ring was a cruel weight he dared not remove lest Inesta mock him for pretending they were ever anything more than a disaster. By the time the knock on the door came to let them know Inesta's traveling companions had arrived, he had lost track of the time and still had nothing to say.

Inesta was the first to react, answering the door and letting their neighbours inside. From behind him, Ress heard men's voices, the shuffling of trunks, and groans as things were carried away. Inesta moved in and out of the house, giving instructions on what should be packed in the carriage and how without breaking her possessions.

"That's the last of it," he heard Inesta say.

Closing his eyes, Ress listened to her heels click across the floor. Hands grasped his shoulders and turned him around. His gaze met Inesta's despite his thoughts screaming at his eyes to stay closed.

"This is it," she told him. "This is my goodbye." Inesta kissed his cheeks. "If you're ever in Alosaa, come see me. I've left the information for Eloras's on the table in the bedroom." Her lips brushed his with a chaste kiss. "Thank you for everything you've done, and for letting me go."

She released him and rushed from the house, slamming the door shut.

"What just happened?" Ress asked eventually, surprised to hear his voice faint and dazed. He had no idea how long he had been standing there, staring at the floor, the warmth of Inesta's kiss fading into nothing.

Tash squeezed his shoulder. "I think you need to sit down." He glanced at the kitchen. "Actually, I think you need a change of scenery. Come on."

Ress followed Tash to the porch, unable to focus on anything other than the blurred vision he could not blink away. Somewhere in his flimsy thoughts he registered that they were completely alone, the carriage with Inesta and her things well out of sight, a lost memory disappearing down the road. "I need to get back to the shop. Adren, Bremary, goblets—"

"Yes, and they'll be just as happy to see Ally as they are you. First, we get you to my mother. Then I'll send our mutual sister to deliver the news and have Bremary take you to her place. Cove can worry about the shop and everything else. The last thing you need is to be here or anywhere to do with Ines." Tash guided Ress down the stone path. "They shall come to you, not the other way around."

"She's gone."

"I know."

"For good."

"I know."

"We're the biggest asses in the universe."

"Trust me, I'm aware."

"Are you? Do you realize how horrible we are? There we were protecting her, or thinking we were, and we only made her miserable." Ress matched his stride to Tash's, barely recalling how he had made it from the kitchen to the road. "We're delusional."

"For now, but what you're feeling will fade," Tash murmured. "You'll move on."

"Really? How long does *that* take?"

In the silence that answered, he wondered if there was any point in asking anything else. At the end, he was alone.

Lost in his foggy reality, he already missed her yelling.

Somewhere on the other side of the radiant night sky was there a host of falling stars he could wish upon?

Ress sat back on the wooden swing and gripped the ropes tethering the thick board to the only tree in the backyard. A small push against the ground set him in a gentle sway. After another glance at the grey stones and red boards of Bremary and Covran's home, he let his gaze wander upwards. A curtain of bright purple and pink light spanned the dark sky as if someone had painted it with a broad brush. Blue and green light clung to edges of the other colours, taunting the stars with brilliance. It was one of his favourite parts of autumn, where the universe offered an effervescent show for nights at a time.

Out of habit, he searched for constellations outside the expanse of coloured light. The rear of the Tri-horned Goat and the tip of the tall hat from the Shepherd extended out to the right. To the left, the tusks of the Bird Hunt Boar followed the Flock towards the horizon in the east.

"It must be frustrating for Boar to always chase such a silly set of birds but never catch them," he remembered his sister, Lalaern, saying when she was eleven. *"He must be really hungry! He should just turn around and eat the goat. There's more meat there, anyway. Unless he can't see them — then someone should put some stars in his eyes. I see two over there that aren't doing anything at all! Someone should tell the Goddesses to move them because I think they're lost."*

"You should do it, Lally!" Trenna had insisted. At six years old, her grin had threatened to swallow her small, round face. *"You could be Keeper of the Stars and tell them what to do instead of me!"*

Laughing quietly, Ress stared at the ground and dug his heel into the dirt. He had been nine at the time, playing chase-and-catch with his sisters and cousins while their parents sat on blankets, relaxing under the coloured sky. Things had been simpler then, a blur of days he struggled to remember. Every passing year, he had to reach further as the images faded faster. Voices he had once heard each day grew softer. Most days, he barely recalled his father's voice, but he remembered the tenderness of his father's calloused hands. He had forgotten the sweetest inflections of his mother's singsong tone, but he remembered the scent of her perfume, always stunned when he caught a whiff of it on someone else. His sisters' voices were the most stubborn, clinging to his memories, demanding he never forget.

Wish you were here. He sighed and spun slowly, craning his neck back to watch the thick ropes twisting above him. What he would give to gaze at the stars with his family again and fight over which of them had the best wish whenever a rogue star shot across the sky.

What I'd give for one of their comforting gestures—the ones they give on instinct when someone's at a loss. For years, he had considered such gestures to be useless, too small to help him when his problems were so large. *Now with all of you gone and my problems so massively all-consuming, I'd give my life for one of those gestures. One hug from Mother, one sympathetic smile from Lally... They're the magic in life I stopped appreciating. The cure I threw away.*

Ress stopped turning and lifted his feet. The darkness whirled by as he spun. Branches shook. The tree limb creaked and bounced, ropes untwining quickly and shifting the board beneath him. He breathed deep, savouring the rush.

"Looks like fun."

Eyes struggling to focus, Ress peered in Adren's direction. The back door slammed shut as ce walked the narrow path between the two largest garden beds. Ce fussed with cir shawl before sitting near him at the base of the tree, a small plate in one of cir hands.

"Want some?" Adren held out the plate with a piece of yellow sweet cake buried under orange sprigs and black berries. "Bremary says you didn't eat enough at dinner. She's threatened to shove cake down your throat and sew your mouth shut so you'll swallow."

"She would, too." Ress snorted and waved Adren's offer away. "I'll get some later. In the middle of the night while she's sleeping, just to annoy her."

Adren drew back the plate, flashing him a skeptical glance. "You all right? It's been a tough day." Ce bit into the cake and arched one brow, chewing. "Though considering you were married this morning and single this afternoon, you're doing better than I figured. Cove expected you'd be a mess. We closed up the shop and got here so quick I thought he'd grown wings."

"Family. Nothing like a crisis to show how much they care," Ress murmured. "I'm fine, sort of."

"What does 'sort of' feel like?"

"Like sitting under a field of stars, wondering if any will live forever." Ress focused on the green light as it shifted in the sky. Since dinner, he had thought about Inesta to the point of exhaustion. He had tossed his marriage ring into the well and let it sink with the sentiments that used to make it special. There was nothing to be done, nothing more to think. "Just wishing I could be with my family. That's where I belong. I always have. This is my 'sort of,'" he said softly, "and it feels like a little boy who's gone and grown up against his better judgment, kicking and screaming at the natural order of things."

"I see." Adren dropped cir gaze, hiding a sudden flash of anger and disgust Ress could not understand. What had he said to inspire them?

"What do you think of the house?" he asked, attempting to distract them both from whatever had offended Adren. Perhaps one day ce would tell him what was wrong. "It's been in our family forever. Bremary and Cove took it when their parents moved to be closer to the Hall of the Justice Assembly. Bremary couldn't part with this place." Ress stroked the ropes of the swing, smiling weakly. "I mostly blame this thing — she's always been possessive of it. I know she's only allowing me to swing on it because she feels sorry for me."

"It's hard to let go of what you love. Sometimes it's impossible to walk away from it because as soon as you do, your heart breaks into a thousand little pieces." Adren placed the plate on the ground and raised cir knees to rest cir arms on them. "It's better to fight for it, no matter what you have to do. Home, family, love—they can't go to waste."

As Adren stared into the distance, cir face clouded over with emotions. What was ce thinking? What did ce wish for? Would ce ever wish upon the stars with him?

Face warming, Ress looked away. Inesta was right to leave him. Only half a day had passed since Inesta's departure, and he was back to thinking about Adren in inappropriate ways. He already found it difficult to admit he let Adren stay in the shop because he was attracted to cir. His feelings were more than a matter of sympathy. There was a beauty to Adren, wrapped up in something he had left in his childhood: the allure of the new and the thrill of surprise. Having been caught in the shadows for almost half his life, nothing was pure and beautiful anymore. There was no place for fanciful dreams or wishes.

But being with Adren, even in the silence, Ress rediscovered the boy he used to be, full of wonder. In his youth, he was amazed at the vastness of life. With Adren, his awe was linked to whoever ce really was. Ce reminded him of the innocence and sweet shyness he used to feel inside. The feelings were addictive, healing him as they forced out the feelings of loss over Inesta, callous as that made him.

Let me be callous, then. I don't want to push Adren away. Ress's fingers twitched around the ropes, needing to do something other than hold on. *I've spent most of my life living for other people. I haven't truly lived for myself. I need more than trying to save everyone all the time. What good has it done, anyway? Half the people I love are gone and the other half believe in me so much it makes me inadequate, undeserving. Except you, Adren... you're a bit of light in this storm.* Leaning forward, Ress reached for Adren's cheek, yearning to wipe the sadness from cir face.

He stopped before his fingertips touched cir, his hand hovering with a slight tremble. When Adren gave him a questioning glance, he snapped his hand back.

"Sorry, there was something," he muttered. Ress grimaced as Adren wiped cir cheek with cir sleeve. He was a coward, no matter how much he wanted cir.

Not to lose the chance to spend more time with Adren, he took a shallow breath. "So I was wondering, given your circumstances, if you might be interested in moving... into the house? Mine, I mean. There shouldn't be tension now that Ines is..." Ress cleared his throat. "The extra bedroom would be more comfortable than the shop or any inn. That is if you want to? If you want to stay somewhere else, I can—"

Adren shook cir head. "The house is fine. Thank you." Ce dropped cir gaze. "I wouldn't mind the company. Being on my own... I'm not used to it. Maybe we both need a fresh start?"

Maybe they did, and maybe ce was his new start, someone he wanted to touch and hear at a time when he felt emptier than usual. With Inesta gone, he was acutely aware of the void he held inside. Inesta had distracted him from that emptiness, but going home alone would bury him under it.

Since his first glimpse of Adren, something about cir told him ce could fill the void.

What if I try and end up scaring cir off? I can't possibly be someone ce'd want. I have too many problems, I'm too much of a stranger, and I'm too old. I'm not even that attractive. I can like Adren all I want, but there's no reason for cir to like me back.

Above it all, he was tired. Living in the darkness had taken everything from him. Just once, he wanted to be touched by the light and remember life was more than getting from one day to the next. He wanted to be joyful about taking another breath, not burdened by the reality that he was on purchased time.

Insensitive as it was to move on, he needed to seize the chance to be happy, no matter the risk. If he could show Adren that he cared for cir, maybe ce could find a way past his misgivings and be open to him. Maybe one day he would have a reason to smile again.

CHAPTER SIX

Happy birthday… now kill him.

Adren shifted on the settee, eyeing Ress as he cleaned the hearth in the kitchen, cir gaze pinned to the dingy brown shirt straining across his back. He was a slow-moving target, worsened by the distinctive mope accompanying his limp. One blow to the neck would end him. A knife to the lungs would also work, considering how close he let cir get. His guard was down, not that it had been up as much as ce had anticipated. Did it speak more to a lack of training or lack of care? How had he survived the Shar-denn for twenty-two years?

By selling out our kind and not getting busted, that's how. So here I am, supposed to do everything my betters won't do because they're too scared to try. Settle the score and claim the glory. Be Father's heir and inherit the big nothing Council's left me. At least the person responsible will go down.

Drawing cir glance away, Adren held back a disgruntled sigh. *Maybe not today. It'd be almost too easy. More of a favour, actually.* Ce toyed with the fringe of the black blanket wrapped around cir, staring at the settee cushions, cir eyes out of focus. Since his wife had left, Ress was quieter than usual. To kill him now would put him out of a misery Adren was sure he deserved. *Snitches never deserve happiness. The really dangerous ones don't deserve anything close to it.*

Still, it would be a rash misstep to kill him before ce knew where he hid the plans for weapons and other information that would do bad things in the wrong hands. Retribution was enough for Adren, but not cir father's men. They wanted the evidence cleared to keep their comrades safe—or, at the very least, in their possession so they could sell it to a faction boss with the highest bid. With Rivane imprisoned and the faction leadership shuffling to fill the gap, loyalties were in question. Adren had no more family to claim leadership before one of cir father's men or opponents took over.

Of all the times I need you, Tethe, Mordane. I'd give anything for your ridiculous habit of jumping in at the last moment and staving off disaster. Adren glowered at the cushions, gripping the blanket tight. For all of their annoying habits and inane schemes, ce missed cir brothers more than ce missed home. They had always been in cir life, taking their roles as cir brothers seriously. They were always the first to defend cir when things got rough and the hardest on cir when ce messed up. Whenever ce wanted to try something new or take part in their work, they offered to give cir the chance, never casting cir aside with just a laugh and snide comment like others did. Ce was never coddled by them, never treated as if ce were fragile, but ce was never alone, never far from their watchful eyes. The four years difference in age between Adren and Mordane had led the way to an easier relationship between them than the seven between cir and Tethe, but they forgave each other for the frustrations and strife. They had always found a way around scraped tolerances and tested patience, smoothing them over with sheepish apologies and open displays of affection.

Now, Tethe and Mordane wasted away in confinement with their parents. Were they suffering? Did they think about cir? Did they worry? Were they even alive? Ce knew nothing, and it was devouring things inside ce never knew ce had. If only ce could conjure cir family, whisking them away from their misery.

Instead, ce was stuck with the man who had brought the shackles to them. Even worse, his family fueled Adren's silenced anger, stabbing cir in the heart with the reminder that ce had nothing.

After Ress's wife left, Adren had stayed with Bremary and Covran in their home, biting cir tongue while Bremary coddled Ress. Two days later, Ress returned to his empty house, offering Adren the smaller bedroom without caveats or conditions. In the three days since then, he still had not imposed rules on cir or showed any care that they were still strangers.

Are you lazy or ignorant? Too trusting? Or is this part of some plan to use me? There's something coming, I know it. Adren glimpsed Ress as he carried a bucket of dirty water across the kitchen. *There's a reason your wife left. What did you* really *do to her?*

Guilt struck Adren's gut. The accusation was wrong the moment the words floated through cir mind. Ress needed to pay for his disloyalty, but wishing harm on his wife from his hands was too far. Maliciousness had never been easy for cir, no matter the circumstances. It was why ce never went on hunts with the Shar-denn packs or participated in the reconditioning of wayward members. From an early age, cir father had realized cir value existed in other efforts to take control from the High Council.

Ce was a bleeding heart, an ugly fact ce tried to hide from the rest of the gang, disguising it like everything else ce was.

Now my heart's bleeding all over this rug. Just can't help itself, can it? Even when I'm screaming inside, telling it to stop being such a damn traitor. Adren frowned at the rug peeking out from beneath the hem of cir white dress. Although ce tried not to care, ce felt bad about the lapsed marriage between Inesta and Ress. There was no reason to be sympathetic, but sorrow clung to cir emotions, digging its claws in further the more ce tried to shake it off. Even worse, ce was at a loss for words, not that ce had the right to say anything at all. Not when ce had never been in a romantic relationship, let alone had any attachments outside of family. No one knew what to make of cir—and no one could when cir father ensured no one got close enough to try. Not that anyone wanted to. There was enough about Adren to ward off the most brazen men, and that was without knowing the truth of what ce was. It was just as well: should anyone have dared to brave Rivane's protectiveness and tried to court Adren, ce likely would have refused them or at least put their intentions to a test to weed out the manipulators and puppets.

Forget me. What in the name of the Four are you? Adren glared at Ress, watching him scrub the floor. *Do something—anything—that'll take this feeling away. I despise you with the fury of a thousand suns; I want you to be miserable. Do something that makes me so furious I can't help but kill you. Because what I'm feeling… it can't happen. I can't feel sorry for you. I have to smother you in your sleep and steal your stuff. I have to look you in the eye and slice open your entrails, then sell them to the faction. So do something, you sneaky, docile bastard!*

If ever ce needed to be someone other than cirself, it was now. Ce needed to be cir father's child, everything the Shar-den wanted. Failure was not acceptable.

To see a mark as anything close to human was begging for a slow death.

"I'm going for a walk," Adren announced before swallowing the disgust leaving an acidic taste on cir tongue. To sit there any longer and delay the meeting with cir father's men was dangerous. Ce would not believe Ress was as nice as he acted, nor could ce waste time wondering about him. Nothing had changed since cir arrival in Araveena Ford. Not the intention, not the motivation, not the required end. No rogue emotions or unwelcome thoughts could deter what needed to happen.

Ress lifted his head, appearing dazed. "Sure." He glanced at the kitchen window, the sunlight illuminating his scarred jaw. "Sounds like a good idea, being a nice day and all. I can come with... if you want?"

Why? Adren nearly spat out, biting back the harsh tone. Ce needed to lull him into trusting cir, not keep snapping at him, no matter how good it felt. "Maybe not this time. I need to be alone to think, but thanks."

"Oh." Ress's gaze fell, disappointment splayed across his face. "I should be here when you get back. Then we can figure out this dinner thing. Ines always—" His face reddened and he resumed scrubbing the floor, shifting his weight to and from his injured knee.

"Sure," Adren muttered, confused by his embarrassment. His reactions made no sense.

With one look at the settee, Adren considered discarding the blanket draped around cir but decided against it. The contrast of black on cir white dress spoke to how ce felt right then—a blending of everything ce was inside, soft and stark all at the same time.

Ce toyed with the rings on the chain around cir neck, tempted to put them on cir fingers. The cold metal clamping cir skin would push back the part of cir that wanted to bathe in the silken caress of flower petals, balancing the delicate connection between appearance and inner self. The urge was no different than what ce had felt earlier that morning, binding cir chest before dressing.

Have you even noticed the difference? Adren's face warmed as ce forced cirself to leave the house. What did it matter if Ress noticed what ce did or did not do? If anything, ce needed him not to care. Enough people revealed their opinions about what ce did to feel like cirself. The last thing ce needed was someone new chastising cir for not being like everyone else, fulfilling the supposed rules of who ce ought to be.

One of the only good things about being on my own: no one's telling me I'm wrong. No one's insisting on calling me by my other name and ignoring the one I chose like it's something to be ashamed of. I can be me.

However, that independence did not stop Adren from making mistakes where cir mouth was concerned. It was bad enough that ce had said anything at all to Ress the morning after the fight in the alley. His question about what Adren called cirself was one ce heard frequently, that much was true, and so was the answer ce had given him. As always, Adren had anticipated the conversation, braced to gain his trust in a false rapport.

The rest of it—the bit about cir brothers—had never been on the list of things to talk about. If not for Ress's unexpected kindness, and the horrible way Adren's words seem to flow when they spoke despite what ce felt, Adren never would have revealed anything beyond the topic of words. His compassion was terrifying, and so was Adren's unsettling need to talk about losing cir family. There was no one ce could share the emotions with, no one who wanted to talk about what had happened in a healing way. The lack drowned Adren under heavy, rolling waves of sadness and pushed cir heart further into the dark corners within, enough that ce had babbled to Ress in an accidental moment that had brought a deluge of grief. The only saving grace was the quick realization that ce could mourn the loss of cir brothers while spitting out pointed words at Ress, blaming him with each syllable.

But then him and that insufferable way he has of being nice... Adren ground cir teeth. Even after ce rambled about Tethe and Mordane, imagining what they would put Ress through if they knew the truth, Ress had steered the conversation back towards cir with an empathy he never should have possessed.

In any other world, someone like him could have filled Adren's thoughts with dreams of having everything, being anything, and finally settling in a life completely of cir own making. In another lifetime, maybe everything Adren had put up with in the past would have never happened, and ce could have loved cirself from cir first breath to the last, no mishaps, doubts, or people wanting cir to live in the shadows.

Tightening the blanket around cir shoulders, Adren approached the road and turned left, heading towards the river ce had followed to Araveena Ford after fleeing Elsove Hillock twenty days ago. Ce wanted the freedom to be who ce was without explaining or justifying the whys and how of something ce did not understand. Some days, ce woke up feeling like a woman, overcome with the desire to touch beauty, an insatiable need to float on the breeze like the gentlest fabric, and undeniable want for sweet scents. Sometimes, even within the same day, ce felt like a man, taking comfort in unfeeling, lifeless metal, with a craving for spices that could cleanse cir spirit with their potency, and the urge to dig cir fingers into the earth to soak up its heat.

Other days, ce felt the essence of both, a curious push and pull that found equilibrium, allowing cir to dream in the comfort of feeling whole. Ce was all of it at once, all of the time, unable to pick one over the other for too long. Both and neither, ce was caught in the middle of wishing for parts ce did not have and reveling in who ce was.

The presence of other people only complicated matters further. How ce dressed, cir choice to be called Adren instead of Eradrene, how ce acted—all of it was about showing who ce really was rather than hide. The freedom from being on cir own made existing less of a hassle.

Except freedom came at a price ce could not afford.

Adren's face heated with the depth of cir rage. How dare Ress betray their family and the Shar-denn. They had entrusted him with secrets and given him the means to have influence within the ranks. They had protected his family and taken him back after the High Council arrested him. Barring the fact no one wanted to attack him should he retaliate with weapons they knew nothing about, the Shar-denn not only let him live, they allowed him to continue working. How could he have turned in a faction boss? What else had he done and what were his intentions? Was it a matter of saving himself, or was he trying to dismantle the Shar-denn, one betrayed member at a time?

His reasons were irrelevant, Adren decided. A cold breeze swept down the dirt road from behind cir as ce turned onto a flat, well-trodden path descending to the river, a shortcut to the ruins of an old bridge. At midpoint, thick brush surrounded the path, the twigs of dark, half-bare brambly bushes spilling into the leaf-littered pathway. Long, drooping tree limbs weighted with orange and yellow-black leaves formed an arbour above, riddled with holes that let sunshine through. Purple-winged silverbirds hopped branches, twittering upbeat songs as their outstretched feathers dislodged wilting leaves that swayed to the dry red earth. Past the birdsong was the gurgle of fast-moving water flowing over rocks.

Laughter and loud whoops of excitement flashed through cir thoughts, dancing around fragments of bright, vivid colours moving quickly. Giddy with anticipation dragged up by memory, Adren stroked the wilting leaves of the bushes and surrendered cir worries to a lazy smile. If ce immersed cirself in the recollections, ce could almost feel cir brothers whoosh by cir as they used to as children whenever they cut through the brush on the way to the pond near their home. Merasha had taught all three of them how to swim, insisting that any skill was a skill worth having, even if they never set foot on a ship or fell into a river. More than once, she had accompanied Adren, Mordane, and Tethe on their youthful excursions to the pond, teaching them how to appreciate life and each other. While Merasha had preferred to bask in the sun at the edge of the pond as they splashed and played in the water, her presence was always felt, each water drop reminding Adren of the moments with cir mother. Not only had Merasha taught them to tread water and keep their heads high, she had taught them control. She had given them confidence and mastery over an adversary.

In those same lessons, she had showered them with the steadfast love of a mother, captured in every breath they struggled to take and the tender embraces that rewarded them. Her calm, soothing voice fluttered around Adren's thoughts on small wings of memory, reminding cir to hold onto what hurt inside. Ce could not forget who ce was fighting for; ce had to let the pain drive cir. *Pain means something's wrong*, Merasha had said often, *and that wrong has to be put right before there is peace. No matter what it takes, no matter the sacrifice, we do what we have to do to make that peace. There is no running away, just pushing forward.*

Even if it killed the soul in the process.

Adren pulled cir hands from the bushes as if they had burned cir and picked up cir pace. Where the path ended, flattening into an expanse of moist earth and small rocks on the riverbank, Adren turned left and continued along the waterside. The river was no wider than the length of a modest barn. Trees lined both sides of the waterway, their bright orange and yellow leaves casting distorted reflections across the water. Grey and black rocks lay scattered across the riverbed, the occasional mass of black stone rising above the water like a smooth, polished beacon gleaming in the light. In places where the water looked still, sinewy green stalks reached up between the rocks, their large, flat green pads floating on the water's surface.

The decrepit bridge came into view, its weathered grey stone walls standing on the riverbed on either side. The rusted metal frame was still intact over the river, supporting nothing but a large hole in the middle. The wooden planks were gone, removed or destroyed, leaving only splinters and a reminder.

A flash of colour vanished around the wall nearest Adren. As ce ventured closer, three bodies stepped away from the bridge.

Ce recognized Amelin's bright blond hair first. Short and windswept, the ends curled around his grey-blue scarf and the upturned collar of his grey long coat. When their gazes met, Amelin buried his boyish features into his scarf. With his lips hidden, his hazel eyes did all the smiling. Behind him, Pade shifted restlessly and shoved his gloved hands into the low pockets of his black coat. The loose, tangled strands of his brown hair partially hid his dark tan face and golden eyes.

Beside Amelin, Darus crossed his arms, pulling taut the leather of his brown long coat. His greying brown hair was drawn in a messy tail, revealing his customary dark expression and grey eyes. "Took you long enough," he called out, his voice gruff and low. "We could've done something useful."

"Like what? Get so drunk you find the courage to get my father out of prison?" Adren snorted, stopping three foot lengths from them. "Don't be whining to me. You're the ones who get to gallivant and play heroes in the end. I get the joy of staying here with *him*."

Amelin smirked, his face fully visible. "Having fun, are you?" The higher pitch of his voice complemented his youthful appearance, neither a match to his forty years of age.

"Fun. Right." Adren kicked a stone into the water.

"Hey," Amelin said softly, walking around Adren to wrap an arm around cir shoulders. Adren flinched at the touch, his tightening grasp on cir arm keeping cir from moving away. "Why so glum? You're doing what you wanted to do. Chin up." He lifted cir head with two gentle fingers.

Despite his kind tone, Adren knew Amelin could sell cir as quickly as he could kiss cir. Many women had been seduced by his charms, seeing him as a softhearted boy, only to discover he was devious and took what their flesh could earn. Those same women had found themselves delivered to houses of savage Breakers, battered by Amelin's hands without remorse. Hands that hid every coin he earned from the transactions, building himself a secret fort of wealth. Rivane had warned Adren about Amelin more than once, as much as he had warned cir of Pade and Darus. They could be trusted to do Shar-denn business, but not with anyone's body, heart, or mind.

Adren knocked Amelin's hand away. "I don't need games. I need to get this over with. Ress'll get suspicious, and that'll get us nothing."

Darus snickered. "Testy, testy, little sister. What? He's giving you grief already?"

Yeah, by being too nice. It's so pathetic it hurts. Adren shifted cir weight, digging cir heels into the rocky riverbed. "Something like that."

"So then talk." Pade pushed hair out of his eyes, revealing bushy eyebrows and the healing wound on his left cheek. "Get it done so we can get to business elsewhere."

"It's been over a week since we last saw you, since the snitch beat these two—" Amelin gestured to Pade and Darus, giggling into his scarf. "Should've heard them squealing like little girls over what he did."

Pade flicked his fingers at Amelin. "You try getting knifed in the face, pretty boy. Carve you up myself for the full experience."

"Quit it." Darus threw an annoyed glance over his shoulder. "He got lucky. We weren't full-force, though. Only enough to make him believe our girl was in trouble." He looked at Adren. "Right?"

Adren nodded, gritting cir teeth at Darus's incessant ability to irritate cir whenever he spoke. The scuffle in the alley had left cir bruised, but nothing like the injuries Ress had inflicted on Darus and Pade, whose face would bear the mark from Ress's knife for the rest of his life. The feigned assault had been well-planned after Amelin's meticulous surveillance and Darus's ability to adapt and scheme. They had not anticipated Ress returning to the shop that night, but it worked in their favour. So had Adren's initial visit to the shop, an attempt to capture Ress's attention — a ploy ce had doubted would work despite Amelin's insistence.

Ress had fallen for both schemes, setting fire to Adren's skepticism. Amelin and Darus had wanted to see what Ress would do when faced with a supposed damsel in assumed peril. The rumours circulating the Shar-denn labeled Ress as a bleeding heart, caring too much for others while he drowned in foolish compassion and sputtered lies. The gang was suspicious, troubled by where his misguided sympathies would take him. He was dangerous, giving the Shar-denn more reason to kill him.

"He fell for it, all right. Thought I was the worse for wear and let me stay the night." Adren licked cir lips. "I poked around the village, asking about him. The magistrate's not fond of him. Ress's arrest didn't do him any good here, even if people seem to like him. It's more pretend, I think, especially with how quick they are to divulge details. I know enough about his business and his family to use them if they become an issue." Ce watched the water, contemplating the rest of the news. "We've also had an… adjustment to the timeline. I was lying low before returning to the shop to do a little spying, but he found me."

"Found you?" Pade arched one brow.

"Trying to sleep in the alley." Adren folded cir arms over cir chest. The cloth binding cir chest felt tighter than usual, its sudden coarseness as irritating as the memories lashing cir.

"Wait, *why*?" Amelin stepped back, his wide eyes quick to over-emphasize his surprise.

"Because there weren't many places to stay and I'm broke, you ass," Adren snapped. "Information costs, and you lot didn't leave me much to work with."

Darus grabbed cir wrist. "There's not much to be had, so don't go drawing blood. It's not like we were in charge of the faction coffers."

Adren yanked cir arm back. The seized coffers had been Mordane's responsibility. No doubt the High Council would torture him to get the details of the faction's finances and security. Not that he would surrender the information. Rivane had assigned Mordane to the financial welfare of their faction for a reason: he was infallible, unbreakable, and would sooner sew his lips shut with metal shards than confess.

The coffers were not the only funds on Adren's mind as ce eyed Amelin. Darus's cut of the faction funds was lost in gambling and Pade's in luxurious accommodations and loans, but Amelin's share was available. The fact he had never once offered to take care of cir did not escape cir attention. Amelin acted horrified at Adren sleeping in an alley but never spared a coin in cir direction. His loyalty was to Rivane, but it did not extend to Adren, even if ce was Rivane's youngest child.

The money was not Adren's greatest annoyance. Ce could handle sleeping in an alley. The darkness was soothing, the cold a reminder that ce was still alive and free, able to avenge cir family.

Ress was worse.

The moment he had found cir, all of Adren's thoughts had scattered, flung in multiple directions ending in dead ends and mindless sarcasm. Caught unaware, Adren's first response had been sharp and defensive, attempting to ward Ress off. While Adren had pieced together the right response, fending off his offers to help, Ress had stared at cir with aggravating tenderness. To anyone else, his generosity and thoughtfulness would have been kindness easy to accept.

To Adren, they were every reason to want a piece of his face in cir hands. Ress had ripped Adren's entire life apart but had the audacity to show cir compassion. He had stolen everything but offered cir a comfortable bed, food, and a safe place.

The cruelty in the irony made Adren want to claw out cir own brain.

I accepted only because I need to get close to him, Adren reminded cirself. *I need to find those plans. Maybe even get him to talk. The only way out for him is dead, and I'm the one who's going to do it. I need to. I have to, no matter if I find myself wondering…*

No. Ce could not allow cir thoughts to stray. Ress was nothing more than a walking corpse begging to be reduced to cinders.

"So what does this mean?" Pade scratched the stitches of his cheek wound. "Changes timeline in a good way, I hope."

"It should. I'm closer to him now. I should be able to get what we need, do the deed, and leave without too much attention." Adren shrugged, hoping if ce said the next words with nonchalance, the shocked response would die quicker. "I'm living in his house."

All three men regarded cir as if ce had shifted into a grotesque creature of massive proportions.

"You're—you're—wait, what?" Amelin sputtered.

"Bleeding heart," Darus muttered. "I told you guys it's true. He's an absolute idiot."

"Yes, but a dangerous, likely-to-get-us-killed idiot." Pade pointed at Adren. "Otherwise this one would never be necessary. We'd be able to do the damage ourselves."

He's not that dangerous, Adren wanted to argue. Between the house and the shop, ce saw little to corroborate what the Shar-denn feared was true, unless Ress hid his lethal things in a different place.

Even if ce was right, Ress's circumstances still posed a conundrum. Assumptions and suspicions ran rampant through the Shar-denn, forming the shared opinion that Ress was an informant for the High Council. Yet, unlike other members, he could not be removed as easily.

More complicated still: the faction bosses still wanted what Ress could provide.

Neither ignorant nor inept, he had proven his worth over and over again. After his release from the High Council, Ress had sworn to the faction bosses he had not snitched. Rather, he blamed the raids and arrests on Taldris, a defected gang member. When interrogated by the bosses for more information about his arrest, Ress had insisted he told no one anything, saying the other Shar-denn members had balked and revealed details.

Members who were missing or dead, unable to back Ress's story or prove him a liar.

In his defence, Ress had told the bosses he portrayed himself as a bumbling fool and downplayed what he knew of the gang, using his physical impairments and a convoluted sob story to drive away the High Council's interrogators. He had also promised his honesty to the faction bosses and revealed that hunters would check on him.

Most of his arguments were suspect, but his position in the game between the Shar-denn and the High Council was considered a worthy trap. Gang members could be caught or killed by him, given that Ress designed special weapons for the Shar-denn. There was also a chance he provided the High Council with the same. A clever man would also have kept weapons for himself, and *that* was what they gambled on the most. He had always been deemed too clever.

They could not afford to have any more members arrested in the process. If Ress were removed from existence, it needed to be discreet and efficient. There could not be witnesses or evidence.

There could only be someone like Adren who could make it all disappear.

"Her, us—whatever it takes." Darus shrugged. "All I know is if we do this, we get into Shar history. We'll avenge Rivane and the rest of our boys *and* have the glory of telling the other bosses *we* pitched Ress. We'll do what the cowards can't."

"Plus make a fortune off the plans and goods he's got," Amelin added, a smirk curling his lips. "We'll be rewarded for being *so* resourceful."

"*Then* we'll buy my family out of prison," Adren reminded them, glancing at the water, away from Amelin's creepy smirk. "Or at least pay to get some mouths moving towards the same end."

"Of course." Amelin hugged Adren around the shoulders. "You do your bit and we'll do ours."

"He's right." Pade nodded, his hair falling over his cheeks. "You're our best bet, one of the Shar's best tools. The sharpest weapon we have."

Darus swatted Amelin's arm from Adren and clasped Adren's shoulders. "Use that pretty girl thing you do and bypass his defences. Be all sweet and pitiful, all wounded and innocent.

Then kill him and cover it up. You'll be the perfect murderer. No weapons. No traps to bust. By the time someone realizes what could've happened to him, it'll be done and we'll be gone. You'll have used your weirdness to full effect. Do some good. Make your daddy proud."

His words empowered only the conflict raging inside Adren. Ce was a tool. Not a person, not someone who could use a sympathetic friend, not anything but a means to an end.

Everything ce hated.

Was there a point in trying to be more? What good could come from it? And why was ce thinking about that when ce had a job to do?

Dreams. These thoughts, they're only foolish dreams. I'm the child of a faction boss. We don't get the privilege of dreams. We make people do things. We make the world open their eyes and treasure their lives. We put the Council in their place. There's nothing beyond that. There can't be.

Once more, the words Adren used time and time again to remind cirself to believe in living felt like lies. Falsehoods that tasted sour to cir soul, piercing like rusty, splintered nails on a misguided tongue.

The moment the meeting ended, Darus, Amelin, and Pade hurried down the riverside towards their horses waiting in the woods. They would return to Hilarye, the neighbouring village in the south, keeping distance from Adren until their next meeting in four weeks. Until then, they expected Adren to find the items they desired and kill Ress.

Because sure, it's that easy. Adren sighed and walked the path to the main road. *None of it changes the fact I don't have a home. No one wants a stranger around, and the Shar… they play up to my father real well, but without him, they're scared of me. I know they think I'll get them caught. I can't trust them anyway because the Council and everyone else would pay anything to get a hand on me. What I can do is worth homes, limbs, offspring. No doubt Father's replacement would die to own me. He'd probably rub it in Father's face from the other side of the prison bars just for fun.*

Without family, without home, no place was safe. No one could be trusted. Ce was alone.

What ce would give to never be alone again.

Adren hurried up the path to the road, grumbling as ce headed for Ress's house. For as long as ce could remember, ce had always been surrounded by family and the people who worked for cir father. There was always someone nearby, always someone watching. How much of that was because ce was the child of a faction boss and how much was because of cir strange abilities, ce did not know. Deep down, ce hoped it was about love and not whatever ce was.

The boy-girl thing I can handle, but being a freak... still don't have a grasp on that. With a frown, Adren walked the side of the road with cir head down, ignoring glances from passersby. *Don't know if I'll ever get used to being an aberration. Haven't met anyone else like me, haven't heard of any, and I can't go doing whatever I want because it'll attract attention. So I have a secret I can never share because someone will lock me up, try to control me, or ostracize me for being so abnormal I can never live near anyone ever again. Then I'll be alone forever.*

Ce stopped, a deep pain pooling around cir heart. Forever: such a short word for a long sentence. A punishment ce would never survive, not if dread and loneliness were trustworthy indicators.

That's why I need my family. I'm losing it. Adren closed the gap between the road and Ress's home with rushed steps.

When ce stood before the front doors, ce cursed. *I really am losing it. I just ran to the house where my enemy lives... Ran, as if I wanted to be here.*

Things needed to change, and quick.

Adren entered the house, greeted by the fragrant scent of fresh flowers and quiet noises ce could barely discern. Cir glance flicked from room to room. Where was Ress?

As if hearing cir thoughts, Ress stepped into the doorway of the main bedroom. "You're back." He looked surprised, his hands shifting around a thick, fabric-wrapped parcel. "I, uh— Give me a moment."

Clearing his throat, he shuffled back into the room. On his return, he held three parcels, balancing them in both arms. All three were wrapped in dark mauve fabric and strands of cream-coloured cord tied together in the centre.

He set the parcels on the kitchen table and rubbed his chin, eyelids fluttering as he avoided Adren's gaze. "Bremary just brought these, and I was going to—" Ress rubbed the back of his neck and gestured to the parcels. "Go ahead. Open them."

"Why?" On the way to the kitchen, Adren tossed cir blanket over a settee.

"Because they're yours."

Was it cir imagination, or was Ress blushing? What was wrong with him? His nervousness worried Adren. Strange packages worried cir more.

Ce stood behind one of the chairs, eyeing the parcels. They were large and lumpy, varied in thickness.

"I promise they don't bite," Ress said softly, poking the parcel closest to him. The insides appeared soft, giving with the pressure of his fingertip and springing back into place as he drew away.

Did ce take the chance? Whatever it was seemed harmless. *You're supposed to get his trust, right? Open the damn package.* Adren slid the parcels closer and tugged the cord off the first one before peeling back the soft wrapping.

Cir heartbeat faltered, tripping across rhythms. Ce choked on a breath.

"I figured you could use them," Ress said, his voice still quiet.

Adren looked at him, then inspected the two pieces of clothing in cir hands. One was a dark grey shawl, tightly knit with bronze beads cinching dark grey tassels. The other was a long dress of light pink fabric and black lace, its hem decorated with dark pink embroidery and bright white pearls. The modest neckline dipped, adorned with thin black ribbon over the lace trim. The sleeves cut off at the elbow, finished with black ribbon and three tiers of lace cuffs to cover the rest of the arm. A thin belt of black ribbons encircled the waist and hung low.

The dress fit the latest fashion in Kattal, an expensive garment resembling one cir mother had worn often.

"I—I—" Adren laid the clothes on the table beside the vase of dark orange flowers, a new bouquet since ce had left earlier. Ce stared at the white centres and yellow dots on the underside of the petals, swallowing back the emotions twisting into a ball inside cir. Tears gathered in the corners of cir eyes as ce seethed at his nerve.

How could ce be touched and enraged at the same time? How could ce want to hug him and tear his face off all at once? This was not how it was supposed to be. He had no right to give cir gifts, and ce had no right to accept.

"Here. Try this one next." Ress pushed the smaller of the remaining two parcels towards cir, his eyes bright and hopeful.

Reluctant, Adren unwrapped the next two pieces of clothing. Black pants, expertly crafted with loose legs and a simple waist, and a black shirt laced at the cowl-like neck with long, black cord through gold grommets. The pants were coarse; the shirt soft. Both smelled fresh, as though recently washed and dried.

Ce considered the third parcel, dreading the contents. If the pattern held true, ce already knew what it was. Holding cir breath, ce opened the wrapping and clutched the leather long coat. Black with silver buttons and a generous hood, the coat was new and unblemished, lacking the dust of the red earth and creases from use.

"I know you need to have a choice, so I got you everything." Ress shuffled his feet, staring at the floor. He struggled with his arms, crossing and uncrossing them before drawing his hands behind his back. "They should be a perfect fit. I'm used to choosing clothes for other people."

Words played hiding games with Adren, only one word spilling from cir lips. "Why?"

"Why…?" Confusion and worry spread across Ress's face until he looked at the clothes. "Oh, why these?"

Adren nodded.

Ress let out a ragged breath. "I saw you don't have much and thought you'd like a couple more options." He shrugged, offering a lopsided smile. "I remember you telling Bremary it was your birthday soon. Don't know if I've missed it or if I'm early, but they still count."

Out of everything he had been through the last week, he recalled a trivial detail Adren barely recalled mentioning, one that should have meant nothing to him.

Ce wanted to hate him, more in that moment than any other. Why could ce not muster the rage it took to throw his gifts in his face and walk away?

"Thanks," Adren murmured. "And yeah, I'm twenty-five. Today, actually."

"Good, I didn't miss it." Ress grinned. "Nice to know I still have my timing. Maybe, in the spirit of the birthday thing, you might be willing to try the dinner I'm going to attempt? I can't promise it'll be fancy, but it'll be warm and hopefully taste decent."

"Yeah, sure." Mouth dry, Adren urged cir tongue to work, batting cir lashes to keep tears back. "I'll just get changed."

"Sure. If something doesn't fit, let me know. I can ask Parase to fix it."

With a weak nod, Adren bundled the clothes in cir arms and forced cirself to go to the smaller bedroom. Once inside, ce hurled the clothes at the bed and kicked the door shut.

I can't believe this. Ce leaned against the door and slid down to the floor, knees raised. How could the day have gone from plotting revenge to being showered with gifts by the same man ce was supposed to kill?

*How twisted is it that he—my enemy—would care about my birthday when the men I grew up around didn't mention it at all? They've known me my whole life and not one of them said anything. But he—the clothes—the flowers—*dinner. *He's all but courting me and here I am…*

He had no reason to give cir anything. More than that, he acknowledged who ce was without argument, taking note of cir preferences. Whenever he spoke to cir, his tone and words were respectful. Part of cir wondered if he truly understood how ce felt, needing no more than a single hasty conversation.

Adren folded cir arms and dropped cir head on them. Ce was used to people's ridicule and their struggle to comprehend. Few of the Shardenn members understood. They had dubbed cir situation the "boy-girl thing" since ce was twelve, after ce first started dressing in clothing usually worn by men. Those same men insisted it was because ce wanted to mimic them out of admiration, a tribute to their prowess and power. Then they began to consider it a trait to exploit, encouraging Adren to claim ce had a twin in order to confuse people.

Ress went along with cir needs, never laughing, never shaming. He never made an issue out of them, even when cir own family continued to. There was no need to justify.

Hands clamped around cir head, Adren squeezed cir eyes shut. Three weeks. Cir family had been taken nearly three weeks ago. When ce first arrived in Araveena Ford, ce had been confident. The twelve days following the raid had readied cir, strengthening cir resolve. Ce had helped Darus and Pade secure Ress's location, schemed in their secluded cache house, and spent three days traveling down the riverside on a horse Darus had stabled in Hilarye.

Then eight unpredictable days had happened, threatening everything.

Cir stockpiled confidence was shaking apart. Every morning and night, ce recited the names of cir family a hundred times, forcing cirself to remember the panic of the raid, to feel the terror. Each day, ce recalled the comforts of cir room and the sensation of the lightly scented air passing through the halls of cir family's elaborate house. Ce remembered the dinners, the laughter, the stories—everything ce had tried not to take for granted, knowing that one day, someone could rip it away. Rage ate at cir heart, having dug itself a deep pit in the bowels of the chambers, waiting to strike.

A pit other emotions filled in, suffocating cir rage until it was too weak to fight back.

No amount of confidence could stop the fact that an aggressive front of emotions attacked cir hate and would not stop advancing.

It's his fault. He's the problem. I expected him to be callous. I expected him to throw me into the nearest tavern and be done with me. I never believed anyone when they said he was a bleeding heart. I thought they were lying, but now...

The icy walls keeping cir reason intact were melting. The more time ce spent with Ress, the more ce seemed to be drowning. For all the talk and demands ce had spewed since the raid, cir determination was slipping. The promise to go against who ce was and commit the execution was diminishing into something else.

Why couldn't he be a complete ass? Adren wiped cir face with cir sleeve. Destroying someone who was horrible, nasty, and cruel was easier to justify. The heartless were not missed. Ce had prepared for someone rough, selfish, uncaring, disloyal. Someone who believed he was tough because he could look out for himself. *Because who turns in people and destroys lives when they're nice?* Adren picked at the woven blue rug on the floor. *Yet even nice guys have to die.*

But did they have to be murdered?

Adren gazed at the clothes heaped on the bed. *Happy birthday, freak. Avenge the family or fool yourself into being more than what you aren't. You can choose only one. Just whose side are you on?*

CHAPTER SEVEN

Get out! Don't just watch. Run. Run as fast as you can. Don't let them get you. Don't let them see what you are. Hide. Hide everything.

The raiders were back. Angry, snarling hunters with weapons burst through the doors and smashed the windows. Clanging, screeching metal; shattered blue glass, crunching underfoot. They bounded through the chaos like rabid beasts on the chase, shadows pushing, grabbing. Stomping, shouting, hitting, taking, taking, taking...

"But Mother—"

"Go! Hide!"

"I can't. I can't leave, not you. Not them." I can't—

Adren forced cir eyes open, one hand reaching into the mocking darkness for a mother that was not there.

She'll never be there again. She's gone, she's gone, she's gone away. Alone in a cell for another day.

The sickening voice sang from the dark corners of cir mind. Adren swallowed back tears and plunged cir fists beneath the blankets, shivering as cold fingers touched hot skin. Cir fingertips twitched against cir palm, desperate to hold, caress. Touch. Ce needed a gentle touch. To feel loved again. To put the world right and curl up in its false security.

A foggy voice surfaced from the back of cir mind, babbling, nattering, lost to the haze of the nightmare still clinging to cir thoughts, gorging on fear. Words, so many words, none of them clear. A familiar voice with everything to say and nothing to show shepherded Adren's thoughts to a place deep inside, slamming a gate behind them to banish what devoured cir pinned soul.

Silence descended, blocking the voice, choking the nightmare. A safe quietness, enough to clear cir mind and think—

A scream pierced the inner darkness. Adren winced, clapping cir hands over cir ears. Pitched high, the scathing scream tore at cir insides, shredding memories.

When the second scream sounded, overlapping the first with a grating loudness, Adren sat up, struggling for breath. The screams were new, nothing like the gentle voices ce had heard since childhood, four voices that soothed cir in the moments they were needed most. *Whisper, whisper, whisper,* ce chanted, rocking to the faint pulsing rhythm between the unwavering screams. *Make them go away. Whisper.*

Move, a voice whispered in response, floating above the screams, cutting through the pain. Familiar as it wrapped around all other sounds in cir mind, the voice filled Adren with relief. It was the voice of reason, the voice of a Goddess.

Adren leapt from the bed, scrambling to stand still. All cir body wanted to do was run. Climb. Hide. Tugging at cir bedclothes, a nightshirt and pants borrowed from Bremary and Covran, Adren cursed the chill racing from cir feet to cir neck. Ce grabbed the closest long coat and pulled it on, folding cir arms and settling into the warmth of the soft fabric lining the new leather.

Move, the voice whispered again. Beneath the whisper, the screams dampened. More voices rasped around them, without warning or apparent meaning. They wrought confusion, forcing distance between the calm Adren struggled to grasp and the sanity ce wished for.

Memories of the raid flickered, disjointed images of shadows and weapons in the dark. Bodies running, fighting, falling...

Adren yanked open the door and charged into the sitting room, cir eyes stinging as bright light caught cir by surprise. Moonlight poured over everything in the room, streaming in from the open windows to give a clear view of the furniture and rugs, almost haunting cir, mocking, deriding as it reminded cir of where ce was.

Nowhere near home.

But close enough to cir enemy to share the pain. To end it.

Fists digging into the crooks of cir arms, ce stalked towards the kitchen. Light gleamed off the sharpened knives hanging on the rack near the washbasin. One strike would improve everything. One jab would get revenge. Killing him would be easy, so easy…

Ce stopped short, two foot lengths between cir and the knives.

Too easy, the whispering voice said, louder than the screams dying in the background. *Too easy to fall; too easy to run to where you can never leave. Slip this one time and you will keep sliding.*

And we wouldn't want that. Adren pivoted sharply and walked to the sitting room, cir bare feet cooled by the smooth floor. Once ce reached the hearth along the furthest wall, ce spun around and crossed the length of the open space to the side door leading to the back of the house, then back again, over and over. Inside, the screams stopped and cir ears no longer rang. The voices remained, a dozen or more scraping as they collided, each vying for attention. Fragmented shouts and rough demands offset tearstained pleas and ignored truths, beating the images of bodies into cir thoughts. Living bodies, dead bodies—each one from the past, each a ghost; bodies ce had made disappear without spilling their blood. Killing had never been cir job. Ce stole. Ce hid evidence from dangerous hands. Ce sent the right people and the wrong objects to a new existence. Never had ce killed.

All innocence is lost eventually, Adren remembered Tethe saying when ce was twelve and ready to work for the Shar-denn. *So make it good when you drown it. You can't ever get it back, so make the memory a good one. Be strong, kiss it goodbye, and give it up.*

He never said the same thing about hate.

No, that one we keep. Adren continued to pace, letting the voices rattle and berate choices ce could not take back. The voices chortled at the hate spreading between cir recollections of one bad choice to another. Why was ce *really* in Araveena Ford? Because ce hated Ress or because ce hated cirself for not fighting to save cir family? Why had ce not hurt Ress when ce had the chance? Because there was a measure of merit to his being or because ce was too weak, too *feeling*, too alone? Where was the hate when ce needed it most?

I just want them back. I want to feel safe again. I want a real home, not one I've had thrown at me by him. *He's the reason I'm on the run. He's the reason Council can catch me. He ruined my life!*

Adren padded into the kitchen and leaned against the counter, staring out the window overlooking the gardens in the front yard. Cir fingernails raked the stone countertop. Teeth grinding, ce pushed against the voices with justifications. Heat consumed cir inside and out, the unbidden fire of cir abilities burning from cir core and spiraling out into every limb and pore. Small bumps rose across cir skin. *My family is all I have. There's no one else. There's never anyone else. They'll serve my father but ignore me. They'll lick the ground my brothers walk on but avoid me. I'm always too strange, always so much trouble. Too much of a freak, too unnatural, as if everyone else is so bleeding great. I've got no friends, not unless I buy them. Only family distracted me from the frustration and loneliness. They kept me from the things killing me now.*

A rush of energy swept through cir, stealing cir breath and twisting it onto itself, shoving the breath back down cir throat. In the briefest of moments, death banged on the splintered door to cir soul, yanking cir across the line of consciousness and darkness before shoving cir against the wall of judgment. Frantic shadows clawed cir insides, scraping and screeching, desperate to be let out to play.

Cir magic was awake, demanding to be exploited.

Fingers numbed, ce no longer felt the smooth stone beneath cir hand. Cir skin tingled, weighted and pricked as if a hundred tiny, invisible feet danced over cir body with sharp pins on their shoes. Time ground to a stop, the present choking on the past, sputtering and wailing until breaking free. Weaving around cir, pulling cir into the spaces between the physical and the unseen, time slid over cir skin like a blanket of snow. Moments slipped back in time, falling upon each other. Cir thoughts reversed, memories playing towards their beginning.

Something needed to happen. Someone needed to disappear, scattering into oblivion. Cir magic itched and shrieked to make a new reality.

Ce needed a new future.

I'm alone, Adren seethed, digging cir fingers into cir palms. *I have* nothing. *I certainly can't go to the Council for anything. They'll either arrest me or figure out what I am, then make me do things for them.* He stole *everything, ripped it all away. Hate him, hate him—*

"Adren?" Ress's voice asked from behind cir. Fingers clasped cir shoulder.

"Hands off!" Adren whirled around, thrusting out one hand to push him away. Heat shot into cir fingers, driving against the tightening air until the shield of cir control snapped.

Ce sent him flying towards the wall between the two bedrooms.

Ress hit the wall, back slamming the wood panels, his arms out before him. He slid to the floor, dazed. Cracked wood hung from the wall where he had hit, a dark hole attesting to the force of cir blow.

"Leave me alone! You've done enough," Adren yelled. "You could've kept your mouth shut. You didn't have to snitch. We all make choices, and *you made the wrong one!*" Swiping cir hand towards the knives, ce made a fist, pulling on the air with enough magic to yank them from the wall. As Ress lifted his head, ce thrust cir fist towards him, hurling the knives.

He ducked. The knives dug into the wall around his body, blades sinking deep.

"Adren—"

"No, *don't*. You didn't have to rat out anybody. Of *all* the Shar families, why'd you have to go for mine? What did my father *ever* do to you other than let you help his faction? Mordane made sure you were paid *well* beyond what my father owed—that should've been enough to shut you up!" Adren stomped across the kitchen and stopped midway to Ress. Cir skin blazed, threatening to rip and shred. Outside, every sense screamed that ce was as fire, melting and shriveling, dripping liquid ash. Inside, ce was like ice, growing and pushing for more space, caging rational thought.

Caught between them, ce burned in every way. Agony pounded through cir in waves, echoing the rhythm of cir heart. "You're all wrong. *I'm* all wrong. I can't visit them in prison. I can't see them if they die. And it's all—" ce raised cir hand "—your—" Adren parted cir fingers wide, thrusting cir palm at Ress "—*fault!*"

Chaos erupted around them. Logs in both hearths split, sparked, and burst into purple flames. The bucket of water on the floor by the washbasin hit the ceiling with a thud and somersaulted, its contents raining in every direction. Furniture skidded, squealing across the floor. The settees slammed against one wall, the small tables into another. The kitchen table crashed into the cupboards, shaking shelves and popping doors. Cups tumbled and bounced; clay plates smashed on the ground. The vase of orange flowers shattered, shooting glass across the room.

Silence fell.

Ress lifted his head from under his arms and stared, first at Adren, then the house. His eyes widened, lips working without uttering words.

Adren stumbled back. What had ce done?

No, no, no. I didn't—I couldn't—I'm not supposed to. I—I—

It was too late.

Ce was never supposed to expose what ce could do. No one was supposed to know other than cir family and cir father's most trusted men, of which there were precious few.

In unchecked rage, ce had lost control and shown everything.

To the last person who deserved to know.

"Adren..." Ress groaned and pulled himself up, grimacing as he gripped the doorframe of his bedroom.

Adren ran into cir room and slammed the door shut. Ce threw the bolt and the smaller lock on the door. Until ce figured out what ce needed to do next, ce would not leave the room. No one would come in.

I'm a freak. I destroy things. Adren scurried across the room and crouched in the corner between an armoire and the window. *I'll destroy everything if I'm given the chance. That's all I'm good for.*

Ce watched the play of light and shadow under the door, waiting for Ress to smash it down.

He knocked, instead. "Adren, please, come out." The doorknob rattled. Gentle taps on the door followed. "Please. I won't hurt you. I just— I've got questions, but I won't harm you. I can't."

Wrong. You have and you will.

"Go away!" Adren sank into the corner, scrunching into a ball and hugging cir knees. Ress was not the only one who could do harm. Ce would break him. With one chance and no effort, he would be gone.

The long night gave way to the short light of day, but the shadows remained in Adren. When the pink sunset heralded the oncoming night, ce sat on cir bed and glared at the floor, unfocused and confounded by limited options. Since dinner with Ress the night before, ce had neither eaten nor drunk. Ress had tried several times to lull cir out of the room, but Adren refused. More than once, he spoke of finding someone to help, his voice heavy with desperation.

Shortly before sunset, he had left the house, closing the front door loudly. To lead cir to believe it was safe to venture out of the room, Adren supposed. Was it a trap or kindness? That was the one thing ce could not decide, not that ce wanted to leave the room in either case. The room was safe, a closed box where ce could reconsider cir plans. Five days had passed since cir meeting with Darus, Amelin, and Pade. Five days since the gifts from Ress.

Everything was falling apart.

He thinks he can find someone to help me. Adren leaned forward, elbows on cir knees. Ce focused on the brown armoire across the room, a twin to the armoire at the foot of the bed. *He's a fool. No one can help. Unless they can take it away, there's no point—and that's assuming they don't go running the other way, hollering for my damnation.*

The front door slammed closed.

Adren stiffened. Ress was back, his slow, distinctive footfalls loud as they approached. Two other sets of footsteps joined his, both barely audible.

Sucking in a breath, Adren stood from the bed, cir pink dress falling around cir. One hand up, palm out, ce backed away from the door.

From the other side, Ress spoke to whoever was with him, mumbling his words. Two voices answered back, both male, both muffled.

A knock prompted Adren to remain steady. "Yeah?"

"It's me," Ress answered. "I've brought someone. A priest. On my life, I swear he's safe to talk to."

"Adren," a second voice said softly, slightly higher than Ress's. "You need not fear me. You may, however, call me Tash. I am what he says—a priest from the Temple of the Four." Tash paused as though hoping for a response. "I understand you wish to be left alone, and I'm willing to respect your decision. Just know I am here, and I know what you are. Ress told me what happened, and I know why. I know what allows you to do what you did. If you want me to leave, I will, but if you wish to talk, I pose you no harm. I'm only here to listen."

Adren stared at the door. Was he lying? No one had ever been able to tell cir what ce was. How could a priest ce had never met have answers? If he was lying, ce would have to hide from him, too. He could easily hand cir over to someone who could do damage.

But if he's telling the truth...

"I don't know you," Adren shouted. "I don't trust you. How do I know you won't gut me?"

"I understand your concerns. I'm not asking you to suspend them." Tash's voice remained gentle. "I will not harm you, an oath I will keep to death and the lives beyond. I only want to give you a chance to share your burdens. I will not tell anyone about what you can do. I offer help, but the choice remains yours. Only you can open the door."

A door that should remain locked for all of their sakes.

Still, he says he knows. It's the first time anyone's tried that. Most of the time, they stare or back away or make me feel like I'm some mythical beast. He actually sounds confident. Extra points for talking like a priest, even if he's not real.

"Only if you tell me what I am." Adren crept to the door and waited.

"If that is what you need, I will gladly give it," Tash replied.

Here's to taking a chance. Adren unlocked the door and slid the bolt. As ce opened the door, ce found Ress leaning against the wall between bedrooms, his expression melting from concern to relief. A man of similar height stood beside him, dressed in layers of shimmering red robes. One robe was laced down the front with red cord, while his outer robe was open and unclasped, flowing around him, its flared sleeves hanging to his knuckles. His floor-length veil sparkled gold and white, draped over his shoulder-length brown hair.

"Adren." Tash dipped his head, his blue eyes bright like his smile. Unlike other priests Adren had seen, he kept a trim beard and mustache, neither detracting from his soft features. "I'm honoured to meet you."

I don't know why. Adren eyed him warily, startled by the realization that he waited for an invitation into the room. "Come in?"

"Thank you." With another dip of his head, Tash entered, his movements slow. He glanced at the haphazard state of Adren's things strewn about the room and the mussed bed. "May I sit?"

Aware that Ress remained at the door, Adren crossed the room to the chairs at the small round table in the furthest corner. Ce dragged one chair towards the window and planted it against the wall, facing the door. The next chair ce placed three foot lengths in front of the first, but in the opposite direction. "Please." Adren gestured to the chair facing the window.

Tash sat in the chair and placed his hands on his knees. "Thank you."

"Don't mention it." Adren fell into the chair at the window and glimpsed Ress. Was he too frightened to enter? Would he kick cir out? What was going through his mind?

"As I said, you may call me Tash." Tash held out both hands, his palms up. His sleeves fell back to reveal bracers the colour of his skin. "Thank you for allowing me to see you." He nodded, his gaze flickering to his hands.

Taking the invitation, Adren clasped Tash's fingers.

Emotions surged through cir, slamming every thought against cir skull. Images played behind cir eyes in a collapsing pile of colour and sound, a blurred rush of movement in a pool of light. Names raced between cir ears, chirps and shrill whistles colliding with the sounds of a child then the laughter of a man. In the forefront of cir mind, white light and liquid silver flowed and danced, lacing and knotting to form a delicate web.

In a blinding burst, the light splintered into a cloud of bright white feathers with silver rain.

There was magic at work.

He is mine. Mine, until the end of all time, a feminine voice insisted, its power familiar and impossible to ignore. One voice of the four Adren recognized from cir mind—the voice of one of the Goddesses.

Whispers broke the silence behind the voice. A bird's song played between the whispers, wrapping sweet sounds around their words. Upon the last four notes, an overwhelming wave of love washed through Adren. A pure love that sought everything ce was and stole nothing.

Adren snatched cir hands back. "You're doused in the energy of Emeraliss."

Tash's eyes gleamed. "Yes, I serve Her above all others. She is my patron goddess."

"She chose you."

"Yes."

"Birds. Feathers. Flight..." Names and images fell into place, lining up side by side until ce could piece the pictures together. Snippets of past conversations provided the rest of the answer. Adren's eyes widened before narrowing. "You. You're the one who got away. You're the one who set the Shar-denn nest burning. Halataldris. Traitor, coward. Now you're bound to the Goddess of Love."

"Yes," Tash said quietly, his body tense. "The Shar-denn stopped being my master a long time ago. Now I serve only the Four and the people. Each day is a new opportunity to atone for my crimes by helping those in need." He smiled sadly. "I'd like to help you, if you're willing to accept. Or be a friend, at least, someone who won't judge you. Someone who understands it's not easy being who you are. You bear deep secrets that are hard to keep. They're even harder to bear alone."

The words stole Adren's breath. Hearing him say the same things ce felt killed the accusations ce wanted to hurl at him. How much more did he know?

"You said you knew what I was." Adren swallowed hard, cir mouth dry. "What am I, then?" Ce watched his eyes, waiting for a trace of a lie.

A smirk tugged Tash's lips as he said nothing. After several moments, his smirk faded into a frown. His brow furrowed, his gaze searching cirs. "You don't know, do you?"

"Don't know what?"

"Here I thought you were testing me, but really..." He breathed in. "You don't actually know."

"Again: I don't know what?" Adren leaned back, crossing cir arms in wait.

"That you're Goddess-touched."

"I'm *what*?"

"Goddess-touched," Tash repeated, the corners of his eyes softening.

"Meaning what? Some fancy name for a freak? Because if there's anything I know, it's how to be an aberration. I see a lot of things I don't want to see and do things no one should do."

"No, Adren. No." Tash reached for cir but recoiled instantly. He drew back into his chair and laid his hands in his lap. "You are *not* a freak, but you *are* rare, like all of the Goddess-touched."

"Wait. There's *more*? More like me?"

Tash nodded.

Adren resisted the urge to jump up. Ce perched on the edge of the chair. "Take me to them, please. I need to know—"

"I can't." Tash's gaze fell to the floor. "They are lost to us."

"I don't understand. How do you lose people like me?" Adren slumped forward, forearms on cir knees. "Assuming we *are* people."

"You are, only… different. As for the lost part: it's a long story, one without an ending."

"So then tell it." *I have all day. For this, I have an entire lifetime.* Adren tapped Tash's knee, biting back a grimace at the shock that sparked between them. "Please. I'm sick of being me without having any reason. You're the only one who's ever known or been willing to tell me. We're different *how*?"

"Your bloodlines—they aren't the same as everyone else's. Not fully human." The twisted smile Tash offered resembled an apologetic grimace. "Goddess-touched are descendants of the Goddesses and their consorts. You are human in most ways, but your magic comes from the divine lineage, as does any connection you have to the worlds outside of that. Hearing voices is a common trait. Seeing beyond the seen is another. There are more than a hundred traits and even more abilities, but not all are present in every individual."

"So all these things I've heard… All the times I thought I was losing it… It's real?"

"Every bit of it."

The accident the night before made more sense. The strange voices outside of what ce knew as the four Goddesses were real, whatever they were. "And there are whole lines of these things."

"Each descendant carries the blood and, therefore, the capability. The families of Goddess-touched are considered sacred." Tash smoothed the folds of his robes over his lap, rubbing his palms as though nervous. "The Temples of the Four—the priests such as myself—we are charged with the duty of guiding, protecting, teaching, and serving the Goddess-touched. Providing those from the lineages do not commit crimes against humanity or unforgivable things, we are committed to doing whatever is required of us."

Adren snorted. "If that's true, then how'd you lose them?"

"The priests were not at fault, though it plagues us all the same." Tash held up one hand. "The Goddess-touched are coveted as useful allies and even more useful tools. Many have tried to own them, including the High Council, the Grand Families, the Shar-denn, and a host of others." His head tilted to the side. "What do you know of the Volarsaa War?"

"It was a damn long time ago, for one. Over four hundred years. Kattal became a republic then. We separated from Arminloa because we couldn't take their discrimination and attitude. It wasn't any prettier afterwards, though. No one liked each other, even here in Kattal."

Tash lowered his chin. "A simplified version but no less correct. There were many factors, and yes, there was civil unrest. Everyone had a hand in the war, including the Goddess-touched. Kattal had our families, Arminloa had theirs. While they eventually came to blows, they were not always on opposite sides of the political line. Often they agreed on the same things. Unfortunately, they were pitted against one another during the Volarsaa War. Mouths ran, people pushed, and a divide formed. It worsened the more they invested their efforts until they saw only enemies."

He stood from the chair and walked behind it, gripping the wood bar across the back. "After the fighting subsided and agreements were signed, the families saw what they had done to each other and their countries. They felt abused. They were pawns, moved across borders, used like weapons to control people. To the eternal shame of the Temple," Tash said softly, "the priests couldn't protect them. So the families of both countries made a pact and went into hiding."

Like me. Adren inhaled and let it out slowly.

"No one knows where the families are—if they're even in Kattal or Arminloa anymore. Likewise, no one knows who is Goddess-touched because they hide their magic. For all we know, they've blended into the rest of society, acting like everyone else." Tash stared at the chair, his veil falling forward to frame his face. "The priests used to track the bloodlines, but that information's useless until the families choose to return—*if* they return. It's disheartening because many of those families are born from sacred champions. They are worthy of many things, none of which includes harm or fear."

"What *I* don't understand is why this isn't common knowledge." With a deepened frown, Adren crossed cir arms and slouched back, stretching cir legs. "Our villages have scads of books about the Volarsaa War. My tutors had piles' worth. We all learn from a young age that it was ugly. Patriotism is rammed into our heads by old stories and speeches. At no point are the Goddess-touched *ever* mentioned, anywhere. They weren't mentioned by any priest I've ever met. Otherwise I would've gone running to my parents or the temples, *begging* to know more."

Tash flashed another doleful smile. "One of the benefits of magic: none of that means anything. After their pact, the Goddess-touched families infiltrated everything that mentioned them. They rewrote books and policies. They modified and stole records. They removed their existence to the best of their ability, going so far as to alter the memories of leaders and influential citizens. However, the priests were spared. Our books and ancestral records were hidden. They remain in the sole possession of a

Keeper of the Sacred Assembly, safeguarded in the Sanctum of the Mortal Divine."

"Meaning the Goddess-touched became stories themselves," Adren muttered.

"Yes."

Adren winced. "So no one knows about us? We're all just nothing?"

"Not all. Some stories get passed down, particularly in the most devout families. Apparently the stories didn't make it to your family." Tash's scowl worried Adren. His expression softened, and he sat down again. "Four hundred years is long enough to make people think magic is a myth, a whimsical folktale. It doesn't exist except as a wish, a dream. No one can show them it's real."

"Yet the priests know. I take it you're not allowed to forget?"

"Never. We are instructed that if we come across a Goddess-touched, we are to serve. Even lay down our life in their defence."

"Wait, you have to—" Realization cut through Adren, a chill racing after it. "Are you saying that you—me—this talk—?"

Tash sat on the edge of his seat and held out his hands. When Adren slipped cir hands into his, the shock caused them both to tremble. He caressed cir fingers. "I am bound by my oaths to protect you, yes."

In the doorway, Ress coughed, holding both sides of the doorframe as he sipped breaths.

Ignoring Ress, Tash continued. "I'll keep an eye on you as best I can, and I can help guide you—but only if you accept me. There's nothing that says you have to, but if you wish it, I will." The warmth of his hands forced back the chill pooling in Adren's skin. "I understand the risk you take. I also understand the Shar-denn would want to use your abilities. Covet them. Hoard them. Maybe even compel you to do things you wouldn't ever do otherwise."

Adren bowed cir head at his pointed look. He was neither ignorant nor naïve, understanding more than he might let on.

"There's one thing that confuses me," he said, squeezing cir fingers. "You should already know all of this. Your family should have told you. The families would always tell their descendants who and what they are, especially to keep the secret."

Adren shrugged. "My family doesn't have magic."

Ress crept further into the room, curiosity scrawled across his face.

"If that's true..." Tash breathed out and rubbed cir palms. "Adren, *every* member of these families has magic. If your family doesn't have it..."

I'm not actually from their family, Adren finished.

Doubt pummeled cir memories, teasing and prodding, assaulting images and conversations with little regard for anything but the truth. Ce was the youngest child of Rivane and Merasha, and sibling to Tethe and Mordane. There was never anything else.

Was there?

Swallowing hard, Adren blinked through the onslaught, cir hands limp in Tash's. Cir sight blurred, unfocused as ce struggled to gather the suspicions creeping around fond memories. *The jokes I've heard since I was a kid—the terrible things the Shar guys have said to run me off. All those horrible jokes about me being kidnapped, all because I'm not anything like my parents, or not enough, anyway. All those times Tethe's torn into me when he's enraged at what I've done, saying he should just throw me back into whatever hole Mother and Father dragged me out of. Saying I'm not the truest of true siblings. All of that's the truth, isn't it? That's why I don't resemble anyone in my family.*

"Kidnapped," ce said without thinking. The word blazed on cir tongue, numbing cir insides. "I was taken, wasn't I? All those times Father's men have taunted me with it, they've been telling the truth. They've used it to convince me I'm a freak." Adren shook cir head, unable to believe it, no matter how possible. "All my loyalty, all my love… They never talk about the day I was born. They never have details. But they love me—I know they do—so maybe it's just me being an ass. Still, they could've kidnapped me, right? It sounds like something they'd do, but I can't—I *can't*—"

Tash gripped cir shoulders. "Not necessarily. Maybe it's as simple as adoption. Maybe your blood family couldn't keep you or they died." He lifted Adren's chin. "The Shar-denn does questionable, immoral things, but it doesn't mean they kidnapped you."

"How much do you believe that?" Adren pursed cir lips. "You've been part of the Shar. You did their dirty work. I don't doubt your head's filled with terrible things, too. Horrible things you'll never forget or forgive because they fester in your gut until you're sick every night and can't sleep."

"It doesn't mean you should give up on hope," Tash said quietly. "Or yourself."

"I'm not. I'm confused. And Ress, he's the reason I'm…"

Not going to say the rest of that—not that he hasn't noticed I tried to kill him. Adren caught Ress's pensive expression. Could they talk after what had happened, or was the burden of the truth too heavy?

Movement on the other side of the doorway stole Adren's attention: the third man, the one ce had forgotten about. He crossed through the house from kitchen to sitting room, his head tilted as he stared into the bedroom. One of his hands clutched the hilt of the sword hanging from his hip, his other hand close to the knife at his other hip.

You look Shar-denn. You better damn well not be. Adren regarded him with caution. His black hair hung down his back in a straight tail, and the scruff around his jaws suggested he had not shaved for at least two days. Dressed in all black, his tunic and pants emphasized his muscular frame. The tattoos around his neck raised cir guard higher.

Tash followed Adren's line of sight. "Don't worry about him. He won't harm you."

When Adren slid cir doubtful glance to Tash, he turned in his seat. "Mayr, can you join us?" he called, his words laced with a tone similar to the one cir father used when calling for cir mother.

But are they still my parents?

The thought was more sobering than ce could handle at that moment. If ce could ever handle it.

Mayr entered the room and stopped at Tash's side, his hip touching Tash's arm. He drew a brief caress across Tash's back before grasping the back of the chair.

Adren eyed them for several moments, waiting to see what else they would display. "You're together."

"Yeah. It's always going to be obvious, isn't it?" Mayr gave Adren a crooked, boyish smile. "Apparently I'm horrible at pretending we aren't."

"Married?" Adren asked.

"Sure, you can call it that." Mayr passed his fingertips over Tash's neck before brushing back Tash's veil. "What do you say? Want to be my husband more officially? Sign our lives away?"

Tash smirked. "Your sense of what makes an appropriate proposal fails to astound me."

Mayr's low, rich laugh put Adren at ease only slightly.

As though seeing Adren's doubt, Tash grabbed Mayr's hand and held it in both of his. "You have nothing to fear from him, I promise. If you can invest even a shred of trust in me, you can trust him. Mayr can offer you protection as much as I can." He brushed a kiss over Mayr's knuckles. "I trust no other with my life as much as I do him."

"Thanks," Mayr whispered. His gaze shifted to Adren as he cleared his throat. "Don't mind him. He does this often. Thinks kissing up to me gets him out of anything."

"When I should just kiss you and get everything I want, I suppose?" Tash asked, looking hopeful.

"Honesty will get you everywhere. Sex will get you more."

Adren snorted, unable to hold back a snicker.

Mayr gestured to Adren. "See? That's funny. I'm funny. Sometimes dangerous, but mostly funny. I work really hard at it. *Years* of training. You never know when it's necessary."

Tash stood, appearing tired, as though drained by the conversation. "This is where I should leave. I'll let you rest and think about my offer. I'll stay in Araveena for a few days in case you want to talk more. We can talk about magic or the Shar-denn or anything else—including why the world doesn't swallow us whole."

"Get him started on that and you won't sleep," Mayr muttered. "Too many theories you'll never stop thinking about."

"I'll stop by before we leave," Tash continued, ignoring Mayr. "I won't leave without hearing your decision, either way it leans."

Adren stood, watching Ress slip out of the room.

"If you need anything, all you have to do is ask." Tash grasped cir arms. The shocks between them had stopped, though Adren had not noticed when. Perhaps it meant they were used to each other, or ce had tapped into something he possessed—possibly his connection to Emeraliss. Ce felt more at peace than ce had for months. "Ress knows how to contact me. If you ever need help and can't wait for me—or if you can't *get* to me—go to *any* Temple of the Four. Request to see the priestess who oversees the temple, and tell *only she* what you are. Ask her to send for Brother Halataldris. She will grant you refuge, protection, and everything you need until I arrive."

"Thank you," Adren murmured.

"You're welcome." Tash hesitated. "Since we share the Shar in common: I know what it's like being there and here, on both sides of that boundary. One side is criminal and loathing, the other freedom and difficult to manage. I'll do what I can for you, if that's what you need. There may also be a way we can figure out which bloodline you come from. I can talk to the Keeper in charge of the Sanctum. I could also work on getting you protection from the High Council—" He stiffened as Adren shrank back. "*Without* dragging you in to see them. If you want out of the Shar, the Council could let you be. I can try, if you want."

The offer sounded like a dream, even less attainable than Tash realized. It was a sore point, a cruel reminder ce had done things the High Council would not forgive. Other than the destruction of evidence and bodies, ce was partly responsible for the new explosives the Shar-denn used, a fact the authorities would not excuse easily. No one had said how many people were killed with the weapons ce had been told to create, but ce expected the number would escalate.

"Thanks. I'll think about everything." Adren followed Tash and Mayr to the bedroom door, forcing a smile as they moved into the sitting room. Once they reached the settees, ce closed the door and turned around, pressing cir back against the door. After everything that had been said, only one question hung above all others, irrational and doomed: how could ce ever have Ress's trust now?

CHAPTER EIGHT

Making peace with his shattered pride and blurred self-preservation would require more effort than tinkering with a silver chain. For survival's sake, he should have been on the run, not sitting at the kitchen table with pliers and chain, pretending he was dedicated to his work. It was ludicrous. So far gone over the line of ridiculous there was no more line to be seen.

So ridiculous I went running to Tash for help. Ress grumbled under his breath, tightening the chain around his fingers. *I hope he didn't make things worse.*

He glanced at the closed door to Adren's bedroom. Tash and Mayr had lingered after the discussion with Adren, eating a cold, hastily prepared dinner with Ress before leaving. Adren was still in hiding, revealing nothing of what ce intended to do. With the moon rising higher as time seemed to pass slower, Ress had relied on work to keep busy. The house was clean, furniture moved, and everything but the vase and broken dishes restored. There was not much else to do but wait. Although a quiet voice deep inside told him to flee, he refused.

Makes about as much sense as getting help from the same person who turned me into the authorities.

Except Tash was the only person he thought might know how Adren could throw him across a room with the wave of cir hand. After Adren's attack, Ress had swallowed what little pride he could salvage and run to Tash's parents. In the middle of the night, stunned and confused, he had woken them and Allaysia, then begged them to send a message to Tash. His exact words were lost to the haze of his frazzled state at the time, but he knew the result of his inconsiderate actions: Kilienn had ridden to the Temple of the Four closest to Araveena Ford and given the message to the priests. Even in the darkness of early morning, they had sent a messenger to Dahena. The message had reached Tash by noon; Tash and Mayr arrived just before sunset.

I was desperate, and he's a priest. They're supposed to protect people and know everything. There's no one else I could ask, especially not without putting Adren in danger. Just because ce tried to kill me…

None of it compared to what he had done to Adren.

The moment ce had mentioned Mordane, Ress's memories pieced together what he had been too ignorant to see. Rivane had hired Ress three years ago, instructing him to forge and transport shipments of illicit weapons: two crates of throwing stars and barbed maces, one of which was exported to Arminloa while the other was delivered to Rivane's estate in Elsove Hillock.

Six months later, Ress was arrested.

His time with Rivane's family had been limited. He knew Rivane had three children but had met only Mordane. Never had he seen Rivane's daughter, Eradrene, or thought much about her. No one had mentioned Eradrene preferred to be called Adren and refused to be seen as a daughter. Nor had anyone told him part of the family had escaped arrest. Two months ago, he had reported Rivane to High Council and walked away, hoping the name would pacify the councilmen for another handful of months. Of the names he'd had left to play, Rivane's was one he cared little for. Ress owed Rivane nothing. They belonged to different factions, regardless of the alliances. Giving up the name of a boss he had no further dealings with had been a fair trade for his life, particularly since his loyalty was supposed to be to his own faction's boss, Traise. From Rathen's disinterest in talking about the issue, Ress had assumed Rivane's family had either been captured or the High Council intended to wait and catch Rivane in the act.

No wonder he had sensed rage and slips of anger from Adren. Revenge was ugly, but living with the betrayer was worse. He was surprised he could still draw breath.

His guilt surprised him more.

He should have been terrified and scrambling to safer quarters. Instead, he felt terrible and responsible, sympathetic to Adren's need to be there. The loss of family was agony enough, but the possibility ce had been kidnapped and used by the Shar-denn worsened the circumstances. To control someone like a Goddess-touched granted power the gang should not have.

If ce could do that kind of damage when ce's snapping at me, imagine what someone like cir could do to everyone else. I've seen the women and children the Shar's captured and broken. I wouldn't put it past them to have taken cir. Magic can't be made, but it should be protected.

Like Adren.

Ress flung the chain across the table. The metal links slid across the wood and dropped to the floor.

He covered his face with both hands. Despite what he had done, in spite of knowing who and what ce was, he cared for Adren. Why? How? The answers to both questions were unfathomable. Adren's pain equally pained him. Cir rage saddened him. The situation was far enough past wrong that nothing could make it better.

His desire to protect Adren was more frustrating. Before the incident in the kitchen, he had wanted to take care of cir. He delighted in offering Adren gifts, including his trust. Never had he been attracted to anyone the way he sought Adren. Aware ce could leave eventually, he had wanted them to talk deeply, laugh continuously, and live unapologetically. The attack should have quelled all of those feelings and wants.

It had the opposite effect. The knowledge he had hurt Adren drove the desire to care for cir so deep into his heart, it had become a need. The urge to do better and be more was overwhelming, only faintly resembling what he felt for Inesta. Even with the truth between them, he was drawn in, unwilling to leave.

Of course, if I ask Tash what's wrong with me, he'll probably say it's something damned foolish like love.

Ress groaned, folding his arms and resting his head on them. Caring for the person most likely to kill him was the last thing he needed. Just as ridiculous was the fact he had known Adren for almost two weeks. That was not enough time to start falling in love.

Was it?

He pushed up and shuffled to the other end of the table to retrieve the chain. Whatever his problem, he was letting Adren stay. The decision flirted with disaster, screaming of trouble. Of all the reasons ce could be there, they whittled down to the same thing: to get rid of him.

And he was doing nothing to stop it.

Death's coming anyway. Eventually this borrowed time is going to come due. Ress stared at the tools on the table and toyed with the chain, lacing it around his fingers. *I may as well die doing the right thing rather than hurt someone else. So if Adren's here to do damage, let cir. I'd rather go at cir hands than anyone else's.*

The bedroom door creaked open behind him. Ress held his breath, listening for Adren's footsteps. None came.

"Why did you bring Tash here?" Adren's question was almost too quiet to hear.

Turning his head, Ress remained still, glimpsing Adren in the doorway. "Because you needed him."

"I could've killed you. I *tried* to kill you. If I hadn't missed, you'd be dead."

But you did miss. Then you stayed. All of that says something—maybe. I still don't know what. Ress laid the chain on the table and spun around. Slow and confident, he approached Adren. To his surprise, ce still wore the pink dress and black coat he had given cir. *Here I expected you'd want to burn them.* He stopped, leaving more than an arm's length of space between them.

Adren looked tired, dark bags under cir eyes suggesting ce had not slept in the last two days. Cir hair was still loose and disheveled. "Why would you help me? What kind of fool does *anything* for someone who aims knives at their head?" Hesitant, ce stepped towards him, watching his hands as though expecting him to strike.

I won't do that to you. That's not who I am, he wanted to argue, fighting the pain stabbing a fork in his emotions. To think Adren believed he would go that far… it hurt something fierce, but that was the way of the Shar-denn: they returned hit for hit until someone lost everything.

Unless they stopped fighting altogether.

"Can I…" Ress shifted his feet. His request would sound more ludicrous once it left his mouth, he was certain. Sometimes the right action was the most irrational. "Can I hug you?"

Adren's brow furrowed. "I don't get it…?"

"Just… can I? It's not a trick," he added softly. When he stepped forward, Adren straightened but did not move. As he drew cir into a gentle hold, Adren stiffened and inhaled sharply.

The hard embrace back stunned him, stealing his breath.

"Why don't you turn me in?" Adren's arms slid up his waist, cir voice a whisper against his ear. "You have enough to have me imprisoned or worse, so why don't you?"

"I don't want to." Ress buried his face in cir shoulder, taking in the faint, bittersweet scent clinging to cir neck. "Why didn't you kill me or hurt my cousins?"

It took him a moment to realize ce was shaking. "I thought I wanted to. I thought…" Adren gripped the back of his shirt, the heels of cir palms digging into his back. "Make me hate you. Hurt me and make me hate you like I did before. Stop being kind and thoughtful and someone I want to spend time with."

Adren pulled back and cupped Ress's face in both hands. "Don't give me hope. Don't treat me like you want me here. I can't do what I need to do when it's like this. I can't avenge my family when I like the things you do for me. I have to be like they are: cold and angry. I can't be me. I can't think about what I might want or like or need. Not when it doesn't help them."

"Maybe it isn't about helping them." Ress drew his thumb through over cir jaw. "Maybe it's about helping you. As difficult as it is to believe, maybe you're not supposed to be like them. Maybe you're exactly who you're supposed to be."

Ce hugged him again. "Stop," Adren whispered hoarsely. "Just stop. Hope makes me think I don't have to make you pay. Hope reminds me there's more than anger and hate. I don't deserve it."

"Neither do I, but you've given me the same."

"And you're a fool." Adren leaned cir forehead against his chin. "Don't feed the beast inside me, the one that thinks I can do better. Don't rob me of the Shar-denn morality that says

I can't ever forgive you. That I can't save you. I made promises I need to keep. I have duties to fulfill."

Ress breathed deep and ran his hands down Adren's arms. "So keep them." Considering how close he had let Adren get, perhaps ce deserved to be the one who took his life. He had let his guard slip. The longer he held cir, the more vulnerable he became.

"How can you say ridiculously asinine stuff like that?" Confusion spread across Adren's face as ce straightened. "You have family. You have a life. You know the penalty for what you've done is death. You can't want that."

"I don't," Ress said, tucking Adren's hair behind cir ear, "but I don't want to keep hurting you. I'm sorry what I did made you hate me. If we had met at any other time, under any other circumstance, I wouldn't have said anything to Council. I would've lied."

Adren's breath hitched. "You'd have lied... for me?"

"In a heartbeat."

"You're such an ass," Adren whispered. Ce backed into cir room, disappearing around the corner towards the bed.

The sigh Ress was holding back tumbled out. His suspicions were right about why ce was there. For all he knew, ce was pretending to be affected, lulling him into a trap.

Except for the way ce had clung to him and cir pleading gaze, betraying the battle ce fought inside. He could not be cir champion and end that fight, but he could offer weapons in the way of options.

Taking his chances, Ress stepped into the bedroom. Adren lay on the bed on cir side, facing the wall to Ress's left, cir arms tucked under cir pillow. He sat on the edge of the mattress, staring at the back of cir head. With a tentative hand, he stroked cir hair. "If you can't forgive me, and you can't kill me," he whispered, "at least share your pain with me. Let me take it on."

"You're not supposed to care," Adren mumbled. "We're supposed to be on different sides."

"I know, but I've never been good at following the rules."

As Adren rolled onto cir back, ce glared at him. "That's not funny."

"It wasn't supposed to be." Ress withdrew his hand. "I know who I am, and I can take responsibility for my actions when I want to."

Adren caught his fingers and guided them to cir temple. "Then start here. Start with what haunts me. What you gave to me. Then tell me why I have it at all. Tell me why you sent the Council's mongrels after us. Make me understand. You said you'd have lied for me. If that's true, you should be able to tell me the truth. You owe me that much."

Yes, he did, and after months of keeping it a secret, perhaps it was time to confess his transgressions to someone who understood the rules of the game they lived. There was no point in lying—he was already caught.

"You won't like the story," Ress murmured. "It's a shallow tale of a man who believed he could do some good for Kattal. A tired, cornered, coward of a man who thought selling out the people he had the least to do with could save lives, including his own. He was prodded for names and those were the ones he could give without bringing the wrath of his own faction down on him. Because he likes to think he believes in justice. He likes to think he can make the world better, one arrest at a time."

Anger flickered in Adren's eyes. Or was it disappointment?

"I'll make you a deal." Ress tilted his head. "If you promise to eat something, I'll tell you more about me. I can't tell you anything if you're unconscious."

Adren snorted. "You're just trying to get out of it."

"No, I'm not. I'm hungry and looking for someone to join me for a snack so I don't feel like a complete glutton." He dared to smile as Adren allowed him to pull cir up until they sat face to face. "Besides, it gives you something to throw at me if you don't like what you're hearing."

"It's a wonder the Shar's kept you—you're insane."

Ress shrugged and stood, bringing Adren to cir feet. "They made me as much as they made you. It'll never be pretty." He leaned into Adren, his face close to cirs. "I don't know how to fix this, but I'll try, even if it's one small thing at a time. I don't blame you for wanting payback. I deserve a lot worse. But maybe there's something better for both of us, something greater than what the Shar believes in. Maybe, just maybe, we can find it together if we're willing to try a little insanity."

Lifting his arm in invitation, he expected to be slapped away.

When Adren accepted his offer and led him from the room, he almost tripped in surprise. For better or for worse, he was giving into the delicate thread of hope tugging on his heart. Where that thread ended, he had no idea, but he was giving Adren the power to control it. Only time would tell if ce cut that thread or tied it down.

Three weeks later and I'm still breathing. Ress peered at Adren as they stepped out of the spice shop and into the busy, sunlit alley towards the village square. *At least I think I am. Sometimes when I look at cir...*

He shifted the green basket in his hand, the heavy contents pushing down one side. They had spent every day together since ce had decided to stay, even after hearing his pitiful excuses for turning in cir family. Adren had taken the confession with equal measures of spite, disgust, understanding, and mercy, no less than he had expected and no more than he had hoped. Each day he awoke was a blessing, giving him the chance to know Adren better, as much as ce would allow. Some days, ce was content to talk and laugh. Other days, ce was reserved and preferred to observe more than speak. Even on those days, he learned something new about cir. Mostly because he was looking.

"So *why* did you buy that much koneer spice?" Adren matched Ress's steps up the alley, weaving around villagers.

Ress glanced at Adren's black coat and the hood pooled below the tight bun of cir braided hair. His gaze traveled down cir black shirt and pants before moving back up to the rings on cir fingers. The clothes tipped him off to how Adren felt, preparing him for the quiet, sarcastic tones and particular preferences. "I figured you'd appreciate it."

"What gave you that idea?"

"Considering it's that kind of day—" Ress tugged on the sleeve of Adren's coat. "You have a specific palate, and I'm taking care of it. Yesterday was berries and honey. Today's the complete opposite. Not that I'm complaining," he added quietly, almost wishing ce could not hear it. The last thing he wanted was to scare Adren off by coming on too strong without consideration for cir feelings. Their relationship was already strange and complicated enough.

He almost sighed in relief with Adren's silence. Perhaps ce had not heard his words after all.

Adren curled cir arm around his, the contact sending a chill through him. "Thanks," ce muttered, staring at the shops instead of returning his gaze.

They continued through the alley, quiet and tense. Around them, villagers and merchants bustled between the shops and alley in a blur of colour and chattering voices. Once in the village square, they were surrounded by more of the same. Painted shop signs swung with the changing direction of the wind. Doors opened and closed, unleashing the faint sound of tinkering bells into the air. Bright red, green, and yellow pennants on the merchants' carts flapped as people surveyed the goods on display. The square was alive, filled with laughter and the sounds of business, dressed in the trappings of a thriving village.

Out of habit, Ress's attention wandered towards the metal shop. Bremary and Covran had not hesitated to run the shop for the day, one of the many since Inesta had left. They assumed he avoided the shop because Inesta had worked there.

Eventually he would be honest and tell them it was because he wanted to pursue a new life, one that included Adren for however long ce remained.

Their time together was not infinite. Before he lost everything, he wanted to enjoy the little he had. It was why he dined with Tash's family every week, timed with Tash's visits with Adren, and why he had given his testament of final wishes to Mayr. In the possession of someone who not only enforced laws but had a personal interest in Tash's life, the testament would ensure that with Ress's death, his cousins would be taken care of. He had named Kilienn and Covran the executors of his testament, hoping that whatever was left could benefit at least some of his family.

I just hope it isn't too soon. Emotions danced around his heart, threatening to kick the thoughts in his head. Although he and Adren had gotten along for several days, they could not ignore their circumstances. Hope could guide his days, but it would not keep him chained to ignorance. No matter how much he gave, Adren could still take his life.

Leave it to me to let my death in through the front door and make peace with it before it drags me under.

"Let's go over here," he suggested, steering Adren to a cart with flowers and circular wreaths decorated with ribbons, strands of beads, and leaves. *We're supposed to be having a good time. Me thinking the worst can't be part of this. It might be the truth, but even the truth needs to be told to shove off sometimes.* "See anything you want?"

Adren's gaze swept over the flowers until cir fingers landed on a wreath: fragrant, red, tear-shaped petals arranged in starburst patterns on large black leaves, all interlaced with dark orange ribbon and bright orange glass beads. "Not really." Ce drew cir hand back and gave him a weak smile, cir attention lingering on the wreath. "Got some things on my mind. It's not a smother-me-in-flowers kind of day."

"Dare I ask?"

"Just things, mostly to do with… you know." Adren flicked cir wrist. "Things Tash said."

"Harming or helping?"

"Helping, for the most part. Whatever harm there's been, it's been my fault." Adren stepped closer to the cart and fingered the wreath again. "I knew it when I agreed to his offer. I'd rather know who I am than turn him away because it hurts. At least he's patient, understanding. He gets the… other things." An implicative glance filled the silence with words neither of them could utter in public. "I don't have to make things up. Sometimes he knows what I'm going to say before I say it."

"He spent ten years having to anticipate," Ress said, "and more years before that being damn annoying, like he can read minds."

Adren laughed low. "You never know. I wouldn't mind being able to do that."

"I wouldn't mind, either."

"What? Me read minds? Or you read them?"

"Either. It'd making saying things a lot easier."

"Like what? Sounds pointed to me."

Ress's face warmed. "Nothing."

"Pretty thin lie you have there."

"It's nothing." Ress pretended to be distracted by the blue flowers near his elbow. When Adren looked away, he let out a breath. He was being a fool. Time was fleeting and easily wasted on uncertainty and lost chances. There was no time for any of it.

As Adren stepped to the side, Ress grasped cir hand. With their hands lowered between them, he interlaced their fingers partway, hoping the subtle message did not result in a punch to the face or worse.

Adren stiffened, flushing as ce glanced at the cart. After a moment's hesitation, ce moved closer to him until their arms pressed together. Cir hand clasped his, locking their fingers tighter.

The young woman tending the flower cart eyed them but said nothing. Behind them, whispers of Inesta wafted with the breeze from passersby. Two elderly women in light, woolen shawls and long dark skirts approached the cart on the other side of Adren. There was no mistaking their scowls at Ress, their stares flickering between him and Adren.

"We should go," Adren muttered, wrenching cir hand free of his. Ce flicked cir fingers at the women. "Too many eyes coming out of their sockets." The women sneered and perused the other side of the cart.

"One last thing." Ress sifted through the coins in his pocket before slipping a silver twicepin and four bronze quartermarks into the merchant woman's hand. He placed the wreath Adren favoured into the basket, rearranging the other items to hold it in place. "Now we're good."

"You should've left it," Adren told him on their way to the alley leading back to the house. "I didn't ask you to get it."

"You didn't have to." Ress shrugged. "You might not have wanted it today, but I've always got one foot in tomorrow." He choked back the realization ce had yet to move away. "It might be the most beautiful thing to you in the morning."

"Why should you—" A sigh cut off Adren's words. "Never mind. I'll just say thanks and leave it there."

"Because where else would you go with that?"

"A swat in the ribs, maybe. I can be rough with the best of them."

Ress smirked. "Maybe with your brothers. Maybe even with your father's lackeys."

"What's with this 'maybe' business?" Adren tugged him to a stop at the other end of the alley. "They taught me to scrap, so I scrapped. They didn't take pity on me or let me win. I had to fight for it."

"Hey, far be it from me to doubt your training. I vaguely remember saving you from a beating in the alley. This alley, actually."

Adren's face blanched. Ce flipped up cir hood and continued towards the road, arms crossed.

Dammit! I went from sweet to ass in no time.

"Adren!" Ress hurried after cir. "I'm sorry. That wasn't fair," he apologized, matching cir strides, once more admiring cir alternating grace and swagger.

"Not that anything between us has been fair." Adren peered around cir hood, pain pooled in cir green eyes. "You know what you know."

An awkward silence filled the space between them, casting a tense shroud over the rest of their walk. Ress ignored the curious stares of the neighbours watching them from their yards. No doubt the news of Inesta's departure had finished circulating the village. Now, the villagers waited to see how he would react and would take pleasure in scolding his decisions.

Whatever they make of us, I don't care. It's even less of their business than the rest of my life.

Adren remained quiet even as they entered the house. When ce stopped in the sitting room, looking as though ce wanted to turn around and walk out, Ress set the basket on the kitchen table. He had to atone for his insensitivity, no excuses.

"Go on, show me." He stepped into the open space between the kitchen and the sitting room. "Show me what they taught you."

Ce spun around. "What?"

"Come on, you heard me." Ress beckoned with one hand. "Throw a shot."

"Right, like I'm falling for that."

"What? Afraid I can beat you?" Ress smirked and shoved his hands into his pants pockets. "I mean, I only have one good leg and all. But sure, go ahead and forfeit. I'll—"

Adren lunged at him. Ce gripped his arms and pushed while hooking one leg around his, catching him behind the knee. Ress fell, his back slamming against the floor.

Dropping to one knee on top of him, Adren clutched his collar, cir other fist pulled back. "Any further requests?"

"Yeah, don't leave yourself open." In a fluid movement, Ress grabbed Adren's raised fist and drew cir into him as he rolled them. Straddled over cir hips, he pressed Adren against the floor, pinning cir wrists above cir head with both hands. "Just saying."

"Thanks for caring."

"Can't help myself." Ress released one of cir hands. "I'm nothing but—"

Cir hand shot to his throat. In a tight grasp, Adren twisted his head and yanked on his hand still around cir wrist. They struggled until ce rammed cir knee into his gut and flipped him onto his back. Adren sat on his stomach and held down his wrists. "Talk. You're all talk. Who taught you all the bad manners and sloppy habits?"

"Tash, mostly. I might've made some of it up, though."

"I bet." Face red, Adren huffed and ripped cir gaze away. Staring at the basket on the kitchen table, ce appeared lost in thought. The pressure of Adren's hands on his wrists lightened. Tension eased from cir body. As Adren faced him again, cir features softened. The concern in cir eyes was thicker than the confusion in cir voice. "What is this?"

"What's what?"

"This. You and me. On the floor. Holding hands at a stupid cart. What is this?"

Even if he'd had the answer, Ress could not have said a word. His tongue refused to work properly, his thoughts stumbling and falling into a chaotic mass of things he wanted to say. "I don't know."

"Then tell me about *her*." Adren released his wrists and sat straight, straddling his hips. "Talk to me about Inesta. Aren't you missing her? She's been gone for a little more than a month. If you loved her, why are you wasting time with me? She can't be that forgettable, that easy to get over. That's not fair, either."

Ress cupped cir cheek, hesitant and slow. "It's not fair, but it was worse when she and I were together." He fingered the tight strands of Adren's hair. "I miss her, but not the way you think. Our marriage... it locked us down and shoved our hearts out. We were never meant for each other. I don't regret taking care of her, and I won't ever forget her. I'm just sorry we were miserable."

"That's it?"

"Afraid so. There's a part of me that wishes we could have worked, but I know there's better." Ress drew his fingertips along Adren's jaw. "I figure if someone like Tash could find someone who honestly cares for him, no matter what he's done, I can, too. Even though they're from two different sides of the law, they're still together." He pulled his hand back. "Now that I think I've finally found the chance for more, I want to take it, my past be damned. I'd rather share my future with someone I shouldn't than be alone."

Adren stiffened. "Are you saying what I think…?" A blush crept across cir face. "I don't know how to do this, especially when you… me… It's a bad idea."

"Maybe it is, but that doesn't stop the truth."

"Which is?"

"I like you a little too much. Enemy or friend, doesn't seem to matter. I see you. I'm drawn to you. I'm perfectly happy being right here with you, even knowing the ugly truth. I like you, and it gets worse every day. Hate me all you want, but I'm headed in the other direction and wishing you'd come with me." Ress traced the shape of Adren's chin with his thumb, bracing himself to hear whatever would bring the peaceful moment crashing down.

Ce clutched his wrist, keeping his touch on cir skin. "I don't hate you," Adren murmured, "and that's the problem." With gentle fingers, ce brushed hair across his forehead, scowling. "I like you a little too much—so much I stayed when I should've run."

Ress let out his breath. Relief flooded his emotions until he realized Adren saying the words was as terrifying as cir killing him.

"Is that what this is, then?" Adren's fingertips trailed down his temple. "You and me trading likes until we get tired, or is there something more?"

"Maybe, if you want there to be. If you want, we could…" *What?* Ress berated himself, unable to find the words. *We could what? Lie around doing nothing all day and merely exist? Hold hands and giggle and act like youths? Be something we're not and pretend to forget everything else?*

Adren's body tensed before ce scrambled onto cir knees. "I've never done this before. I don't know how to—I don't want to—I can't do that, I can't—" Ce shuddered and moved to stand.

"Wait, hold on." Ress caught Adren by the hand. "Can't do what?"

"Be your—do things—that." Adren gripped his thigh, close enough to his groin to make a point. "I'm not ready to go there, to do it. Hold my hand all you want, but I'm not sucking your—"

"Whoa, whoa, whoa. No, no, no. That's not what I mean. *At all*." Pulling Adren's hand from his leg, Ress eased cir down onto him, cir legs on either side of his waist. He held Adren's hands in both of his. "I was trying to say we could spend time together as maybe something a little more… romantically inclined. Or we could work on being really good friends if that's what you want—nothing else on the side of that, I swear. I'm not looking for anyone to suck any part of me. I don't need it. I don't particularly want it. That's not how I want to spend our time."

"I'm supposed to believe that?"

"Yes, because it's true."

"So we *aren't* having this conversation because you want me to be your whore?"

"No. I don't want you to be anyone's whore." Ress caressed Adren's cheek. "But I would like to hold you and say ridiculous things to make you smile. I'd like to give you things that'll make you happy. I want to hear more about you growing up, and how you feel, and what you want. I want to get to know you more than anyone else does. I wouldn't mind you staying and treating this house like your own."

He cupped both hands around cir face. "I went through the motions with Inesta, being her lover, but it didn't do anything for me. It's not who I am. I want you here, but not to warm my bed—not like that. You steal my attention the moment you walk into the room or speak or laugh or do anything, and I'm pretty sure you're digging my heart out of my chest every time we talk." Ress slid his fingers over Adren's hair, teasing strands free. "I'd like to be selfish and have more, if it's something you might want, too—and I want you to know it."

"I know it now," Adren whispered, drawing cir fingertips down his chest. "Why would you give me the time of day, given what you know?

I'm twisted up inside. Half the time I don't know who I am. What is there to want?"

"Real answer?"

"Yes."

"Even if it's pathetic?"

"Yes."

"And doesn't make sense."

"Would you stop stalling and tell me already?"

Moving slow to keep Adren in place, Ress sat up and wrapped his arms around cir waist. "Here it is, then, the disgusting truth," he murmured, fighting the urge to unbraid Adren's hair. "Whenever you're in one of your dresses and you're laughing and giggling like everything's perfect, you remind me of a flower on the cusp of full bloom, desperate to stay in the light, yearning to be seen past the trees and all the other beautiful things around you. You don't want to be lost to the distractions or be a blur in the chaos. You want to be seen and appreciated. I get that, and I see you. I want to bring the sun to you. I forget the other things exist because you spin the world around you."

Beneath the leather coat, Ress drew his hands up Adren's back, catching cir tremble as his touch slipped across cir spine. "Then when you're like this, serious and calm and ready to defend, you remind me of a bottle made of dark glass in the instant before it shatters. It's the anticipation, the need to get close. I know the contents will remain, just splattered everywhere, but I want to save the shell from being destroyed. It's better to save it before it falls apart than to put it back together," he said, his lips close to Adren's. "Not only will it never be the same, it risks losing a piece. Lose that piece and the bottle will never be whole again."

Adren swallowed hard and looped cir arms around his neck. "You're right: that doesn't make sense, no more than the rest of me. It just sounds more beautiful." Ce pressed cir forehead to his. "Give me something else, something that makes sense. Bring the light and save the glass."

"How do you feel about a kiss?"

"I don't know. Never tried it before," Adren whispered. "Maybe we should find out."

The space closed between them as Ress's lips took to Adren's gently, enough to taste savoury skin and feel the rush of breath through their slightly parted lips. He coaxed cir, silently asking for more with a light push ce returned. The kiss never strayed from being chaste and sweet.

Ress pulled away first. "Did that help, or am I going to be punched in the head?"

"Get back here, or I'll punch you somewhere else," Adren said, tugging him back to cir.

"Sounds fair to me." He yielded to Adren's kiss, holding cir tighter as ce sank further into him. In that moment, he knew he would spend the rest of his life making up for what he had taken from Adren, earning every kiss ce brushed across his lips.

Of everything he had taken from the Shardenn, of everything he hated about it, ce was the one person he wanted to keep around, consequences be damned.

CHAPTER NINE

For every physical urge demanding ce move away from Ress, Adren's other needs instructed cir to stay. Moving meant prying his arm from cir waist and drawing cir legs from his. Neither sounded satisfactory, even if parts of cir were numb, cir muscles threatened to cramp in protest, and cir torso was stiff from sleeping with a binding on.

Behind cir, Ress breathed quiet and slow, his lips close enough to warm Adren's earlobe every time he exhaled. He was still asleep, his body heavy against cirs, keeping them in place on the half of the bed nearest the door. They were both still dressed, their discarded boots and knives abandoned in the sitting room. Adren's coat lay on the floor beside the settee after being discarded during their first bout of kisses before dinner.

After dinner, during the second round of more passionate kisses, they had stumbled into Adren's bedroom and fallen onto the bed, their greedy lips stealing breaths without apology. Once exhausted, they had curled up together and drifted to sleep. Now they were disheveled and more restricted by fabric than Adren preferred.

That's where a single kiss gets us. Adren peered at Ress over cir shoulder. Locks of his dark hair fell into his face, almost hiding the movement under his eyelid. He looked peaceful, his features enhanced in the soft morning light. His scarred jaw was buried in the pillow, the mark a curious part of him that did nothing to deter Adren's fondness for staring at his lips and yearning for one of his gentle touches.

Sentimental as it was, ce wanted to push his hair back and kiss him again. Part of cir needed to wish him good morning and hear his soothing voice in return. *That still requires moving.* It was a necessary evil ce was not ready to confront, not when lying in his arms felt perfect. Intimacy stilled the chaos inside, his embrace filling cir with a calm ce craved. Their first kiss had awakened a curious, adventurous beast inside Adren, but lying together lulled it into complacency.

Maybe it was because they got on better than they should have, though the newness of it... that pushed hard at cir thoughts, laughing quietly in the back of cir mind at how ce wanted to explain it all away. As though anything in cir life was making sense lately.

I've never been here before. Never... like this. Intimate. Touchy. Personal. It's... disturbing, and about seven years of awkward crammed into a few moments of pretending like I know what I'm doing.

Adren frowned as ce focused on the light flutter of Ress's lashes. It was unnerving, not knowing where they went from that point, or how to get there. Ce had never expected to fall for anyone, let alone get close to them, or even want them close to cir, not when trust always meant opening cirself up for rejection. *But Ress... he really jams that up. Bastard.*

Ce snorted softly, unable to stop imagining cir fingers playing across his brow, wondering how he would respond to such a soft touch waking him from the dream holding him in its clutches. Fear, ce was used to that. Being denied, turned down, pushed away—ce was used to that, too. So much rejection, with cir entire life built on a foundation of *no* and *not good enough* and *not like that*.

Meanwhile, freedom seemed to come with its own difficulties, leaving cir fumbling for a way through.

For all of cir twenty-five years, ce certainly felt more and more like ce was eighteen all over again, stumbling over what to do with life. Being so close to someone—*wanting* them to be even closer to cir—was a far cry from normal. Ce shared enough in common with Ress that telling the truth came more easily now he knew who ce was, but not without that hint of terror that shook cir even now. Sharing so much in common usually meant ce had to back away to save cirself, at least in the Shar-denn where darkness fed on darkness in a never-ending cycle. The shadows that haunted cir only ever grew bigger and threatened to take over what precious little good there was. Always a hunt. Always a death. Always that unspoken misery.

Shar-denn freedom was just another word for their tiny little rust-ridden cage of mistrust and agony no one ever wanted to talk about, a slow, festering poison Adren had always felt but never named for fear of being silenced permanently.

Though maybe, just maybe, that was why ce was with Ress now, unwilling to leave his side, as risky as their situation was. He hated that silence, loathed that cage, and threatened to pick the locks just to get out—everything ce wished ce could do on cir own. It was everything ce wanted to grab onto with both hands and runaway with, holding it closer than anything else in life, protecting it from any danger.

This was the kick ce needed. This was the fight in cir soul. This was a soft light in the dark.

And maybe ce would even dare to enjoy it.

Frustrated with waiting, tired of fighting what ce wanted to do for fear of making a mistake, Adren draped cir arm over Ress's and held his hand, cir gentle stroke over his fingers surprisingly soothing. As simple as it was, the touch offered even more than the calm ce needed right then, gifting cir with a rush of memories worth every moment of heat and compromised clarity. Recollection toyed with Adren, playing cir emotions for all they were worth as ce remembered how Ress and cir had ended up in the same bed, sharing the same space without fear of what the morning would bring.

There was no stopping the small smile that curved cir lips right then, or the warmth that pooled in cir chest. What was a subtle gesture of affection in the market had blossomed into less timid forms of affection by nightfall, and ce regretted none of it. Together they were driving stakes through the ruthless darkness that separated them, breaking through the pain that wanted to keep them enemies.

Not that I miss Mother and Father and my brothers any less. I just care for him a little more than I did.

Every tenet of the Shar-denn would cry sacrilege if they knew.

Tethe and Mordane would be disgusted. Father would be enraged. Mother… she'd pat me on the back and lecture me on disappointment. The enemy can't get to you, ever. You don't let anyone carve up your heart. You don't let anyone in who doesn't deserve to be there. You don't give into anyone who hasn't earned it.

While cir family rotted in prison or died on the execution dais, Adren's soul took refuge in Ress's tenderness.

Somewhere fate's laughing itself into oblivion. Adren cuddled further into Ress, throwing off his breathing pattern. Hips shifting, he tightened his grip around cir. Protective and comforting, his embrace was the simplest embodiment of all the things he said he wanted to offer Adren. His hold was not the cold touch of the Shar-denn or the isolation of emptiness. There were no demands, no ransom, no ultimatums. There were choices, alternatives, and opportunities of equal value. Rather than waking every morning and forcing cirself to remember how hate felt, Adren could hold onto who ce was. Death did not have to be cir first thought of the day and last regret at night. A bleeding heart's power came from love, and ce wanted to keep it that way. To fulfill every desire, wish, and rule of the Shar-denn would kill that part of cir.

The part I need to treasure most. Adren peered at Ress again, surprised to find his dark eyes open.

"Morning," he murmured, kissing the crook of cir neck before yawning into cir shoulder. "How are you feeling?"

Adren rolled onto cir back and swept hair out of his face. "Like myself—or at least how I want to feel."

"Mm, I understand." With another yawn, Ress propped himself up on his elbow. "The only times I feel that way these days is when I'm getting people away from the Shar."

Silence fell between them, heavy with meaning and question. They watched each other, not moving.

He expected cir to break the silence first, Adren realized.

"What's that supposed to mean?" Ce turned to face him, his expression saying more than ce could comprehend.

Ress brushed Adren's braid over cir shoulder. "You're right: I do owe you the truth, especially since we're here... like this." He cupped cir cheek. "It might run you off. You might decide it's not worth staying. You might think it's heinous and walk out the door. For all I know, you'll turn me in to the Shar enforcers." His thumb glided over cir lips. "But I'm tired of lying. If this is ever going to go anywhere, I need to know it's real."

"So say it." Adren traced the line of his jaw with one fingertip. "Don't hold back."

Turning onto his back, he rested his hands on his chest as he stared at the ceiling beams. "You already know I've played informant, but you don't know the rest. I'm not Shar, not in my heart. Never have been. The bastards only think I am because they nearly tore out my kneecap. But I've played the game, too." Ress returned his gaze to Adren. "I love to sabotage their sorry asses."

"Meaning what, exactly?"

"He who coordinates the shipments can make them disappear."

Propped up on both elbows, Adren struggled to stay silent. Without coercion or striking a deal, he was giving cir the confession that every faction boss and gang member would pay to hear. "What are we talking? Big? Small?"

"The big stuff. The important stuff. Some of the weapons I don't think the Shar should have—or anyone, really. Mostly it's been the people. Women and children. I never could stomach that particular variety of vomit-inducing filth," he muttered. "I change schedules and drops and move things around. I make them fail. I make things go missing. I twist up the routes and finer details. Then I fill the transport rosters with guys I know are naïve enough to believe whatever I tell them. I set other Shar-denn members up for the fall. Sometimes they fall hard—as in never breathe again." Ress drew his hands down his face. "I keep jabbing a knife in the knee of the Shar like they did to me and poison the well while I'm at it."

How dare you, you ungrateful—

Adren sucked in a sharp breath. The feelings twisting cir insides left a foul, acidic taste in cir mouth. The part of cir belonging to the Shar-denn insisted ce drag him to the enforcers. In the back of cir mind, ce heard cir father and brothers commanding ce get justice. Had they heard the confession, they would have beaten Ress to one moment away from death, let him recover, and then invited other faction bosses to the next round until he could no longer scream for mercy. For generations, the Shar-denn had fought hard and long to have control over their lives and stand up to the High Council's imperfect system. No one would take their freedom and power away.

Ce hated being entrusted with the truth. Of all the things Ress could tell cir, he chose those that would get him tortured in the worst ways. Why would he dare? The amount of trust he put into cir kicked Adren in the gut.

The part of cir that needed to leave the gang stood fast, wanting to safeguard his trust and keep his secrets. How could ce fault him for wanting to save innocent people? How could ce punish him for doing what truly was the right thing?

Especially since I could've been one of those children they stole. Adren played with the wrinkled, white sheet beneath them. To think poorly of cir parents stung, cir loyalty burning under the pressure of doubt and suspicion. Still, ce could not ignore the truth: cir parents could have kidnapped cir, no different than when they instructed their gang members to do the same thing to someone else. Or the fact that both Rivane and Merasha knew what happened within the slavery ring, allowing men like Amelin to do whatever they pleased while Rivane accepted a substantial portion of the profits to fund other illegal activities.

What made Adren any less likely to have been taken like the people Ress saved? If anything, ce would have been an exceptional child worth stealing, no matter what cir parents had to give up. *Was I locked in a box? Did they ever think of sending me to the Breakers to be housetrained? If I had been, wouldn't I have wanted someone to save me? Wouldn't I have seen him as a hero if he* had *saved me and returned me to my real family? He's probably a hero to those women and children, to their families, even if they don't know he did it. I don't have any right to turn him in, none at all.*

In a long string of expletives, Adren cursed the Shar-denn. Cir first thought had been to berate Ress and turn to what cir family would do. That was wrong, backwards, twisted. No matter how good ce thought ce could be—despite cir sympathy for others—cir instinct was to think like the people who routinely harmed others for what power it gave them. How could they have gotten deep enough under cir skin to compel Adren to defend them so easily and without thought? Ce might have been innocent, too, and they had corrupted cir.

Yet all this time, all these years... Memories were quick to answer Adren's dejection, tossing cheerful images around like pillows, attempting to soften the blow. Contentment pushed against cir disappointment as ce recalled being five years old, lying on a blanket flattened on soft red grass, cir belly full from a picnic feast with cir parents and brothers. Beside cir, Rivane lying on his back, pointing at the clouds and laughing as they named each shape together, spinning tales of the faces they saw in the sky. Fanciful stories that had made cir heart soar, as light and inspiring as when cir mother's graceful fingers moved over a harp, creating ethereal melodies that lifted Adren's spirit.

Despite all of their love and affections, Adren could not put it past cir parents to have kidnapped cir. Ce could not disregard what ce knew of Rivane's determination and Merasha's stubbornness. When they wanted something, they got it. Their loyalty to the Shar-denn was not to be scoffed at: when they believed something or someone would benefit the gang, they did whatever was necessary to obtain that advantage. No republic law would stop them. No morality outside of the Shar-denn's ideals would dissuade them. A Goddess-touched child would have elevated their status within the Shar-denn, providing them not only with a measure of protection others could not combat, but furthering their reputation and commanding ultimate respect for their achievements.

They were Shar-denn, first and foremost, criminals to their core. No sweet memory could wash the blood from their hands.

Maybe the separation from cir family was a good thing. Maybe talking with Tash and feeling something for Ress was a better path. Maybe ce needed to change—a feat possible only when ce was on cir own, away from the darkness and bitter sense of entitlement.

Maybe ce needed to get in touch with cir humanity and sing the praises of mercy.

"What happens to them?" Adren asked, licking cir lips. "The women and children, I mean."

Ress faced cir. "Sometimes I've met them somewhere. Other times, I've sent someone I can trust. There aren't many, but I can always rely on the priests. Lately I've sent hunters to take care of the few shipments the Shar's let me handle. I don't like them, but at least they've got their priorities straight. We smuggle people into a new life. If we're lucky, they have families we can take them to. We get them clothes, funds, food, shelter, protection. Everything. Then we make sure someone pays the price without it coming back to me."

His palm hovered above Adren's cheek as though he were afraid to touch. "You come from deep in the Shar, so I don't expect you to understand. I've tried to make changes where I can, without getting killed. I can't help if I'm dead. I also can't sit by and let the Shar get away with a hundred different forms of murder. I'm not a patriot by any means, just human. They can call me a bleeding heart all they want," he said, "because it's true. I never agreed to hurt people. I only agreed to survive."

When Ress pulled his hand away, Adren caught it. Ce pressed his palm to cir jaw and splayed his fingers, slipping cir fingers between his. "I might've been raised by them, but it doesn't mean I can't understand. It also doesn't mean I can't keep your secrets, because I will. I won't tell them."

His gaze searched cirs. "I want to believe that. I want to believe you're the one I'm supposed to be telling this to. I *want* you to be the one who won't throw me out or turn me in or kill me for caring. Promise me I can trust you. I want to love you, but I need to trust you."

Words caught in Adren's throat. Ce had been prepared to say yes, but the moment he mentioned love, no reply was adequate enough.

"Trust me," Adren whispered, stroking his hair. "I won't hurt you like that. I can't. If that isn't enough, trust this: you know what I am, and you know I'm not in prison when I should be. You could turn me in and the Council would probably forgive you anything. But I'm still here, trusting you won't do that do me. I have everything to lose and nothing to gain except you."

The truth stung as Adren heard cir own words. Whatever cir motivations were before, they were now locked up, the key of determination thrown away. Hearing of Ress's transgressions was one thing, but seeing his reasons was another. Perhaps he could help cir, too.

He already is helping, though. I see in him what I want—what no one else has wanted to give. He sees me. Doesn't look past, doesn't look through, just sees me, even better than Mordane does. And I don't want to lose it—I can't lose it. I want to know if there's more; if we could be more.

Emeraliss, give me strength.

Adren kissed Ress's lips, soft and slow, teasing his bottom lip. "We should get up."

Ress grunted and flopped back onto the other half of the bed. "Don't know if I like that idea. It means responsibility. To dos. Stuff. Don't know if I really want to do stuff today."

With a laugh, Adren sat up on the edge of the bed, cir bare feet digging into the woven blue rug on the floor. Ce tugged on the collar of cir shirt, loosening the stays before pulling the shirt over cir head. Tossing the shirt at the footboard of the bed, Adren glanced over cir shoulder. "Help me unbind?"

Silent, Ress knelt behind cir. "If you want me to." He caressed the bare skin of Adren's shoulder, stopping above the faded brown cloth wrapped around cir chest several times.

Adren's heartbeat faltered with his touch. "Please." Ce drew his hands around cir, guiding his fingertips to the small metal pin between cir breasts.

Without help, he uncapped the pin and withdrew it. The cloth loosened, one end falling to cir waist as the rest shifted downwards. After placing the pin on the bed, Ress grasped the trailing end. He worked with steady movements, his arms slipping under Adren's to unwind the cloth. Each time he reached around, Adren held cir breath.

Shivers surged through Adren to the rhythm he created. No one had helped with the process before, a single constant ce had come to rely on even when everything else in life was uncertain. There had never been anyone there to help. Ce had started binding cir breasts as an adolescent, just after cir thirteenth birthday, and everything after that had been a matter of doing whatever ce could think of to feel more like cirself. Almost everyone ce knew scoffed at what ce did to feel more male, not one of them stopping to understand or even truly listen to cir—enough that ce had wanted to stop talking about it altogether. Without anyone to guide cir or offer advice that was more than *stop doing it and we'll stop harassing you*, ce had made everything up as ce went.

And while Ress and Tash assured cir they knew of other people who were like Adren, including members of the High Council ce had never heard a kind word about, a piece of cir continued to doubt them both, regardless of how much ce wanted to believe. No matter how many times Tash told cir of the different words other people used like ce did, no matter how many times he insisted their goddess Hastal would completely understand and approve with every blessing She had, Adren struggled to let go of the soul-slicing jeers and the derisive snorts that had plagued cir adolescence and nearly every day since. They echoed in cir thoughts without any measure of mercy, the lingering ghosts of voices that only dealt hurt and anger.

So many years of denial, of laughter and scolding and misery. So many years of being shoved aside and hearing no... More than once, cir brothers had threatened to yank cir bindings off. They had been particularly annoyed whenever Adren scrapped and trained shirtless, wearing only the binding.

Meanwhile Ress doesn't bat a lash. As he unraveled the binding's last layer, Adren savoured how safe ce felt. Ress worked the fabric as though it were normal for him, his breath dancing across cir shoulders.

The end of the fabric fell away, quickly gathered in his hand. He offered the mass of thin fabric to cir.

Ce tossed the binding to the end of the bed and grabbed his fingers. Before he could ask, Adren cupped his hands over cir breasts. "Thank you."

Ress caught his breath and coughed. "You're welcome." His palms moved to support cir breasts from beneath, his thumbs stroking cir hardened nipples.

Adren bit back a moan and leaned into him. Ce liked what they had already—the kisses, the embraces, the chaste touches—but ce liked his touch there, too. Imagining how his hands would feel elsewhere took no effort.

I'm not ready for it. It's not what he wants, either. The rest of it leads to things I can't afford and don't want. As much as I don't consider myself all-girl, my body doesn't agree completely. No matter how man I feel, some things are stuck. I'm not bringing any kid into the world that's like me, and that's what this leads to. Nature's cruel enough. I can't give that much. To anyone.

Adren brought Ress's hands to cir lips and kissed his knuckles. They would take the slow path, a comfortable pace. While ce wanted to be touched in all ways, ce would settle for cir own means. Given Ress's disinterest in sexual play, Adren was certain ce had all the time ce needed to figure out what ce wanted.

That did not stop cir from trembling as he trailed his fingers down cir left side.

"What's this?" Ress fingered the silver and gold tattoo on Adren's ribs, above the waist of cir pants. He traced the curves of the image: a skull on a bed of leaves with a crown of flowers on its head. "I'm not familiar with these inks."

"It used to be black and green, but the colours started fading the night I got it." Adren cleared cir throat. "A couple days later, it was silver and gold. It changed all by itself."

The questing fingers stopped on cir hip. "That's a first."

"I know. No one had heard of anything like it before. Now I'm wondering if it has something to do with being Goddess-touched."

"Have you asked Tash?"

"Not yet." They had not had time to discuss the trivial matter of a tattoo.

Ress kissed Adren's cheek and shuffled off the bed. "You could ask him this afternoon. For now—" He bent down to tease cir skin with small kisses from the bottom of the tattoo to the top. When he straightened, he grinned. "We'll keep it between us."

As he turned away to wash and dress, Adren let out the breath ce had sucked in. His simple actions made cir feel wanted. In a perfect world, they could have everything. They could leave the Shar-denn and forge a new life together, their relationship strung together by a series of simple actions that conveyed love, whether it be friendship or something else altogether. They could talk, laugh, and exist without a second thought.

Except we don't live in a perfect world, and there isn't any running from the Shar.

Dread twisted in cir stomach. Life would never be that easy.

"Aren't you afraid to be seen with me? Seen at all? You're a walking dead man."

Waiting for Tash to answer, Adren peered at Ress and Mayr. They remained more than a dozen foot lengths behind, walking slowly and talking too quiet for Adren to hear. Neither looked pleased as their gazes flickered, scanning for trouble.

"Some risks are necessary." Tash continued along the riverbank with a slow stride. "If we always surrendered to fear, we'd never do anything."

"You're either courageous or just one damn ridiculous fool." Adren clenched cir jaws, cir gaze sliding towards Tash. "Sorry. That didn't come out right."

Tash raised his hand, smirking. "No, you're right, though sometimes the two meld into one. The bravest act can be full of foolish and the other way around. I'm apparently both on a regular basis. However, without that part of me, I'd never be a priest. I'd never be here."

"Walking with me?"

"Breathing."

"Ah." Adren matched Tash's steps as ce watched ripples move in the water from falling leaves. Their stroll along the river was Tash's idea, a way to get fresh air while avoiding other people. Since their first conversation, they had met every week for two days, sometimes three. Mayr always came with him and stayed close, but not close enough to smother Adren with his presence. Ample space was granted for cir to speak with Tash, and though ce found it difficult to believe some of what came up in the discussions, other matters were clear. None of them knew who cir blood family was, but Tash held onto the belief they would one day, saying the future had saved hope from the past.

All that mattered to Adren was the present. How could ce balance family and self without losing either? How could ce hold onto peace when others demanded chaos?

"Here's a question for you, not that I expect you have an answer." Adren pulled Tash to a stop. Night after night, ce had wanted to ask someone the one question plaguing cir most. The answer alone could define who ce was and what ce was meant to be, assuming anyone had the answer at all. "Ress. The fact he's alive. Why couldn't I kill him?"

Ce drew back, not wanting to sully Tash's soft robes. "I was set on doing it. For weeks, I could taste it, feel it. It was all I could dream about. Then as soon as I had the chance, I couldn't. I was *this* close, but I failed." Adren slipped cir hands into cir coat pockets as they resumed walking. "I couldn't do it physically. I couldn't make myself commit. And I'm not talking about choice. That's part of it, sure, but this..." Adren shook cir head. "The knives were supposed to go *into* him, not around, and after that, I wanted to punish him. I wanted him gone. It was just me and him and my anger, just standing there, ready to make him hurt. I swear that's what I meant to do, but something... something happened," ce whispered. "Like my magic took over completely, leaving me there to deal with it. It destroyed his house but left him safe. It took all my rage and sent it everywhere except onto him, no matter what I wanted. Or what I thought I wanted," Adren mumbled, "and I really don't get it. I couldn't control my magic—I couldn't control *me*. I swear choice had nothing to do with it, at least not consciously. For the first time, I had no choice. Whatever it did, it did on its own, but how? *How?*"

Chin lowered, Tash nodded. "I've inquired with the Keeper I mentioned before, and he's teaching me more about the Goddess-touched. I have a theory about why things aren't what you expected." As he stopped, he turned Adren towards him. "I think you might be one of Emeraliss's descendants. I can't prove it, and for all of my asking, Emeraliss isn't answering. However, it could explain several things, including why we were in Araveena at the same time." He clutched Adren's shoulders. "If you are, it could mean the love you bear for other beings trumps your ability to harm. You value life and love, not death and hate, and you can't go against the divinity in your blood. You can't deny Emeraliss's place in your life, steering you in the right direction."

"Is that why the Four talk to me—to keep me in line and make me fail when I'm about to do something really foolish?"

"You could think of it like that, yes. Though maybe not so much *make* you fail as... strongly encourage. The Goddesses rather enjoy the idea of free will."

"So I'm not just seeing what I want to see?"

"Not where magic is concerned." Tash's smile lit up his eyes. "Though I can't speak to the terrible plan inherent in living with Ress."

Adren snickered. "You should say that a little louder. See how he reacts."

"I'll save it for later. We have a lot of time to make up for, but I don't need to do it all at once."

"Can I ask you another question, then?"

"Absolutely."

"You told me before you've killed people."

Tash tensed and pulled his hands back. "Yes. It was part of my role in the Shar."

"How do you get over something like that? How could you leave it behind and start over? It can't be that easy."

"No, it's not. I still struggle," Tash admitted softly. "The cruelty of the past is still part of me. I'll never escape it, but I decided a long time ago it wouldn't destroy who I could be. It's not a matter of getting over it, but striving to do better. To do as much good as possible and tip the scales."

"I suppose it applies to me, too, Goddess-touched or not," Adren muttered. Ce had not expected his answer to be any different, though ce had hoped for more. The decisions ce faced were difficult enough without worrying about how ce would deal with regret.

Tash clasped cir arms. "Don't let my journey hinder yours. These things take time, but we don't have to do it alone." He glanced at Mayr and Ress with an affectionate smile. "I've learned to share the burden, and that's what helps the most. Instead of keeping the darkness pent up and bearing the weight alone, I've given into someone who wants to help. Someone who cares so much they not only shift the load, they break it into smaller pieces. He trades hope for pain until we can both carry the weight without harm. So while there's no magical solution, there is a touch of magic in what I've found."

Like Ress does. I don't know how, but he takes it all. Adren wanted to believe Ress could be that someone for cir. Ce yearned for everything Tash described, especially if that someone accepted all of cir, without question, fight, or fear. Most people were quick to dismiss cir, but not Ress, the one who should have feared cir the most.

Caught between two worlds, how would they make it work?

"I want out," Adren whispered. "I'm not proud of what I've done. Now I'm part of some race I still don't know much about, but I feel like I'm less than them. Less than everyone else." Ce tilted cir head. "My magic is so strange. When I make things disappear, everything slows down and moves in reverse, like I undo time, one invisible fragment after another. No one's ever understood what happens or why I can't make things appear. I have to work with what exists already. I can move things, break them, put them back together. I can change things, but I can't create. When I'm doing it, I feel powerful, but when I'm thinking about it, talking about it, I feel useless."

"It's not a measure of usefulness," Tash argued. "Each individual has different capabilities, but there's no shame in that. Or perhaps it's because you don't know how. It took you years to master what you *can* do."

"Because no one helped me. My family didn't know how any of it worked." Letting out a frustrated breath, Adren stared over Tash's shoulder to the water. "All of this… it's making me wonder if leaving the Shar is what I have to do. I'm starting to think I needed to be on the outside to see past it. That world was all I knew, my whole life, but now that I've seen what I could have outside of it… I'm not sure I want to go back. Was that how it was for you?"

"No. I had my family to ground me."

"So I'm alone in this?"

"You're *not* alone. You want to see the world, there's nothing unusual in that."

"I already know what the Shar has to offer." Adren gritted cir teeth. "I'll never be anything more than a lackey or a liability. I'm not meant to be our faction's boss, and I never wanted to be. It'd mean me doing more of what I don't want to do. But if I'm not faction boss, I'll always have to tiptoe around who is. It's not unusual for a new boss to exterminate the former boss's family to avoid conflicts in loyalty."

Tash's gaze fell. "I know. I've seen it happen."

"So how do I go back? How do I even go forward?" Adren picked up a smooth, grey stone from the grass beside cir and rolled it in cir hands. "I'm starting to think this is what my parents tried to keep me from. They never wanted me to find out what the rest of the world was really like." Ce threw the stone at the river. The moment the stone touched the water, cir body tingled and pulled taut. Under cir skin, ce felt the strain of the water's surface breaking and rippling outwards, the chaos smashing apart peace. "I was never allowed to speak to a priest alone. I wasn't really allowed to be in the presence of priests, at all. I never thought about it much before, but now I wonder if my parents wanted me to stay ignorant and alone."

Adren bit cir bottom lip. "You told me the priests learn about people like me. If I'd spent enough time with a priest, what are the chances they'd have figured it out?"

Tash breathed in. "It isn't as easy as that, unfortunately. Though if a priest had heard or seen what you can do, they would've known immediately. The tattoo you showed me earlier would have told them the same."

"Dammit." Adren kicked the ground, scattering leaves towards the river. No wonder cir parents kept cir a secret. Anything else would have shoved the truth in cir face.

Yet I care for them. I'm cursing their names and loving them all the same.

"What's wrong with me?" ce murmured. "How can I still want my family even though they could've kidnapped me and kept me isolated so I'd never know I wasn't the only one?"

"Nothing's wrong with you. It's not something you can easily let go."

You're telling me. You come here, tell me they're alive, more or less intact, and I still want to rescue them, even if it is foolish... and brave, two things that shouldn't be paired together. Adren rested cir face in cir hands. Nothing about the conversation solved the problem of what ce would tell cir father's men in a week. Darus and the others would never let cir leave the Shardenn.

As much as ce wanted to ask Tash for his help with them, ce was far from ready to tell anyone ce was not working alone. There had to be a way ce could drive the others off while saving Ress and cirself. Ce wanted to see the world, not be kept in the dark about it. Ce wanted to know if ce could be more than always stuck in the middle.

Tash pried Adren's fingers from cir face. "It's all right to want out. No matter what they think, the Shar doesn't have to control you. You *can* give yourself permission to leave. I gave myself that permission and took what they stole from me. I believe you can, too, if you want it." He held cir face in his hands. "I'll be here on the other side—we'll all be here—but you're the only one who can cut the tie."

Adren turned away. *You're giving me the knife, but do I have the strength to use it?*

With one decision, ce could die just as quickly as ce was saved.

I shouldn't be here. This isn't going to be good.

Adren leaned against the broken wall of the abandoned bridge, listening to the river and watching the sunlit trees for movement. As promised, ce was attending the meeting with Darus, Amelin, and Pade, alone and ready to give an update. This time, ce was fully armed, carrying knives in cir boots and in the sheath at cir thigh, hidden by cir old long coat. The meeting would be the first time seeing cir father's men since ce attacked Ress; the first time since cir first kiss a week ago. What was ce going to tell them?

I'm such a fool. I should've told Ress the truth. Or Tash. Or even Mayr. I should've told someone who could've talked me out of this—or given me a good lie, at least. But no, I had to do it on my own.

Gaze flicking from tree to tree of browning orange leaves and decaying canopy, Adren wished things could have been different. Ce never should have agreed to work with Darus's plan, Amelin's greed, and Pade's interest in inflicting pain. Cir father had chosen them to fulfill specific tasks for their faction and family. They had served him well and gotten along with cir brothers, a perfect fit for the Shar-denn.

Ce trusted none of them.

Had ce controlled who served the faction, Darus, Amelin, and Pade would never have been near cir family. Something about each of them always put cir on edge. Perhaps it was the way they looked at cir. Or the way they called cir "she" and "her" with sarcasm and laughter in their voices. Maybe it was the way they could say all the right things but their eyes said otherwise.

Still, ce could not turn them in, nor could ce allow them to be harmed. They were the only piece of family ce had left, cir lifeline to the Shardenn. Even if they had taken advantage of cir panic and desperation after the raid, ce had to protect them. Such was the promise ce had made cir father and brothers when ce turned eighteen. With Adren's abilities came responsibility, Rivane had said, and ce owed the rest of the faction that responsibility. Adren had sworn to keep their identities secret and protect their families. On cir word, ce would never act against them unless they broke the rules of the gang first.

Even then, I might as well keep them safe for Father's sake. They can still find a way to get everyone out of prison. I doubt Amelin actually cares about it, but Darus and Pade... they've always done what they've said they'd do. Maybe I can use some of Amelin's talk against him and get him to foot the fees. Remind him how much Tethe loved drinking with him and sleazing over women. They were friends. Maybe that'll mean something with the right angle.

A low, warbling whistle sounded from Adren's right, on the other side of the stone wall.

When ce peered around the side, ce found Darus, his brown long coat skimming the rocks of the riverbank as he approached. Amelin and Pade followed behind, their faces covered by black scarves with the ends tucked into their coats.

"Nice of you to join us." Darus stopped at Adren's side, flashing a small grin. "It's been too long. I think Amelin's missed you."

Amelin nudged Adren back from the wall to hug cir around the shoulders. He tugged his scarf down, freeing the curled ends of his blond hair. Laying his head on Adren's shoulder, he nuzzled cir cheek. "Family's a terrible thing to be without. You know how it is." He pouted. "Are we there yet? Can we kill the bastard and go now?"

"Yeah, because it's time to change Ame's nappies and shove a funnel down his throat so he'll shut up," Pade grumbled, pulling down his scarf and sweeping back his dark hair. The wound on his cheek had healed, leaving a dark scar. "So? We good? Can we finally stow the goods and start selling? I'd love to start spreading word of the snitch's demise."

Under their scrutiny, Adren fought the need to shuffle cir feet. It was bad enough Amelin held cir tighter whenever ce shifted. "Not yet."

"'Not yet,'" Darus echoed dryly. "What does *that* mean?"

"It means I don't have what we're after. It's been... difficult."

"And again, what does that mean?" Darus crossed his arms. "Four weeks, Adren, plus whatever else you've had. This could've been done in a matter of days. You're *living* in his *house*. It should be so painfully easy, a child could do it. A blinded *and gagged* child. You're seriously telling me you don't have anything useful?"

Adren shrugged, hoping the mix of truth and lies was good enough. "Ress keeps his work stored well. I haven't found the weapons or plans. Looked and looked, but haven't been able to find anything good. I'm starting to wonder if he keeps the information around or just commits it to memory. Or gives it to someone to keep or dispose of."

"Huh, that's interesting. That means you're empty handed *and* he's still alive." Darus stepped closer to Adren.

Amelin's arm slipped up to Adren's neck, keeping cir in place.

"What *I* find particularly funny," Darus continued, "is that this is *really* simple stuff. Clear objectives, close quarters. Not nearly as complicated as the things we've done for your father. Certainly nothing kids couldn't do if given the right incentive." His bittersweet breath flowed over Adren's lips as he leaned forward. "You're the daughter of a boss, trained and

338

capable. We've seen you work with much more *difficult* plans. So it's hilarious to hear you've got nothing, especially when I have the funniest feeling you're lying."

Amelin's grip tightened around Adren's neck. "Our sense of humour has limits," he murmured, squeezing until Adren could barely breathe.

Adren's hand snaked under cir coat to cir knife. "Not lying," ce rasped, unsheathing the knife slowly. If ce had to, ce would ram the blade into Amelin's thigh. "Just stuck."

Darus yanked cir knife hand up. "As if this is any help." He snatched the knife and tossed it to the ground. "Let's be honest: we know you won't use your freaky abilities against us. You swore to daddy you wouldn't, not ever. We were all there. You're bound by oath to *protect* us. You wouldn't want to betray daddy, would you? So let's try this again."

"I... told you. Diffi—"

"No, no. Don't care. You had your chance." Darus stepped back. "Pade? Spell it out for us, would you?"

Pade moved to where Darus had stood and grabbed Adren's chin. "You have three days. Three. *You* will kill Ress—with or without the weapons and plans—or we will do it. Except if *we* have to do it, we're not going to be in the sharing mood... except for a note to Council with your name, your whereabouts, and some incentive. A list of things we've seen you do will get their attention, I'm sure." He smiled. "That's assuming you *don't* get skinned by the rest of the Shar once they find out how much you've failed."

Adren swallowed hard and looked away.

Pade snatched cir face back into place, his golden gaze locked to cirs. Amelin's breath warmed cir ear, his lips traveling over cir skin.

"You know the rules, *Eradrene*." Amelin kissed cir neck, his touch nauseating. "You're the daughter of a boss—this is *your* responsibility. You swore your blood oaths to the faction. You swore your life to your father. If the family ship goes down and you're the only one left, *you're* the one who's supposed to fix it. So if you won't get justice for your old man, if *you* won't set things right, someone else has to. And that someone is obligated to get rid of you, too, because you'll be considered a traitor."

"The only way for you to even out the miscarriage of loyalty is to be loyal to Rivane— to your entire faction—and do the right thing," Darus said. "Otherwise they'll be hunting you, and we won't do a damn thing to stop it." He spit at the ground near cir feet. "We'll take you down, little sister, and I won't be feeling any pain about it. We've tolerated you up to now. Your father is our main concern. Tethe and Mordane, too. You're alive because they wanted you to be. If you betray them, you'll take the fall, boss's daughter or no." With a snide smile, he gestured to cir hands. "Use your fancy little freaky abilities against us all you want—at least a quarter of our faction knows what we're up to. If we don't come back, they'll come looking. If they find you but not us… it won't be pretty."

Pade released Adren. "Either play by the Shar rules or don't. Just remember that if you don't, you're dead."

Adren choked as Amelin squeezed cir neck. "Don't make us hurt you, precious. That'd be embarrassing." Amelin kissed cir cheek and thrust Adren aside.

Coughing and sputtering, Adren rubbed cir throat, easing the pain away. Inside, ce screamed. Thoughts blurred, stumbling over one another, frantic in their search for a safe, dark space to cry and beg.

There would be no mercy. No compassion. No understanding. The rules of the gang were clear, and Adren's role inside those rules was fixed. If ce did not do as dictated, the factions would turn against cir, especially whoever took over as leader in their own faction.

"Three days." Darus lowered his chin. "You know where to get a hold of us, and we'll be watching. Get it done, send us a message. We all go home. If you're *extra* lucky, we won't go telling Rivane how much you're failing him. Got it?"

"Yes," Adren replied hoarsely.

To cir relief, all three turned away and returned to their horses.

Adren leaned against the wall and banged cir fist against the stone, cursing cir foolishness. *Of course they'd pick the Shar's rules over me. What in the Four's name was I expecting? A party? They've tolerated me.* Tolerated. *They'll sell me just like that. They'll keep to the rules and tenets and charters and everything I don't care about. I want my family back but not all those gods-awful rules.*

Except ce knew the truth: to get cir family back, ce had to honour the Shar-denn game. They were connected, considered one in the same, not separate. If ce refused, ce could never go back. If others in their faction knew of Adren's mission, ce could not easily dispose of Darus, Pade, and Amelin.

Not that I could anyway. Adren lifted cir hands to stare at cir fingers. *I don't kill.*

Yet ce had the power to kill Ress.

All I have to do is stay and we'll both be targets. If I leave—and if I tell him to leave—we might have a chance. A small chance, but a chance nonetheless. Except…

They could not leave together. Fleeing from the Shar-denn as an individual was difficult enough; hiding as two would put them in more danger. Not that Ress would leave willingly, nor *could* he leave. He cared too much for his family. Even more, he was legally bound to Araveena Ford, or so he had told Adren after confessing his role as an informant. Of the two of them, only Adren could leave.

Realization drove a stake through what remained of cir heart. Ress had to stay.

Ce had to go.

If Ress stayed, the High Council and their bounty hunters would protect him. He could petition the High Council to send him to a safer place. At worst, he could seek refuge in a temple.

But if he left, the High Council would hunt him. If he escaped with Adren, they would be chased and miserable, open to more pain and suffering. They would never be happy; they would never be left to live in peace. Paranoia would divide them, forcing them to constantly look over their shoulder, pack their things, and keep running. They would blame each other. They would consider each other enemies. In the end, the High Council or Shar-denn would take him and leave Adren alone. Ress would be imprisoned or executed, the latter being the most likely.

If Adren stayed, ce would bring more attention than they could afford. Ress would never stay with cir, not with the trouble it meant. Not when someone could point out where Adren was and have cir dragged to High Council in chains, only to be imprisoned or used like the other Goddess-touched. Not when the Shar-denn would have two traitors to dispose of and would find the means to do so. They would always feel the need to hide and nearly kill each other with the frustration of being stuck in one place. Ce would bring more trouble to Araveena Ford, putting its families in danger. There would be no buying cir safety, no matter what Ress could do. What he had done was dangerous enough, but Adren's position in the Shar-denn was higher than his, making cir transgressions worse. Not only did ce know more, ce had done more. Of the two of them, ce was worth the most.

If ce left on cir own, they had a better chance at survival. Twisted and painful as it was, they could stay alive.

So could what they felt.

Ress had survived before Adren found him, and there was a chance he could survive once ce left. Ce would not be the reason he got hurt. Nor would ce beg the authorities to intervene or stay in a temple. Those options would end in harm for the people who helped cir.

Running away, that's what I've got. If Tash could do it, maybe I can, too.

The battle could not be clearer: exact revenge to buy cir family their freedom or run and save someone who cared for cir no matter what ce did, regardless of who ce was, and offered the softer, sweeter life ce wished for. Ce could not have both. Ce had to choose.

No matter the decision, the trap was set. The risks were inevitable. In the end, only one thing mattered, the facts boiled down to one simple truth:

Caught between bleak futures built on all manners of wrong, ce would go down doing what was right.

CHAPTER TEN

He should do something nice for Adren, that night and not a day later.

No, something romantic, Ress corrected, prodding the narrow clasps on a gold bracelet. *Nice is for when you're making friends. I'm kind of hoping we're slightly past that part.* Smirking, he leaned back on his stool and held the bracelet up. Its white jewels reflected the sunlight, casting faint colours across the workroom walls. *Because I definitely don't go kissing friends with so much eagerness, not even Ines.*

The smirk dissipated as he lowered the bracelet. Inesta. The part of him that cared for her tugged and whispered, scolding him without offering quarter. No, it was not fair that while she surrendered everything to find a new life, he took up with someone else. Still, it was how things were, unbidden and unexpected. Although he thought of Inesta several times each day, wondering if her new life gave her what she sought, he needed more than grieving for someone he had never been right for, not in the way either of them needed. Someone he had never fallen for, not honestly, not completely.

Sometimes love was never enough, especially if it meant being miserable.

But Adren… Ce was there, willing to pursue something honest and real, even with their unconventional circumstances built from disturbing choices. They understood each other in ways no one else could, coming from the same darkness that took everything they had and left them with so little they could be proud of. Instead of mourning lost years, he now delighted in the brighter future with someone who knew exactly what he was up against—someone who was willing to brave those malicious shadows that bit back deeply with a rough-handed fight of their own.

Which is why I need to dig into my ridiculously romantic side and pull out something really good—something I haven't done before. Something I never did for Ines. Hand-me-down gestures won't cut it. It needs to be something special, but what's with the wooing thing, anyway? He scowled at his fingers as realization crept suspiciously around his new-found optimism. *I don't know a damn thing about courtship. Ines and me skipped all the cute stuff and went straight to marriage, but even that ceremony wasn't dripping in sentiment. Now, with Adren… the slower we go, the longer we drag the simplest gestures out, the tighter ce's got me coiled. Like I'm getting to know everything ce is inside with every unending kiss and lingering glance and extended silence—everything that could be lost if we push too fast.*

He never wanted it to end. Wrapped up in the essence of Adren's spirit, willfully surrendering to cir, he was at peace, content. Before Adren, he had dreaded the nights, knowing he returned home to a quiet house and unhappy life. With Adren there, laughter and easy chatter filled the house again. Every stolen moment away from mundane chores to kiss or embrace was exciting. There were no apologies. They had put the dark truths aside and focused on trust.

Ress laid the bracelet on the workbench and gazed at his palm. Even a week later, he felt the sensation of Adren's bindings on his skin. He had not expected Adren to trust him that much, certainly not that quickly. When he had kissed cir during their play fight, he had only wanted to know how ce tasted. The kisses afterwards had been a pleasant surprise.

It was Adren's request to help unbind cir that had seized his heart and shocked his thoughts.

For Adren to have asked him to remove the bindings and touch cir skin spoke volumes. The request could not have been made lightly, not when it left cir vulnerable. The fabric was more than threads: it was a part of Adren, a meaningful piece of cirself.

Since then, Adren had asked for his help with binding and unbinding, and he obeyed without hesitation. Although he did not deserve cir trust, he was going to work hard to keep it.

"Thinking of someone you'd rather be touching than playing around here?"

Bremary's voice sent Ress's thoughts scampering into separate corners. She slipped into the workroom, her mauve and black lace dress sweeping across the floor. Her hair was twisted back in small sections and tied with bright green, pink, and yellow ribbons that trailed down her back.

"I've noticed your dazed face when you think no one's looking," she continued, leaning against the doorframe. Silent laughter crinkled the corners of her brown eyes. "You're happier every day. I don't even remember seeing you like this with Inesta. You're getting goofy, almost deliriously joyful. I'm pretty sure I know why. I've noticed." Bremary slapped his shoulder. "Stop it. I don't think Cove can take this much happiness. He'll keel over if he thinks you're stealing his role as the lovesick fool."

"Maybe it's time for a change. I can be in love and he can be serious. Might find himself settling down if he did." Ress grinned. "Then you can finally lay flat that girl you've been chasing after."

"As if he has anything to do with it." Bremary kicked at the hem of her skirt, a faint blush colouring her tan skin. "Besides, we're talking about you." Lips pursed, she tilted her head.

"I'm right about you and Adren, then. And since you dropped the word first… It's love?"

"Maybe. I don't know what else to call it."

"Whatever it is, it's doing good things for you." Bremary stroked Ress's hair, her cold fingertips stopping at his nape. "I hate talking ill of Ines, but I won't lie and say I don't like seeing you this way. You've always had a beautiful smile, just like our mothers. It's nice to see it more often now. Not to mention you're walking taller these days. Maybe even with a bit more jaunt." She pulled away. "Or maybe I'm seeing what I want to see. It's better than what I thought would happen if Ines left. Though it was quick, I'll give you that. Adren wasn't the reason you and Ines… you know?"

"No. I never cheated on Ines. Should anyone argue otherwise, I'll make them regret it." Picking up the bracelet, Ress examined the clasps, satisfied they were mended and tight. "It's merely how the timing worked out. Fate being funny."

"So it's real, this thing you've got now? It's not you using someone to heal? Hiding from what happened?"

"Bremary," Ress warned softly. "I started feeling something for Adren before Ines left, but I didn't do anything about it." He looked Bremary in the eye. "This isn't me using Adren. This is me finding someone I actually want to be with and seeing where it goes for sake of being happy. Perhaps it's too early to be talking about love, but I want to hope. I want to be more than someone's shield and second option."

Bremary kissed his forehead. "Just don't get hurt in the process, and don't hold back. Give it everything you have."

"That's what I'm planning on." Glancing at his hands, Ress frowned. "Except I'm stuck on the finer details of how. I don't want to treat Adren like Ines. I want to give Adren more, but I don't even know what that means. I thought I was giving everything before. I'm floundering here, trying to figure out how to court Adren properly. Any ideas?"

She snickered. "My poor big cousin. You've been married so long you don't know how to be someone's perfect dream." Her features softened as she patted his shoulder. "First piece of advice: don't over-think it. Let it come to you. Second piece of advice? It's in the little things."

"Yeah, I know *that*, but what do you do when you gave your ex-wife all the little things?"

"Find new ones?"

"You're *so* incredibly helpful."

"Oh, you wanted *help*. Here I thought you were peddling rhetoric thoughts." Bremary grinned. "Flowers?"

"Do it weekly."

"Dinner?"

"I cook every night. Adren doesn't know how."

"Sweets?"

"And spices. Done them both."

"You've already done the something nice to wear, twice over." Bremary scowled. "Jewelry? Adren wears rings and bracelets."

"Haven't done it yet, but two things come to mind. One, I did it often with Ines, and two—" Ress held up the bracelet. "—kind of obvious, don't you think? Isn't that a lack of imagination?"

"Not if it was the right piece," a low, feminine voice added from around the corner of the doorway. "Not the birthstone type, or the named things, or anything easy. Something no one else could possibly have or give." Kirra stepped into the room, covered by her black cloak. Her grey shawl pooled around her neck, revealing two long tails of blonde hair.

Ress jumped up, knocking the stool back. He had not heard her enter the shop. Nor had Covran announced her arrival from where he worked at the front desk, having taken over for Adren after ce left for a walk.

With one gloved hand, Kirra motioned for him to sit. "Relax. No games. I thought I'd help. Girl problems?"

"Romantic interest is more accurate," Ress corrected, hesitant to sit. At least Kirra seemed more like herself, the false voice and personality left behind for the moment. She was almost tolerable.

"Ah, the all-annoying thing so many of us fall for. I feel for you." Kirra offered him a kind smile. "Jewelry's good but it needs to be personal. Put everything you have into it. Tie your heart to it. Don't do cute, and don't do clever or smart. Find the essence of what you really want to say and you'll get there. Don't need jewels. Don't need fancy. Just something so unique you'd never be able to make it again."

That was the most generous answer Kirra had ever given him. "Personal experience, I take it?"

Kirra shrugged. "Intuition."

"Well, you've got me sold." Bremary clasped her hands and swayed as she eyed Kirra. "Want to intuition yourself into working here?"

The lewd gaze Kirra raked over Bremary was far from subtle. "Only if you'll play my inspiration," she said, biting her bottom lip.

Bremary's face turned multiple shades of crimson. "I'm going to help Cove." She hurried out the door before Kirra could touch her.

"Guess that was a *bit* much," Kirra muttered. "I could swear she was eyeing me before."

"Maybe she was." Ress sat on the stool, the heels of his boots hooked on the bar along the bottom. "She's more of a chaser, though. Turn things around and she gets funny. She likes being forward but prefers subtle in return."

"Yeah, I don't do subtle." Kirra's golden eyes narrowed. "I also don't do the fluffy prey thing."

"I can't imagine why not."

Kirra lifted her arms, her cloak parting to reveal shin-high boots, black leather pants, and a black bodice covered with crisscrossed straps and silver buckles. "Right?" She dropped her arms. "Though I wouldn't mind finding out how sharp her claws are."

To keep the conversation from getting more awkward, Ress cleared his throat. "You're here to tell me what, exactly?"

"It's straight to business, then." Kirra grasped her hips and leaned forward. "R wants to see you tonight, midnight, here. The usual check in."

Ress nodded his understanding. While he had no new information for Rathen, there would be questions about the future. At no point would he mention Adren. He would not tolerate Rathen mishandling cir. The meeting would keep to his work with the Shar-denn only.

"Well, that was easy." Frowning, Kirra peered into the shop. "It's different than the last time I was here. What you do?"

"Got divorced," Ress answered dryly.

"Oh." Kirra spun on her heel. "Sorry?"

"If you want to be."

"That good, huh?"

"Oh, yeah. Just great."

"Her fault or yours?"

"Both."

"Ouch. Sounds like a good time to stop prying." Kirra draped her shawl over her head and closed her cloak. "Catch you next time, then. Fill in the rest."

The next moment, she flounced out of the room and left the shop.

"You can leave, too, Ress," Bremary shouted from the front. "Go home and get some of that thing with no official name yet."

"And what in the Four's name is that?" Covran grumbled loudly, followed by a huff and grunt.

"Might as well. I'm done with this anyway." Ress placed the bracelet into a wooden box and snapped the lid shut. The shop would close soon, and Bremary did not need him there. Perhaps leaving would give him the chance to start thinking on Kirra's suggestion before he saw Adren. Ce should have returned to the house from cir walk.

He moved the bracelet to the pile of finished orders, setting the small box on top of the others. Maybe the next time, he could go with cir and they could take a walk together. They could wander along the river, taking their time, holding hands.

Or is the river a thing for Adren and Tash now? I don't know. Where do I fit in the matters of the Goddess-touched?

Shrugging off the question, Ress cleared the tools off the workbench and dusted with a rag. With the space ready for the next day, he passed through the shop, turning down the sleeves of his brown shirt. "I'll head out. Mind if we see you tonight?" *Because I don't want Adren to be alone when I meet with Rathen.*

Bremary stopped counting receipts and leaned against the desk. "Sure. Come 'round for dinner. I wouldn't mind playing coins after." She stared pointedly at her brother. "Assuming you're ready to make good on the threat to trump me at Crowns and Fools? I've got the disc with your name on it burning a hole in my stash: blue-faced Fool on red-footed Knave. Please tell me I can play it. It's like the sex you've been having with yourself all these years, just less messy."

Covran shoved her. "I wonder why *that* is?" He faced Ress. "Please tell me you'll be my mate in this game. I'll work alone every day next week so you can do whatever you want. If you love me at all, you'll help me beat her and take the pot."

Ress snickered, already imagining how the game would go. Bremary never took competition lightly. She always played for keeps. "Fine. Count me in."

"Ha!" On his way around the desk, Covran stuck out his tongue at Bremary. "See you at the table."

Before he could hear the rest of the bantering, Ress hurried out of the shop. The conversation would only end in tears of exasperation.

As he rushed home, thoughts of Adren replaced those of his cousins. He hoped Adren welcomed the impromptu visit with them. Ce liked his family. At least he thought ce did. Adren had never said otherwise nor had ce recoiled from Bremary's attempts to include cir.

We should probably talk about that, he realized, ambling up the stone pathway to the front doors. *Maybe we need to set some boundaries before I overstep the imaginary line.* Pushing open the door, he promised himself to broach the subject before they left for dinner.

"Adren?" Ress closed the door. "Did I beat you home?"

Silence answered.

But not perfect silence: faint noises sounded in the direction of Adren's bedroom. A soft click. A rustle. A sniffle. A ragged breath.

Something was wrong.

Ress charged across the sitting room. "Adren?"

He froze in the bedroom doorway. Adren stood beside cir bed, dressed in cir old long coat, shirt, and pants. Green eyes red and swollen, tears streamed down cir cheeks. In one hand was cir satchel; in cir other hand, cir white dress and red shawl, folded and ready to be packed. The clothes he had given cir lay on the bed, neat and flat as though in presentation.

Or apology.

"Adren—"

"Don't." Adren shoved cir dress and shawl into the satchel. "I can't stay."

Ress caught his breath before he choked. "Can't stay?"

"Yes, as in leaving." Adren pulled a small, white, leather-bound book from underneath cir mattress—a gift from Tash to record cir thoughts. Ce worked the book into the satchel, burying it deep.

"Wait. I don't understand."

"You wouldn't. I never wanted you to."

"Adren, *wait*." Closing the space between them, Ress reached for Adren's satchel. His fingers grazed the bag before ce yanked it away. "Don't leave. Whatever I did, I'm sorry."

"It's too late now. It's too late for everything… except running."

"From *what*?"

Adren's mouth opened, the answer hanging in the air.

Ce busied cirself the next instant, packing the rest of cir things. "I can't do this. If I leave now, it'll put a couple days between us. It'll be safer this way."

"Safer? Adren!" Ress snatched the strap of the satchel and tugged hard, wrestling the bag from cir. As his arms snapped back, the satchel slammed into his chest. He tossed it onto the bed and grabbed Adren. Ce struggled in his grasp, pushing him away. "Tell me what's wrong."

"You're a dead man, don't you get that?" Adren tore away from him. "I'm even deader than you. If you let me go, there's a chance we won't be so dead!" Ce pushed his chest with both hands, sending him stumbling back into the wall beside the bed. "I'm not the only one who's after you. I never have been. Now they're collecting."

Ress cursed silently. Had he not been tripping on hope and tangled up in awe, he would have realized Adren was not alone. If ce knew what he had done, others would know and want payback, too. Adren was merely the frontline assault.

I know better and I still slipped. Now ce's running because I was too ignorant to see past my own wants. Too caught up in what could be that I lost track of what is.

"Explain it to me." Hands out, he moved towards Adren with slow steps. "Don't go like this. Tell me."

"Tell you *what*? That three of my father's men and I concocted a plan to steal your stuff, take your head, and sell everything?" Adren wiped cir eyes on the sleeve of cir coat and glowered at his outstretched palms. "We know you're working on new weapons. *I* was supposed to get the plans for them. *I* was supposed to get close to you to get whatever else you had. The first day I came into your shop, you were supposed to see me. The assault in the alley was never real. Darus and Pade weren't really hurting me, but you got Pade good. He wants to return the favour for carving his face. Then after..." Ce shook cir head. "It was supposed to be so easy. Find the stuff, take the stuff, kill you, leave. But I couldn't. Everything since has been outside of any plan because I couldn't get rid of you," Adren whispered. "I still can't, so they're going to gut you and get rid of me. They're following every rule the Shar has. I have to go."

Of course that's what they want. His death was worth something to the Shar-denn, but they valued his work more, knowing the staggering number of dead bodies it would leave behind. "You're the child of a boss, Adren. They're supposed to protect you."

"Not when I promised to do the one thing I'm supposed to do and ended up doing nothing." Adren gripped his wrists, holding him in place. "You're an enemy. You've committed grave offences against the bosses and our brothers and sisters, all punishable by torture and execution. *I'm* one of the elite, promised to enforce punishment and take down our enemies. Showing you mercy means I'm committing those offences, too. Letting you live voids my rights. I'm a traitor to my family, my upbringing, and our laws. If you live, I die. You've been in the Shar long enough to know that."

And long enough to have forgotten it. Ress felt the blood drain from his face. Of all the rules the Shar-denn followed, he had kept what he needed and discarded care of the rest. He had never needed to recall the rules that applied to faction bosses and their families. Those had been the concern of Tash, Nimae, and Varen, given their proximity to the leaders.

Now those rules meant everything. They would steal what little light he had managed to protect in his life.

Loving Adren condemned them both.

"They're coming in three days," Adren continued. "Darus, Amelin, and Pade. They've worked for my father since they were boys— their fathers worked for him, too. Darus is leadership. He likes to play at being my father's left hand and gets all the good missions, so he's a big problem. Pade's quiet, stealthy. He's easily lost in the shadows, so watch for knives in the dark. As for Amelin—he's the charmer, one of the ones who snares women and children and sends them on for housetraining. One of those guys you'd love to gut for what he does to them." Ce grabbed cir satchel and clasped it shut. "I've left you descriptions of what they look like on the table in the kitchen. There's a letter. It's all there, everything I've said and more."

Adren slipped the satchel over cir head and turned. Ress jumped into the doorway. "Don't do this."

Adren growled and swiped his shoulder. Ress threw up both arms and gripped the doorframe, digging his nails into the wood. Even if the frame came apart and splinters jammed under his fingernails, he would hang on.

"Let me leave. This isn't the time to be a fool!" Adren pushed on his chest. When it failed to budge him, ce yanked on his collar. "If I run quick and hide really well, they won't get me. I can steal attention from you long enough for you to get your damn backside to safer ground. Even if they split up to chase us both, there's a better chance we'll survive because they won't attack you alone. *I'm* the key to killing you safely until they get a mob careless enough to try. *I'm* more of a threat to them and the Shar with what I know. They'll come for me first. Without me—"

"Without you, this house is empty and so is my life." Ress clenched his teeth and clutched the doorframe tighter. Wood split, lifting from the wall. Nails scraped his skin. His injured knee blazed with sharp, stabbing pains radiating outwards. "You don't need to lecture me on how the Shar works. I know what they're bastard enough to do."

"I can't do this right now." Adren closed one hand around his neck. "I've got nothing else. *Nothing.* No home, no safety, no family to protect me. If I don't leave, the Shar gets me and I die doing what they want. I'm tired of that. I'm sick of being whatever someone else wants me to be." Adren reeled cir arm back and paused, fist aimed downwards. "Get out of the way or I'll hit everything you value."

"Then you'd better start by smacking yourself in the face." Ress pushed off the doorframe, launching himself at Adren. He grabbed cir hands before ce punched him. "You don't have nothing. You have *a lot* of somethings, including me. Safety might be difficult to manage, but I'll do anything. Just don't leave. Not like this." He kissed Adren's whitened knuckles. "There's got to be another way."

"The only way out is dead."

"Tash is still breathing."

Adren tugged cir hands from his. "We'll never be happy. If we're not dead, all we have is running. It'll never stop. That's not a life; it's a living death sentence. Whatever you think we have will die with it. We'll be as miserable as you were with Inesta."

Ress drew Adren into him and cradled cir head against his chest. His mind twisted on itself, desperate to find a solution between losses. Adren could not stay, nor could he let cir go. There was no one he could trust to take cir in, not when ce was Goddess-touched and in a questionable state. *Especially when most people can't fend off the people coming for us.*

If he left with Adren, he would leave Bremary, Covran, Tash's family, and the village to fend for themselves. *Not to mention the other lovely complications. Where would we go? Where's 'safe' for us? I can't leave without permission. I can't really trust anyone, not with my life and certainly not where ce's concerned. We'd have to get rid of anyone coming to get us to cover our tracks. I'm not good at doing these things alone.*

How could staying and dying or running and dying be their only options?

"There's got to be something," he whispered, swinging back and forth gently, holding Adren closer. "Give me a bit of time. Put a little faith in your divine blood. Maybe between them, we'll find a way out."

They had to leave Araveena Ford, both of them, everything else be damned.

And that's the plan. Solid as anything can be when it's full of holes and bending under the weight of foolish hope. Ress tipped back in his chair and stretched his legs across the corner of his desk. He swept a glance across his dark office, pausing on the dim moonlight creeping in from under the door. *Ridiculous beyond measure with whispers of sunny logic, that's what this is. A trap set for an optimist by a realist fool, but a trap, nonetheless. If Rivane's men want me, they'll have to work harder. If they want Adren, they'll have to lay down their lives and kiss eternity hello. If there's anything about this situation they've got right, it's that it's not going to be easy.*

The plan had every chance of being more difficult than he anticipated. There were too many variables, too many people to involve. Unlike the covert missions of sabotage, he could not execute this plan alone. If Adren was to have any chance of leaving the Shar-denn, intact and protected without anyone pursuing, they needed help.

That help will probably turn around and throw me in prison, but we're out of ideal options. He scowled at the door, listening for the soft sounds of someone breaking into the shop. Given Rathen's low opinion of anyone who broke the law, Ress could imagine how pleased Rathen would be to haul him to a prison in an inhospitable region of Kattal. All because he lacked the permission to leave Araveena Ford in order to save a life.

"Permission be damned, too," he muttered, grimacing as he shifted his knees. He needed to get Adren out now, not whenever the councilmen found the time to debate and *maybe* approve his request to leave. "I've already damaged Adren's life. I can't keep adding to it."

Nor could he repeat what had happened with Inesta. Adren leaving would hurt worse.

Focused on the light under the door, Ress hoped Adren fulfilled cir to promise to stay until his plan was complete. After tearing into his thoughts all evening, considering options and discarding all but the most impossible ideas, it took Ress almost as long to convince Adren to agree to his plan. Much of what needed to happen hinged on Adren's capabilities and determination. Ce needed to play the role ce had in the Shar-denn, regardless of doubt or discomfort. The plan was ridiculous enough to be unpredictable and barely legal enough to save Adren.

Assuming ce did not leave in the middle of the night, one reason he had left Adren with Bremary and Covran while he met with Rathen. The other reason was to keep Adren and Rathen separated. They could not meet before they set the plan in motion. No one could get a hint of Adren's identity until someone was there to protect cir—someone no bounty hunter could touch.

Shadows devoured the light under the door. The doorknob turned quietly.

The door opened, followed by a soft grunt and Rathen's cloaked figure. "That's a first," Rathen murmured, closing the door.

Ress struck a match to light the candle next to him on the edge of the desk. The yellow glow bathed the room, shadows flickering around them. "It was bound to happen." He blew out the match and tossed it down. "Especially when we need to talk."

Rathen pushed back his hood and tousled his blond hair. "Sounds like a reason to keep one eye pinned on you permanently. What you do?"

"Nothing yet."

"Great, you're going to kill me with suspense."

"Lucky for you I'm not interested killing you at all." Ress nodded at Rathen. "Business first. You gave all the information to Council?"

"No. I cleaned the Council latrines with the papers. Whoops."

"Stuff it. This isn't one of our damn meetings where you insult me, I give you information, and you run off feeling good about yourself." Ress drew his legs down and sat straight. "Things aren't good. They aren't like they used to be. I've got problems you need to know about."

"So I've heard." Rathen's tone was uncharacteristically soft. He rocked on his heels, his cloak and dark long coat swaying with him. "K says you've split from your girl. I don't know whether to say sorry or congratulations."

Surprised he would care, Ress blinked as he considered his next words. "You should be careful with that compassion, hunter. You might as well lock it back up—you're not going to like what I need to tell you. More like ask."

"*Please*, don't tell me it's a favour. I don't *do* favours."

Ress ground his teeth. He hated asking for favours just as much, but protection and refuge came with the price of choking on pride and bathing in humility.

"So don't think of it as a favour. Consider it part of your job." Ress opened the bottom drawer of his desk and removed the brown leather case containing folded letters. Hesitant, he held the flat case towards Rathen. "I need you to deliver a letter to Priest Halataldris, as quickly as you can. If you leave now, he'll get it well before breakfast. He lives in the temple in—"

"Dahena. Yeah, I know. I also know he's staked claim to the bed of Dahe's Head Guard. Don't think I haven't been keeping an eye on him. I don't trust him any more than I do you." Rathen curled his lip at the leather case. "Do I *look* like a messenger?"

"No, you look like you're not old enough to be playing with yourself." Ress thrust the letters out further. "Take them, unless you know any messengers who could kill an assailant with one hand if they tried to steal these? If not, you're all I've got."

Rathen regarded Ress with a tight-lipped expression. He snatched the case and tucked it inside his coat. "Sensitive details, then."

"Yeah. Sensitive as in could get people killed, including someone who doesn't deserve it." Ress held up his hand. "Not me, though I wouldn't mind living through this."

"Are you going to tell me what 'this' is?"

Ress stared at Rathen's chest. "Not here and not out loud. There's no time. I need you to deliver the letter and go along with it, assuming you care about saving lives." He gestured to Rathen's pocket with his chin. "There's a letter in there for you and K. It says everything you need to know. What I can tell you right now is there's something in it for you. You want criminals? You want gang members? Then deliver, read, and work with me."

"What's the thing you're not saying?" One of Rathen's blond brows arched. "I bet it's the part I'm not going to like."

"You might want to up your bet. You'd make a fortune."

"Spit it out, then." Rathen held up both hands and stepped back. "If you want my help, if you're going to drag K into this, I want to know at least that much."

Ress let out a frustrated breath. They were wasting time. "I'm leaving Araveena."

"Ha! Right. Good luck with that." Arms crossed, Rathen snorted and pursed his lips.

"You can get someone else's help if you want to break Council rules. I like getting paid, thanks."

"Yeah? Then *you* can tell them why you passed up on the chance to haul in three of Faction Boss Rivane's men. One leadership, one defence, and one inside the slavery ring. All of them close to the top." Ress fisted his hands, his nails digging into his palms. "Shove the rules down my throat all you want, but I'll take my chances and violate the terms of my release. I don't have time to ask permission from Council. They'll have to wait until we get to safety. Otherwise, you can kiss this informant's ass goodbye and let the Shar keep taking citizen's lives, including someone who can give you loads of new information. *That's* what's at stake here. *That's* the life we need to save—someone who can help the cause. Someone we can't afford to lose. So you choose, hero. Help me help Council or leave me to rot."

"Always the damn clever ones," Rathen muttered. "I swear you do it so I'll never work again."

"Be the smart, clever one, then. Keep your job and rub the Shar's nose in it. You can talk your way out of punishment. Council can't afford to lose you, but I'm losing value as an informant. The Shar *knows* I'm helping Council, and they're out for blood. I'm not useful here, not anymore. Let me be useful somewhere else, even if I'm locked up."

Silent, Rathen watched Ress with a pensive gaze, his lips contorting and twitching. "This someone of yours must be special if you're willing to hang your bare ass out to be ripped off. Cota's got teeth and Severn's got claws—the rest of Council will let them to tear you apart."

"Then let them. I'm overdue, anyway."

"You're a fool," Rathen mumbled, "but a fool with a point." He covered his face with his hood. "Consider your letters delivered."

"Immediately. No delay."

"Yeah, yeah. I'll wake him and the boyfriend up and shove it in their sleepy faces."

"Thank you." Ress snuffed the candle before Rathen slipped out the door and closed it. Although he could not trust Rathen any more than he trusted Tash, he wanted to. He was reasonably certain neither would harm Adren. Tash was obligated to protect Adren; Rathen was obligated to arrest criminals and take them to their judgment, especially when they violated the nation. While no one needed to care about Ress, he believed they would see Adren as innocent. In drawing on their empathy for Adren's circumstances, he could take Adren to a safer place. He was no one's hero, but maybe he could be someone special to Adren.

Ress crept to the door and opened it slowly, casting a long look over the workroom. Metal gleamed in the white light. Crystals glistened. Leaves clung to windows above before dancing with the breeze, floating away with pieces of his memory. Half his life had been spent in the forge and the shop. They were his family's legacy, the pride of multiple generations. Every nook, every cranny, every flaw, every perfection—he knew all the details. He cherished the scent, the warmth, the silence.

And he was leaving it all.

With a sigh deep enough to hurl sadness into the pit of his stomach, he closed the door, his fingers lingering on the cool knob. Only two things offered him comfort: the fact that he was leaving the shop to Covran and Bremary, and the hope that in leaving, he could be loved by the one person he needed it from.

Here's to fighting for it. Win or lose, I did it for the right reason. Goddesses, grant us mercy, because no one else will.

CHAPTER ELEVEN

Would anyone show up, or would they ignore Ress's request for help?

Adren strolled through the market, eyeing the wares and merchants, waiting for something to go wrong. Tired from staying up all night, skeptical about Ress's plan, ce worried he was investing too much into an idea that would fail. Already late afternoon, they had yet to find out if Ress's letters had roused support. Sending the letter via bounty hunter was bad enough; expecting anyone to arrive the next night, willing to help, was ludicrous. The act was too rash, placing too much faith in people Adren could not trust, save Tash and perhaps Mayr, who acted liked they cared about cir.

Here's the chance to see how much they think of me. Adren crossed cir arms, pulling into cirself. Ce buried cir face in the cowl of cir shirt and drifted towards the outer edge of the village square. Attention straying to the windows of the metal shop, Adren glimpsed Bremary at the desk in the front. More than likely, Ress and Covran were in the back, working as though the day were not their last together. Doing what he loved was how Ress wanted to leave things, how he wanted to abandon Araveena Ford.

At least he has something else to do. The Shar's the only thing I've ever known. Where do I go from here? I don't do crafty things. I don't have any talent except for maybe asking too many questions and being mouthy. Even if we manage to get out of here, what do I do? Sit around and stare at people all day? Walk pretty and play snitch? I can't be a priest's pet. I won't be anyone's pet. 'We'll figure it out later,' he says. Yeah, that's great. He knows exactly who he is and what he can do. Meanwhile, I'm only part god. No pressure.

Ce needed more than later. Ce needed a finely detailed map and painfully exuberant guide to explain what a life without the Shardenn could be.

Part of Adren wished no one would respond to Ress's message with help. Doubt bludgeoned the parts of cir that wanted out. Ce did not want to be rescued and given refuge—and certainly not as though ce deserved it. Terrifying uncertainty waited on the other side of a rescue. Constant nightmares of danger plagued cir, mocking cir daydreams. What if ce failed? What if ce was an obvious fraud, only able to pretend to be civil and normal but never truly worthy of the rights and privileges granted to innocent citizens? Ress had earned a portion of those rights and privileges back, despite his affiliations.

All Adren had earned was a grimy cell and stale meals.

How could Tash stand doing this, being between two worlds? How did he leave the one and give himself over to the other? It was a conversation they would have again in the near future—and keep having, Adren sensed, assuming ce survived Ress's plan.

Adren's gaze crawled over the alleyways and road into the village square, pausing on the shadows and dark corners. Recognizing nothing out of the ordinary, ce sighed. Why had ce bothered to leave the house? Ce had told Ress ce was better off somewhere far from Araveena Ford. Not loitering in the square, searching for people who would never show.

One step from whirling around and fleeing down the alley towards the house, Adren cast a last look over the market.

Red, shimmering fabric with gold thread gleamed in the sunlight, a bolt of beauty draped over an arm covered in stark black sleeve and bracer. Hesitant but hopeful, Adren followed the curved limb towards the owner's face.

Mayr.

Somehow, he had crept into the market without cir noticing. He hovered beside a farmer's overflowing cart with a woman at his side, inspecting several bundled herbs. The woman wore a black cloak, hiding the rest of her clothes. A grey shawl covered most of the tight curls of her blonde hair, except for those around her pretty, unpainted face.

As though sensing Adren, Mayr turned his head in cir direction and lowered his chin. In a gradual slide of his gaze, he peered at Adren, his expression dark and firm. His arm rose to his chest, directing cir attention to the red fabric.

The next instant, he stepped around the furthest end of the cart and pulled the blonde woman with him, laughing as he snatched a handful of orange vegetables. Face brightening as he flicked his long braid over his shoulder, he avoided facing Adren's direction.

The display told Adren everything ce needed to know: he was there, as was Tash and whoever else they had persuaded to join them.

The plan was in play.

So am I. I can't believe we're going through with this. Ress is out of his mind, and his friends are just as far gone as he is. I'm running away with a bunch of fools.

Ce could do worse.

Because the choices aren't getting any better. Foolish men with the law on their side or vindictive criminals who'd gut me faster than they can say Father's name? At least the law-kissers are nice and give me a place to sleep.

Turning and walking slowly towards the messenger's shop at the opposite end of the village square, Adren reached into the pocket inside cir coat. The hard corners of the folded letter to Darus, Pade, and Amelin scraped cir fingertips, reminding cir to keep a steady pace and give nothing away. With each step, ce stole glances in different directions. Was Amelin there, watching and waiting for cir to act? Was Pade hiding behind a wall or curtained window, tracking cir movements?

Unable to take the chance, Adren carried onward, pretending to be lost in thought. When ce entered the messenger's shop, ce ignored the patrons standing and chattering at the side, papers and baskets in hand. The shop was small, its dark, black wood panels contrasted by bright green curtains and white banners with salutations in bright yellow paint. In the centre of the shop, four long wooden desks sat in a square, their corners buried by stacks of papers. Four pristinely dressed clerks sat inside the square, their backs to one another, each already serving a customer or ready to take another.

Adren approached the first clerk ce saw: a young woman with light brown hair, dark eyes, and a kind smile. She held out her hand, the bell sleeves of her yellow dress sweeping over the desk. "How can I help you?" the woman asked with a singsong tone.

"This needs to go to Hilarye." Adren placed the letter on the desk with one gold tenpin coin and two silver twicepins, more than enough to cover the expense without many questions.

"Immediately, and in-person, not left with a third party."

The clerk nodded, picking up the note with her left hand. She raised her right arm and snapped her fingers, gesturing to a lanky, dark-dressed man with a long, blond beard and grey cap standing in the corner to Adren's left. "We can handle it right now. This one just got in."

The man drew closer. Adren surveyed his dirt-covered boots, faded brown coat, and wrinkled pants and shirt. He took the letter from the clerk. "Who and where in Hilarye?"

"Surad Grey," Adren answered. "Herald's High Inn."

"Fitting, that." The messenger tipped his cap. "Consider it done." He snatched both twicepins from the desk. "Thanks for your patronage. I don't mind dining well tonight." The messenger grinned and hurried from the shop.

"I hate when he does that." The clerk smiled at Adren. "He'll get it there, don't you worry. Anything else I can do?"

"That's it."

"Lovely. Enjoy the rest of the day. I hear we're expecting a beautiful sunset."

"Thanks." Adren left the shop, battling the weight of deception. The clerk had been too happy for cir liking, too willing to participate in a lie she knew nothing about. *If this is doing the right thing, shouldn't I feel better?*

It was too late to question what they were doing. Ce had committed to luring cir father's men into a trap. The letter said everything they wanted to hear, the intention clear between the vague terms: ce would kill Ress that night, and when the deed was done, ce would meet Darus, Pade, and Amelin to prove it. As far as they needed to know, everything they wanted for the Shar-denn would come to pass by dawn.

A dawn Adren dreaded with every breath ce had.

The only way out is dead.

"You can do this. You *have* to do this." In the darkness of the chilled bedroom, Ress leaned forward on the bed and gripped Adren's shoulders, his whispers barely audible. "Kill me, Adren. We're past midnight. Kill me and it'll be over."

Then we'll begin.

Adren moved away. Ress could not be all over cir, not while ce wanted to punch something to numb the pain inside. Every thought buried cir pride deeper. Every memory screamed at cir betrayal. There would be no going back, no way to face cir parents without shame.

Because I'm about to tear into their hearts with a blunt axe.

A necessary death, a small voice reminded cir, a soothing whisper behind the chaos. *Embrace death and step through the mirror of judgment to birth life. Blood remains thicker than the water in lies.*

Especially blood birthed from the divine.

The Shar-denn could not control cir any longer. Ce needed to learn whose blood ce shared. Ce wanted more than simply following orders and rules—and certainly more than just shutting cir mouth and keeping quiet, unable to question any of it. Although the need to save cir parents and brothers had not lessened, ce needed a new way, a new set of rules. The thought of their demise in a dank cell made cir sick, but ce could not save them their way, breaking the laws and condemning cirself to the life they had chosen for cir. If ce wanted to be seen as more than a common criminal, ce had to treat cirself as more first. The rescue would have to wait.

"Fine." Adren pushed Ress until he lay on the bed, cir gloved hand flattened on his chest. His heart beat strong as he grinned. "You're dead. Now stay down or I'll kill you for real." Ce rolled from the bed and smoothed cir dress and long coat. With one hand, Adren mussed cir hair, the red strands loosely tied back with black ribbon. Never had ce felt more and less like cirself. In every aspect of cir life, ce was caught between sides, each choice offering a vast difference from the next. Inside, every part of cir pushed hard and pulled taut, strangling from the core.

The road to having peace was choosing only one. One life, one self, one chance.

Adren grabbed the thick white candle from the bedside table and rushed from the room. Steps light, ce crossed through the sitting room to the front entryway. Cir skin crawled with the sensation of gazes clinging to cir from between cracks in the doorways. Whispers floated on the darkness, a floorboard creaking as ce opened one door. Past the cold air weighted by white puffs of cir breath, ce saw only the moonlit houses across the road and plants swaying in modest gardens. Ce held the candle at arm's length, far enough that anyone on the road could see it. Gradually ce set the candle on the top porch step and turned back into the house, closing the door.

The first step in the plan was complete. The unlit candle stated cir intention to follow through on Ress's demise. After the display, Darus, Pade, and Amelin would be waiting to meet Adren at the house.

With proof.

Cir stomach churned, cir gaze on the black metal chest beside the kitchen hearth. By the time ce had returned from the market, the chest had been on the table, left by one of the bounty hunters. Aware of what the chest contained, ce had avoided the kitchen until Ress returned from the shop.

You can't avoid it now. If you don't take it, they won't believe you hurt him and the whole thing falls apart. They'll only come inside if they think he's dead.

Ce returned to Ress's bedroom and kneeled on the bed. "Slash, slash, slash," Adren whispered, brushing a quick kiss across his lips. "I'm killing you in your sleep—a knife to the throat so you can't scream for help. Then I'm going to take your arm and make you bleed out even faster."

"Damn, that's going to hurt." Ress clutched cir head with both hands and coaxed a slower, deeper kiss from Adren. His lips lingered as he eased back, his fingers sliding around the back of cir neck. "Try not to make a huge mess. I actually like this place."

"Stay dead while I finish hacking you apart and I'll give it real consideration."

"Please don't hold this over my head for the rest of my life."

"Quit it. You're not funny." Adren pushed up from the bed. Gruesome and inappropriate, his humour was one of the only things making the situation bearable. If he was joking around, he still cared. If he was stealing kisses, he still wanted cir.

Hold onto that, Adren told cirself on the way to the kitchen hearth. *Freedom is good, but sharing it with someone who gives a damn is better.*

Sucking in a breath, ce unlatched the metal chest and flipped the lid. The thick stench of blood filled the air, worsened by the weight of death surrounding the severed limb inside. Wrapped in three layers of blood-soaked linens lay a man's left forearm and hand, cut from the elbow, still encased in a shirt sleeve. A dead man's leftovers, Ress had assured cir, taken from a prisoner's corpse.

Adren covered cir nose with cir arm, nose crinkled. If fate was kind, it would give cir a life away from dead bodies. Withstanding them was never easy. Ce would rather be surrounded by life than dallying with death.

To get there, ce would have to ensure morbid circumstances worked in their favour. The severed limb already bore the Shar-denn skull and fist symbol, the tattoo a close match to Ress's, due to the diligence of the bounty hunters. All ce had to do was show the limb to Darus, Amelin, and Pade and convince them it was real enough to entice them into the house.

"Time to go." Adren removed the linens and arm before slamming the chest shut and returning to the front doors. The blood was wet, its original moisture sustained by the watered down red dye Ress had added. Even through the thin leather of cir gloves, ce felt heat emanating from the skin from the fire they had kept going after dinner and the heat trapped inside the chest afterwards. Although not perfect in recreation, it would be enough. It had to be.

Ignoring the raspy whispers muffled by doors and the cloaked body creeping along the wall of the sitting room, Adren slipped onto the porch and closed the door tight. Ce laid the limb on the porch along the edge, beside the railing post left of the steps. After picking up the candle and holding it high as though inspecting it, Adren sat in the wicker rocking chair in the middle of the porch with the candle beside cir. Ce did not move. Ce barely breathed, listening for sounds that did not belong. The other houses were dark inside, seeming so devoid of life, closed doors keeping the inhabitants safer than they realized. Leaves fluttered across the ground, dancing around wilted plants. Beside cir, the window shutters sparkled like silver stars on a vibrant blue ocean.

Only the three shadowy figures walking up the road ruined the tranquility. Keeping close to the gates and railings of the house lots, they moved together as one unit with little space between them.

Once they reached the house directly across the road, the figures turned abruptly and continued towards Adren. They passed under the silver archway, rustling the leaves of the vines. None of their skin was visible, hidden under hoods, gloves, and long coats with the collars up over their scarves.

"It's done, then?" the first figure asked gruffly, ascending the porch steps. The others stopped on the bottom step. When he tugged back his hood to reveal his eyes, Darus glared at Adren. "You indicated there'd be proof."

Adren gestured to the bloody linens. "Dead men don't need arms."

Darus leaned down and peeled back the linens. "Took the one with the mark, did you?" He shuffled aside to allow Pade and Amelin around the porch railing.

"Dead traitors don't need brandings."

"Especially when they didn't honour them in life." Darus flipped the linens over the limb. "Welcome to the new day, kids. We're down one nasty piece of trouble." His gaze returned to Adren. "We're good?"

"We're good." Adren stood. "Now that I've kept *my* end, can we *please* get the rest of his rubbish and get out of here?" Ce jutted cir thumb towards the house. "Let's go in and grab the good stuff. There's not much, but some of it might fetch something. And wouldn't you know," ce said with a smirk, "he carries the keys to his shop everywhere he goes. Just begging to be mugged."

"Why, little sister," Amelin said, almost breathless, "are you suggesting we *raid* something?" He snickered. "It starts with pillaging, ends with riches. Finally seeing that bit of your father in you."

Darus grunted. "We can discuss it later. In the meantime, grab the goods, grab the key, grab the body. We leave tonight. The closest cache house is ready for us. I'd rather not waste their time or ours, especially since we need to figure out who's getting first call on the corpse. I'd say our new boss, but rumours say there's still a blood match waiting to happen, so we're staying solo for now."

"Until Rivane gets out," Pade corrected. "Then it'll be all-out war on whoever's stupid enough to take his place."

"Shall we continue nattering like children or are we going?" Adren pushed past Darus and opened both front doors. "Less talk, more do." Ce stepped over the threshold, glowering at them. "Or are you getting useless without someone giving you orders?"

"Watch yourself," Darus warned, following Adren inside. "You're a long way from earning the right to use that lip."

"Still an infant," Pade muttered from beside Darus. "Fetch a rattle, Ame."

Adren ventured into the sitting room, holding cir head high. Shadows filled spaces where there had been nothing before. "Great. Give me something I can shove down your throat and shut you up." Ce stopped between the settees and peered over cir shoulder, glimpsing bodies behind the doors. "Close the damn door while you're at it. We're not inviting the neighbours."

"Bossy infant." Amelin laughed and closed both doors behind him. "Just when you think they're grown—"

He gasped, choking on his words, struggling against the arm wrapped around his throat.

"Should've fetched the damn rattle," Mayr murmured, his voice carrying over the slapping noise of Amelin fighting back.

Boots scuffed the floor. Shadows launched from the corners, reaching, grabbing, barreling into Darus and Pade as they scrambled. Cursing and shouting, Darus and Pade battled the fists pummeling them to the ground. They lunged and kicked, biting and punching anything they could reach. For every hand they assaulted, another took its place, forcing them to their knees.

"Go on, keep snarling," a woman yelled, ripping off Darus's scarf: Kirra, the blonde Adren had seen in the market with Mayr, now dressed in a leather long coat. She pulled the scarf taut, the ends coiled tight around her hands. "Get it out before we get you in cuffs. I like my prisoners *silent*."

"Come on, be honest: that's how you like your men." The soldier beside Kirra laughed and jerked Darus's head back by the hair, her other hand beckoning for the scarf. "Give it over. I'll gag him. That'll make it real silent. Shove it so far, he won't bother anyone again."

"And that's overkill, not justice."

Tash's voice silenced the fray. The hiss of a match sounded and a yellow glow filled Ress's bedroom. Tash entered the doorway, the elegance of his vestments and dark red long coat with flared sleeves a stark contrast to the ugly scene around them.

As everyone paused to stare at Tash, Ress stepped out from behind him, carrying a small metal lamp. Dressed to travel, Ress's brown long coat dusted the tips of his shin-high boots and hung open, revealing the gold tips of the knives in his boots. Two Shar-denn knives: one his and the other that of the faction boss who had conscripted him.

Adren gazed at the others in the room. Mayr's arm remained around Amelin's throat as he dragged him into the kitchen. The more Amelin struggled and resisted, Mayr's grip tightened with added pressure from his other arm. Amelin's face was deep red, his eyelids drooping as the rest of his body weakened.

Near the kitchen table, Darus and Pade were surrounded. On their knees with their hands locked behind their heads, they were held in place by Kirra, Rathen, two Kattal soldiers dressed in heavy green tunics and dark pants, and four guards in dark clothes that had come with Mayr and Tash.

Rathen twisted Pade's wrists down and yanked him up. "We wouldn't want to piss all over justice, would we?" One of the soldiers offered him a pair of thick metal cuffs connected by a short chain. "Come on. You're going to see daddy Rivane again, all nice and cozy in a private prison cell. You should be *thrilled*." He snatched the cuffs and jammed Pade's hands through them. Pade grimaced and growled, fighting the cuffs until Rathen punched his forearm and twisted harder.

"Up yours." Darus spat at Rathen's feet, twisting as a guard clamped cuffs around his wrists.

Smirking, Rathen squeezed Pade's cuffs closed. "You're nowhere near pretty enough to be anywhere *near* my ass. Try another orifice."

"I think it's time to be leaving," Ress said, moving to Adren's side. Tash took the lamp from Ress and placed it on the table. "Everyone has things under control here?"

Mayr kicked Amelin's knees out from under him and slammed Amelin to the ground, ramming Amelin's face to the floor and breaking his nose. He dug his heel into the back of Amelin's neck, shifting his weight onto Amelin's spine. Two guards scurried to cuff Amelin. "Absolutely. Go." His attention shifted to Tash, his features softening with an uneasy smile. "Be careful, and be quick. May the Goddesses protect you."

Ress took Adren's hand and led cir towards the front doors as Tash followed close behind. Everything they needed was already in the carriage waiting for them in the village square. They had packed only what they required. Most of the additional pieces were small items from Ress's family he could not part with. They would return and reclaim the rest of his possessions later, once they had a permanent place to live. Though when that would be, neither Adren nor Ress knew. Even if they found a home in a remote corner of the republic, they would never be safe.

Adren clutched Ress's fingers tighter. Those worries were for after dawn, when they were safe within the walls of the Temple of the Four.

"We'll run, fast as we can. Don't stop until you're in the carriage." Ress grabbed the door handle and kissed Adren's cheek. "Then I vote we take a nap. It's going to be a long ride."

"Even longer the more you stall," Tash murmured.

"Fine." Ress rolled his eyes and opened the door. "We're going, Your Holy Impatientness."

"Or not," a raspy voice said.

A fist punched through the doorway, aimed at Ress's face.

Ress's head snapped back, his jaw taking the hit. He stumbled, knocking into Adren as Tash yanked cir aside.

Growling, Adren pulled the knife from the sheath at cir thigh, ready to stab the men standing on the porch. At least two, from what ce could tell. The man in front of Ress was tall and muscular, covered by long coat and cloak. Dark hair fell around his shoulders in tight curls, framing the skull fragments tattooed on his face. Beside him, kicking open the second door, was a shorter, broader man with similar curly hair, the daggers tattooed around his neck signifying a dozen years of service to the Shardenn.

Savo and Simar, Adren recalled, the oldest of the family of five brothers who worked for Darus. Men ce rarely saw outside the times they had accompanied cir brothers to faction meetings.

"Thought we'd say hello." Simar seized Ress's coat collar and hauled him outside. Whirling, he threw Ress against the porch railing.

Wood cracked and splintered, splitting under Ress's back. He tumbled onto the porch, boards creaking under the sudden force.

Before Ress could get his footing, Simar threw punches into Ress's face, hoisting him up by the shirt to keep him in place. "That's—" Simar punched Ress's jaw. "—for being—" A punch to Ress's right eye. "—a snitch."

One hard shot to the throat forced Ress to slump back. The back of his head hit the porch.

"Ass!" Adren shot forward, knife brandished at Savo's grinning face.

Tash jerked cir back before ce crossed the threshold, dragging cir against him. "Don't!"

Savo stepped inside, filling the doorway. The side door near the bedrooms burst open, hinges squealing in protest. More than a dozen men charged into the kitchen with weapons, hollering and jabbing at the soldiers scrambling from the kitchen table, drawing their swords.

Laughter filled the house, bringing the chaos to a standstill. Darus leaned against the table, his cuffs and chain rattling with the shaking of his body. "We decided we'd bring friends, make this a party." He threw an amused glance at Adren. "You can't set traps worth my spit. Stop trying. While you're at it, stop breathing."

With his nod, chaos erupted again. Darus hopped onto the table and kicked Rathen with both feet, shoving him away from Pade. Kirra punched Pade in the neck as he fumbled to stay upright. The soldiers and guards lunged at the Shar-denn assailants, swords striking, hitting anything they could. Bodies tumbled and collided in a blurred melee to the sound of shouts and growls.

Knife in hand, Mayr rushed Savo. Dodging Savo's fist, he sank to the ground to stab Savo's thigh. "Go!" He motioned at Tash before jumping up, spinning around, and elbowing Savo in the chest. When Savo groaned and wrapped his arms tight around Mayr, Mayr stamped Savo's foot and pulled hard, wrenching Savo's body to the side and down. They toppled to the floor together, clearing the doorway.

Grip tight around cir hand, Tash hurried Adren onto the porch. Simar and Ress wrestled to their left, rolling over the damaged boards, exchanging punches to their bloody faces and ribs. Three dark figures in cloaks trampled the gardens, hurrying through the yard and up the porch steps.

"Stay." Tash shoved Adren to the right.

Ce tripped over the clay flower pots in the dark corner. Crashing into the post joining the railings, Adren smashed cir wrist on the house, knocking the knife from cir hand.

Adren scrambled and ducked, grabbing the knife before it fell through the crack between the porch and house. Ce clambered back, avoiding the feet threatening to crush cir fingers in Tash's scuffle with the assailants. Weight shifted and broad shoulders lowered, Tash struck one man and then another, punching their throats and battering their exposed torsos. As one lunged at him, Tash bent down and rammed his shoulder into the attacker's gut, pushing him back. The assailant fell over Simar and Ress then sprawled across the porch with Tash's veil in his hand.

His partner stunned, the second man yanked Tash up and drove his fist towards Tash's jaw.

The next instant, the attacker's arm was twisted behind his back with Tash forcing it higher. Tash dragged the man to the porch steps and threw him onto the pathway, sending him rolling through the flattened garden.

From inside the house, voices yelled insults and hollered for help. Swords skittered across the floor. Limbs snapped, furniture crashed, glass shattered. Darus squirmed under Rathen's weight, struggling to escape the fists pounding his face. Kirra smashed a chair over Pade's head, two of the legs flying in opposite directions as the back cracked. Mayr kneeled on Savo's back, trying to cuff Savo's hands with bloody fingers, forcing Savo's thumbs back and twisting his wrists until he complied. Bodies moved too quickly to get an accurate count.

Outside, Tash hauled Ress up by both arms. Both of them kicked Simar, sending him reeling towards the other end of the porch. The man who had ripped off Tash's veil stood, the fabric easily forgotten as he tossed the tattered veil into the garden. He charged, snarling as he reached for Tash.

Stepping aside, Tash turned and snapped his arm back. His upper arm struck his attacker's neck, an awkward blow to the throat that stole the man's breath and sent him back, choking.

The assailant hit the house and collapsed, frantically grappling the wall to pull himself up.

"If you have *any* measure of intelligence, you'll stay where I put you." Tash grasped the man's chin, forcing him to look up. "Stay. Down." He shoved the man aside before steadying Ress against the doorframe.

Blood flowed from Ress's nose, down his split lips, and dripped onto his ruined clothes. Light illuminated Tash's bleeding knuckles as he tore the hem from one of his robes and offered it to Ress to wipe his face. Tash tore the hems from his other robes and wrapped them around his knuckles, flexing his fingers with a grimace.

I was supposed to run with them. I was supposed to leave. Adren glanced inside the house. Bodies toppled over, adding to the piles of limp forms already on the floor. While everyone was immersed in the fight, ce could have jumped over the porch railing and fled for the carriage. *Instead, I'm standing here, useless and lost while a priest takes all the hits. This isn't right. I'm supposed to be fighting, not letting some priest dictate what I don't do.*

Eyes narrowed, jaws clenched, Adren glanced at the houses across the road. People stood on their porches, lamps in hand, gaping at the commotion.

Great, just what we need.

Adren sheathed cir knife. "We should—"

Simar jumped up, yelling as he staggered across the porch and launched at Tash. The moment he dragged Tash down and rolled towards Adren, two of the other assailants charged Ress. They grabbed him by the coat and threw him onto the porch. Grips heavy on his shoulders, they forced Ress to his knees, ramming his injured knee into the splintered boards.

"One last thing—" One of the men hissed, jerking a knife from his belt. Ress squirmed as the man snatched his wrist and slashed Ress's sleeves. Peeling back the fabric, he held Ress's arm towards the moon. "You can't have this."

The blade sliced through Ress's forearm, slashing the skull tattoo. Blood overwhelmed the fissure, streaming down his skin and pooling on his knees. Ress pulled and pushed, yelling his pain and choking.

Heat surged through Adren's skin, scorching the last of cir willingness to be peaceful and compliant. Anger blazed in cir core, whirling in an erratic dance with rage, caged by screams for retribution. *Enough!*

Every promise ce had made the Shar-denn crumbled inside cir soul, the warped pieces scattering and falling into the void between cir loyalties. Oaths once sealed with absolute trust were undone, rendered irretrievable and irreplaceable, never to be whole again. *This is the choice I have to make. The one I can't take back.*

Between the Shar-denn's illusion of safety and Ress's life, ce chose life.

Ce was done with the lies.

Adren forced out cir breath until none was left, pushing against the tortuous instinct to inhale. Ce slipped into the doorway, hands raised, palms out, ready to take. Eyes squeezed shut, ce listened past Ress's screams and weakened protests of the others still fighting, focusing on the murky whispers on the other side of the violence. Voices ce felt more than heard, their words translated through cir magic, not cir mind. Energy raced through every vein, danced around every nerve, giddy and greedy, feeding on promises of liberty. Intention tugged and tightened, melding need, want, and hope into the single ball of bright white flame growing in the centre of cir mind. Silence played tag with the darkness within, pulling time into cir like an old friend.

There was no one else, nothing else. Just cir and the threat of destruction, stealing what was precious.

Fingers twisting, body tingling with agony between an invisible shroud of fire and a chill bouncing around cir insides, Adren thought only of the Shar-denn members. Their faces and anger filled cir mind as ce toyed with the air, teasing out the feel of them, pulling on the weight of their vengeance and coiling it around cir hands. Deafened to the noise of the fight, ce heard their hearts beating, a chorus pulsing deep in cir mind. Wispy shadows of their spirits danced around cir, heavy and blackened, shrouded in waste and lies. Ce could almost reach out and stroke their icy limbs, aching to welcome them into a new trap.

A divine trap coated in the thick honey of justice, so much sweeter than the simplicity of revenge.

The Shar-denn would fall.

Tugging on the air, Adren fingered the strands leading to each of the Shar-denn fighters, playing the threads of their spirits like shattering, out-of-tune instruments. Ce tasted the bitterness of their crimes, the unsavoury truth blistering beneath cir skin. The pain they had exacted on innocent people tasted sour, gritty on cir tongue and greasy to the soul. The blood they had spilled was metallic and rough, difficult to swallow, drowning cir in the flood of their hate. Ce choked on the stench of their greed and disdain.

Justice be done.

Eyes opening wide, Adren lowered cir head, clenching cir fists. *Your waking moments are mine; your darkness is yours. Justice is served.*

Yanking cir hands inwards, Adren crossed cir arms, bringing the heavy air down.

With it, the remaining Shar-denn members, their bodies collapsing into motionless heaps.

No one moved. Lost to confusion, the conscious struggled to catch their breaths.

"What in the Four's gods-damned sanity was that?" Rathen stumbled, pushing up from the floor beside Pade. He scowled at Adren before helping Kirra to her feet.

"Your chance to get them and go." Adren breathed out, relieved to see the men lying on the porch near Ress. "They shouldn't be dead, only unconscious. I don't know for how long, so move quickly." Cir glance skipped over the porch to Tash, lying in the corner under Simar. "I've never done that before," ce said quietly, holding Tash's sympathetic gaze as he pushed Simar off and stood. "I don't know if…"

Exhaustion swept over cir. Knees buckling, Adren reached for the doorframe.

Mayr hurried to catch cir. "Got you," he murmured, hoisting Adren up with his arm behind cir back.

"I wanted to get them off him."

"I know." Mayr shifted Adren's weight, guiding cir arm around his neck. "Think about it later. Right now, you've got a carriage to catch. Come on." He looked over his shoulder at Rathen. "You get the rest cuffed. I'll get the cart and be back to help with the wounds."

"Divide and conquer. I like it." Kirra huffed, blowing hair out of her eyes before caressing her scraped cheek. "Mind if I kick a few for fun?"

"Don't care."

"Whatever would Steward Dahe say?"

"'Kick them for me.'" Mayr snorted, guiding Adren onto the porch. "I still don't care."

"Just checking," Kirra called, "since you're the only legal bureaucratic proxy here. It's your fault if I mess it up."

"So don't mess it up. And next time you call me bureaucratic, I'm going to kick your ass," Mayr threatened before he sat Adren on the steps and straightened. "*No one* calls me a bureaucrat. It makes me cry." He turned towards Ress and kneeled, placing his hand over Ress's as Ress clutched his wounded forearm.

Tash rushed into the house. A moment later, he returned with towels. "Here," he said, sinking to his knees, wincing as he bumped into Ress. "Only until I find needle and thread." He pried Ress's hand away and wrapped the towels around his forearm. Blood soaked the layers of yellow linen.

"Storage room," Ress said through clenched teeth, cradling his arm to his chest. "Wood box, green ribbon around the handle. Last case to the left, second shelf."

As Tash rose, Mayr eased him back down. "I'll get it. Stay here." After a scowl at the limp bodies lying around them and a glare at Tash, Mayr disappeared into the house.

"So, brother," Ress mumbled, "how much do you love me?"

Pressing harder on Ress's wound, Tash tilted his head. "Why?"

"What are the odds I could get you to knock me out?"

"Slim."

"Damn you."

"No, curse me. Damning means I still have some sort of redemption at the Goddesses' discretion. Curses can last forever, goddesses or no, and they're messier."

"Double damn you." Ress hissed and curled his body, only to groan and struggle into a new position. "I forgot how much this hurts."

Adren felt cir heart sink. *All of this is my fault. If I'd never come...*

Ce would never know what ce was or have the chance to see through the cage the Shar-denn had built around cir. They wanted cir to believe they were everything ce needed and could ever have. They had convinced cir the gang's side was the only side worth fighting for, even if ce was never truly happy or fully cirself.

Who was wrong or right was not the issue weighing most on cir—where ce belonged was. All the questions that had plagued cir since childhood, all the worries ce was too different to belong, could finally find a place to rest.

Meanwhile, tonight could've killed the people with the answers.

Then give back a piece of life, a small voice told cir, gentle like a breeze. The voice of a Goddess:

warm on the inside, determined on the outside, as liquid as the soothing energy flowing through Adren's body.

"Here, let me." Adren crawled onto the porch beside Ress and coaxed him into surrendering his arm. Clasping his hand, ce willed the lukewarm sensation through cir fingers. Thick waves cascaded through cir and washed over him in a faint glimmer of silver light, ebbing and flowing between them. His pain trickled into cir, weaving its way up Adren in a web until dissipating near cir heart. Ce imagined his skin as it was before, and as ce concentrated on images of a knife moving in reverse, ce pushed against time as the knife retracted from him, tugging on the threads of the past to weave a new reality.

Once the pain subsided, Adren unwound the towels and stroked Ress's forearm. The skin was red and raw. A misshapen scar split the skull in two, but the wound no longer bled.

"I'm sorry it isn't fully healed, and I don't think I can fix much else. I'm too tired," Adren muttered, cir head swimming. Exhaustion overtook cir again. Behind cir, Mayr returned with the box and a lit candle. To cir relief, he set both down without asking questions. "It's good enough for us to get going."

Save for the rare occasions as a child, ce had never healed someone else. Those early attempts had resulted in cir being chastised for helping, partly because cir family valued independence and challenge, and partly because they worried ce would be discovered. Cir experience at healing had ended with cirself, isolated to cuts that were too stubborn to heal quickly.

Tash gripped Adren's fingers. "It's more than anyone could have asked, but you're right: we need to leave." With Mayr's help, he pulled Ress up. "As fast as we can manage."

Mayr offered Adren his hand, but ce pushed him away and stood on cir own. Ce needed to stay strong. That much ce would take from cir family, no matter which side of the law they were on.

"You two go ahead." Tash drew Ress's uninjured arm around his shoulders and held him close as they descended the steps. "We'll meet you there."

Mayr followed them with Adren. He grunted and kicked a stone off the path. "Not going to happen."

"Mayr—"

"No. The last time I sent you off by yourself, you handed out beatings on a porch. So give it up. The answer's no."

Sighing, Tash guided Ress to the road. They both limped, though Ress's damaged leg showed the most distress. Despite their injuries, they hobbled up the empty road quicker than Adren expected, flanked by Mayr as Adren drifted to Ress's side. Although they passed people who stood outside of their homes, no one offered to assist. Instead, the onlookers stepped back towards their houses and kept silent. Not that ce expected any different or wanted more.

Their trek through the alley towards the village square was just as uneventful. When they exited and moved around the merchant carts, Adren recognized Covran standing at the dais in the centre of the quiet square. A cloak and hood hid most of him, but the moonlight illuminated his face. Beside him waited an older man who resembled Tash in build and the way his wavy hair hung loose around his shoulders, his body hidden by a cloak. Tash's father, ce assumed.

They were not alone. Next to the flagpole sat a closed carriage, simple and small with unmarked doors and a team of four dark horses. Two cloaked guards sat up front, one with the reins in his hands, while two guards waited on horses beside the carriage. A large, open cart waited beside the carriage, hooked up to a team of six horses. Empty except for the straw inside, the cart and the four Kattal soldiers with it were ready to take the gang members to see the High Council.

"You look like you've been on the wrong end of something." Covran hopped off the dais on their approach, reaching for Ress. "Making friends again?" He slipped between Ress and

Adren, leaning to lift Ress's arm around his shoulders and help him to the carriage.

"You know me. Can't stop people from making my face pretty." Ress winced and bit back a cry as they stopped at the carriage. "Just wish they'd learn to do it with pillows."

"Get to the temple and I'm sure they'll have all the pillows you could ever need," Tash's father said, opening the carriage door wide.

"A room full." Tash assisted Ress up the two narrow steps and into the carriage, pushing from behind. "I'll barter away a week's worth of my prayer meals for all the softest ones if it'll stop you from doing something foolish."

Ress shuffled to the end of the cushioned seat facing the horses. "And stop giving you competition? Where's the fun in that?"

"Adren, would you?" Tash motioned to Ress. "It's been a long time since we shared a carriage. I might be tempted to forget all vows and pitch him out the window."

Adren climbed into the carriage beside Ress. Large enough for four people to sit upright without bumping knees, the inside of the carriage was simple like the outside. The curtains on the small windows were closed, and the dark cushions were smooth and soft, though not comfortable enough to sleep on for an extended period of time.

When Adren clasped Ress's hand, he squeezed gently and lifted their fingers onto his shaking knee. "I'm sorry," ce murmured.

"For what?" Pain scrawled across Ress's face. "It wasn't your fault they weren't clueless. Or that I wasn't smart enough to think that far."

"I know. It's just…" Adren sighed. *Complicated. It's just complicated. None of this has gone the way it was planned.*

Ce glanced at Tash, catching him in a tender kiss with Mayr. Tearing cir gaze away, Adren focused on the door hinges. *Let's add that to the list of things I never want to do again: nearly getting a priest killed. Guess he wasn't joking when he said they're supposed to protect people like me. I think we might have to set some boundaries.*

The carriage creaked and swayed as Tash climbed in and sat opposite Ress. "No more dallying. Sister Kee and Brother Armamae are waiting for us."

"Get there safe. *No. More. Hitting.*" Mayr closed the door partially and leaned against it. "I'll come to the temple once we're done with Council. Be there. *All* of you." He closed the door completely, plunging them into darkness, save for a sliver of light between the curtains.

"Can't say I'll be able to go anywhere else." When the carriage rolled forward, jolting back and forth, Ress cursed, holding his ribs. "I think those asses beat everything that holds everything else in me together. How good are your healers?"

"Better than the two of us deserve," Tash said softly. "You two should rest before then. We'll arrive in Dahena around sunrise. There's plenty of time to close your eyes and prepare for what's to come. I'm afraid sanctuary might require vast effort on your part, both in adapting to change and exercising tolerance." He touched Adren's knee. "It's best to sleep now. I'll keep watch."

"Hero," Ress muttered, shifting further into the corner as the carriage wheels assumed a smooth rhythm. Curling his arm around Adren's shoulders, he pulled cir in and rested his chin on cir head. "All hail the glory that's carriage sleep."

Settled against him, ce listened quietly as his short, ragged breaths became longer and deeper. Adren considered the multitude of changes that would bury them: a temporary home, potentially dangerous strangers, new expectations, and not a single guarantee—not even where the two of them were concerned. But Ress spoke of trust, hope, and a future. Everything ce lacked in the Shar-denn. If the words were not enough to bait cir emotions and desire, the fact he was fleeing Araveena Ford with cir said everything cir heart wanted to hear. The risks were high, his life in danger, and yet he had the courage to run to protect cir.

In return, he made no demands and took nothing by force. He gave what Adren had only wished of having, seeing who ce truly was.

For once, ce was in the right place at the right time with the right people, doing the right thing.

How many years had ce spent at odds with cirself? How many times had ce poked the beast within, seeing the fragmented realities of what ce was and who ce could never be? How long had it taken before ce accepted the lie that the Shar-denn was the only home ce needed?

All at the expense of losing myself to them. And I didn't even like it, not even a little. I only pretended I did, so good I convinced myself. Now I can start again and build new realities. Or live the ones I really want, with at least one person who believes in me. Someone who doesn't see me as just one thing or another, but recognizes the whole. Someone who doesn't tell me to change. He hasn't even asked. Not once. No matter the day, he sees me. No matter what I'm capable of, he's with me. Never asks me to be something else. Only asks me to stay.

Adren peered through the crack between the curtains, watching blurred shapes pass by. For most of cir life, ce had been forced to define cirself. Never had ce liked the options, always at the mercy of limitation and someone else's opinion of what ce should be. Ce was a mix of dichotomies, unable to choose one or the other, or to walk the fine line between.

Before Ress, ce had struggled with the fight for balance within cirself and who ce was for others. The days ce had belonged to the Shar-denn outnumbered the days ce belonged to cirself. Cir family had demanded ce do things that battled who ce was inside, drawing out the identity they wanted and pushing the rest aside.

Those days were over.

Whatever happened, ce had made cir choice and Ress had made his, linking their futures. The Shar-denn could not have either of them. They belonged to themselves. They belonged to each other. Anything else was settling for less.

Never again.

Closing cir eyes, Adren's thoughts drifted towards the calm voices in cir mind, singsong and soothing. It felt like going home. Loving, carefree, happy—everything ce wanted to be.

On the other side of sunrise, a new life awaited.

CHAPTER TWELVE

His freedom could end any moment, going out in a flash of darkness.

Ress bit down against a groan and shifted his weight, leaning harder on his cane. *Chairs. Would it kill Council to get some measly chairs? I'll damn well stand before them in there, but honestly, right now...*

Every part of him hurt, even after the attention from the healers in the temple. Their kindness had poked and prodded him since his arrival in Dahena four days ago, drowning him in the heady scent of ointments and repugnant herbs to kill the pain. The bandages around his ribs and his salve-slathered forearm were nothing compared to the tight brace around his inflamed knee. After being rammed into the porch, his knee had twisted and caught the boards wrong, forcing the joint out of alignment. Wish as he may for it to heal quickly and completely, his future included more sitting and a reduction in heroic antics. Even Adren's attempts at healing him had met their match, failing to produce anything but frustration.

The wait in the High Council Hall did not improve matters. While he appreciated the High Council waiting four days before summoning him and Adren, the worst part was standing in the antechamber to Council Chambers, staring at the massive, elaborately carved doors and wondering what judgment waited on the other side. None of them were there for a simple meeting. This was a hearing, a chance for the High Council to punish Ress and Adren for crimes against the republic.

There was no bandage or ointment for the wounds High Council would inflict.

Shuffling back from Tash and Adren, Ress glanced around the entrance hall. The room was as open and sumptuous as the rest of the building. Sunlight passed through the glass mosaic of the high ceiling, bathing the white and grey marble walls with a many-coloured tinge, blending greens and mauves with blues and pinks. Large paintings of Kattal's landscape and historic ships adorned the walls, the bronze frames mounted above long beds of green ferns and creeping vines. Dried red and yellow petals lay scattered across the garden beds as though they had not merely wilted and fallen from the bare red plants between the ferns. Someone carefully tended the gardens, balancing natural processes with controlling behaviour.

Then again, that's the dirty truth of us all. Ress's gaze fell on Rathen, Kirra, and Mayr. They stood off to the side of the room with their arms crossed as they eyed the doors. From what he understood, they had already received a verbal lashing for their actions in Araveena Ford. Though the matter was not yet finished—the councilmen could always extend their displeasure into a formal castigation.

He turned away, guilt gnawing on his sympathy. They could have refused to help him and saved themselves. Instead, they had incurred their own injuries and pushed the rules on consorting with criminals. Bruised on the inside and out, their easy tones and playful glances were stowed away. The hearing was as much a judgment of them as it was of Ress and Adren.

Then there's Priestess Kee. Ress watched the black-haired priestess pace around the room. Her red robes trailed along the floor as she passed Mayr, Rathen, and Kirra before making her way towards Ress, Adren, and Tash. Kee was silent, her hands clasped before her, a pristine veil draped perfectly over her head. Steady and composed, her dark eyes revealed nothing of her thoughts. Since taking refuge in the temple she managed as their chosen Overseer, Ress had confessed all of his transgressions to her.

His admission had taken almost an entire day, almost as long as Adren's.

The disclosure made him feel no better, though it had secured his refuge in the temple. Tash swore Kee's declaration of mercy at that morning's prayer circle was trustworthy. When Kee granted amnesty, Tash had insisted, it was not done lightly nor was it flimsy. For however long they remained in the temple and abided by the priests' rules, they were untouchable.

From what Ress saw, he did not doubt Kee could withstand the fight to keep the amnesty intact. In her mid-fifties, Kee's staunch bearing was complemented by stubbornness in her tone. Other priests revered her for upholding their ideals with solemn devotion.

He could imagine what that loyalty looked like against the High Council.

We might be going in with scrapes and bruises, but who knows who'll lose limbs in there. Ress smirked, entertained by the fanciful images his mind tossed out. It was the only thing truly funny about the situation; the only amusement he could hold onto. Otherwise there was nothing stopping his hope from surrendering.

He owed people more than that. Adren, his family—even Tash.

Ress slid his gaze back to Tash and Adren. After their past, he never expected to owe Tash for any reason. Now each day whispered of a debt he could not repay.

Or maybe it's balancing things between us, wiping all the debts clean. We can't go back to being children, but maybe this is how we start again. Maybe our brotherly oath still means something.

Without a doubt, their oath meant something to Adren. Caught between running from wrong and finding right, Adren needed what the priests offered. Ce needed Tash's attention and advice no less than ce needed comfort. The transition would never be easy, but at least ce had the opportunity.

"So they're kind enough to send us a personal invitation to be reamed out, but they'll make us wait until we die of boredom." Adren crossed cir arms and scuffed cir heel across the floor. "Part of how they weed out the salvageable ones?"

"Perhaps." Tash smiled, the dark circles around his eyes as noticeable as his bruised cheek. "Our matters *do* take up a lot of parchment."

Adren grunted, tapping cir fingertips on cir long coat. "Figures I'd be punished for taking up too much time and resources."

"Adren, don't take it to heart," Tash admonished softly. "Here, give me your hands."

One of Adren's brows rose in question as ce complied.

Tash grasped Adren's hands, stroking cir knuckles with his thumbs. "Breathe with me, deep, slow. Keep your eyes on mine." Together they inhaled and exhaled, ignoring Ress's restlessness. "Find that quiet place inside, that safe void between darkness and light. Rest there and look into the darkness. Lay your thoughts down and free yourself of their weight. Let them go, become weightless. Empty yourself." Their long breaths continued, synched and quiet as Tash spoke. "Now peer into the light, feel its strength. Feel the peace there, waiting for a home. Gather up that peace and embrace it tightly. Let it whisper, let it soothe. When you breathe out, give it all of that breath, slow, steady, and deep. When you breathe in, take its breath into you, calm, pure, and serene. Become one. Become you."

Grip tightening, Tash lowered his chin. "The Council is tough, blunt, and they can be condescending and unkind. But they are fair, honest, and they will give you a chance to speak. This is a hearing, not a final judgment. They will allow you to say what you need to."

When Adren opened cir mouth, Tash clasped cir hands between his. "You have to remain calm. Speak honestly, respectfully, and take time to answer. They'll respect that, even if it doesn't seem like it. No matter what they do—yell, speak out of turn, talk down to you—you *must* keep calm and be honest. Earn their graces first. Don't demand anything—they don't respond well to that."

With a light hand, Tash gestured to Kee. "We will be with you the entire time. The Council cannot kick us out. Everyone else here knows the rules. We know each other's roles and duties. I am your advocate, and the councilmen know it. Sister Kee will fight for you, and she is a talented champion. You should also know that Council hasn't dealt with a Goddess-touched in a long while. They need a bit of leeway, just as you do. They'll take things better if they're shown compassion, hard as it is for you to give. Promise me you'll try."

Adren's lips twisted. "I can't promise it'll work, but I'll try. I can do that." Ce smiled sheepishly. "In the meantime, can we keep doing that breathing thing?"

Tash smirked and repositioned their hands. They breathed together, finding the same pace as before.

"Really wish I had some of those candles right now," Adren muttered. "The scented ones I have in the temple. They're calming. I'm pretty sure they help me sleep better."

"I didn't realize you liked them." Amusement brightened Tash's face. "I'll bring you more later."

"I'd appreciate that." Adren drew cir hands away. "I'm going to light a bunch of them and drink. A lot. Sounds like a good way to unwind after this."

Ress snorted, imagining Adren surrounded by candles and appreciating the need to relax. They would all need to unwind after the meeting. He suspected no one would be spared political wrath.

"In that case," Tash said, "I'll bring you another type of candle and the libation that complements it best. The ones you have don't go so well with alcohol, just steeped herbs."

"However do you know that?" Ress returned Tash's playful glance.

"Experience. Wisdom. Nausea and a bucket."

Adren laughed for the first time that day, the sound playing through Ress and leaving behind relief.

"Laughter is good. Keep that." Kee stopped at Adren's side, eyeing Ress up and down, her lips pursed as her gaze passed over his legs.

Ress knew that look—the one that disagreed with his judgment. No doubt she wanted to insist once more that she request Council set a chair out for him during the hearing, not that he would use it, and he had told her as much twice already. He intended to take the hits just as he was and make the councilmen look up at him from their cushy chairs while they condemned him. They already looked down on him in both law and opinion, but he refused to make it any easier for them physically. He still had that much control over the situation, free to go down as he damn well desired, as upright as he could manage, even though he knew he would spend the rest of the night and the next day confined to sitting or lying down, more than likely unconscious from the never-ending burn that traveled from head to rather angry toe. He trusted the priests with his suffering and vulnerability, but never the Council. That was one advantage he would never give them. The choice remained his, and he would fight them for it all the way to the end.

To his relief, Kee said nothing, though she gave him a nod before facing Adren. "Come, walk with me," Kee said. "Let's discuss what else to keep." She lifted her hand to Adren's arm, hesitant to touch.

No different than the other priests. They act like Adren's made of brittle glass. Ress offered Adren a lopsided smile as ce drifted away with Kee. His stare remained on them as they strolled close to the walls. Since leaving Araveena Ford, he had watched everyone around Adren. All it would take was one wrong person to take Adren away, one wrong move, one word. Strangers were enemies until proven friends, and they were low on friends.

"No harm will come to cir," Tash murmured, stepping closer to Ress.

"From you, maybe," Ress mumbled, "but you're not everyone else." He studied Kee's rigid posture and the tension in Adren's shoulders. "Can't blame me for worrying about how this is going down. I've dreaded this meeting since we left home. I don't think I'll come back from it."

"Then expect to be surprised."

Taken by Tash's flat, smug tone, Ress snapped his focus onto him.

"Sister Kee's going to fight for Adren, but she'll fight just as hard for *you*." Close enough for Ress to feel his breath, Tash lowered his voice. "After what you told her, she's convinced you've earned amnesty. Sister Kee doesn't see you as a criminal—she thinks you're a blessing from the Four, sent to wreak havoc on the Shar. She thinks you're here to make them hurt."

How Tash said the words without choking or laughing, Ress could not fathom. How could a priestess spare him that much faith? "I told you to stop being an optimist. You daydream too much."

"And you too little." Annoyance pinched Tash's expression. "She doesn't believe you have a dark heart. She'll play every justification she has. You just have to *let her*." He raised his hand, cutting off Ress's reply. "I know it's difficult, but you *have* to let Sister Kee fight for you. You want out? She'll get you there. Just don't get in her way, yeah?"

There he is, that guy I used to know—thinks he has all the answers, all the gall, all the orders. It wouldn't take much to prove you wrong, brother. Please tell me you're right this time, you and your special little world of nothing-we-can't-fix priests.

Gaze falling, Ress nodded.

Tash gripped the back of Ress's neck, the rough touch forcing Ress to look him in the eye. "Yeah?"

Ress squeezed his cane and straightened. "Yeah, fine."

"Good." Tash clapped Ress's neck gently.

In the same instant, the doors to the Council Chambers swung open. Spice-scented air wafted into the antechamber to the sound of multiple voices, none of them clear.

A small man waited in the doorway in a long, dark green tunic and black pants, almost lost between the doors towering over him. Young with an unblemished complexion and straw-coloured hair, he appeared more like a child of ten than an official herald.

"You may enter," the man announced, his deep voice affirming his adulthood. He pulled one of the doors open all the way. "In the case of Ress of Araveena Ford and Adren of Elsove Hillock, the High Council of Kattal bids you fair day and honourable resolve."

Ress remained still, relieved as Kee and Adren stepped behind him. They waited in silence, allowing Mayr, Rathen, and Kirra to enter the room in a blur of black clothes. When Tash tapped Ress's elbow, Ress limped through the doorway, grateful the two guards at the doors remained stationary. He reached behind him, holding his breath until Adren grasped his hand and moved beside him. They entered the room together, flanked by Tash and Kee. Behind them, the doors closed.

The Council Chambers was enormous relative to the antechamber and boasted a single window: a large circle of uncoloured glass in the centre of the ceiling that naturally drew one's glance upward. Five gold shields adorned three of the white walls, each as tall as him and wide like the double-door entrance, representing a different tract: Gailarin, Alosaa, Lasael, Eruelme, and Riaes. In the wall to Ress's left was a solitary door made of smooth metal, bolted and barricaded with two guards on either side.

Afraid to ask where the door led, Ress stopped and faced the table in the centre of the room. Long and black, the table accommodated all twelve councilmen in a line facing the main entrance. Every councilman wore an intricate silver and emerald chain of office around their neck and a leather long coat specific to their position. Parchment sat in small piles before each of the chattering councilmen, with more stacks beneath the table. Two men and three women bustled around the table in lavish, bright clothes, swapping parchments with select councilmen. Once they finished, the group scurried to the edge of the Council Chambers.

Of the twelve councilmen, Ress was concerned with only two: Cota, Councilman of Law and Justice; and Severn, Councilman of Public Protection. They sat in the middle of the group, their stern expressions darker than the rest.

The moment Cota stood, the voices in the room silenced.

"Considering all but one of you are familiar with our proceedings, I will keep my opening remarks short. I am Councilman Cota Dalenvrae, the chief minister of Kattal's laws and overseer of justice." Cota's pale green gaze passed over the room, lingering on Adren and Ress. The jagged scar on the left side of his face reminded Ress of his own scars. Darker than the umber skin around it, the injury was clearly visible, as though on display. Cota's short brown hair parted where the scar began at his temple, and the low collar of his white tunic revealed the curved end around his jaw.

Showing it because of pride or intimidation tactic? Ress suspected it was both, inspecting Cota's charcoal grey coat and black pants tucked into knee-high black boots. Like all the coats donned by the councilmen, Cota's bore the emblem of the High Council on the back: a shield presented between two bearcats in rampant stance. The silver emblem on Cota's coat matched the elaborate pattern of silver vines that spiraled around the shield then traveled along the side of the arms to the cuffs. The silver caught the light in small doses, giving a glint to the dull leather. Nothing about Cota was inconspicuous. He wanted to be seen.

"We are gathered to hear what you have to say about your circumstances, Ress, son of Sebina and Telumic, and Adren, child of Merasha and Rivane," Cota continued, his husky voice carrying through the room. "This is not the final hearing, nor our final judgment. We will hold further hearings until we reach a resolution. Today, we wish to address the matters that have led us to this point. We retain the right to speak to multiple parties on *any* matter pertaining to your persons, so it is best to speak the truth. Lies are easily snuffed out; lives more easily so."

The final words were meant for Adren, Ress realized, following Cota's hardened stare to Adren's paling face.

"We formally recognize your advocates, Priestess Kee, Priest Halataldris." Cota inclined his head with each name. "You are welcome to speak and be heard." He gestured to the black-haired woman to his left. "For now, I will defer my inquisitions and speculations and give the floor to Councilman Severn, the chief minister of Kattal's protective services and public security. Councilman?" His ornate chain of office clinked on the table as he reclaimed his seat and retrieved his quill.

Severn stood, her fingertips grazing the polished table. The metal rings on her right hand held Ress's attention. Thick and bronze, the rings were fused together, forming a weapon often worn by Shar-denn members. The comfort with which she wore the bronze knuckles gave him pause.

The whole point, he suspected, peering at her long, dark hair and wide, accusation-filled eyes. She was not given to elaborate shows with little significance. Like Cota, her choices were calculated. The metal knuckles were not a trinket. They were a warning, no different than her attire: black tunic and pants, black boots fastened with gold chains up to her thigh, and a dark red long coat with black emblem and elaborate black vines. The emeralds in her chain of office were the only softness.

Having been interrogated by Severn countless times, Ress understood why his aunt Herias liked her. Neither of them took anyone's foolishness easily.

That and the expression on Severn's face suggested she was about to rip out internal organs.

"Thank you, Councilman." Severn's glance flicked from one face to another. "I have questions for all of you. No one will feel left out. As is custom, I shall begin with the officers of the law." Anger flashed across her face as her gaze settled on Mayr. "You have the highest status here, Head of the Dahe Guard, so I'll interrogate you first."

Ress shuddered at her icy tone. As Mayr bowed his head and stepped forward, Ress imagined what appendage Severn intended to destroy.

"I'm surprised your Tract Steward is absent." Severn crossed her arms. "These are her citizens, after all, criminals within her borders. Furthermore, their crimes have occurred within *her* jurisdiction." Her narrow lips pursed. "Or are you hiding something? Perhaps hiding from Steward Dahe? Did you do something you don't want her knowing about?"

Back tensing, Mayr flicked his braided hair over his shoulder. "No, Councilman," he responded, drawing his hands behind his back. "Steward Dahe is aware of *all* my actions. She knows why I'm here. I asked her not to attend. If you want a meeting with both of us, you're free to request it, but I figured this meeting has nothing to do with her, not yet."

"Who are you to decide that?" Severn's glare shifted towards Tash. "Taking matters into your own hands again, are we?"

Mayr gripped his left wrist and rolled his shoulders back. "Given the nature of those present, I asked Aeley to stay home. I was entrusted with sensitive information and asked to keep confidentiality. I'm keeping my word."

"So you're confessing to protecting known criminals and being in their confidence?"

"That's not what I said."

"Sounds like it to me."

"And it seems I babbled, so let me try again: Aeley knows *exactly* what I've done and why, and she gave me the go ahead." Mayr's tone hardened but did not rise. He squeezed his left wrist. "Aeley knew I was in contact with a Council informant and a suspected member of the Shar-denn. I told her when I first met them, and she approved our continued meetings. Should either of them have hurt anyone, we'd have acted. Though it would've been difficult considering said suspected member was under a priest's protection, restricting us from kicking their heads in."

Severn's eyes narrowed. "Thank you for that lovely image. I suppose you'll say she knew of the events in Araveena?"

"Like she was there. I painted her a real pretty picture and I'll give the same to you." Mayr's left hand was white, the fingers of his right hand flexing around his wrist. "I told her of Ress's request for extraction and the chance to capture more Shar bastards. Aeley told me to take any necessary action to make the arrests and bring *your invaluable* informant to safety. She doesn't have any reason to distrust me, so go ahead, talk to her. While you're at it, feel free to ask her if we agreed to keep our hands off the priest's charge. We think a lot alike, Ae and me."

"Except she knows when to stop being cocky," Cota interjected. "I appreciate your honesty, but you're no replacement for your

Tract Steward, on *any* level. While I value the sanctity of an oath, you should always encourage your superiors to personally participate and question your alliances. Question your loyalties. Question what is doing right by Kattal and what is doing right by loved ones."

Cota rubbed his chin, his slick gaze alternating between Mayr and Tash with grimy suspicion. "You're young, Guard Mayr. I don't expect perfection, but you're playing a dangerous game. I respect your need to serve Kattal and her people. I respect your duty to family and friends. One day, however, you'll have to choose between masters. You'll be forced to choose between explicit loyalty to our rules or loyalty to the Temple—or to someone else completely. They may seem to be on the same side now, but they won't always."

Ress clenched his jaws, grinding his teeth at the glower Cota shot Tash. Mayr and Tash had helped capture more than a dozen Shar-denn members, including three of high rank, and the High Council was accusing them of playing favourites?

The awkward silence grew tenser as Mayr looked over his shoulder to Tash. His grey eyes were dark and angry, his lips pressed hard in a thin line. Tash appeared no happier.

"I don't excuse negligence lightly, even when the lines are blurred." Severn jabbed the table with one finger. "It is your *duty* to tell us these things. You knew of the arrests in Elsove Hillock and our efforts to locate the missing family member. You *know* we must approve of any plans to extract informants. Not only did you violate these rules, you *knew* Ress harboured an *extremely* dangerous person and never said a word. For weeks, you *all* knew where Adren was and never mentioned it. I can guess at why not."

"Councilman—"

"No." Severn cut Mayr off with a raised hand. "I'm not convinced we *shouldn't* strip your rank. Pretending the laws don't apply to you won't be so fun then."

Kirra stepped forward and flung her arm across Mayr's chest as though shielding him. "Councilman Severn, may I speak?"

Severn took a deep breath and blinked. "You may."

"We don't doubt he messed up somewhere," Kirra argued, patting Mayr's shoulder, "but we all messed up, me and Rathen included. I'd like to argue that maybe we *didn't* mess up in the grand scheme of justice. That's what this hearing's about, right? Justice?" She huffed lightly, brushing her blonde hair across her forehead. "We didn't have time to get your approval. It was either run to you or run after a few good marks. Knowing how much we need to get these bastards in prison, we thought we'd catch the filth first and ask for your kindness later because we're saving lives. Saving families."

Kirra motioned to Ress. "Because of him, we've got a lot of squirmy little slugs gnawing on prison bars. I'm happy we dragged in that disgusting slaver—I'd have broken a few more laws to get him. Adren helped with that, in several ways. Without cir, we wouldn't have had such a good chance. I don't think it's fair to punish a Head Guard for doing his Steward's bidding when we were doing yours in what little time we had. Had we delayed and worried about permission—which often takes *at least* a day, just to be honest—we could've lost them. So maybe we could share the blame?"

Ress sucked in a breath, watching the silent exchange between Kirra and Severn. He waited for Severn's harsh reprimands to turn onto Kirra.

"I'll consider it," Severn said eventually, eyeing Kirra, "though we're going to have our own talk, you, me, and Rathen. A refresher on protocol and the fact I don't sleep. You *still* should've come to me. I could've rushed the approval through if I'd known the players."

"Yes, Councilman, I humbly apologize on our behalf," Kirra answered, bowing her head.

Stunned, Ress shuffled his feet to ease the burning ache in his knee. If anyone else was surprised to see Severn back down, they hid it well.

"We won't waste any more of Council's time with wrist slaps." Severn faced Ress and Adren. "Before Councilman Cota takes over, I'll speak to the state of our prisoners. Rivane and family are in solitary until the end of their trials. After their judgments, we'll see if they're still alive to be kept elsewhere." The glare Severn cast Adren was as threatening as her tone. "That includes you. If you wish to join them, we certainly have a cell available."

Adren stepped forward, cir hands in fists. Kee pushed cir back, one finger pressed to her lips.

"The others are with the rest of the prisoners," Severn continued. "Darus and Pade are putting up a good fight. Amelin, on the other hand—" A smirk sparked a light in her dark eyes. "He's found himself a permanent bed in the infirmary. Once his coma breaks, he'll face the same scrutiny as the others. Though it appears the other prisoners have made his judgment clear."

Her expression darkening, Severn stared at Adren. "All of them have indicated we should investigate you. If you hoped they'd keep your secret, you're wrong. We're aware of what you can do. Don't think we're not educated in your kind, and don't get too comfortable. You're not a god, merely a descendant. You're judged the same as everyone else."

And you're just a politician. You're not that special, sweetheart. Ress grasped Adren's hand, offering cir an apologetic grimace. Flushed, Adren cast him a pained glance. They both wanted to fight back.

To Ress's relief, Severn sat down. "Councilman?"

Cota read over the parchment in his hands. "Before we question you, we are giving you both a chance to speak. You may state your case with as little or as much as you please, but consider your words carefully. They will be recorded for further use. Honesty will hurt more than false testimony, but it serves you better."

Flicking his attention towards Ress, Cota fingered the parchment. "We will start with you, Ress. We've already heard your former transgressions. Councilman Severn has debriefed us on your activities as an informant. We can skip all of that. If you wish to speak, you may focus only on the recent events. You may begin."

"Thank you, Councilman." Ress cleared his throat and shifted his cane from one hand to the other. The faces of the councilmen blurred together, a dull palette of disinterest and annoyance coloured with curiosity and criticism. Mayr, Rathen, and Kirra spared him lukewarm glances. Only Tash and Kee offered encouragement, placing their hands on his shoulders. "I've said plenty before, so I'll keep this short: I chose to leave Araveena and violate the terms of my release. I knowingly harboured someone the Council wanted to arrest. I involved officers of the law, placing them in danger."

He drew Adren close and intertwined their fingers. "I'd do it again, knowing what was at stake. I've played by your rules and ruined the lives of those I love. I've outstayed my welcome in the Shar-denn. Still, I was going to keep abiding by your rules—right up until Adren revealed ce was in danger, then I had to act. Ce intended to kill me but didn't, even though I'd earned that death." Ress's glance fluttered over Adren's paled face. "Truth is, Adren's as much Shar as I am, maybe even less. For all the pain ce could cause, ce doesn't do it. In different circumstances, in a better environment, ce'd be an upstanding citizen. If it helps, you should know Adren saved all of us in Araveena, and ce's saved me a few times now. When everything fell apart, Adren put it right."

Ress rocked on his heels. "I beg you to give Adren a chance like you did me. You got names out of me, but Adren can give you more. Ce's willing, and I'm promising to help. Rivane and Merasha didn't give cir much of a choice. When you're in the Shar, they're all-consuming, all-dictating. They decide what's best, rip you apart, and blind you to everything else, no matter what you want. But if you ask Adren what ce wants, you'll be pleased. You'll see an ally. You'll see the chance to make a difference." Wincing as Adren clutched his hand too tight, cir rings digging into his skin, Ress met Cota's gaze. "And that's what I'd like to say."

Cota drew his fist across his lips, regarding Ress with a raised brow. "You are aware you spent your entire statement defending Adren and condemning yourself, yes?"

"Yes, sir."

"You retract nothing?"

"No, sir."

"Very well, let the record stand." Amusement flashed across Cota's features as he tapped the parchment beneath his palm. "Adren, would you like to make a statement?"

Adren looked at Ress, Tash, and Kee. "Yes."

Cota gestured to cir. "The floor is yours."

"Thank you," Adren muttered. When Kee whispered and urged cir with a hand on cir shoulder, Adren moved forward. "I don't know how this works, but I know how to tell the truth." Ce faced Severn. "My family helped run the Shar-denn. My father's been a boss for more than thirty years, and I assisted him. I broke all sorts of laws. I won't lie about it, just like I won't lie about what I am. I can't change that. If those bastards in prison are using me to make themselves feel better, fine. I don't enjoy being attacked because I broke Shar laws."

Adren continued slowly, taking a breath and another step forward. "That's the thing, though: I broke Shar laws. I wanted out. Yes, my family raised me to believe that's the world I belonged to. For most of my life, I believed I did, but not completely. I treasured my family hard, even when it violated who I was, even when I wanted to say no. But this—fleeing with Ress—this was me saying no. Hard to believe, I'm sure, but every bit true."

Ce gave Ress a weak smile. "I messed up, and I'll own that. My family might've boxed me into the Shar, but I made choices I wish I could take back. While I've never killed, I didn't stop anyone, not like Ress. I should know—*he* stopped *me*. I thought he'd taken my choices away, but I was wrong. He gave me more. I'm kind of hoping that doesn't end today. I'd like to know what it feels like to help people. I'd like to know what it's like being one of the good guys." Adren dug cir toe into the floor, lowering cir gaze. "If that means telling you everything and showing you *exactly* what I have to offer, I'll do it, because some people here make me want to be worthy of life. They might've broken laws to save my sorry ass, but even when they're following the laws, they're pretty damn inspiring."

Kissing Adren's forehead, Ress curled his arm around cir back. He glimpsed Kirra and Mayr's smiles before they turned away.

The snicker from one of the councilmen, however, was uncalled for.

"How touching," Severn drawled, leaning forward on her elbows. "Such a shame your parents couldn't be so thoughtful. Your brothers aren't any less kind. It seems whenever they go to say 'Councilman' it comes out 'bitch'. Nice to see your education surpasses theirs, even if you've earned your graces in the bedroom."

Adren clenched cir hands, cir face red. "You self-righteous—"

Tash grabbed cir arm. "Calm," he whispered, pulling Adren back. "Respect."

"But she's pissing all over us," Adren argued.

"She does that to half the people who come in here." Anger flickered in Tash's eyes. "You saw her with Mayr—and he's on her side."

Adren let out a frustrated breath, glaring at Severn.

"Be careful, Adren. Your family traits are slipping." Severn stood and tapped the table. "You want to be deserving of mercy? Give us one good reason. *One.* Not one that's sweet and pretty or whispered to you by a lover. Don't stand there looking all wounded, like you're going to put your fist through our faces. Your brother tried that—he hasn't been able to move his fists since."

Severn jabbed her finger towards Adren, wisps of her black hair framing her dark features. "We've got enough of your kind running the streets, ruining lives. Shar-denn filth that do whatever they damn well please. Do I care if you're not the one hurting children and making widows left, right, and centre? No, but you're part of it. You could've stopped it, but you *didn't*. You want to be a 'good guy'? Then tell me you'd be happy to serve time in prison. I've got a set of cuffs with your name on them. Tell me you'd wear them to prove your new loyalty. Tell me you'd stand in the stocks for days and rot in your own filth. *Show* me you want it."

As Adren stepped forward, Kee pushed cir back.

"Your statement is finished." Kee moved to stand in front of Adren and Ress. "Councilman Cota, High Council, you have heard their statements. They are open and honest, admitting guilt and intent. They have asked for forgiveness. This is their first hearing, and they have exercised great responsibility and integrity. And, being their first hearing, I hereby declare the Temple of the Four is taking them under the wing of amnesty." She motioned to Tash. "Brother Halataldris, myself, and our brethren have taken responsibility for Adren and Ress. They are under our protection. Your brash requests for imprisonment are unacceptable, as is verbal assault."

"You have *got* to be joking," Severn grumbled, crossing her arms. "You saved that for this *exact* moment, didn't you?"

"If you suggest I play a game, Councilman, I promise you I don't." Kee lifted her chin and clasped her hands before her. "It was in their best interest to make their statements free of our influence, but now the Temple must intervene. We have heard the detailed stories of their circumstances and have granted them clemency. Brother Halataldris and I are here to secure a *mutual* amnesty agreement."

"*Mutual?*" Severn thrust out her hand. "I get him, but Adren has to answer to cir crimes, no different than the rest of the family. Who's to say Adren isn't here to sabotage us? To take information back to the Shar-denn and hurt more people? Are you willing to risk everyone's life for *that*?"

"No, but that is not the risk here," Kee argued, her voice hard and even. "The risk is imprisoning an ally. Someone who could take all that fear you carry and put it to rest; someone who can step into their birthright and pull out a warrior. Our most needed heroes are not born but nurtured, and often their journey is wrought with choices they would have made differently. Yet those who rise above adversity nevertheless are not only the stronger for it, they share that strength with others to heal what wounds us. Surely you will not alienate such an ally because your heart is turning so cold, it cannot offer forgiveness?"

"Because my heart is—" Severn muttered, tilting her head. "Forgiveness is earned, priestess, and whatever *fear* I carry is because I've seen too many people hurt because some gang thinks it's owed something. There's so many, we can't keep up."

"Try trust, then."

"*Trust?* Like what you're giving them?" Severn pointed at Ress and Adren. "So they've told you everything they've done, have they? Did it ever occur to you they could be lying? Did you even check? Or is faith *that* ignorant?"

"Of course we verified their stories. If Council reviews yesterday's visitor roster at the prison where Adren's family is, you will see that two priests and I were there."

Before Severn could argue, Kee raised her hand. "Now, Councilman Cota, you said we were welcome to speak?" When Cota nodded, Kee spoke lightly. "Then here is *our* statement. We respect the right of the High Council to hear the confessions in full and prepare terms of judgment. We believe in justice. However, we also believe in forgiveness should the soul desire it. I deeply believe Adren is seeking redemption. Likewise, I believe Ress has already paid his dues. They will attend your hearings, but we will be at every one to keep them peaceful.

"Furthermore," Kee continued, lowering her hand, "Adren and Ress are fully aware of the stipulations of our amnesty. *Both* will act within the same terms Brother Halataldris faced when he first came to us. Together, they will aid the community and atone for their transgressions, at the discretion of the Temple. The agreements have already been struck. Do not make a liar out of me, Councilman Severn, and keep your verbal executioner's blade on lock down."

More than one councilman gaped.

"You may join our agreement or not," Kee said, "though if you agree, every party will reap greater benefits. If you don't, we'll have many more meetings like this—unless you enjoy getting nowhere?"

Silence filled the room. No one moved. Severn and Kee stared each other down, dueling within the long, awkward pause. Cota was flushed like his colleagues, all of them focused on Severn.

With his next breath, Ress prayed he and Adren survived the battle.

Stumbling out of the meeting, Ress swore he had lost five years of his life.

"They should've just hacked off my arms and legs and beat me with them," Ress grumbled, sliding his glance towards Tash and Mayr as their group left the Council Chambers. "It would've achieved the same damn thing."

Rathen snorted and draped his arm around Kirra's shoulders, guiding her out of the doorway before the herald shut the doors. "They want you to *feel* what they're saying, just in case you weren't listening." He shrugged. "Though you're still alive, so you're bellyaching why?"

Good point. Ress squeezed Adren's hand and hobbled beside cir, aware of Kee behind them. Both he and Adren were more than alive: they were safe from prison and execution unless they violated Kee's rules. Despite conflicts in opinions, the majority of High Council had agreed to the amnesty. Ress and Adren would remain with the priests, neither free nor condemned.

"Guess we missed the party."

The unfamiliar voice stopped Ress, surprise jolting him back. Two women approached from the other end of the antechamber. The tall woman to his left wore her dark blonde hair pulled back from her face. Beneath a brown cloak that matched her eyes, she wore dark pants, shin-high boots, a white shirt, and a sword at her waist. The woman beside her was shorter with dark, loosely curled hair and dark grey eyes. Dressed in a lavish burgundy gown and cloak with wide black ribbons, the brunette appeared unarmed.

Walking up to Mayr, the blonde held up two dark brown wine bottles. Tied around the neck of each bottle were white ribbons and a large white bow. "We figured you could use these." She offered one bottle to Mayr. "Something tells me you earned it."

"I told you not to come, Ae," Mayr scolded, accepting the bottle and rolling it in his hands. "It's beautiful." He hugged the bottle in both arms. "Mmm. My favourite anti-Council medicine. Hey—you—" As Tash grinned and reached for the bottle, Mayr slapped Tash's hand away. "Get your hands off! Steal the other one."

Tash's laugh was as wicked as the gleam in his eyes. "If you want—but if you really enjoy this one, we could share it later." He whispered in Mayr's ear, one of his hands drawing Mayr in by the hip.

Mayr handed the bottle to Tash. "You win. Keep it for when we're naked."

Ress coughed and faced the women again.

"Oh, right. Aeley, Lira—" Mayr gestured to Ress and Adren. "—the ones Severn's busting bollocks over."

"Was it really that bad?" Lira's grey gaze fell on Ress and Adren, her features bright with silent laughter. "He's prone to exaggeration."

"No, this one hurt *bad*." Kirra jutted her thumb at Mayr. "Your boy took a few good hits. The rest of us did, too."

Mayr scowled at Aeley. "I told you to stay *home*."

"No, you said you didn't want me '*there*,'" Aeley argued. "You didn't say *anything* about me being *here*."

"You're smart when you're being cute." Mayr kissed Aeley's cheek. "Thanks."

Aeley clutched his shirt as he pulled back, her expression solemn. "Do I have to haul your ass out of prison soon or are we good?"

With a sigh, Mayr rolled his eyes. "Yeah, we're good. Expect Severn to come calling, though. She's got a hundred ways to skin me for being obnoxiously autonomous."

Lira snickered. "We need to get you home before you start the next war. That's my job— stop trying to steal it." She wrapped her arm around Mayr's. "Come, escort us out. Try being a gentleman and maybe they won't bust your other parts."

"Always so thoughtful," Mayr murmured, kissing Lira's head. "Just until we get home, then I'm not responsible for whatever happens." He wound Aeley's arm around his and led them towards the hallway, peering over his shoulder. "Anyone want to join?"

Rathen and Kirra followed with casual strides, their hands in their coat pockets. "No, we've got a new hunt," Rathen answered. "We'll get everyone else settled in the temple then we're off."

"We shan't keep you any longer than necessary." Kee nodded at Adren and urged cir towards the door. "Thank you for your testimonies today. They are greatly appreciated." She ushered Adren from the room, followed by Mayr, Aeley, and Lira.

Once Rathen and Kirra stepped into the corridor, Ress limped towards the doorway.

Tash clasped Ress's elbow. "Wait."

Recognizing the serious tone, Ress stopped. "Yeah?"

"Are you all right? After that, I mean?"

"Am I all right with being alive? Absolutely." Ress laughed. "Priestess Kee—she's something special."

"Don't we know it. She's to the Temple as Severn is to Council—a metal fist to the gut. Our temple elected her as our Overseer for that very reason, among her other talents for keeping order. I respect her for it."

"Meanwhile, I get the impression Mayr doesn't. He's practically verging on despise."

"He has his reasons." Tash stared at the floor. "It was a misunderstanding: a misinterpretation. But I can't force forgiveness. Some things have to stay how they are." He glanced at Ress. "You and me, however, that's already changing. What happened in Araveena had to happen. All of it."

Ress sighed. Painful as the ordeal was, he hoped Tash was right. "You're sure everything's in order there?"

"Everyone's all right, I promise. The guards sent to Araveena are protecting our families like they're supposed to." Tash squeezed Ress's elbow. "If the Shar attacks, we'll hear about it, but Bremary, Cove, my family—none of them will be harmed."

"If only Ines could be so lucky," Ress murmured. "I wish she had a guard."

Tash took a ragged breath. He withdrew a folded piece of parchment from inside his long coat and caressed it with his thumb. "It's already done."

"What?"

"Weeks ago, just after she left," Tash said softly. "Mayr sent a message to Rosayra, wife and Head Guard for Steward Oaren in Alosaa. He called in a personal favour, asking her to keep an eye on Ines, and Rosayra agreed. Their guards are watching over Ines, enough to be a pain in the Shar's guts but not disrupting her life. She's safe, Ress. She's being taken care of."

Tash held out the note. In the centre was Ress's name in black ink. "Ines sent this."

Dread punched Ress hard, his chest pained under the weight. He opened the note, braced for what hate filled it.

A dried blue flower with yellow streaks fell out. Even pressed flat, the patterns on the petals looked identical to those of the flower he had given Inesta on their wedding day—the flower she had worn in her hair at the ceremony and feast until it fell out while dancing.

Catching the flower between his fingers, he read the message above her name:

Thank you.

Ress's heart all but fell out of his chest. No other words could have said as much as they did. No other meaning could have hurt in the same way. No other message could have made his heart feel that much lighter. They both were free.

"Are you good now?" Tash rubbed Ress's arm.

"Yeah," Ress said quietly, folding the parchment. He tucked the flower inside and slipped the letter into his coat pocket. Although he was better than good, he had no words to explain it.

Tash steered Ress towards the corridor, the wine bottle in his other hand. "I'm supposed to get Adren a strong drink. I'd like you to join us. We'll finally get you inebriated."

"And you call yourself a priest? Isn't there a sacred hand slap in there somewhere?"

"We haven't thrown out *all* of the small pleasures in life. We're allowed certain things in moderation." Tash lowered his head. "Brother Armamae can out-drink all of us," he whispered. "So can Sister Kee. Just don't tell anyone. It might bolster her image."

Ress laughed as they entered the hallway, his hand sneaking into his pocket to finger Inesta's letter. In one small package, he had his happier ending. In two short words, he had more freedom than even the High Council had offered. In letting Inesta go, he had taken back his heart. With one letter of mercy, Inesta had given him permission to embrace Adren fully.

Embrace Adren he would.

Hobbling through the bright white corridor as fast as his body allowed, Ress brushed past the splendorous arrangements of orange, gold, and mauve-black flowers in the massive vases to his right, situated between the series of stained-glass windows that looked onto an exquisite courtyard. In a matter of moments that burned with every step, he closed the fifty paces between him and Adren, cir attention still on Kee as they lingered in the middle of the hallway, engrossed in quiet discussion.

Without a word, Ress grabbed Adren's hand and playfully twirled cir around as if they were about to dance.

"What—" Adren started, losing cir balance and stumbling into him.

Ress pulled cir close, quick to cut off any further questions with a kiss, its tenderness a gentle tingle on his lips before feisty longing drove it deeper. Fate had spared him and Adren a dozen forms of heartbreak that day, granting them what he hoped were a wealth of days to explore what they could be together. Whatever pity the Goddesses had taken upon them, for whatever reason the universe saw fit to offer them a new life, he would accept it without question.

"Just thought I'd mark the occasion," Ress said huskily against Adren's lips.

Adren laughed, a soothing calm that Ress had begun to crave, especially in the silence. "Consider it marked," ce muttered, wrapping cir arms around his neck as ce stole a kiss weighted with demand and promise.

The path they walked into their uncertain future would not be easy, but it was theirs. From this moment, life meant something. It meant everything.

So did every heartbeat that tripped on love.

EPILOGUE

He had expected to have a private meeting with Tract Steward Dahe one day, but not in the temple chamber he shared with Adren.

Ress waited at the window as Aeley swept into the small room behind Tash and Mayr. Adren stared at him from where ce stood beside the bed they had shared for the last three weeks, "what do I do?" written across cir features. They were not prepared to receive an unannounced guest, let alone defend themselves if the Tract Steward interrogated them. What did she want?

As Mayr closed the door, hiding four of the Dahe guards standing in the corridor, Ress tensed. The last thing they needed was to be taken to prison.

"Tract Steward," Ress greeted, inclining his head. With a glower at Tash, he hoped their relationship was not falling apart again. He'd had enough of betrayal and lies. Refuge in the temple gave him a chance to revisit truth and honesty, and dedicate himself to living both.

Aeley regarded him silently, her pink lips never loosening from her smirk. Her hands shifted beneath her brown cloak as she removed her gloves, the leather dark like the rest of her clothes. Everything about her was a stark contrast to the bright white marble of the temple walls and the joyful, pious lives of the priests who had welcomed Ress and Adren with kindness and wonder.

"Ress." Aeley cocked her head to the side, the loose tail of her blonde hair falling over her shoulder. "Adren."

Adren nodded weakly. Ce twined cir fingers in the folds of the white dress the priests had given cir before slipping cir hands into the pockets of cir red long coat, another gift from the priests and a match to Tash's. Cir glance darted from Tash to Ress then to Mayr before finally returning to Aeley.

"Relax," Aeley said, raising one of her hands. "No one's in trouble. No one's dragging you out of here. Well, at least not without your agreement." She stepped back, gesturing to the walls with the flick of her wrist. "Not much, is it? Perhaps a little cramped for two?"

While Ress would not argue about the size of the chamber or its lack of decoration, he dared not complain. The room was clean, contained pristine furniture, and provided a calm, well-lit space away from the bustle of priests and unwanted attention. A warm bed piled with soft blankets and pillows was nothing to scoff at, no matter how simple the wooden frame and headboard. Given their few possessions, he and

Adren easily made the dresser, armoire, and bedside table work. The small, round table and two chairs in the corner of the room nearest the window provided a place for them to eat a meal together.

"We make do." Ress shifted his feet and crossed his arms. "I've been in worse."

"Mm, so I've heard. Can't beat the luxury of a prison cell, although..." A mischievous grin replaced Aeley's smirk, her eyes gleaming. "Maybe we can do a *little* better: a room in my home."

Ress's face warmed. What kind of joke were they playing? "Pardon?"

"I'm officially extending an invitation to both of you to live at the estate." Aeley clasped her hands, her expression solemn. "I've discussed this with the required parties. I feel it's the best course of action given your individual circumstances. It's the safer option for the two of you *and* the priests."

Her features softened with a look at Adren. "I understand you're in a precarious position, not only because of your family, but because of something you can't control. I'm also aware the Council knows about both but aren't spreading the word. Your father's men did you no favours," she murmured, loud enough for only those in the room to hear. "I swear on the lives of those I hold dear I will keep your circumstances secret, but they can't be ignored. We agree," she added, motioning to Tash and Mayr, "that you'll be safest at the estate with my guards. If anyone's foolish enough to attack you there, they deserve the damage we'll deal them."

Ress could feel Adren's apprehension. "It's a nice offer," ce started, "but…"

"Walking into my house is like walking straight into the Council's prison?" Aeley smiled gently. "Yeah, I know, but I've heard enough about Ress to know what the real story is. I'm willing to work with that. As for you, Adren, you put me into a tough place, but I was born stubborn. Tash makes compelling arguments, and I'm willing to listen. I'll abide by the Temple's deal for your amnesty."

"Council won't like it." Ress leaned against the window frame, tugging on the thin, white curtains. "They're still having a fit that I left."

"That's normal. They have fits over everything." Aeley waved the concerns away. "They've already agreed I should take you in. If you're under my supervision, they're less likely to paint a target on your back." Her smirk returned as she lowered her chin. "The Council's informed me of the terms of your next position. We've got a room you can use for whatever you want. Always locked, always stocked with materials you need. It's all yours."

The offer was tempting. With his role as an informant compromised, Ress had offered the High Council another option: weapons and information for their militant forces. He had the designs for the weapons the Shar-denn wanted to use, and he knew their tactics. Combined with Adren's knowledge of the new explosives and other strategies, they could provide the Kattal forces with things no one else would give them.

To his relief, the High Council had agreed it was a worthwhile venture.

Having a private workroom could mean more, giving him a place to work on other projects. Although he had left the metal shop behind, he had not abandoned the smith in him. While he appreciated the generosity of the village smith for loaning him a small space to create the pieces Mayr had paid him to craft, he missed the feel of his own workroom and forge.

Except this isn't about me. Ress gazed at Adren. In truth, he would feel better if ce was guarded, even if those guards were Aeley's. Rivane's men would not be the last people after him, and the price on his life would have increased after taking Adren. They needed to be prepared for anything to happen.

Ress slid his focus to Tash and Mayr. *I get it, that undeniable need to do anything to protect who you love, even if it means surrendering. For Adren, I'll do that and more. Ce's the only good thing to come from the Shar. These weeks with cir have been more open and honest than any single day with Ines. I can't lose Adren. I won't.*

Head inclined towards Adren, he shrugged. They could at least try the new arrangement.

"I guess..." Adren cleared cir throat. "I wouldn't mind getting out of here." Ce raised cir hands towards Tash. "Not that I don't appreciate what everyone's done. It's just with all the priests and the worshippers and everything Goddess *all the time*, it's a bit—"

"Much?" Tash nodded. "I've seen it wearing on you, and I've explained it to Aeley. It's one of the reasons I asked her to consider making this offer."

"Oh." Adren's glance dropped to the floor. "I guess all that's left is to say yes."

"We can move you today," Aeley said, "and discuss taking you back to Araveena to retrieve more of your things. Just say the word."

After a final look at Adren, Ress sighed. "Sure."

Aeley backed towards the door. "Good, now these two can stop bothering me about it." She slapped Mayr's shoulder before opening the door. "I'll inform Priestess Kee. Then I'll tell Haydin we're welcoming extra bodies and let you do whatever you need to do. He'll have everything ready before you arrive." With a hint of a flounce, she entered the corridor and disappeared around the corner, followed by all but two of her guards.

"We'll leave, too." Tash pulled Mayr by the hand. "Give you time to pack."

The door closed behind them, leaving the room silent.

"How does this kind of thing keep happening?" Adren whispered. "I feel like I'm being bounced across lines as they're being undrawn."

Ress crossed the room to draw cir into his arms. "Welcome to my life." He kissed the crook of cir neck, his lips lingering as he savoured cir scent. "Never as planned. Always revising the rules. Kind of like right now."

Not to waste the moment, he reached beneath his shirt for the gold chain around his neck. Before Adren could question, he drew the chain over his head and held it up, allowing the glassy stone it bore to dangle in front of Adren's eyes.

"Something new," he said. "Something no one else has. You didn't take my heart, but you still have it. I'm giving it to you, and those of others who care about you."

When Adren lifted cir hand, he slipped the heart-shaped stone into cir palm. Dark pink with tiny fissures filled with amber glass, the stone was smooth and perfectly cut, locked inside an elegant gold cage following the curves of the heart. The stone was from a larger shard given to him by Priestess Kee. *"From the Shatterlands, during my Uldana Trials,"* she had said.

Only when he had told Tash did he discover the significance: in giving him the shard, Kee

454

had given him a piece of herself, one she had suffered to retrieve to prove herself as a priestess. The small chunk of shard Kee had encouraged him to take was a gift to honour the first Goddess-touched they had met in decades, a subtle reminder that Adren was precious.

Too precious to keep caged.

"As alone as you've felt," Ress murmured, leaning into Adren, "you'll never be alone again. You've got me. You've got them. Now you've got a place where we can both belong, just as we are."

Adren hugged him around the neck. Cir green eyes appeared to glow in the sunlight, the gold rings around cir irises as rich as the gold cage in cir fist. "Sounds like a perfect plan. I'm with you, from start to finish." Ce pressed their foreheads together. "If the only way out is dead, I'm willing to go there with you. To the end."

To the end, wherever that may be, Ress promised, savouring Adren's touch as though it were the first. *But for right now, you're my new beginning, from one breath to the next. A second chance at doing things the way I should've done the first time around.*

A fragile chance at a future they needed to safeguard no matter what, magical in its own right but so vulnerable it terrified him. On their own, they had been condemned to walk the dark path alone, always searching for a way out. Together, they had a chance at actually living, perhaps even for the first time since they were children, chipped pieces of their bruised souls restored by the promising whispers of freedom and gentle hands that offered help, not harm.

Drawing Adren close, Ress held cir tight, his face buried in cir shoulder, scared to let go but just as relieved ce was still there. Still trusting. Still with him despite the uncertainties. *This is our second chance at the lives we should've had. Our choice. Our only way forward. Ours. For however long we have. For however long we can manage.*

Ours.

FIN

PLAYLIST FOR *BLOOD BORNE*

(Artists and songs are listed in alphabetical order)

Themes:
Whole-book theme:
MS MR – Hurricane

Adren theme:
The Weeknd – Devil May Cry

Ress theme:
MS MR – All the Things Lost

Ress & Adren theme:
Lacuna Coil – Within Me

Ress & Inesta theme:
Ellie Goulding – Heal

Rest of the Playlist!
A Great Big World – Say Something (feat. Christina Aguilera)
Alexandre Desplat – Lily's Theme (from the film, "Harry Potter & the Deathly Hallows")

Blue Foundation – Eyes on Fire
Breaking Benjamin – What Lies Beneath
Breaking Benjamin – Without You (Acoustic)

City and Colour – Day Old Hate
City and Colour – Ladies and Gentlemen
City and Colour – Two Coins

Ellie Goulding – Scream It Out
Emily Browning – Sweet Dreams (Are Made of This)
Emjay – Falling in Love
Emjay – Flying to The Moon
Emjay – In Your Arms
Evanescence – My Immortal

Fefe Dobson – Bye Bye Boyfriend

Garbage – Stroke of Luck

Hurt – Falls Apart
Hurt – House Carpenter
Hurt – Overdose

Joseph Trapanese – Amity (from the film, "Insurgent")
Joseph Trapanese – Beyond the Wall (from the film, "Allegiant")
Joseph Trapanese – Candor (from "Insurgent")

Joseph Trapanese – The Council (from "Allegiant")
Joseph Trapanese – You're Worth It (from "Insurgent")

Klaypex – Rain (feat. Sara Kay)

Lacuna Coil – Falling
Lacuna Coil – Falling Again
Lacuna Coil – The Ghost Woman and the Hunter
Lana Del Rey – Money Power Glory
Lana Del Rey – Music to Watch Boys To
Lia Ices – Grown Unknown
Lia Ices – Ice Wine
Loreena McKennitt – Breaking the Silence
Loreena McKennitt – Samain Night
Loreena McKennitt – The Old Ways

Maroon 5 – Come Away to the Water (feat. Rozzi Crane)
MS MR – Bones

Of Monsters and Men – Silhouettes

Rammstein – Asche zu Asche
Rammstein – Du Hast
Rammstein – Mein Herz Brennt

Sia – Elastic Heart (feat. The Weeknd and Diplo)
SOHN – Bloodflows

Staind – Epiphany
Staind – It's Been Awhile
Staind – Outside
Stereophonics – Maybe Tomorrow

The Weeknd – The Town

THE REPUBLIC CONTINUES IN *SOULBOUND*

In a relationship that violates rules and expectations, Mayr and Tash have found their perfect match in each other. Despite their fears and difficult pasts, they hope for a shared future with security and a family. When Mayr's secret first love, Arieve, proposes they create that family with her, it seems dreams could become reality.

But life is complicated, and so is the delicate balance between duty and love. While Mayr protects the Dahe family at all costs, Tash is determined to succeed as a priest. Both positions require sacrifice, forcing their relationship into painful choices. To make matters worse, criminals lurk in the shadows, seeking revenge on them and those they guard.

The life they want risks losing everything—including Arieve and each other. Even if they can have it all, keeping it may take more than they can give.

AUTHOR'S NOTE

Welcome to the darker side of The Republic! It's a bit grimy, a little bitey, and it's on a downward spiral. I enjoyed writing this one—I hope you've enjoyed it, too, whether you're new to my work or if you've been with the series over the years! Adren and Ress are a couple of firsts for me: Adren is my first non-binary/genderqueer character, while Ress is my first asexual main character. (Brother Armamae from *Four* is aromantic asexual, but he's part of the supporting cast).

Blood Borne is the second part of a trilogy inside the larger series: *Four*, *Blood Borne*, and the next book, *Soulbound*, all go together. I've learned so much while writing them, especially things about their world I didn't know until they hit the page. While the previous books set up circumstances, *Blood Borne* really kicks things into gear. On one hand, it's about being a survivor and trying being a good person despite terrible circumstances. Ress and Adren are driven to go forward even when they're falling apart and giving up, watching horrible things happen, knowing they can only do so much without losing absolutely everything.

On the other hand, it's about them being seen and accepted for who they are, and about rising up from oppression and harmful emotional and mental conditioning to do what's right, even when it hurts. And for Adren, it's a journey away from domestic abuse and the power games ce's been forced to endure under cir parents' roof, a toxic environment ce's needed to escape for a long time but hasn't had anyone to turn to for help. It very much reminds me of the line from Bobbie Gentry's song (and Reba McEntire's cover), *Fancy*:

"If you want out, well, it's up to you".

That's pretty much Adren and Ress in a nutshell. They've had themselves up to this point, so when they get together… it's more like kindred spirits finally meeting.

Having said that, I *can* say this isn't the end of Adren and Ress. They stick around, wreak some havoc. They still have growth to go through, especially with each other, because their relationship is so new and different for them. This is first romantic connection Adren has had with anyone, and ce's cautious, especially with everything else going on. The romance between them is small and fragile right now, but it has the potential to grow deeper. They just need some time and a lot of trust!

There are major developments coming, though... and they're in the eye of the storm because the Shar-denn isn't playing around. There are also questions and matters that have been left open in the story, and they'll be answered as the series goes along. Adren's birth family? What Ress knows that could sink the entire country? Where Nimae's gone? It's coming, I promise!

And the Goddess-touched... they've opened up an entire new set of circumstances, because where magic goes, trouble usually follows. Not only has it given me a chance to really dig into their nation's history, I've come up with entirely new characters and situations I'm so jazzed to write about. Though with all of that comes more of the heavier side of the series, which includes further looks into the Shar-denn and their activities. It's not going to be pretty, and the angst is going to be on tap for a while.

Thank you to everyone who brought *Blood Borne* to life! Such deep, warm thanks go to Sam, Megan, and Sasha at Less Than Three Press for getting it out there originally, then cheering it on. Your support still means everything. <3

Thanks, also, to Constance Blye for the editing on the first edition and Natasha Snow for the amazing cover that captures everything about the story! Once again, you rocked this one right out of the park. Keep working that magic! And Raelynn Marie, THAT MAP! It's so beautiful and perfect.

And thanks to the folks on Tumblr for their personal insights—Anagnori, Ask a Non-binary, Chris, and Taz. Adren never would've happened without what you've shared with the world, and I'm ever so grateful.

Also, thanks to my partner for whom Adren is a big deal—thanks for putting up with my writer ways and night schedule and overwhelming note-writing! I didn't consciously set out to write someone who identified like my partner, but it happened ("write what you know" has never seemed truer), and it's done good things for us. While Adren struggles with the rest of cir identity, cir gender is one thing ce knows for certain, and ce lives that without apology, which is really important at a time when everything has gone to toxic depths. Nothing about Adren's life has gone right, but ce's going to carry on and fight. In the end, *Blood Borne* is a chance for those who are often overlooked to shine in their own story because everyone's got one. They just need the chance to tell it.

And finally, big, gargantuan thanks to you, readers! This series doesn't go anywhere without you. <3 If you're interested in learning more about what I'm currently working on, hop on over to my website or find me on social media! My links are on the very last page.

I love hearing from readers, so feel free to say hi and happy reading. ^_^

Blessings and peace to you all,

Archer

ALSO BY ARCHER KAY LEAH

THE REPUBLIC SERIES
A Question of Counsel (The Republic, book 1)
Four (The Republic, book 2)
Blood Borne (The Republic, book 3)
Soulbound (The Republic, book 4)

NOVELS
For the Clan

NOVELLAS
Heart, Lace, and Soul
Of Kindred and Stardust

ABOUT *THE REPUBLIC* SERIES

Welcome to *The Republic*, high fantasy romances for across the LGBTQA+ spectrum, where love, fight, and hope are at the very core, entwined with the lives of romantic partners, friends, and families... and maybe a few lifelong enemies, too. Come step into their world where games linger and foul play is afoot!

● ● ●

Democracy. Family. Loyalty. Honour.
The perfect system.

Freedom. Belonging. Unity.
The perfect illusion.

With the right people and the right price, the Republic of Kattal can be brought to its knees.

Peace and security are never a guarantee when greed and lies threaten the balance. Fear and control know no bounds; and sacred tenets don't keep the monsters away. The right to choose can be a nightmare.

But for every line crossed, someone waits on the other side, ready to push back.

In justice, there is wisdom. In wisdom, there is protection. In it all, there is love. Maybe it means saving a village; maybe it means saving someone you can't live without. Sometimes it's just about doing the right thing and learning to love yourself.

Magic may lurk in the shadows.
Crime may never sleep.
But love doesn't back down.

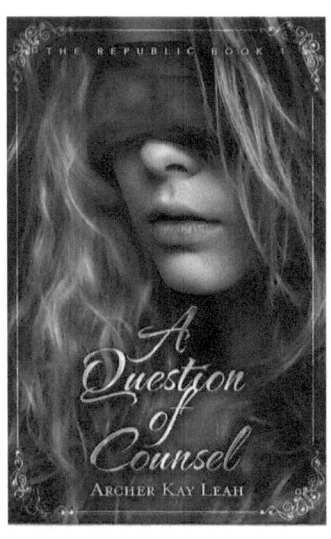

ABOUT THE AUTHOR

Archer Kay Leah was raised in Canada, growing up in a port town at a time when it was starting to become more diverse, both visibly and vocally. Combined with the variety of interests found in Archer's family and the never-ending need to be creative, this diversity inspired a love for toying with characters and their relationships, exploring new experiences and difficult situations.

Archer most enjoys writing speculative fiction and is engaged in a very particular love affair with fantasy, especially when it is dark and emotionally charged. When not reading and writing for work or play, Archer is a geek with too many hobbies and keeps busy with other creative endeavors, a music addiction, and whatever else comes along. Archer lives in London, Ontario with a non-binary partner who loves video games, composing music, and all things out there in the vast space of the universe.

Website: archerkayleah.wordpress.com
Goodreads: goodreads.com/ArcherKayLeah
Facebook: facebook.com/ArcherKayLeah
Twitter: twitter.com/archerkayleah